by the Rebel

CARA COLTER
MICHELLE DOUGLAS
JACKIE BRAUN

Published in Great Britain 2013
by Mills & Boon, an imprint of Harlequin (UK) Limited,
Eton House, 18-24 Paradise Road, Richmond, Surrey TW9 1SR

The Playboy's Plain Jane, *The Loner's Guarded Heart* and *Moonlight and Roses* were first published in Great Britain by Harlequin (UK) Limited.

ISBN: 978 0 263 90563 2
ebook ISBN: 978 1 472 00136 8

05-0813

Harlequin (UK) policy is to use papers that are natural, renewable and recyclable products and made from wood grown in sustainable forests. The logging and manufacturing processes conform to the legal environmental regulations of the country of origin.

Printed and bound in Spain
by Blackprint CPI, Barcelona

THE PLAYBOY'S PLAIN JANE

BY
CARA COLTER

A few words from **Cara Colter** about writing this book: "I love flowers. To me, one of the most luxurious feelings in the world is to have a lovely fresh bouquet on the dining room table. I even have a special light fixture that I can turn on just to spotlight the arrangement. The house might be a mess, a deadline fast looming, but when I see those flowers, breathe in their scent, for a moment my soul goes still and I feel my world as sacred."

Cara and her real-life hero, Rob, live on an acreage in British Columbia. Their cat, Hunter, graciously shares his house with them. They own seven horses, including two new "babies"—Weiner and Schnitzel—a pair of Fjord cross colts. Visit Cara (and the horses, cat and Rob) at her website: www.Cara-Colter.com.

To my daughter-in-law, Crissy Martin,
a true original,
funny, sensitive, spunky, beautiful.

CHAPTER ONE

"…AND I THINK a few lilies," Mrs. Johnson said sadly, "Gertrude did love lilies."

Katie's eyes slid to the clock. Nearly one o'clock. She couldn't very well stop midorder—especially for something as sensitive as a funeral wreath—to go look out the window. But when Mrs. Johnson had come in a full ten minutes ago, she had indicated she was in a hurry. They should have been done by now!

Aware of a certain despicable powerlessness, Katie set down her pen. Well, she did own The Flower Girl, after all. She was the boss. If she wanted to go look out the window, she could do that!

"Excuse me for just a sec," she said. "Something in the window, um, needs my immediate attention."

Ignoring Mrs. Johnson's bewildered glance toward a window that held an eye-catching display of nonattention-needing spring bouquets, Katie stepped out from behind the counter, walked swiftly to the window. She toyed with a vase of bright phlox that represented the new hopes and sweet dreams of the coming of spring.

Right on time, the man she despised more than any

other rounded the corner of First Street, onto Davis. Dylan McKinnon was coming fast, a man who would have scorned the word *jogging*. He was running flat-out, arms and legs pumping, his dark hair wind ruffled.

She felt the bottom fall out of her stomach. Today he was wearing a hooded black jacket, with no sleeves, the absolutely perfect outfit for a man with muscles like that. His arms rippled with easy strength, the line of his triceps, hard cut and sweat beaded, did a funny thing to Katie's breathing.

The jacket was designed to show off his attributes, obviously. As were the shorts, showing the perfect line of legs that were strong and hard with lean male muscle.

Pathetic, she chided herself, knowing darn well it was not Dylan McKinnon she despised, but her own weakness.

He was trouble with a million-dollar grin, but it just didn't make him any less bewitching.

His hair, the rich dark color of espresso, was a touch too long. It made her think ridiculous thoughts of the long-ago Scottish warriors who, with a name like McKinnon, had been Dylan's ancestors.

He had a strong nose, and a faintly clefted chin, high cheekbones that were whisker roughened today. And stamped across those perfect, breath-stealing features was an expression of fierce determination, an almost frightening singleness of focus.

His eyes, framed with a sinful abundance of black, soot-dipped lash, and bluer than the sky right before the sun faded from it, had that look of a man who was looking inward to his own strength, as well as outward at his world.

Katie hated how she loved to watch him run, but

Dylan McKinnon wasn't the most eligible bachelor in Hillsboro, Ontario, for no reason.

Don't stop, she silently begged as he slowed near her window. She pulled back so that he wouldn't see she had watched, darted for the counter as she read his intention to come into her store. He opened the door just as she managed to get behind the cash register and slam her glasses back on her face.

She peeked up over the rims of her spectacles at him, trying to hide the raggedness of her breathing from her unscheduled sprint behind the counter.

"I'm just taking an order," she said, no-nonsense, *professional.* "I'll be with you shortly."

The grin erased some of the warrior from his face, but the lifted eyebrow reinforced it, said as clearly as though he had spoken, *No mere woman has ever kept the great McKinnon waiting.*

She pursed her lips to let him know others might be bowled over by his charms, but she was not. She did feel weakly compelled to watch his daily run, which he surely never had to know. He had to wait in line like everyone else.

Mrs. Johnson, however, wrecked Katie's intention to humble him. Obvious recognition dawned in her face. "Oh, no," she said breathlessly, forgetting her hurry, "You go first, Mr. McKinnon."

"Dylan, please. Are you sure?" He smiled at Mrs. Johnson with chocolate-melting charm.

"Oh," she stammered. "Of course, I'm sure."

"Katie, my lady," he said, stepping up to the counter, with his all-male swagger.

She steeled herself against that smile. "Mr. McKinnon."

"What do you think of the new jacket?" he asked, just as if he hadn't jumped the line, just as if he wasn't taking another customer's time.

She glanced at it, saw close-up the way it showed every line of muscle in his arm, and gulped. As she dragged her eyes back up to his face, she saw the distinctive red Daredevils emblem on his chest. When she met his eyes, she was pretty sure he was conceited enough to know exactly what she thought of his new jacket. Now she wouldn't have given him the pleasure of telling him, even if there were goblins waiting in the back room to cut out her tongue if she uttered a lie.

"I would think, by definition, a jacket should have sleeves."

He frowned at her. "It's a running jacket. You want your arms free when you run. Plus, you don't want to overheat. Our engineers designed it. It's going into production next week."

"It has a hood," she pointed out.

"Uh, yeah?"

"So, your head might get cold, but your arms won't?"

He scowled at her. "Part of the reason it's designed without sleeves is the sweat issue."

"Sweat?" she echoed, hoping it didn't sound as if she was saying a dirty word.

"It's easier to clean an undershirt than the whole jacket." He unzipped, as if he was actually considering demonstrating, and it seemed as if her life had reached a new low. She was discussing undershirts with Dylan McKinnon.

She held up her hand before he managed to get the jacket off, and he lifted his eyebrows at her, faintly mocking, as if he had guessed she was too long without a man and given to swooning.

"Well," she said brightly, trying to hide her wild discomfort, "what can I do for you today?"

"Katie, my lady, I need you to just send a little something to, uh—"

"Heather," she said stiffly.

He grinned. "Yeah, Heather. Thanks."

"Message?" she asked.

"Uh—"

Katie rapidly calculated in her head. This was Heather's third bouquet. "Something like, Sorry I forgot?" she prompted him.

If he was the least contrite that his fickle heart was so predictable, he did not show it. He nodded, grinned at her with *approval.* "Perfect. Oh, and maybe send a little something to Tara, too."

Since his time with Heather was drawing to a close, she guessed cynically. Tara was always on the back burner. Poor Tara. Poor Heather.

He turned, gave Mrs. Johnson a friendly salute and went out the door. The flower shop, which had seemed cheerful and cozy only moments before, seemed faded and gray, hopelessly dreary, as if he had swept every bit of color and energy out of the room with him.

"Was that really Daredevil Dylan McKinnon of the Toronto Blue Jays?" Mrs. Johnson asked, wide-eyed.

Dylan McKinnon had not thrown a baseball in more than five years. In fact, in Katie's opinion, he had managed to parlay the shortest career in professional baseball in history into quite a bit more celebrity than he deserved.

"None other," she said reluctantly.

"My," Mrs. Johnson said. "My."

Young. Old. Whatever. Dylan McKinnon simply had that indefinable *thing* that made him irresistible to the opposite sex.

Pheromones, Katie told herself. He was emitting them with his sweat, a primitive, silent mating call that commanded a woman to choose the biggest, the strongest, the toughest. When he was that handsome, as well, the average woman had very little chance against him. For one with at least a modicum of brains, however, there was no excuse. Though there was no telling what would have happened if he had managed to get the jacket off!

Weakling, she berated herself silently. Outwardly she said "Now about Gertrude's wreath. What kind of lilies—"

"Does he live around here?" Mrs. Johnson asked eagerly. "My granddaughter is a great fan."

If you love your granddaughter, keep her away from that man. "I don't think he lives around here," Katie offered stiffly. In fact, the head office for his wildly successful sporting goods line was located behind a discreet bronze plaque that read McKinnon two doors down, but Katie saw no reason she should offer that. She'd never be able to find a parking spot if the location of the daredevil's office and empire became public knowledge to his rabid fans.

"Gertrude's flowers?" she prompted.

"Oh, yes."

"Since she liked lilies, what would you think of lily of the valley?" Katie asked. "They signify a return to happiness."

"Oh, my dear, that is so lovely. Thank you. One of the reasons I shop here is because you know these things."

In Victorian times, people had always associated meanings with flowers. Katie, as the flower girl, knew those meanings and loved working them into her arrangements.

"It will be a beautiful wreath," she promised. Already she could see the lilies woven together with babies' breath.

But she could also see Heather Richards's bouquet. Perhaps a few snapdragons scattered among yellow roses. A warning of deception and a decrease in love—not that a woman like Heather was ever going to get the meaning.

Like most of the women Dylan McKinnon showed interest in, if they hadn't had celebrity status before they showed up on his arm, they certainly did after. Heather, however, had held minor celebrity status before, as Miss Hillsboro Bikini. Katie would send some azaleas to Tara: *take care of yourself.*

"Dylan seemed to know you," Mrs. Johnson said, almost as if her mind had drifted right along with Katie's. And right back to him. "He did call you Katie, my lady."

"Mr. McKinnon is a very good customer."

"I think it's very sweet that he has a pet name for you."

"Well, Mr. McKinnon is a man who has being sweet to women down to a fine art." And she should know. She had been handling his flower orders since she had opened her shop two doors down from him, just over a year ago.

She didn't want to be mean-spirited about it, because Dylan McKinnon had always been nothing but charming to her. He had charm down to a science: when she was in the room with him it was hard not to give in to the heady sense that she was the only girl in his world, that he truly *cared* about her, that he genuinely found her interesting.

But, of course, that was precisely why he could get any woman he batted those amazing lashes at. Besides, he was one of her best customers, and he didn't just give her a great deal of business, but also spin-off business. Almost all his old girlfriends enjoyed the quality and imaginativeness of her flower arrangements so much that they became her customers.

But she was sure Mrs. Johnson wouldn't look quite so smitten—ready to deliver her granddaughter in gift wrap and a bow—if she knew the truth.

Despite the *appearance* of kindness, the truth could be told in the way a man ordered his flowers.

These ones for Heather for example. It was the third time he'd ordered flowers for her. That would make this the make-up bouquet. He'd probably forgotten lunch or left her in the lurch at the opera. Perhaps a few asters, which signified an afterthought, mixed with the snap-dragons and roses.

If he followed his pattern, and there was no reason to believe he would not, there would be one more delivery of flowers—the-nice-knowing-you-bouquet—and then Heather would be history, along with the dozen or so others that Dylan had romanced.

A dozen women in a year. That was one a month. It was disgraceful.

And then there were the girls who waited in the wings, who received the occasional bouquet when lust-of-the-month was cooling: Tara, Sarah, Janet, and Margot. Add to that there was a special someone he chose flowers for himself, every Friday without fail.

Sending his flowers was like having a rather embarrassing personal look at his little black book!

It was absolutely shameful, Katie thought, that she could see through that man so clearly, despise his devil-may-care attitude with women, and still run to the window every day to watch the pure poetry of him running, still feel herself blush when he smiled at her or teased her, still feel that disastrous sense of *yearning* that had always meant nothing but trouble in her well-ordered life.

Dylan McKinnon walked through his office doors, checked his watch. A mile in six and a half minutes. Not bad for a guy about to turn twenty-seven. Not bad at all. His pulse was already back to normal.

He glanced around the reception area with satisfaction. The decor was rich and sensuous, deep-brown leather sofas, a genuine Turkish rug, good art, low lighting. A pot of Katie's flowers, peach-colored roses that seemed to glow with an inner light, was on the reception desk. All in all, he thought his office was not too bad for a guy who had not even finished college.

"Could you call Erin in design?" he said to the receptionist. "Just tell her I think we should consider making the hood on this jacket removable before it goes into production." What about zip-on sleeves, since by *definition* a jacket had sleeves? "Actually, have her call me."

"All right," the receptionist said.

Margot was a gorgeous girl; married, thankfully. He did not date women who were married or who worked for him, clearly demonstrating what an ethical guy he was, something that would surprise the hell out of Katie, the flower girl.

Dylan shook off the little shiver of unexpected regret he felt. What did he care if Katie's disapproval of him telegraphed through her ramrod-stiff spine every time he walked in her store? It was *entertaining,* he told himself sternly. He'd thought, once or twice, of asking her out—he knew from casual conversations over the year he'd known her, she was single, and something about her intrigued—but she was way more complicated than the kind of girl he liked.

The receptionist apologetically handed him a ream of pink message slips. "One from your dad, one from your sister," she said. "The rest from Miss Richards."

"Ah," he said, and stuffed them in his pocket. He didn't want to talk to his dad today. Probably not tomorrow, either. As for Heather, okay, so he'd missed her last night. She'd wanted him to go to a fashion show. Real men didn't go to fashion shows. He'd implied he *might* attend to avoid sulking or arguments, but he'd never promised he would accompany her. Apparently he had only postponed the inevitable.

He'd gotten in from the sports pub that he was a part owner of to see his answering machine blinking in a frenzy. Each message from her; each one more screechy than the last.

Heather was beginning to give him a headache. Right on schedule. How come girls like Heather always acted like, well, Heather? Possessive, high maintenance, predictable.

Predictable.

That's what he was to Katie, the flower lady. He didn't really know whether to be annoyed or amused that she had his number so completely.

Still, how had she known what to write on that card for Heather?

The little minx was psychic. And darned smart. And hilariously transparent. He had thought she was going to faint when he'd nearly taken his jacket off in front of her. She had a quality of naïveté about her that was refreshing. Intriguing. She'd told him once, tight-lipped and reluctant to part with anything that might be construed as personal information, that she was divorced. Funny, for someone who had "forever girl" written all over her.

The fact that he was predictable to someone who was a little less than worldly, despite her divorce, was somewhat troubling.

Rather than be troubled, he picked the least of the three evils on his messages and called Tara.

"Hey, sis," he said when she answered. "How are you?" He could hear his fourteen-month-old nephew, Jake, howling in the background.

Tara, never one for small talk, said, "Call Dad, for Pete's sake. What is wrong with you?"

His sister was seven years older than him. He had long-ago accepted that she was never going to look at him as a world-class athlete or as Hillsboro's most successful entrepreneur. She was just going to see her little brother, who needed to be bullied into doing what was right. What she perceived was right.

"And for heaven's sake, Dylan, who is that woman you are being photographed with? A new low, even for you. Miss Hillsboro Mud Wrestler? Sheesh."

"She is not Miss Hillsboro Mud Wrestler!" he protested. Only his sister would see a girl like Heather as a new low. The guys at Doofus's Pub knew the truth. Heather was *hot.*

"Dylan, call Dad. And find a decent girl. Oh, never mind. I doubt if you could find a decent girl who would go out with you. Honestly, you are too old to be a captive of your hormones, and too young to be having a midlife crisis. Mom's sick. She isn't going to get any better, and you can't change that by racing your motorcycle or dating every bimbo in Hillsboro. And beyond."

"I'm not trying to change anything," he said coolly indignant.

"Humph," she said with disbelief.

Don't ask her, he ordered himself, but he asked anyway, casually, as if he couldn't care less. "How would you define decent?"

"Wholesome. Sweet. *Smart* would be a nice change. I have to go. Jake just ate an African violet. Do you think that's poisonous?"

I'm sure it's nothing compared to your tongue. He refrained from saying it. "Bye, sis."

"Only someone who loves you as much as me would tell you the truth."

"Thanks," he said dryly.

Still, as he hung up, he reluctantly recognized the gift of her honesty. Too many people fawned over him, but refreshingly, his sister was not one of them.

And neither was Katie Pritchard, who, when he thought about it, was the only woman he knew who even remotely would fit his sister's definition of *decent.*

He ordered a ton of flowers from her, even before someone told him she sent secret messages in with the blossoms. But so far not one person on the receiving end had said a single word about secret messages.

Still, despite the lack of secret messages, he liked going into her little shop. It was like an oasis in the middle of the city. Perversely, he *liked* it that while she could barely contain her disapproval of him she still nearly fainted when he threatened to do something perfectly normal, like remove his jacket.

He liked bugging her. He liked *sparring* with her. Okay, in the past year he had played with the fact most women found him, well, irresistible, but not nearly on the level he had Katie believing. He'd taken to going in there when he was bored and sending flowers to his sister. Also on the receiving end of bouquets were his PR manager, Sarah, and Sister Janet, the nun who ran the boys and girls club. Sometimes Dylan ordered flowers just to see Katie's lips twitch with disapproval when he said, "Just put 'From Dylan with love.'" Even the flowers on the reception desk right now had arrived with that card, addressed to Margot, which he'd quickly discarded.

And, of course, once a week, he went in and she let him go into the refrigerated back room and pick out his own bouquet from the buckets of blossoms there. She would never admit it, but he knew no one else was allowed into that back room. He never told her anything about that bouquet, or who it was for, and Katie did not ask, but probably assumed the worst of him.

Katie found him predictable. Katie, who looked as if she was trying out for librarian of the year.

Every time she saw him, she put those glasses on that made her look stern and formidable. And the dresses!

Just because she was the flower girl, did that mean there was some kind of rule that she had to wear flowered dresses, the kind with lace collars, and that tied at the back? She had curves under there, but for some reason she had decided not to be attractive. She wore flat black shoes, as if she was ashamed of her height, which he thought was amazing. Didn't she know models were tall and skinny, just like her? Okay, most of them had a little more in the chest department, but at least hers looked real.

It all added up to one thing. *Decent.*

He smiled evilly, wondering how the flower girl would feel if she knew he had covertly studied her chest and pronounced it authentic?

She'd probably throw a vase of flowers right at his head.

At the thought of little Miss Calm and Cool and Composed being riled enough to throw something, Dylan felt the oddest little shiver. Challenge? He'd always been a man who had a hard time backing down from a challenge.

His sister had said a decent girl wouldn't go out with him. So much easier to focus on that than to think about the other things Tara had said, or about calling his father. Besides if a decent girl would go out with him that would make Tara wrong about everything.

Why not Katie? He'd always been reluctantly intrigued by her, even though she was no obvious beauty. She was cute, in that deliberately understated way of hers, and he realized he liked her hair: light brown, shiny, wisps of it falling out of her ponytail. Still, she *could* smile more often, wear a dusting of makeup to draw some attention to those amazing hazel eyes, but no, she *chose* to make herself look dowdy.

She did fit his sister's definition of decent. Wholesome she was. And smart? He was willing to bet she knew the name of the current mayor of Hillsboro, and who the prime minister of Canada was, too. She would know how to balance her checkbook, where to get the best deal on toilet paper—though if you even mentioned toilet paper around her she would probably turn all snooty—and the titles of at least three Steinbeck novels.

He was just as willing to bet she wouldn't know a basketball great from a hockey sensation. He liked how she seemed unsettled around him, but did her darnedest to hide it. He was pretty sure she watched him run every day.

So, Katie thought he was predictable? So, his Tara didn't think a decent girl would go out with him?

If there was one thing Dylan McKinnon excelled at it was being unpredictable. It was doing the unexpected. It was taking people by surprise. That was what had made him a superb athlete and now an excellent businessman. He always kept his edge.

His phone rang. It was the receptionist.

"Heather on the line."

"I'm not here."

He'd talk to Heather after she got her flowers. That should calm her down enough to be reasonable. There had been a hockey game on TV last night. No one in their right mind would have expected him to go to a fashion show instead of watching hockey. It was nearly the end of the season!

Heather had promised him girls modeling underwear, but the truth was he didn't care. He was growing weary of his own game.

Secretly, he didn't care if he never saw one more woman strutting around in her underwear again. One more top that showed a belly button, or one more pair of figure-hugging jeans. He didn't care if he never saw one more body piercing, one more head of excruciatingly blond hair, one more set of suspiciously inflated breasts.

He felt like a man trying to care about all the things the wealthy successful businessman ex-athlete was supposed to care about, but somehow his sister was right. He wasn't outrunning anything. His heart wasn't in it anymore. He wanted, no, yearned for something different. He wanted to be *surprised* for a change, instead of always being the one surprising others.

He thought of her again, of Katie, of those enormous hazel eyes, intelligent, wary, behind those glasses.

On an impulse he picked up the phone, rolled through his Rolodex, punched out her number.

"The Flower Girl."

"Hey, Katie, my lady, Dylan."

Silence.

Then, ever so politely, "Yes?"

"Would you—" What was he doing? Had he been on the verge of asking her out for dinner? Katie, the flower girl? He felt an uncharacteristic hesitation.

"Yes?"

"Uh, name three Steinbeck novels for me? I'm doing a questionnaire. I could win a prize. A year's worth of free coffee from my favorite café." He lied with such ease, another talent that Katie would disapprove of heartily.

"You don't know the names of three of Steinbeck's novels?" she asked, just a hint of pity in her cool voice.

"You know. Dumb jock."

"Oh." She said, as if she *did* know, as if it had completely slipped her mind—or it didn't count—that he ran a multi-million-dollar business. "Which ones would you like? The most well-known ones? The first ones? Last ones?"

"Any old three."

"Hmm. *East of Eden. The Grapes of Wrath. Of Mice and Men.* Though, personally, I'd have to say I think his finest work was a short story called 'The Chrysanthemums.' "

He laughed. "That figures. About flowers, right?"

"About an unhappy marriage."

"Is there any other kind?" he asked, keeping his tone light. In actual fact, his parents had enjoyed an extraordinary union—until unexpectedly the "worse" part of the better-or-worse equation had hit and his father had turned into a man Dylan didn't even know.

She was silent, and he realized he'd hit a little too close to home, a reminder of why he couldn't ever ask her out. She was sensitive and sweet, and he was, well, not.

And then she said, softly, with admirable bravery given the fact she had presumably not had a good marriage, at all, "I like to hope."

Oh-oh! A girl who liked to hope, despite the fact divorce was part of her history. Still, if she *hoped* you'd think she'd try just a little harder to *attract.*

"Not for myself personally," she added, her voice suddenly strangled. "I mean, I just want to believe, somewhere, somehow, someone is happy. Together. With another someone."

He snorted, a sound redolent with the cynicism he had been nurturing for the past year.

The word *hope* used in any conversation pertaining to marriage should be more than enough to scare any devoted bachelor near to death, but he'd always had trouble with risk assessment once he'd set a challenge for himself.

If anything, a jolt of fear sent him forward rather than back. That was why Dylan had skied every black diamond run at Whistler Blackcomb. He had bungee-jumped off the New River Gorge Bridge in Virginia on Bridge Day. He planned to sign up for a tour on the Space Shuttle the first year his company grossed five hundred million dollars. Dylan McKinnon prided himself in the fact he was afraid of nothing. He'd *earned* the nickname "Daredevil."

He took chances. That's why he was where he was today.

It was also the reason his baseball career had ended almost before it started, the voice of reason tried to remind him.

He overrode the voice of reason, took a deep breath, spat it out. "Would you like to go for dinner sometime?"

Silence.

"Katie? Are you there?"

"You haven't even sent the fourth bouquet to Heather yet," she said.

"The what?"

"The fourth one. The nice-to-know-you-I'm-such-a-great-guy-I'm-sending-flowers-but-I'm-moving-on one."

He felt a shiver go up and down his spine. How was it that Katie knew him so well? He thought of the year he had known her, those intelligent eyes scrutinizing him, missing nothing. Assessing, mostly correctly, that he was a self-centered, selfish kind of guy.

"Okay," he said. "Send it. Instead of the I'm-sorry one."

"I already sent that one."

Little Miss Efficient. "Okay, send the other one, too, then."

"Do you want the message to read, 'It's been great knowing you. I wish you all the best'?"

He *had* become predictable. Hell. "Sure," he said, "That's fine."

"Anything else?"

"You tell me. Am I available now that the fourth bouquet is being sent?"

"Of course you are," she said sweetly.

Sweet had been one of the components his sister had used to define decent.

"Great. When would you like to go for dinner?"

"Never," she said firmly.

He was stunned, but he realized there was only one reason little miss Katie Wholesome would have said no to him. And it wasn't what his sister had said, either, that no decent girl would go out with him!

"You have a guy, huh?"

Pause. "Actually, I have a customer. If you'll excuse me." And then she hung up. Katie Pritchard hung up on him.

He set down the phone, stunned. And then he began to laugh. Be careful what you wish for, he thought. He'd wished for a surprise, and she had delivered him one.

He'd just been rejected by Katie, the flower girl. He should have been fuming.

But for the first time in a long time he felt challenged. He could make her say *yes.*

Then what, he asked himself? A funny question for a man who absolutely prided himself in *not* asking questions about the future when it came to his dealings with the opposite sex.

Despite the rather racy divorcée title, Katie would be the kind of girl who didn't go out with a guy without a chaperone, a written contract and a rule book. The perfect girl to invite to dinner at his sister's house. That was the *then what,* and nothing beyond that.

So why did his mind ask, *What would it be like to kiss her?*

"Buddy," he told himself, "what are you playing with?"

For some reason, even though she was pretending to be the plainest girl in Hillsboro, he could picture her lips, *exactly.* They were wide and plump, and even without a hint of lipstick on them, they practically begged a man to taste them.

He tried to think what Heather's lips looked like. All he could think of was red grease smeared on his shirt collar. He shuddered, even though Heather was not a girl who would normally make a man shudder.

"Playing with Katie is like toying with a saint," he warned himself. But he was already aware that he felt purposeful. Katie intrigued him, and he wanted her to come out for dinner with him. He was also about to prove to his sister how wrong she could be. About everything.

Now, how was he going to convince Katie to go out with him? He bet it wouldn't be hard at all. If he applied a little pressure to that initial resistance, she'd cave in to his charm like an old mine collapsing.

An old mine collapsing, he told himself happily. *Take that, Steinbeck.*

CHAPTER TWO

"NEVER!" Katie repeated, slamming down the phone and glaring at it.

What had that been all about, anyway? Whatever it was, she hadn't liked it one little bit. Why was Dylan McKinnon asking her out?

To be completely honest, it was a moment she had fantasized about since she had moved in next door to him, but like most fantasies, when it actually happened, the collision with reality was not pretty. Going out with him would *wreck* everything.

Because he only went out with people temporarily.

And then it would be over. Really over. No more Dylan dropping by her shop to tease her, to order flowers, to ruffle her feathers, to remind her of the fickleness of men. Dylan, without her really knowing it, had helped take her mind off the death of her marriage.

The death of—she stopped herself. She was not thinking about that death.

Two years since she and Marcus had parted ways. In the past year, the flower shop had given her a sense of putting her life back together. Whether she liked it or not, Dylan had been part of that.

It occurred to her that if Dylan's running by her window and unexpected drop-bys had become such a highlight in her life, she really had allowed herself to become pathetic.

As if to underscore that discovery, she suddenly caught a glimpse of herself in the mirror—no makeup, hair drawn back in a careless ponytail, and that dress. It was truly hideous, and she knew it. But when she had opened The Flower Girl she had convinced herself to take on a persona, she had shopped for vintage dresses that would underscore the image she was trying to create: back-to-nature, wholesome, flower child.

But underneath she was aware of another motive. Fear. She didn't want to be attractive anymore. She wanted to protect herself from all the things that being attractive to men meant.

It meant being asked out. Participating in the dance of life. It might mean a heart opening again, hope breathing back to life.

I like to hope, she had foolishly said to Dylan.

But the truth was the last thing she wanted was to *hope.* Ever since the breakup of her parents' marriage when she was nine, she had dreamed of a little house and her own little family. Dreamed of a bassinet and a sweet-smelling baby—

Katie slammed the door on those thoughts. Dylan had asked her out for dinner, and already some renegade part of herself wanted to *hope.* She congratulated herself on having the strength to say no before it went one breath further.

As egotistical as he was, even Dylan McKinnon had to understand *never.*

She sighed. Dylan was a disruptive force in the universe. The female part of the universe. Specifically, her part of the universe.

She glanced at the clock. Close enough to quitting time to shut the doors. She closed up and made a decision to head to a movie. Distract herself with something like a political thriller that had nothing to do with romance, love, babies. All those things that could cut so deeply.

But, as she was leaving her business, so was he. Despite her effort to turn the lock more quickly, pretend she didn't see him, *escape,* her fingers were suddenly fumbling, and there he was looking over her shoulder.

"Hey," he said, taking the keys from her, turning the lock, handing them back, "I think we're going to redesign the jacket."

She was annoyed that she had to see him again so soon after declaring *never,* and even more annoyed that she shivered with awareness at that brief touch of his hand. Still, she could be relieved that he seemed to have already forgotten he had asked her out. That's how much it had meant to him.

"Make the hood detachable, sleeves that zip on."

He was too close to her; she liked the protection of her counter separating them. The cool scent of mountain breezes wafted from him, his eyes were intent on hers. She struggled to know what he was talking about, and then realized he was back to the jacket she had seen him running in. She didn't care about his jacket. She wanted to get away from him. Desperately. How dare he look so glorious without half trying? How dare he make her so aware she was looking a little frumpy today? How dare he make her care, when she had managed to care about so little for so long?

"I don't like clothes with zip-on parts," she said, then instantly regretted offering her opinion, when it did not forward her goal of getting away.

He frowned at her. "Why not?"

"Because they're confusing and hard to use," she said.

He eyed her. "You're not particularly coordinated. Remember the time you dropped the vase of roses? Slipped on the ice out there, and I had to help you up? Or how about the time you tripped over that piece of carpet and went flying?"

His eyes crinkled at the corners when he smiled. He was aging, just like everybody else. So, he was the one other man in the universe, besides Richard Gere, who could make eye crinkles look sexy.

"Thank you for bringing up all of my happier memories," she said, annoyed. It was really unfair that he could make her feel as embarrassed as if that had happened yesterday. Of course, he never had to know it was him who brought about that self-conscious awkwardness!

"So, no offense, but you're not exactly the person we're designing for."

"That's too bad," she said, coolly, "because I'm average, just like most of the people who buy your clothing are average. They're going for a run around the block, or taking their dog out for a walk. They want to look athletic, but it doesn't necessarily mean they are. They aren't getting ready for the Olympics or the Blue Jays training camp."

He was glowering at her, which was so much better than the sexy eye-crinkle smile, so she continued.

"So, then it starts raining, and where are your sleeves and your hood if they're detachable? Making nice lumps in your pockets? Or at home on the entryway table? Within three months I would have lost at least one of the sleeves, and probably the hood."

He sighed. "We need you on the design team. Want a job?"

"No."

"Okay, want to go grab a burger, then?"

She eyed him narrowly. Ridiculous to think he had given up on his dinner invitation. He had the innocent look down pat, but when he wanted something, she was willing to bet he had the tenacious predator spirit of a shark! "I already told you no to dinner."

"Grabbing a burger is not exactly dinner," he said. "Market research. The smartest girl I know can help me with my jacket design."

"I am not the smartest girl you know!" Oh boy, relegated to the position of the smart one. Almost as dreadful as being relegated to the position of a friend but never a girlfriend.

"Yup, you are."

"Well then you don't know very many girls."

"We both know that's a lie," he said smoothly.

"Okay, you don't know very many girls who hang out at the library instead of at Doofus's Pub and Grill."

"You don't have to say that as if it's a dirty word. I'm a part owner in Doofus's."

Which explained why a place with a name like Doofus's could be so wildly successful. The man had the

Midas touch—not that she wanted to weaken herself any further by contemplating his touch. She had to be strong.

Hard, with him gazing at her from under the silky tangle of his soot-dark eyelashes. "Do *you* hang out at the library?" he asked.

How could he say that in a tone that made her feel as if he'd asked something way too personal, like the color of her underwear. She could feel an uncomfortable blush starting. "You don't have to say *that* as if it's a dirty word. The library is beautiful. Have you ever been to the Hillsboro Library?"

"Have you ever been to Doofus's?" he shot back.

"Oh, look," she said, changing the subject deftly, "it's starting to rain. And me without my zip-on sleeves. I've got to go, Dylan. See you at the library sometime."

But his hand on her sleeve stopped her. It was not a momentous occasion, a casual touch, but it was the second one in as many minutes. But given she had not wanted to even *think* about his touch, it seemed impossibly cruel that she now was experiencing it again. He probably touched people—girl people—like that all the time. But the easy and unconscious strength in his touch, the sizzle of heat, made her heart pound right up into her throat, made her feel weak and vulnerable, made her ache with a treacherous longing.

"Tell me something about you," he said. "One thing. Anything you want."

"I just did. I like the library." No wonder he had a woman a month! When he said that, his eyes fastened on her face so intently, it felt as if he really wanted to know! She *knew* it was a line, so she hated herself for feeling honored by his interest.

"Something else," he said.

"I live with three males," she said, no reason to tell him they were cats.

He laughed. "I bet they're cats."

The thing you had to remember about Dylan McKinnon was that underneath all that easygoing charm, he was razor sharp. She glanced down at herself to see if had completed her glamorous look today with cat hair, but didn't, thankfully, see any.

"I'm divorced," she reminded him, hoping that failure would be enough to scare him off, unless he enjoyed the horrible stereotype some men had of a divorced woman, a woman who had known the pleasures of the marital bed, and now did not: *hungry.*

"That is a surprise about you," he said. "I would have never guessed divorced."

Had she succeeded in making herself look so frumpy that he didn't believe anyone would have married her? If that was true, what was his sudden interest in her?

"Why not?" she demanded.

"I don't know. You seem like a decent girl."

"Divorced women are indecent?" she asked, and then found herself blushing, looking furiously away from him.

"Sorry." He touched her chin. He had to quit touching her! "I didn't mean it like that. You just seem like the kind of woman who would say forever and mean it."

"I did mean it!" she said, with far more feeling than she would have liked.

"So it was his fault."

She was not going to have this way-too-intimate conversation with Dylan McKinnon on a chance meeting on a public street.

"Does it have to be somebody's fault?" she asked woodenly. Who, after all, could predict how people would react to tragedy? She had miscarried the baby she wanted so badly. It had all unraveled from there.

Sometimes, when she couldn't sleep at night, she tormented herself by wondering if it had been unraveling already, and if she had hoped the baby would somehow glue it back together, give her someone to love in the face of a husband who was distant, from a life that was so far from the fairy tale she had dreamed for herself. This was exactly why she now dedicated her life to her business. Business was not *painful.* It did not cause introspection. It did not leave time for self-pity or self-analysis.

"Come grab a burger with me at Doofus's," he said, and laid a persuasive hand on her wrist.

She heard something gentle in his voice, knew she had not succeeded in keeping her pain out of her eyes.

"They make a mean burger."

"I'm a vegetarian."

"Really?" he said skeptically.

"If I went there, would you come to the library after?" she said, sliding her arm out from under his touch as if she was making a sneak escape from a cobra. Maybe the best defense was an offense. He'd be about as likely to visit a library as she would be to visit a turkey shoot. Still, as he contemplated her, her heart was acting as if she was in a position of life-threatening danger, racing at about thirteen million beats per minute.

"Sure. I'll come to the library. I *like* doing different things. Surprising myself."

Right. He just had all the answers. He'd never go to

the library, just say he was going to, and then send a bouquet of flowers when he didn't show.

"Why are you doing this?" she asked, folding her rescued limbs over her chest, protectively.

He sighed, looked away, ran a hand through the rich darkness of his hair. "I want a change," he said, and she was pretty sure he surprised them both with his sincerity.

Still, to be asked out because he needed a change from his bevy of bimbos? It was insulting!

"And you'd like a new toy to play with," she guessed, with a shake of her head.

He regarded her thoughtfully. "I bet your husband didn't deserve you. He probably wasn't worth the sadness I saw in your eyes when you mentioned your divorce."

The comment was unexpected, his voice quiet and serious, a side of him she had never seen.

Dylan McKinnon's charm was dangerous when he was all playful and boyish. But it turned downright lethal when he became serious, the cast of his face suddenly accentuating the firmness around his mouth, the strength in the cut of his cheekbones and chin.

"I have to go," she said.

She whirled away from him. Her eyes were stinging.

"Hey, Katie," he said, jogging up beside her now, blocking her attempt to escape from all his sympathy with some dignity, "I'm sorry, I didn't mean to hurt you."

"Would you go away? Guys like you always hurt girls like me."

He stopped. Stared at her. She saw her arrow had hit.

"Not every man is going to be like your ex-husband," he said evenly.

"How do you know? You didn't know him." *Or me.*

The truth was it didn't really matter if Dylan was like Marcus, if she was still like her. It was herself she didn't trust after her whole life had fallen apart. She did not trust herself to make good choices, and certainly not to be able to survive that kind of pain ever again.

But it was true Dylan was nothing like Marcus had been. Dylan had his faults, but he didn't try to hide any of them. If anything, he seemed to celebrate them. He didn't seem to have any secrets, unless she counted that one bouquet that he picked himself every week and delivered himself.

Other than that her remark about guys like him hurting girls like her was really undeserved. He had been her most loyal customer. He'd always only been kind to her, funny and charming. He'd helped her pick up the glass that time she had broken the rose vase. He had a gift for making her feel oddly pretty—or at least interesting—even on her ugliest days. He was aggravatingly sure of himself, yes, but he never crossed that line into conceit.

"Come have a hamburger," he said. "No strings attached. I promise I'll make you laugh."

"How can you promise that?" she said, aware suddenly that she *ached* to laugh. To feel light and unburdened. To forget that she had failed at marriage and miscarried a baby. In his eyes she thought she glimpsed something of herself she had lost, a woman who had been carefree and laughter filled. She longed, suddenly, to be that woman again, even if only for a little while.

The pull of being returned to a happier self was too strong to resist.

"Okay," she said, "A hamburger. To reassure you that

I'm not in any danger of turning into a tragic cat lady. And maybe to give you a few ideas for a jacket that people won't lose the sleeves of. And then that's the end of this. Am I clear?"

He nodded with patent insincerity.

She looked at her watch. She could make a quick trip to the mall before she met him. If sympathy had in any way motivated this invitation, there would be nothing like a new pair of jeans and a slinky top to convince him—and herself—that she was not in need of it.

"I'll meet you. In an hour. At Doofus's."

"Perfect," he said, and smiled that slow, sexy utterly sincere smile that had convinced a zillion women before her they were the only one that mattered to him.

It was once she was safe in her car, away from the mesmerizing magnetism of him, that she allowed herself to look hard at the terrible truth he did not know…or maybe he did.

She had a crush on him! That was why she watched him run every day! Look at how easily he had overcome her objections! She had vowed one moment she was never going out to dinner with him, and broken that vow within minutes of having made it.

"I can't do this," she realized.

Because what if—okay it was way out there—but what if they developed feelings for each other? What if she fell in love with him, and he with her? What if all her fairy-tale fantasies roared back to life?

And what if she lost *again?*

"I cannot survive another loss," she whispered. So much safer to have an unrealistic crush on a man, to watch him run, to keep a safe enough distance that each of his faults remained crystal clear, not blurred by the beauty of his physique, his eyes, the totally unexpected firmness in his voice, when he'd said, "I bet he didn't deserve you."

No. Here was the thing she was going to have to realize with her and with men, whether it was Marcus Pritchard, who had seemed safe and stable, or Dylan McKinnon, who seemed dangerous, but who called to some part of her that wanted an adventure. Her judgment was just plain bad.

Some people had good instincts. They knew good people from bad, they knew which horse to bet on, they got a chill up and down their spine if the airplane they were about to board was going to crash.

Katie did not consider herself one of those people. Not anymore. The girl most likely to stay married forever was now divorced. Following her heart the first time had led her to heartbreak. But had it been her heart she had followed, or a desperate need to believe in family after her own had broken apart?

She wanted to impress Dylan that she could look great in hip-hugging jeans and tops that showed a little décolleté? She had to fight that impulse and do the exact opposite! She didn't need to upgrade her wardrobe! She needed to downplay it even more than it was downplayed now.

So, instead of driving to the mall, she drove home. Her three cats, Motley, Crew, and Bartholomew greeted her at the door with enthusiasm that could have only been earned by a tragic cat person.

Though it was still early, she reached way into the back of her closet, found her ugliest, frumpiest and most comfortable flannel pajamas. She heated a frozen pizza in the microwave and finally looked up the number of Doofus's.

"Is Dylan McKinnon there?"

"Who's asking?"

The question said it all. It was asked warily, as if the bartender fielded dozens of these calls. Women, infatuated beyond pride, beyond reason, calling for Dylan, after hearing he hung out there.

"Um, I was supposed to meet him there in a few minutes. Could you tell him I can't make it?"

"You're standing up Dylan McKinnon? Who are you? Leticia Manning?"

The mention of the young and very gorgeous Canadian actress served as a reminder of the kind of woman Dylan *really* went out with, the status of the kind of women he really went out with. Katie Pritchard was a plain Jane. He was a playboy. She needed to remember that.

"Unless he's expecting more than one woman to meet him tonight—" a possibility? "—he'll know who I am!" she said, slammed down the phone, and took a bite of her pizza. It tasted exactly like cardboard. Bartholomew climbed on her lap and she broke off a piece and fed it to him. He purred and sighed and kneaded her with his paws.

Which begged the question—what was so wrong with being a crazy cat lady? She'd send Dylan a bouquet of flowers tomorrow by way of apology. After all, he did it all the time.

Dylan took a sip of his beer, put the nine ball in the side pocket and glanced at the door. The smug sense of self-congratulation that he had felt ever since he'd so easily changed her mind about coming here was dissipating. Was she coming or not? He was a little unsettled by how tense he felt now that it was getting later and she wasn't here. Katie was not the "fashionably late" kind of gal. It was raining quite hard now. The streets would be slick. Did her lack of coordination extend to her driving? Had she—

"Hey, boss," Cy called, "your lady friend ain't coming. She just called."

Rafe Miller looked up from the pool table, guffawed with great enjoyment. "Hey, Dill, you been stood up!"

Dylan liked coming to Doofus's because it was just a local watering hole. It was staffed by people he'd known for a long time. Most of the clients were his buddies. No one here was the least impressed with his celebrity, which at the moment, for one of the first times in his memory, he was sorry for. Guys who really knew you had no respect; they didn't know when to back off.

"Are you seeing Leticia Manning?" Cy asked.

More guffaws.

Dylan glared at him.

"Because she was snooty sounding, just like Leticia Manning."

Well, that left absolutely no question about who had called.

"Want me to cancel your burger?" Cy said helpfully.

"Hell, no." That would make it too much like he cared. And he didn't. Though when he'd seen that pain flash through her eyes at the mention of her divorce, he had cared, for a second. He had sincerely wanted to make her laugh, not just prove to his sister—and himself—that a decent girl would so go out with him.

Then there was the possibility she was teaching him a little lesson. She'd been sending his flowers too long. She knew he stood people up sometimes. She knew he'd let down Heather last night. It would be just like Katie to want him to know how it felt.

And the truth was it didn't feel very good.

Tonight he'd been the one who had learned something, whether she'd intended it or not. It didn't feel too good to be the one left waiting. Dumped. Stood up. Imagine Katie Pritchard being the girl who taught him that!

But he doubted Katie was trying to teach him anything. She was terrified, plain and simple. Marriage had burned her.

He thought of his parents. Maybe marriage burned everyone, given enough time. Which was why, for the past year, he'd been intent on not getting serious, not committing, not caring. Katie needed to learn just that. You could still live, without risking your heart. He bet he could have made her laugh. He bet he could show her laughing again didn't have to mean hurting again.

If he was so determined to tangle his life with hers a little more deeply it occurred to him it was going to require more of him than he had required of himself before. He would actually have to think a bit about her, not just about himself. He would have to be a better man.

Right there at Doofus's, with the tang of beer in the air, and pool balls clacking, Dylan McKinnon had an epiphany.

This is what his sister had tried to tell him: that he could be more. That he had not expected enough of himself. That to get a decent girl to even have dinner with him he had to be a decent man, someone capable of putting another person's interests ahead of his own, capable of venturing out of a place where he risked nothing.

His sister had seen a painful truth. Dylan McKinnon was known as being fearless. But in the area of caring about other people, he was not fearless at all.

He was not the man his mother would have wanted him to be.

So, it was a good thing Katie hadn't shown. Because that type of total attitude shift was the type of thing a man wanted to think about long and hard before he committed to it. Dylan didn't want to be a better man. He liked the man he was just fine. As far as erasing that flit of sorrow from the flower lady's eyes, he was the wrong man for the job.

"Rack 'em, Rafe. Cy, bring everyone a drink."

"What are we celebrating?" Cy asked, suspiciously.

"Freedom," Dylan said, remembering he'd ordered the kiss-off bouquet for Heather today, too.

That announcement was followed by some serious whistling and whooping.

But for all that he tried, and hard, to catch the mood of his own celebration, in the back of his mind a single word worried him.

Terrified.

And he just wasn't giving up on her that easily. Not even, damn it, if it did require that he be a better man.

The fact that a bright bouquet of flowers awaited him on his desk when he arrived the next morning only made him more determined. He flicked the card open.

"Sorry I couldn't make it last night, Love K."

Well, at least he'd taught her something in the year he'd known her!

He sat down and thought. Obviously, a burger at a sports bar had limited appeal to Katie. He'd always been able to count on his own appeal to convince women to take a leap out of their comfort zone, but Katie just wasn't most women. He needed a Plan B.

What would be irresistible to her? It was humbling to realize for Katie it was not him! Dylan McKinnon had become accustomed to being irresistible to women!

Whether she knew it or not, Katie had thrown down the gauntlet.

He was going to help her get back in the swing of things whether she liked it or not! To prove to his sister he could be a decent guy. Or maybe to prove it to himself.

By midafternoon he had two tickets to the most sought after event in Canada—the NHL All-Star hockey game.

He went into her store. She glanced up, looked back down hurriedly. She was blushing. "Sorry I couldn't make it last night. Something came up."

"What?"

She glared at him, annoyed he was rude enough to push. "Sanity."

He reminded himself, firmly, of his goal. One outing, or two, to make her feel attractive. Confident. *Happy.* To be who he guessed she once had been. He'd just help her get her feet wet again, so she didn't end up a tragic cat lady.

He guessed she had never been gorgeous, but lovely in some way that transcended whatever the current trend or fad was. She'd always had a way of holding herself that had seemed proud, as if she was above caring what others thought.

He'd just be a knight, for once in his life, show her

that she didn't have to roll over and die since her marriage had failed.

Looking at her, he realized she seemed to have worked extra hard at not being attractive today. The dress was billowing around her like a tent city, and her hair was pulled back a little too tightly from her face. Not a scrap of makeup, though now that he'd noticed her lips he realized she didn't really need it.

"Thanks for the flowers," he said.

"You were supposed to think it was funny."

"Ha-ha," he said.

She glared at him again. That was more like it, the green suddenly dancing to life in those multicolored eyes, snapping with color.

"So what can I do for you today?" she said. "Heather has been history for a full twelve hours or so. Someone else on the radar?"

If he told her she was on the radar, she'd run. He wouldn't catch her until Alaska, and then she'd probably throw herself into the Bering Sea and start swimming. It was an unusual experience for him to be having this kind of reaction from someone of the female persuasion.

"Um, no. I'm going to take a break for a while."

She was punching flowers into some sort of foam thing, but she lifted her eyes, looked at him, squinted.

"Uh-huh," she said, skeptical and not even trying to hide it.

"Here's what I was thinking. Maybe while I took a break, you could do a few things with me. Like the All-Star Game next weekend in Toronto."

Getting tickets to that game was like winning a

lottery, and he waited for her face to light up. Maybe she'd even come around the counter and give him a hug!

He was a little surprised by how much he would like to be hugged by Katie.

But instead of her face lighting up, she stabbed herself in the pad of her thumb with a rose thorn, glared at it, distracted.

"The what?" She stuck her thumb in her mouth and sucked. She really did not have to wear lipstick. Even watching her suck on that thumb was almost erotic. That was impossible! Look how the girl was dressed. He had just finished dating Miss Hillsboro Bikini, and never once felt the bottom falling out of his world like this.

Well, impossible or not, there was no denying how he was reacting.

"Haven't you got a Band-Aid?" he suggested, just a bit too much snap in his voice.

"Oh, it's just a little prick. They happen all the time. So, what kind of game is it you have tickets for?" she asked.

"Hockey," he said. Obviously she was in a completely different world than him if she didn't know that! "Canada's national game," he supplied when she looked blank. "Our passion, our pastime, our reason to be, during the long months of winter. You know the game?"

She took her thumb out of her mouth, thank goodness, went back to her flower arrangement. "Oh."

She wouldn't sound so unenthused if she knew what it took to get those tickets!

"The best players from the Western and Eastern Conferences get together and play each other. Every great player in the league on the ice at the same time." He began to name names.

She looked as if what he was discussing was about as interesting as choosing between steel-cut and quick cook oats for breakfast.

"Everybody wants tickets to that game," he snapped, feeling his patience begin to wane. He was being a knight, for goodness' sake. Why was she having such difficulty recognizing that?

"Oh," she said again, her vocabulary suddenly irritatingly limited.

"I could probably sell them on the Internet for a thousand bucks a pop."

"Oh, well then," she said, "don't waste them on me."

"It wouldn't be a waste," he sputtered. "You'd have fun. I guarantee it."

"You can't guarantee something like that!"

"Why is having a simple conversation with you like crossing a minefield?"

"Because I'm not blinking my eyelids at you with the devotion of a golden retriever?"

Well, there was that! "Katie, don't be impossible. I've got these great tickets to this great event. I know *in your heart* you want to say yes. Just say yes."

"You don't know the first thing about my heart."

Actually, he did. He'd seen a whole lot of things about her heart in one split second last night. That's why he was standing here trying so damned hard to be a decent guy. Obviously it was a bad fit for him. "That's what I mean about the minefield."

"Look, Dylan," she said with extravagant patience, as if he was a small child, "I know most girls would fall

all over themselves to do just about anything you suggested, including dogsled naked in the Yukon in the dead of winter, but I don't like hockey."

"Well, how do you feel about dogsledding naked, then?"

Ah, there was that blush again.

"Would you stop it? I don't want to go anywhere with you!"

"That hurts."

Oh, he saw that slowed her down a little bit: that he was a living breathing human being with feelings, not just some cavalier playboy.

But it only slowed her down briefly. "Don't even pretend my saying no would hurt you. Just go pick someone else out of your lineup of ten thousand hopefuls."

"I told you I'm taking a break."

"Well, I told you, not with me!"

"Give me one good reason!" he demanded.

"Okay. Going out with you is too public. I don't want my picture on the front page of the *Morning Globe,* I don't want the gossip columnist dissecting what I wear, and my hair."

"Then we'll go someplace private."

"No! Dylan, I don't want anything to change. I like the way my life is right now. You might think it looks dull and boring, but I like it."

There, he thought, he'd given it his best shot. He had tried to rescue the maiden in distress and failed. She had no desire to be rescued, he could go back to being superficial and self-centered, content in the knowledge he had tried.

She'd almost convinced him, but then he looked

more closely as she jabbed the last rose into the flower arrangement and managed to prick herself again.

She glanced at him, and looked quickly away.

And that's when he knew she was lying. She didn't prick herself all the time. She pricked herself when she was distracted.

She didn't like her life the way it was now. She'd settled. Katie really wanted all kinds of things out of life: dazzling things, things that made her heart beat faster, made her wake up in the morning and want to dance with whatever life offered that day.

She was afraid to hope.

And he was more determined than ever to give that back to her. But this was going to be the hard part, figuring out what was irresistible to her, not to him.

He walked back to his office, put the tickets on Margot's desk.

"Treat hubby to a night out," he said gruffly. Almost at his office he turned and looked back at her.

"And figure out what is the perfect date. Not for a guy. For a girl. What would be an absolutely irresistible outing to any woman? Ask your girlfriends. Get back to me."

His receptionist was looking at him as if he'd lost his mind. He stepped into his office and slammed the door.

Later, just to show Miss Snooty next door what she was missing in the excitement department, he got on his motorcycle and pulled a wheelie right in front of her window. Just in case she'd missed the first one, he went around the block and came back and did another one. Then just for good measure, he zipped back the other way.

As always, he was completely predictable to her.

The drapes of The Flower Girl were firmly closed.

CHAPTER THREE

KATIE could hear the sound of the motorcycle coming back down the street, the sudden change in engine pitch warning her Dylan was going to pop it up again.

She firmly closed the curtains.

Good grief! You would think no one had ever said no to that man. Of course, look at him. There was a chance, and a darn good one, that no one ever *had* said no to him. Or at least no one female!

And no wonder. It was not just hard to say no! A woman had to manually override all the biological and chemical systems in her entire body. And then, to add to the complexity of the task, she had to exercise steely control over her emotions.

Saying no to Dylan McKinnon was not fun and it was not easy. And he knew it! Imagine him leaning over that counter, dropping his voice a dreamy notch, looking straight into her eyes and saying as clearly as if he could see her soul, *I know, in your heart, you want to say yes.*

Of course she wanted to say yes! Thankfully she had a policy in place for dealing with him. In the interest of self-preservation, she had developed a new number-one rule: do exactly the opposite of what she *wanted* to do.

It was necessary. Her very survival felt as if it depended on saying no to him. For some reason she had shown up as a blip on Dylan McKinnon's radar. He had decided she *needed* something that he could give her.

But a hockey game? She considered hockey a barbaric, thinly disguised upgrade of the gladiator ring. Saying *yes* would be that first chip out of her soul: pretending she liked something she didn't to please him, becoming something other than what she was just to spend time at his side!

Even the way Dylan worded his invitation to attend that hockey game with him underscored the wisdom of her rejecting it. He was off women, but she'd do? He wanted a change, so she would be a slightly interesting distraction?

A girl just had to have some pride, and Katie knew that better than anyone. She knew how much pride you had to have to come to a small town after a failed marriage. And she knew she had a fragile hold on self-preservation. She could care about that man, and she simply did not want to. She had managed to put her life back together, barely, once, but she was pretty sure she couldn't do it again.

Still, the past year had made her privy to some important knowledge about Dylan. His passions were furious and frantic, but thankfully short-lived. As Hillsboro's most famous son, his every passing fancy, from motorcycle racing to whitewater rafting was carefully documented. He never stuck to anything for very long. He needed a fast pace, plenty of excitement, and if he didn't find them, he moved on. It was his modus operandi for life. From sending his flowers for the past year, Katie knew it was doubly true for the romantic part of his life.

He sent four bouquets during the course of a relationship. The first was his nice-to-meet-you, I'm-interested. The second, usually followed fairly closely on the heels of the first, and she was pretty sure it was the great-sex bouquet. Third, came the sorry-I-forgot, which he didn't really mean, and then the fourth was the goodbye bouquet. The cycle of a relationship that would probably take a normal person a year to play out—or at the very least a few months—he could complete in weeks.

Katie tried to sew warnings into the bouquets, bachelor buttons to signify celibacy for instance, but nobody paid the least bit of attention to the secret meanings of flowers these days, more's the pity.

There were two notable exceptions to Dylan's flower sending and his short attention span, one was the one bouquet he came in for once a week and chose himself.

He had never told her who it was for, but at some time she had let him start choosing his own flowers for it, even though her refrigerator room was sacred to her. Naturally, he had no idea of the meanings of what he was selecting, and yet he unerringly chose flowers like white chrysanthemums, which stood for truth, or daisies, which stood for purity and a loyal love. She never pressed about who the bouquet was for. His choice always seemed so somber, it did not seem possible it was a romantic bouquet.

The other exception to his short attention span was his business. In fact his drive, his restless nature, probably did him nothing but good when it came to running his wildly successful company, Daredevils.

He was constantly testing, developing and innovating. He loved the challenge of new products and new projects, which meant he was always on the cutting edge of business. He'd found the perfect line of work for his boundless energy. But those same qualities put him on the cutting edge of relationships, too, and not in a good way. He did the cutting!

The motorcycle roared by again, and against her better judgment she went and slid open one vertical pleat of her shades a half centimeter or so. He was wearing a distressed black leather jacket, jeans, no helmet. He looked more like a throwback to those renegades women always lost their hearts to—pirates and highwaymen—than Hillsboro's most celebrated success story.

Dylan gunned the bike to a dangerous speed, his silken dark hair flattened against his head, his eyes narrowed to a squint of pure focus. In a motion that looked effortless, he lifted the front wheel of that menacing two-wheeled machine off the ground. He made it rear so that he looked more like a knight on a rearing stallion than a perpetual boy with a penchant for black leather. For a moment he was suspended in time—reckless, strong, sure of himself—and then the front wheel crashed back to earth, he braced himself to absorb the impact and was gone down the street.

Dammit! She knew what he was doing was immature! Silly, even. Her head knew that! But her heart was beating hard, recognizing the preening of the male animal, reacting to it with a sheer animal longing of its own.

"I should call the police," she declared primly, even as she recognized her own lack of conviction. "I'm sure he's being dangerous. It's illegal not to wear a helmet."

That, she thought firmly, was just one more reason she had to say no to him. It was a classical and insurmountable difference between them. If she ever got on a motorcycle without a helmet, the anxiety of getting a head injury or getting a ticket would spoil it for her. Obviously it was taking chances that made the experience fun for him, that put him on the edge of pure excitement.

Here he came again, but instead of popping it up this time, he slowed down and pulled into a vacant parking spot outside her shop.

She ordered herself to drop the curtain, but was caught in the poetry of watching him dismount, throwing that long, beautiful leg up and over the engine.

She prayed he was going back to work, and not—

Her shop door squeaked open. She pretended a sudden intense interest in rearranging the flowers in the pot in the window, letting her hand rest on the white heather, which promised protection. But also could mean dreams come true. She hastily turned her attention to a different pot of flowers.

"Dark in here, Katie-my-lady."

She glanced at him, and then quickly away. She had to keep remembering his restless nature when he turned the full intensity of those blue eyes on her. Blue like sapphires, like deep ocean water, like every pirate and highwayman who had ridden before him.

"These flowers in the window were wilting. That's why I closed the drapes."

"Uh-huh."

"What do you want?"

"Play hooky with me," he said. "Come for a motorcycle ride."

One of the flowers snapped off in her hand. She stared at it. A pink carnation, rife with its multitude of meanings: fascination, a woman's love, I can't forget you, you are always on my mind.

She dropped the flower on the floor and stammered, "Are you crazy? You've just demonstrated to the whole neighborhood how you ride that thing!"

"Oh, were you watching? I could have sworn your drapes were closed."

It was like being caught red-handed at the cookie jar!

He bent and picked up the flower, smelled it, drawing its fragrance deep inside himself, his eyes never leaving hers. There was no way he could discern the secrets of that flower. He held it out to her, but she shook her head as if it was inconsequential, as if it meant nothing to her.

Absently, he threaded the carnation through the button hole of his leather jacket. How many men could do that with such casual panache? Wear a flower on their leather?

"We could cruise out of town," he said, just as if she had not refused him. "The fields are all turning green, the trees are budding. I bet we'd see pussy willows. Babies, too, calves and ducks, little colts and fillies trying out their long legs."

She could feel herself weakening, his voice a brush that painted pictures of a world she wanted to see. She knew spring was here: so many wonderful flowers becoming available locally, but somehow she had missed the *essence* of spring's arrival, its promise: gray and brown turning to green, plants long dormant bravely blooming again, sudden furious storms giving way to sunshine. It was the season of hope.

In fact, Dylan McKinnon was making her feel as if she had missed the essence of everything for a long, long time. He looked so good, standing there so full of confidence, the scent of leather in the air, his hair windswept, his eyes on her so intently.

She could almost imagine how it would feel to go with him, to feel the powerful purr of that bike vibrating through her, to wrap her arms tightly around his waist, to mold herself to his power and confidence, *feel* them, *feel* him in such an intoxicatingly intimate way.

"Say yes," he whispered. "You know you want to do something wild and crazy."

Yes. Yes. Yes.

"No!" The vow. Do the opposite of what she wanted. "I did something wild and crazy once. It involved saying yes, too. And it was a mistake."

They both knew she was referring to her marriage.

"You can't go through life without making mistakes, Katie."

"You can sure as hell try." It was because of his bad influence on her that she was using bad language. If she let this go any further, there was no telling what his influence would do. She would become a different woman than the one she was today.

She could picture herself with her head thrown back, laughing into the wind, while she clung to the motorcycle and him. Sensuous. Exhilarated. On fire with life. Willing to take chances.

Heartbroken! she snapped back at all those dreamy voices.

"Everybody makes mistakes, Katie. You learn from them, you let them make you better, and you move on."

"You with the charmed life!"

For a moment something so sad crossed his face that she was taken aback. But then he grinned, all devil-may-care charm again, and she could almost, but not quite, convince herself that she'd imagined it.

"What mistakes have you made?" she said. Oh, boy! She was getting sucked into this conversation when it was the last thing she wanted.

"Jumping out of an airplane a few months after signing my Blue Jays contract probably wasn't one of my more brilliant decisions," he said.

Was it that memory that had caused that brief sadness to chase across his features?

"So, why'd you do it?" All of Hillsboro still talked of his legendary jump. He'd agreed to do it as a fund-raiser for the local chapter of Big Brothers. Something had gone dreadfully wrong. He'd broken his arm in three places, ended his career as a pitcher before it had ever really even started. All of Hillsboro had gone into mourning over the misfortune of their most favored son.

He smiled. "I did it because I *wanted* to."

His lack of regret over the incident seemed to be genuine, but it proved exactly what she had already decided about *wanting.*

"Wanting is not a reliable compass with which to set the course of your life," she told him sternly. "You made an impulse choice that ruined your career."

He touched one of the flowers in the window, absently. Surprise, surprise, a red rose. *Passion.* His fingers caressed the petal with such tenderness that she could not help but wonder if it wouldn't be worth it. To give in. Just once. To give in to the impulse to play with the most dangerous fire of all: passion.

"You could look at it as an impulse choice that ruined my career," he agreed mildly. Thankfully, he decided to leave the rose alone. "I prefer to think a series of events played out that led me to my true calling."

She was startled by that. She had no awareness that he had moved on from his brush with fame without looking back, the same as he moved on with everything else. She shivered.

She didn't really want to know that about him. Nor did she want to start thinking about the events of her own life in ways that took down her protective barriers, instead of putting them up, in ways that made her more open to the vagaries of life, instead of battened down against them.

Mostly she didn't want to think about how that finger, tender on the petals of a rose, would feel if it brushed the fullness of her bottom lip.

Gathering all of her strength, she said, "I am not getting on that motorcycle with you. I like living!"

"Do you?" he asked softly, the faintest mocking disbelief in his tone. "Do you, Katie, my lady?" And with that, he turned on his heel and left her.

But the question he asked seemed to remain, burning deeper and deeper into her heart, her mind, her soul. *Did she?*

Did she like the nice safe predictable world she had created for herself? Were her flowers and her cats and her love of the library and her visits with her mother enough?

The road she had not taken teased her, the choice she had not made pulled at her, tantalized her, tormented her.

Katie could imagine how the wind would have felt in her face, the touch of sunlight on her cheeks. She could imagine laughter-filled moments, clinging to him on the back of his bike; relying on him to keep her safe. She felt intense regret for the courage she lacked.

She pulled herself to her senses. Ha, as if Dylan McKinnon could be relied on to keep anyone safe! Safe was the least likely word association that would come up in the same sentence as Daredevil Dylan McKinnon.

Then again, a little voice whispered to her, *maybe safety was entirely overrated.* She decided, uncaring of how childish it was, that she hated him.

Which, of course, was the safe choice. So much safer than loving him. Or anybody or anything else.

It occurred to her that if he had even noticed the hideousness of her outfit, it had not deterred him one little bit.

She had to do better. Tomorrow she was wearing her Indian cotton smock dress. And she'd look through that old trunk in the attic. She was sure there were flowered pink and green overalls in there. Of course, that was assuming he was dropping by again tomorrow, and in the days after that, too.

Considering she had decided she hated him, why was she looking forward to the possibility so much?

A charmed life, thought Dylan, hanging up the phone a few days later after his morning call to the nursing home. He contemplated Katie's assessment of him. In some ways it was so true. But he lived with another truth now.

He would trade it all—every single success he had ever enjoyed—to have one day to spend with his mother the way she used to be. After his mom's speedy decline into Alzheimer's, his father had made the unspeakable decision, last year, to put her in a home.

His grief was not just for his mother, but for the death of what he had believed. He had believed that someday he would have what his parents had, a quiet, steady kind of love that raised children and paid bills, that lived up to the vows they had taken, a love that stayed forever.

Instead his father, his model of what Dylan thought a man should be, had bailed.

His mother didn't even seem to know she had been betrayed. She was oblivious to her own illness, a blessing. The only thing that seemed to bring that spark to her eyes that Dylan remembered so well, were the flowers he brought her once a week. And then, only for the moment it took to name them, before the spark was gone, and she was looking at him blankly, as if to say, "Who are you?"

A knock on the door, Margot popped in.

"Sorry, a bad time?"

He had always disliked it when people could read him. It made him feel vulnerable. Margot was getting good at it. Katie had developed a disquieting gift for seeing through his fearless facade to what lay underneath. Maybe he should be remembering that when he was so intent on rescuing her, so intent on proving he could get a decent girl. That there might be a personal price to pay.

No, he was good at protecting himself. He proved it by grinning at Margot, seeing the faint worried crease on her forehead disappear with relief. "No, of course it's not a bad time," he assured her. He nodded toward his in-office basketball hoop. "I just missed a few. You know how I hate that."

"Here's the, er, research you asked me to do." Margot seemed uncharacteristically uncertain as she placed an untidy mountain of papers in front of him.

He didn't remember asking her to do any research, except maybe about the new running jacket. Puzzled, he picked up the first paper on the stack, and flinched. It had a title on it, like a high school essay. It said "My Dream Date with Dylan McKinnon."

Whatever he'd asked her for, Margot had misinterpreted it. Or maybe not. He couldn't remember exactly what he'd said to her.

Sheesh. Katie Pritchard had him rattled.

"Thanks," he said, and Margot looked pleased and left him alone with the monster he'd created.

Now because Katie had him rattled, Dylan's receptionist had presented him, pleased with herself, with a sheaf of papers from Lord knew where—girlfriends, acquaintances, women on the street—all of whom were just a little too eager to share highly personal information about themselves and what they liked to do in their spare time.

He looked at the stack of papers, rifled through. Tidy, messy, typed, printed, handwritten, perfumed. Someone extremely original had submitted her ideas written in red felt pen on a pair of panties. He disposed of the panties and wanted to just throw the rest of this self-created mess out, too.

But then again, there might be something in here—one small idea—that would help him unlock the fortress that was Katie.

He began to read the essay entitled My Dream Date

with Dylan McKinnon. Considering that it was quite neatly typed and double spaced, he wasn't ready for what it said. He was no prude, but he was shocked. He hastily crumpled up the paper and threw it in the garbage along with the panties.

Then he wondered if he should have done that. If he got any more frustrated with Katie, an evening with Ursula, a bottle of spray whipping cream, and a bed wrapped in plastic, might be a balm.

No, he left it in the garbage, reminded himself of the new *decent* Dylan, forced himself to read through the rest of the papers on his desk. Some of them had some ideas that were not half bad: a night at the ice hotel in Quebec, for one.

Not that he'd even think of asking Katie to spend the night with him, because she wasn't that kind of girl, but a *tour* of the ice hotel, and a few drinks of vodka out of ice mugs after the tour had a certain appeal. It was original, and what more perfect date for someone who was proving she could not be easily melted by his charms?

Plus, he liked the idea of feeding Katie a bit of vodka, straight up. He'd be willing to bet he could figure out what she was *really* thinking then.

The idea was taking hold, but then he looked at his calendar. It was spring, and a warm one at that. The ice hotel was probably nothing more than a mud puddle now. Maybe it could be a possibility for next year.

Next year? How long did he think it was going to take to bring Katie around? He thought of the stubborn look on her face when he'd invited her out on his motorcycle. He sighed. It well could be next year. He filed the ice-hotel idea in case he needed it later.

Margot came back in with something else.

"Is that what you meant?" she asked uncertainly, gesturing at the untidy stack of mismatched papers in front of him. "I wasn't quite sure what you wanted when you asked me to canvas my friends about a perfect date."

Ursula was a friend of Margot's? Good grief. His secretary had a whole secret life...that he absolutely didn't want to know about!

"Hey," he said brightly, "I wasn't quite sure myself. Just tossing out ideas. It wasn't actually for me, personally."

"I told my cousin the, um, personal item was a little over the top, but again, I didn't quite know what you were asking for."

"I thought Daredevils should try and take a hard look at how to grow our female market. I was interested in how women think. What they like. Tap into their secret romantic desires as part of a marketing scheme." He was babbling, and he let his voice drift off. "You know."

She looked, ever so faintly, skeptical. "You seem to have a pretty good grasp on what women like."

"I just needed some original ideas. I wanted to think outside the box." His box anyway, because to date, not a single item in his little box of tricks seemed to have even the remotest appeal to Katie.

"This isn't about business, is it?" Margot guessed suddenly, her eyebrow lifted, her hand on her hip.

He coughed, glowered at her, took a sudden interest in tossing a foam basketball from the dozen or so he kept on his desk through the hoop above his office door.

"I've never seen you like this," Margot said.

"Like what?" he said defensively. He missed the basket with his second effort, too. He had not missed that basket for at least three months, no matter what he had said to Margot earlier.

"I don't know. A little unsure. I hesitate to use the word *desperate* but it comes to mind. Have you met somebody special?"

"No!" he said. Despite the quickness of his reply and the empathy of it, a little smile appeared on Margot's lips. *Knowing.* His fear of being easy to read grew.

"Somebody has you rattled," she said, not without delight, when he missed the basket for the third time. It was horrible that she had stumbled on his exact turn of phrase for how Katie Pritchard was making him feel.

"That's not it at all!" he said.

"Boy, I'd like to see the girl that has you in a knot like this."

"I…am…not…in…a…knot." He said each word very slowly and deliberately. If Margot had seen what the girl who had him in a knot was wearing today she probably would have died laughing. Katie had had on some kind of horrible wrinkled smock that made her look pregnant.

But the outfit was deceptive, because it made her look like the kind of girl who should have fallen all over herself when he suggested in-line skating in the park. Instead, she had slipped her glasses down her nose and looked at him, regally astonished by the audacity of his invitation, as if she was the queen.

"I'm not dressed for skating," she'd said, just as if it wouldn't have been a blessing to wreck that dress in whatever way she could.

"It doesn't have to be today," he'd countered, registering he might be making progress. It had not been an out-and-out no.

"In-line skating," she'd said, making him hold his breath when it seemed as if she might be seriously contemplating the suggestion. But then, "No, sorry, it's not on my list of the one hundred things I have to do before I die," she'd said.

"You have a list?"

She'd gone quiet.

"Come on, Katie, give. Tell me just one thing on it."

"No."

"Why not?"

"Because it would become part of this ridiculous campaign you're on, and before I knew it I'd find myself riding an elephant in Africa."

"Is that on your list?" he asked. He couldn't have been more surprised. She didn't even want to ride a motorcycle right here in North America!

"It was just an example."

"You sure like to play your cards close to your chest." Which, since he'd mentioned it, he snuck a quick look at. Gorgeous curves, neatly disguised by the wrinkly sack she was wearing. He looked up. She was blushing. With any other girl that might mean progress, but with her you never could tell. More likely his sneaked peek had set him back a few squares. Since he had yet to get past "go," that was a depressing thought.

To offset the depression, he said, aware he was pleading, "Just tell me one thing off your hundred must-do's. I promise I won't use it. I'll never mention it again." He gave her his Boy Scout honor look, which was practically guaranteed to win the instant trust of fifty per cent of the human race—the female fifty per cent.

She had fixed those enormous hazel eyes on him—

they had taken on a shade of gold today—and looked hard at him over the rims of her glasses. No one looked at him the way Katie did. The rest of the world saw the image: successful, driven, fun loving, daring, but it always felt as if she stripped him to his soul. The rest of the world fell for whatever he wanted them to believe he was, but not her.

Still, when she gave him that look, so intense, so stripping, the ugliness of whatever outfit she was wearing suddenly faded. It was an irony that he didn't completely understand that the uglier she dressed, the more he felt as if he could *see* her.

She shrugged. "I'd like to swim with dolphins," she admitted, but reluctantly. He was sorry he'd promised he wouldn't use it to convince her to go out with him, because he had suddenly, desperately, wanted to see her swim with dolphins.

Hopefully in a bikini, though he was startled to discover that was not his main motivation. He wanted to see her in a pool with dolphins: laughing at their silly grins, stroking their snouts, mimicking their chatter. He wanted to see her happy, uninhibited, sun kissed. Free.

Had she been that once? Before her marriage had shut something down in her? He wanted to see her like that!

Okay, the bikini would be a bonus. Though judging from what she was wearing at the moment, Katie in a bikini was a pipe dream. If she owned a bathing suit at all, it was probably akin to a bathing costume from the twenties, complete with pantaloons.

"I'm going to put that on my list, too," he'd said, amazed by how deeply he meant it.

"You promised you wouldn't do that!" she said, and

actually looked pleased because she had assumed he had broken his word so quickly.

"Not with you," he said. "I'm putting swimming with dolphins on my list to do by myself someday."

For a moment in her eyes, he saw the answer to why he was keeping at this when she wanted him to believe he would never succeed. She had *flinched,* actually hurt that he didn't want to pursue the dolphin swimming with her.

She'd snorted, though, to cover up that momentary lapse in her defenses. "You don't have a list."

"Okay, so I'm going to start one."

"And you don't do things by yourself. If you ever swim with dolphins, I bet you have a woman with you. A gorgeous one, not the least bit shy about falling out of a bikini that is three sizes too small for her."

"You're talking about Heather," he sulked. "It's over. You should know. You sent the flowers." No need to tell Katie the flowers had been dumped on the seat of his open convertible. It would probably up her estimation of Heather by a few notches.

"Dylan," she said patiently, "your women are largely interchangeable, which is why I am determined not to become one of them."

"Planet Earth calling Dylan," Margot said, giving him a bemused look.

"Sorry. I was thinking about something. But that doesn't mean I'm in a knot!"

"Of course you aren't in a knot," Margot said soothingly. "Want some advice?"

"No."

Margot ignored him. "Just be yourself."

Well, that was easier said then done because as his

sister had very rudely pointed out to him, in the past year he had become someone none of them knew. He was trying to find his way back to himself, and somehow, in a way he did not quite fully understand, Katie could help him back to that. In the same way he could help her back to the woman he sensed she once had been. But trying to get through to a woman who did not want to be gotten through to was brand-new and totally frustrating territory for him.

He waited for Margot to leave, picked up yet another letter from the pile. This wasn't half-bad. Celeste's dream date was a trip to the city, a quiet dinner, live theater, and a horse-drawn carriage ride afterward. He made a few calls. There was lots going on in Toronto, just a short drive away, but for live-theater options he narrowed it down to *The Phantom of the Opera* or a light romantic comedy called *The Prince and the Nanny.*

Both sounded equally as oppressive to him, so what girl could resist that? For a moment, Margot's voice sounded inside his head, *Just be yourself,* but he managed to quash it. He'd already tried being himself, with the motorcycle and the in-line skating offer.

No, this was much better. He'd go to her world. Not today, though. He didn't want to seem too eager or too persistent. He didn't want her to think he was a stalker, after all.

Still, the next afternoon he felt like a warrior girding his loins as he began the long walk to the business next door.

CHAPTER FOUR

THE GODS hated her. There was no other reason she was being subjected to such torture. In the last ten days Dylan had pulled out all stops. He was making it so much harder to say no to him that he no longer seemed to even notice what she was wearing! No matter how hideous the outfit—and many of them were plenty hideous—he seemed to see her. He seemed to see right through all the disguises to who she really was.

Still, despite that, it was more than evident to Katie that this had become a game to him. Dylan McKinnon was a competitor and a formidable one. He did not lose, he did not take no for an answer.

But he also took no prisoners. She knew that from a year of sending flowers for him. That fourth goodbye bouquet was as inevitable as the coming of the darkness after a day of luscious sunshine. Her effort to protect her heart from him had triggered his most competitive impulses.

She'd been invited to six different plays, all of which she wanted desperately to see. She'd been invited hiking, fishing and in-line skating. She'd been invited to dinners, sporting events, to meet celebrities. Oh, and she couldn't forget the motorcycle ride, over which she still felt a crippling regret, a swooshing sensation in her stomach, every time she thought of that glorious afternoon that had not been.

Still, the barrage was beginning to tell on her. It was getting so that she jumped every time the door to her shop opened. She was feeling like a nervous wreck, her very skin seemed to tingle, in the way that limbs that had gone numb tingled when they came back to life.

That's what was happening to her, whether she wanted it to or not. She had a feeling of being acutely, vibrantly alive.

Alive in a way she had not felt alive in a long, long time. She had not even been aware of the hibernation state she had fallen into, until he came along, woken her up, made demands of her, challenged her.

She glanced at the clock. Nearly one. She sidled over to the window. There he was, right on schedule. While she looked worse and worse—albeit deliberately—he looked better and better.

Today he was wearing jogging pants that hung low on his hips, an old Blue Jays jersey with no sleeves, a ball cap pulled low over his eyes against the brilliance of the spring day. Despite how new the days of spring were, Dylan was beginning to look sun-kissed, golden. It wasn't even possible. He had to be artificially tanning. She could never respect a man who used a tanning bed.

Was Dylan stopping?

Her traitorous heart hammered as if it couldn't care a less whether he used a tanning bed! He *was* slowing. The wild beat of her heart reminded her what it was to feel so *alive.*

She made a mad dash for the security of her counter—she was going to be in better shape than him if this kept up—and made a great show of stuffing flowers into a bouquet that she had no order for. Begonias for beware. Tuberoses for dangerous pleasures. And then her fickle fingers plucked a pink camellia—for longing—out of one of the jugs. And some gloxinia for love at first sight.

She had left her door open today, and so the bell didn't even ring warning her he was there, looking at her. She smelled him.

A scent more delicious than the aroma of spring that wafted through her door—masculine, tangy, mountain pure—and enveloped her.

"I like the way you look when you work," he decided after a long moment.

How could he possibly not notice these overalls? Any reasonable man would have seen overalls printed with huge pink peonies and vibrant green vines as a deterrent, but not him.

Peonies symbolized shame, which is what she felt about her inability to control the wild thudding of her heart as soon as he was around. They had other meanings, too. *Happy life. Happy marriage.* She had dared to dream those dreams once. She was over it.

She shoved the flower arrangement away from herself. *Don't ask.* "And how do I look when I work?"

"Intense. As if those flowers speak a language and you understand it."

"Hmm." She glanced at the bouquet. It spoke a language all right. It told her she was a woman dangerously divided.

"And also you stick your tongue out when you work."

"I do not!"

"Umm-hmm, caught right between your front teeth, like this."

She looked at his tongue. A mistake.

"I see you managed to lose the sleeves for your shirt," she said, not wanting him to notice that she was a woman who looked at a man's tongue and understood the meaning of pink camellia in a way she never quite had before.

"I ripped them off. By the way, we're completely bogged down on that jacket design. Runners *like* no sleeves."

Especially runners built like him. No sleeves. Show off those newly tanned arms. Get any girl you wanted.

Naturally that was the only reason for his persistence. No one had played hard-to-get with him before. Though she didn't feel as if she was *playing*. Running for her life was more like it. If she ran any harder, she was going to have to start looking for a sleeveless jacket of her own!

"Are you tanning?" she said, as if that was the mystery she was trying to solve by looking at his bare arms for far too long.

"Tanning? Even I haven't hit the beach yet."

"Not that kind of tanning!" *The vain kind.*

He actually threw back his head and laughed. "Katie, you have me so wrong. I'm not that kind of guy."

That's exactly what she was afraid of. That she wanted him—no, desperately needed for him—to be vain and self-centered, and that he wasn't. A part of her was always insisting it knew exactly who he was.

"Tell me you can't picture me in a tanning bed," he pleaded.

She wasn't even sure what a tanning bed involved beyond absurd self-involvement. Nudity? She could feel a blush that was going to put that pink camellia to shame moving up her neck.

"So, what can I do for you today?" she asked, all brisk professionalism.

"Say yes," he said, placing both hands and his elbows on the counter, leaning over it, fixing his gaze on her.

"You haven't asked me anything yet!" Except if she could picture him on a tanning bed, and she was not saying yes to that! Even if, despite her best efforts to stop it cold, a sneaky picture was trying to crowd into her head.

"I know, but just to surprise me, say yes."

"Is it your birthday?"

"No."

"Then I have no occasion to surprise you."

"Would you surprise me if it was my birthday?"

She was hit with an illuminating moment of self-knowledge. She was coming to love these little conversational sparring matches. She only pretended to hate them. She only pretended to herself that she wanted him to keep on running by her door. In some part of her, that she might have been just as content to keep a secret from herself, she would be devastated if he stopped popping in.

He was delivering what she needed most, even if she wanted it the least: he was delivering the unexpected; he was shaking up her comfy, safe little world; he was making her *want* again.

Dylan McKinnon was a born tease, a born charmer. He had a great sense of humor and a delightful sense of mischief. Whether she wanted to admit it or not, these spontaneous, unscheduled interchanges added spark to her day, brightness to her world, a lightness to her step. Not that she would ever let him see anything beyond her aggravation.

"No, I wouldn't surprise you even if it was your birthday. I'm not the kind of person who does surprises well."

She knew, even if he wouldn't admit it, that was the biggest surprise of all to him. That anybody could say no to him. Some days it was all that gave her strength. Knowing if she ever weakened and said yes, it would be the beginning of the end. Before she knew it she'd be getting the equivalent of the fourth bouquet—the nice-knowing-you bouquet.

"*Au contraire,* Katie, my lady, I think you are full of the most amazing surprises."

His voice had gone soft, his gaze suddenly intent, stripping. He did this—went from teasing to serious in the blink of an eye. It left her feeling off balance, unsettled. *Alive.*

"I assure you, I am not full of surprises." But hadn't she just surprised herself by acknowledging how she was coming to look forward to his visits?

He shrugged, unconvinced. "Do you want to know when my birthday is?"

He was back to playful again, and he wagged his eyebrows at her with such exaggerated hopefulness she had to bite her tongue to keep from laughing.

"If I did want to know your birth date," she said, struggling for composure, "I could find an old baseball card, I'm sure. Just think, I could find out all kinds of interesting information about you. How much you weigh, how tall you are, all your baseball stats. I could be just like all the other girls."

"No you couldn't," he said, serious again, quiet. "You could never be like the other girls, Katie."

She didn't know if that was a good thing or a bad thing, and she was not going to let him know she cared by asking!

He sighed, looked at her with aggravation, then smiled as if he'd hit a home run. "What would you think about hitting opening day at the Ice Hotel, in Quebec? Coincidentally, it coincides with my birthday. Approximately."

She scowled at him. Looked over his shoulder. Today was the first day it had been warm enough to leave her door open, spring warmth creeping in, full of promise. It was not the kind of day that normal people thought about ice hotels.

She had seen pictures of the Ice Hotel. It was magnificent: every piece of the structure, from walls, to floors, to beds, to vodka glasses carved out of ice. Seeing the ice hotel was on her list of one hundred things she wanted to do someday, right along with swimming with dolphins. How had he managed to stumble onto something from her list?

She eyed him suspiciously. He was a man driven. He probably broke into her apartment when she wasn't there and found her list.

Then she sighed. How much easier all this would be if she really could believe the worst of him. That he tanned. That he stalked. But no matter how badly she wanted to believe it to protect herself, she had that sense again, of knowing him.

She had a weird kind of trust in him even if he had spoiled the Ice Hotel for her.

Somehow, now, knowing she would be seeing it alone, when she had been invited to see it with him wrecked it for her. She would never be able to see those caribou-skin-covered beds now without wondering—

"No," she said, and her voice sounded just a teensy bit shrieky.

"Hey, it's not until next year."

"Dylan, you strike me as the man least likely to plan for something a year in advance."

"Not true. I mean, okay, I might have a slight problem with birthdays, but other than that I'm quite good at planning ahead. The next line of Daredevils jackets, for instance, will come out a year from now. If we can ever decide on a design."

"Well, the answer is still no."

"Ah," he said with a sad and insincere shake of his head, "Shot down again."

"Dylan, I wish you'd stop this."

"No, you don't," he said softly, suddenly serious again.

She folded her arms firmly over the bright pink peonies on her chest, but it didn't matter how she tried to hide those peonies. That was her shameful truth. She didn't really want this to stop, and it was nothing but embarrassing that he saw that so, so clearly.

If she really wanted it to stop, after all, she'd just say yes to something. Anything. Motorcycles or rollerblading or dinner and dancing. And then this whole thing would follow a very predictable pattern, the age-old formula for every story. It would have a beginning. A middle. And an end.

An end, as in stopped. Over. He probably wouldn't even drop in here anymore.

"I'm not going out with you, Dylan," she said. "Not ever. You must have better things to do with your time than pester me."

"Ah, Katie, my lady, oddly enough I've come to adore pestering you."

"That's what I was afraid of," she said solemnly.

He laughed. His laughter was beautiful, it twinkled through his eyes, showed the whiteness of his teeth, the strong column of his throat. He laughed from his belly, with sincere enjoyment, a contagious *joie de vivre*. But his laughter just made her more aware of how much she stood to lose the moment she said yes.

Sitting at his desk, throwing foam basketballs at his net and missing with heart-wrenching regularity, Dylan McKinnon was struck by inspiration.

He realized he had been going about this the wrong way. He'd asked Margot to find out for him what girls liked, and gotten more than what he bargained for when their answers had poured in. He'd tried to talk Katie into doing what he liked, but with the same result.

But he had always known she wasn't like any other girl he'd ever met. Her ability to say no to him being an unfortunate case in point.

It was time to tackle this differently.

He thought about what he knew about Katie for sure. He knew she was heartbroken.

Aside from that he knew she liked books and possibly cats. She was devoted to the library.

She wanted to swim with dolphins. And he knew

he'd seen just the tiniest flicker of interest in her eye when he'd mentioned the Ice Hotel.

Absently he did an Internet search. Cats + books + libraries.

Astonishingly he got a hit, and it was close to home, too. The gods had taken pity on him, seen the worthiness of his mission. Because there it was, as simple as that: the event she would find irresistible. The Toronto Public Library was hosting a fund-raising meet and greet with famous cat cartoonist Tac Revol. Tickets, naturally, were sold out, an obstacle that meant absolutely nothing to Daredevil Dylan McKinnon. By the end of the week, he had them.

He walked into her store, practically swaggering with confidence. He paused and studied her. She was trying not to acknowledge him. Could she possibly be miffed that he had not been in here every day? Oh, yes, he thought happily, that seemed to be a distinct possibility! Did she look different?

Yes, much worse than she had a week ago. She had her hair loose, which was unusual, but the style was uninspiring, lying limp to the curve of a shoulder hidden by a ruffled neckline. The skirt was a multilayered affair in several deep and distressing shades of purple.

She looked everywhere but at him. Then she met his eyes, smiled with bright phoniness, and said, "So, have you met someone new? Time to send out your famous let's-get-to-know-each-other bouquet?"

Ah, so that's why she thought he hadn't been around. "No, I haven't met anyone new," he said.

"Well, time's awasting," she said, still spilling over with phony brightness. "If you're going to keep up your same schedule, a woman a month, for this year, you'll have to get busy."

How right his sister had been. No decent girl wanted to go out with a guy like that.

"One of my clients left me her granddaughter's phone number, even though I advised her not to." Un-Katielike, she was babbling. More hurt that he had not been by than she would ever admit?

He was not even going to answer her about somebody's granddaughter. As if he would ever phone a girl he had never met. No sense telling Katie that. His sister probably would not believe him, either. A man who had turned over a new leaf had to prove it. No one was going to take his word for it. But had he turned over a new leaf? There was that feeling again, of not knowing himself.

Without a word he laid the tickets on the counter.

She glanced at them, and went to push them back. But as her hand touched them, she really looked at the tickets, and her eyes went round. He was very pleased. It was so evident she *coveted* those tickets.

"Tac Revol," she breathed. "Ohmygod. How did you get these? They're harder to come by than two scoops of pistachio on the moon!"

"I thought you might like them," he said solemnly. The look on her face had been what was harder to come by than two scoops of pistachio on the moon. He had managed, finally, to make her happy. The shadow of wariness disappeared from her features.

"For me?" she breathed with disbelief and delight. And then the unexpected happened. She picked up *both* tickets, and began to dance around her shop. She came out from behind the counter and whirled by him hugging *both* tickets to her bosom.

The dress suddenly didn't seem so monstrously ugly as the full skirt moved around her, twirled up to show a beguiling glimpse of legs so long and slender his mouth went dry. Her long hair was doing gypsy things, and the neckline of the blouse had slipped sideways, showing him the creamy perfection of her skin, the curve of her shoulder.

After he'd watched her drop that vase full of roses, and trip over the edge of a rug, he'd always kind of written her off as a klutz. But now he saw how wrong he had been.

She was graceful and sensual, at ease in her body.

But he could see the truth now, so clearly it hurt his head.

True beauty had a shine to it.

A shine that could not be disguised, or manufactured, either.

Katie Pritchard was beautiful.

He registered this fact slowly, stunned. It had been necessary for him to become a better man to even begin to see the truth about her.

Really, now was the time to break it to her that only one ticket was for her. And the other was for her escort. Him.

But somehow he didn't want to stop the dance, kill the radiant smile on her face. And somehow he needed some time alone with this astonishing revelation. Katie was beautiful. In a way that could change a man's life in ways he was not prepared to have it changed.

He thought of what he had come to know about her over the past year, and even more in the past two weeks:

that she was funny and shy and smart and sassy. And eminently decent. He realized exactly why he had avoided girls like her.

"My Mom is going to be in total shock," she told him, finally, stopping in front of him. Her brow was just a little dewy from exertion, her breath was coming in faint pants.

A shameful waste of passion.

"She has tried everything to get tickets to this event," Katie rushed on. "She even offered her first-born child. Which would be me. Oh, I could just kiss you!"

He closed his eyes and puckered up, but nothing happened. When he opened them again, she had whirled away, was in the back room on the phone. He felt an astonishing *yearning* to know what her lips would have tasted like, even though he now knew her to be far more dangerous than he had ever guessed.

Well, to his detriment, he had never shown nearly enough caution around anything dangerous.

"Mom," she said, breathlessly into the phone, "You'll never guess what just happened. I have tickets to Tac Revol!"

He stood there for a moment, letting her excited voice wash over him, thinking maybe he was too late. She already was a crazy cat lady, that was the only type of person who could get so excited about those tickets!

He was aware, suddenly, almost sadly, that he had gotten exactly what he wanted. He had transformed her. This was the moment he had waited for and worked toward. His stated mission was over, except for the going-out-with-him part.

He had *seen* her. Passionate. Laughter filled. Playful.

This moment had come out of nowhere, a gift almost as good as getting to see her swim with dolphins. But what was even more astonishing than having *seen* her was the glimpse of himself. This was the kind of girl a man could fall in love with, before he even knew what had happened.

A woman who loved her mother. He was not sure any of his other recent girlfriends had ever mentioned a mother to him!

Love. He didn't like it that that word had entered his mind in connection with Katie. Thankfully, she was the kind of girl a man like him was not really worthy of since he was not certain he could sustain this new and honorable self for long enough. He might even have bad genetics.

His father had managed a pretext of honor for thirty-five years! His father had taken a vow to love and honor and cherish, through better or worse, and he had broken that vow. He had institutionalized his wife. If that wasn't bad enough, he was reluctant to go and see her. Dylan was willing to bet it had been more than two months since his father had visited his mother. He suspected a new lady friend. And then his sister wondered what was wrong with *him* when he could not bring himself to return his father's calls? The events of his mother's illness had sent Dylan into a state of shock. He could not believe the fabric of a life that had seemed so strong, so real, could be so easily torn. He had become a man who did not believe in anything anymore.

And yet, looking at Katie talking to her own mother, he thought, *A man could believe in that.*

He realized the enormity of his error. He'd told himself he had been trying to give her back something she had lost. Now he saw he had tried to give her back what he missed about himself.

Hope. Belief. Trust.

He was not the man for this task. Foolish to have taken it on.

Katie glanced at him. Suddenly her whole demeanor changed. "Mom, I'll call you back."

"Dylan?"

"Huh?"

"Are you okay?" She came out of the back room, came and stood looking up at him.

He pasted his breeziest smile on his face, tried to see the plain Jane in her. But he saw something else. A girl who needed a man who could be one hundred per cent real. Katie needed someone brave enough to trust her with who he was once he laid down the shield.

He folded his arms over his chest. He wasn't ever having a relationship with her. He'd done the decent thing. He'd given her back her spirit, however briefly. Both of them knew now that it had only been hidden, not lost.

And what of his own spirit?

He was aware of his lack, that he had overdeveloped many sides of his personality: strength, daring, persistence. Others he had managed to totally ignore: sentiment, softness, vulnerability. If he let this thing with Katie go any further, he was going to get to the place where he really hurt, and dammit, he didn't want to go there! He was not the least bit interested in discovering his own humanity, what lay beyond the fearless facade.

He was about fun and danger, and lovely combinations of both. He was not about self-discovery. In fact he could honestly say he hated stuff like that. Nothing could bring on that nice-to-have-known-you bouquet faster than a girlfriend wanting to have a deep and meaningful conversation.

"Dylan, what's wrong?"

"Nothing," he said.

She looked doubtful. "Did you want to see Tac Revol?"

"Excuse me?" he said, lifting an eyebrow at her. "Like, I'd be caught dead at something like that!"

For a moment she looked unconvinced, and then her face relaxed.

"Oh. Of course you wouldn't! You probably don't even know Tac Revol spells Cat Lover, backward. You've just been so persistent. I thought, oh, never mind what I thought." Her smile came back. "So, you don't care if I take my mom?"

"I'm glad you're taking your mom." He ordered himself to stop talking. *McKinnon, get out. Get out with your life. Full retreat.* "I wish I could make my mom so happy. Just one more time."

"Is she gone, Dylan?" she asked softly.

Such a complicated question. "Yes," he said gruffly. She was gone. The mother of his youth, brilliant, witty, warm, loving, capable, sensitive, she was gone. And she was never coming back.

"Oh, I'm so sorry."

Everything brave and fearless in him was collapsing in the face of the light in her eyes, the wariness washed from them, replaced with something so warm, a place a man could lay down his shield and rest his head.

Katie Pritchard was beautiful in a different way than he had ever experienced beautiful before.

Hers was a kind of beauty that changed the things it

touched, made them need to be worthy of her. She was deep and real and genuine, and she'd already been stuck with one guy who wasn't anywhere near worthy of those things, who could not live up to her standard.

And that knowledge of her and what would be required of any man who linked his life with hers, even temporarily, made him feel oddly fragile, as if he had inadvertently touched something sacred. He was aware of feeling the route he was on had taken a dangerous twist and become very, very scary. Scary? But that was impossible. The Daredevil Dylan McKinnon was fearless. A little snip like her was not going to bring him to his knees.

Or maybe she was.

Because she reached up and touched his cheek with her hand, soothingly, as if she understood all the secrets he was not telling her.

And then she kissed him.

Her lips were unspeakably tender, they invited him to tell her everything, they called to the place in him that he had been so fierce about guarding, that he had revealed to no one.

It was a place of burdens and loneliness, and the burdens felt suddenly lighter, and the loneliness felt like it was fog that sun was penetrating.

"If you want to go for coffee sometime," she said, hesitantly.

He reeled back from her. "I have to go out of town for a while," he said, and saw her flinch from the obviousness of the lie.

But he felt as if it was better—far better—to hurt her now than later. The fabric of life, and especially of love, was fragile after all. He could not trust himself not to damage what he saw blossoming in the tenderness of her eyes.

Love. He could not trust himself with love.

CHAPTER FIVE

KATE took up her post beside her window, glanced at the clock. Nearly one o'clock and no Dylan. Just as there had been no Dylan for the past three days. No dropping by her shop, no teasing, no exotic invitations. Ever since she had accepted the tickets from him—and made the mistake of telling him she was available for coffee—it was as if he had dropped off the face of the earth.

The chase was over. For a guy like him it was all about the chase. She knew that from sending his flowers.

He had told her he had to go away, but she could see his red sports car parked right up the street. He certainly didn't have to let her know his schedule!

Still, this *feeling* inside her should serve as a warning. She missed him coming by. Each day she chose an uglier outfit in anticipation of it. Today she had on a pair of daisy-printed culottes and had her hair tied with a matching bandanna. It was a lot of trouble to have gone to if he wasn't going to come by and appreciate it.

For all that she had thought she was winning this game of cat and mouse they had been playing, she now realized she hadn't been at all.

She'd been kidding herself, falling more in love with

him every day. The tickets to the Tac Revol reading had finished her really, swamped her with tenderness for the man she wanted—no, needed—so desperately to hate. And when he had choked up, at the mention of his own mother, it was like the armor around her heart had been pierced irreparably.

And then he'd stopped coming, proving her instincts had been correct. Saying yes to him, inviting him for coffee, was the beginning of the end. Except her end seemed to have come without the stuff that was supposed to come in the middle. Ridiculous to feel regret.

Probably Dylan had seen something in her face that day she took the tickets that had frightened him off. *Girl who cares too much, feels too deeply, capable of sappy behavior over small gestures.*

Good, she tried to convince herself. Good that he had lost interest in his game. She had no hope of coming out the winner in any kind of match with him.

It was five minutes past one. He wasn't coming. He wasn't running today, or if he was he was avoiding her shop.

She felt her heart drop, hated it that she felt her throat close and her eyes prick as if she was going to cry! She would not cry. Her assistant, Mrs. Abercrombie, was working today. People came in all the time!

Stop it! She ordered herself. She'd known all along this was the danger of dancing with a man like that. That is what they had been doing, the last weeks, dancing, circling around each other, jousting.

A dangerous dance, because how could you spend any kind of time with a guy like that and not want more?

Not more of the good looks and charm, not more of the fun-loving playboy persona.

No, more of the other things, the more subtle qualities, the ones he tried to hide. Depth. Gentleness. Compassion. Intelligence.

More of the look in his eyes and on his face when he had said his mother was gone. She had seen who he really was then: a warrior who somehow felt he had failed, who was looking at his arsenal of weapons helplessly, not understanding how they had not worked to hold back the flow of life, to keep pain at bay from those he loved. In that moment, when he had mentioned his mother, she had seen how furiously and fiercely he loved, and she knew just why he was intent on pursuing the superficial.

And she knew just why she wanted to be the one he finally chose to lay down his weapons for, to come home to.

Her heart wanted it so badly. Her head said, pragmatically, *never going to happen.* Katie pulled her shoulders back and shoved out her chin, tucked her hair neatly behind her ears.

She was a divorced woman, not a schoolgirl. She already knew about the daggers hidden in the cloak of love. She had known all along she should not let her defenses down, and she had thought she was succeeding. Now she saw her defenses had started to come down the first day she had given in to the impulse to watch him run.

She had been realistic from the start, she had known he was not a man any intelligent woman should be pinning her hopes on. She had known all along she was a momentary distraction. She had known all along that some girl would come along who was his type—dumb, beautiful and built, a girl who allowed him to keep his fearless facade in place—and that would be the end of his interest in her.

The day was gorgeous, and she needed to focus on that—on the robin singing in the tree outside her window, in the solace of her flowers. She decided to put some buckets of flowers outside the door.

But when Katie looked at her finished display, she knew she wasn't as done thinking about him as she wanted to be. To people walking by it would only look pretty. Not a single soul but her would know what it meant. Unconsciously she had chosen larkspur, primroses, yellow lilies. She had lined her outer windowsill with little garden-ready containers of marigolds.

Dylan's worst character traits were all represented: fickleness, inconsistency, false expectations. The marigolds might have been unfair. She shouldn't really call him cruel—he had given her the Tac Revol tickets—but it did feel cruel that he had lost interest as quickly as he had gained it. That she had come to look forward to him coming by, anticipate it, *live for it,* and he had stopped.

At the last moment she added a bucket of gladiolas to her display. The flower of the gladiators, of warriors, representing strength. True strength, not just physical strength, but strength of spirit. She eyed her choice wondering if it represented her or Dylan.

Without warning, his office door flew open, and Dylan stepped out into the bright sunshine.

For a moment Katie hoped he had seen her, fantasized that he would come over and tell her what urgent matter had kept him away for the past few days.

But he didn't appear to see her at all. Slighted, she went to duck back inside her own door, but something in his demeanor stopped her. He was looking vaguely frantic, his eyes scanning the parked cars, when she could clearly see where he had parked his own car.

Dylan, frantic? She frowned. Something wrong with that picture. He never looked anything but polished—some might go as far as to say perfect—even in his jogging clothes, but he wasn't in his jogging clothes, and he looked faintly disheveled. His shirt was white and crisp, but his tie was undone, his sleeves rolled up. He had left his desk in a hurry.

None of her business, she told herself, but instead of stepping in to the relative safety of her shop, and away from any kind of engagement with him, some kind of automatic pilot took over. She stepped out, touched his arm.

He started, and that's when she realized, despite the rather gaudy outfit she was wearing for his benefit, he hadn't even seen her.

He couldn't have dismissed her that completely from his life in three short days!

"Dylan, what's wrong?"

He looked at her, and she knew she was seeing something she might never see again. Dylan was afraid.

He fumbled with his keys. "The hospital just called. Tara was brought in by ambulance."

Tara. One of his standbys. How had she managed to forget this about him when she was inviting him for coffee?

"They can't locate Sam."

"Sam?"

"My sister, Tara's, husband. They wouldn't say very much on the phone. Or maybe I didn't hear much beyond *scheduled for surgery.*"

"Tara is your sister?" she asked, flabbergasted. And then she saw the look on his face. He had his keys out, and Kate noticed his hand was shaking ever so slightly. She plucked the keys from him.

"I'll drive you. I'll just let Mrs. Abercrombie know I'm leaving."

She expected argument, at least a token protest, but there was none.

"Thanks, Katie," he said, and then he looked at her. Really looked at her, and she knew she could put out all the buckets of larkspur in the world, it wasn't going to change how she felt. The whole world could believe he was a daredevil, beyond fear, if they wanted to. In his eyes in that moment, she saw how deeply he cared for those rare people who were close to him, just as the other day she had seen how he cared about his mother. She saw that he, without hesitation, would lay down his life to protect those he cared about.

She saw, clearly, why he was so quick to get rid of women from his life.

Because he was the kind of man who, when he gave his heart, it took every single thing that he had. Caring so much was the place that weakened him, that made him afraid. No one could understand that fear of being destroyed by love as well as a woman who had lost a baby.

Katie understood she had a job to do. She unlocked the doors of his car, and they got in. She had never been in a car where she felt so low to the ground. She looked at the gear shift, tried not to let her trepidation show.

"I think the quickest way to the hospital—"

She nearly stalled the car getting it out of the parking spot. Gamely she gave it gas, and was astonished by how the amount of power sucked her back into the seat. She slammed on the brakes, adjusted the amount of gas she gave it, tried again. A car behind her honked.

"Have you ever driven a car like this?" he asked uneasily.

"A car's a car," she said grimly, trying to force it into second. The gears ground, and he winced.

"That shows what you know. Katie, pull over. I'll drive." As annoying as it was that her Good Samaritan act had been accepted for less than thirty seconds, at least his preoccupation with her driving was keeping him from being overtaken by worry about his sister.

She wanted to ask exactly what the hospital had told him about his sister, but it seemed like a wiser course just to keep his mind on her driving. And not let him behind the wheel! If she did that, she had no doubt they would be racing through the streets of Hillsboro at record-breaking speeds. He'd probably get pulled over before he got anywhere near the hospital.

"You're not safe to drive right now," she informed him, pulling into the stream of traffic on a busier road. Another horn honked.

"Sheesh, and you are? Did you know sometimes you have this holier-than-thou way of speaking that drives me crazy?"

That could be a good thing, too, right? Lots of women would like to be the ones driving Dylan

McKinnon crazy. Or just driving him. "At least no one will get hurt if we crash at this speed."

"There's that tone again. My sister will be transferred to the old folks' home before we get to the hospital."

She decided to keep with her plan to keep Dylan's mind off his worries. "Tell me about your sister. Are you the only two children?"

"Unfortunately. Tara's seven years older than me, and I would have liked a dozen other siblings to keep her busy. So she wouldn't focus so much on me. She's a menace. Meddlesome. Opinionated. I can't believe a nice guy like Sam married her."

Underneath every single word Katie heard pure love. "You adore her," she surmised.

He glared at her. "She's a pain in the butt."

"You love her madly."

"Whatever."

"You send her flowers all the time."

"Yeah, well, mostly to bug you."

"To make me think you are something you aren't," she deduced softly.

"I'm every bit as bad as you think I am, Katie. Probably worse."

"Uh-huh."

"You were very smart never to go out with me."

"Uh-huh."

"If you don't believe me, ask my sister."

"Okay."

"And quit agreeing with me, for goodness' sake!"

"Are you afraid of something, Mr. Fearless?" But she already knew. He was terrified of the very same thing she was. *Love.* He was terrified because he knew it was a force out of his control. His sister being hurt was a reminder of that. That life could best the warrior when it came to love.

He squinted narrowly at her. “I’m terrified of your driving, actually.”

She was a little rusty with the standard, and after a stop at some lights her takeoff was a bit rough. The car bucked and threw Dylan’s head forward.

“And whatever you’re wearing. You look like you’re going to an audition for the Von Trapp Family singers. What do they call those things?”

“Culottes.” Ah, he was trying so hard not to let her see his heart. But she felt as if she could see it anyway.

“Good name,” he muttered. “Terrifying, right up there with blood culottes.”

A good thing to know about a man, that he could keep his sense of humor, even in a crisis. A good thing to know about a man—that making wisecracks was one of the defenses in the armor around his heart. They finally pulled up to the Hillsboro Hospital at the emergency door. “I’ll let you go in,” she said, “and I’ll go find a parking spot.”

“I don’t want to leave my car with you.”

“Too bad. Pretend it’s valet service.”

He looked as if he wanted to argue, but his concern for his sister got the better of him. He got out, slammed the door, raced to the hospital entrance and disappeared.

She parked the car, but way off in a back lot, not close to any other cars. If it got scratched she was going to be blamed. And then she turned the mirror and winced at what she saw. It was one thing to play the flower girl at work, for her customers, and to bug Dylan, but to go into a public building looking as if she had made an outfit out of curtains and was ready to burst into song!

She removed the scarf, ran her fingers through her hair and shook it. There was, unfortunately, not a thing she could do about the culottes, except hold her head up high, something, thankfully, that she'd had a great deal of practice at.

She went in through the sliding emergency room doors, and had to pause to let her eyes adjust from the bright light outside.

And then she looked around.

She saw Dylan, standing by a window, but he was not alone.

He was holding a baby. The breath went out of her. The baby was nestled against his chest, thumb in mouth, his other hand tracing the outline of Dylan's lips. And if she was not mistaken, Dylan kissed those little fingers, then said something that made the baby lift his head, look at him and smile.

She could see clearly they were related. The child was obviously his sister's baby, Dylan's nephew. The baby's smile showed the promise of being at least as devastating as his uncle's was. In fact, that baby could have been Dylan's son rather than his nephew, their appearance was so similar. Both had hair the color of rich, dark chocolate, amazing blue eyes. The baby, though dimpled, already had the cheekbones and the chin that were going to break hearts.

Katie was completely taken by the contrast of what she was seeing: Dylan so strong and so sure, his arm muscles flexed to hold the baby, so pudgy and powerless, so completely trusting of his uncle.

She stared at Dylan's posture. He was comfortable, relaxed, and yet two things were very evident: his deep love of the child, and the warrior protectiveness he felt toward him.

Again, she could sense how deeply this man loved when he allowed himself to. And Dylan, man least likely to ever make a serious commitment, looked as if he had been born to be a daddy.

But watching them, she suddenly felt her own heartbreak as fresh and as painful as if the wound had happened yesterday.

Once upon a time this had been her dream for herself.

Exactly.

A strong man. A baby. A little house. A swing set. More babies. A sandbox. Cookies baking. Flower beds to supply a home-based fresh-cut flower business.

Only, her dream had died, been shattered, when she had miscarried the baby. A little boy, who would have been just a year or so older than the one in Dylan's arms.

Months in a gray fog, a place of *no* feeling. No tears. No laughter. No joy. No sense of having anything to look forward to. Marcus growing impatient, then distant. More distant than he had been before.

As the memories swamped Katie, she watched a nurse approach Dylan, tiny, perky, all smiles and bubbliness.

The kind of girl Dylan always went for—except that, as a nurse, she was probably smart.

Katie wanted to leave. Her heart hurt in ways she had not thought it could hurt.

This was the hurt she always had known Dylan was capable of inflicting. This was the hurt three days of not seeing him had begun to prepare her for. It was the hurt of a woman who wanted something terribly badly—underscored by the picture he made holding that baby—and it was like wanting two scoops of pistachio on the moon. Not just unrealistic. Impossible. Nonexistent.

She drew in a deep breath, and marched up to him, just as the nurse moved away. "Here are your keys," she said brightly. "I'm going to go. I hope your sister is all right."

"She fell over some toys on the stairs," he said, but he was watching her, carefully. He made no move to take the keys. "Her leg is broken, badly. An orthopedic surgeon is on the way."

"On the way!" she said. "That's great. Well, I must—"

He took a step in to her. "What's the matter?" he asked softly.

The baby was reaching for her hair. He smelled sweet, of talcum and baby soap, and of innocence and hope and dreams.

She couldn't even do the baby bouquets at work. She let Mrs. Abercrombie fill the little blue ceramic boots and the pink stork baskets.

"The matter?" She stepped back from the baby. If he touched her with those little pudgy hands she knew she would shatter into a million pieces, and there would be no putting her back together again. "Nothing."

But her voice wobbled shamefully. She pressed the keys into his hand. "I have to—"

"Katie," he said, his voice gravelly, firm, strong, "Talk to me."

No.

A terrible thing happened. She began to cry. It felt as

if every one of those feelings she'd bottled up after the miscarriage had decided to pick this moment, of all moments, not be dammed one second longer.

It was exactly the kind of demonstration that could absolutely be counted on to horrify a man like Dylan McKinnon.

Only it didn't.

He drew her into him with his free arm, pressed her head against his chest. "Hey," he said, "Hey, it's okay."

The baby was too close now. Touching her, squawking at her like a little bird, tangling his fists in her hair.

She waited to break, to shatter, for her heart to burst into a million pieces.

Standing there with Dylan's arm around her, held fast by his strength, with the sweet-scented baby pulling at her hair and chirping away at her in baby talk, something did shatter. The ice around her heart. Only, behind it was not destruction but warmth. The loveliest warmth burst through her.

She wiped her tears on Dylan's chest, took a step back. "Can I hold him?" she whispered.

The baby came to her so willingly, gurgling and blowing spit bubbles. Her arms closed around him, and she felt his wriggling, beautiful strength.

She felt *life.* In all its mystery and all its magnificence.

She met Dylan's eyes and heard herself saying, her voice brave, "I had a miscarriage. I lost my baby. The marriage didn't make it."

He just looked at her. He didn't try and make it better, but he didn't try and look away, either. He didn't try and change the subject. He didn't offer words that would not and could not help. He just looked at her, and there was something in the look in his eyes that she could hang on to.

"Come on," he finally said. "Let's sit down over here." He guided her to the waiting room, which was blessedly empty, and she took a chair, the baby nestled happily against her. Dylan took the chair beside her, covered her hand with his own.

"What's his name?" she asked.

"Jake."

"I was going to call my baby Jonathon. It was a boy, too."

"Jonathon's a nice name. I think you would have been a good mom. No. A great one." He did not say she was young and there would be more babies, more chances, as if one child could be replaced with another.

"I took it really hard," she told him.

"Would there be any other way to take it?" he asked softly.

"Marcus, my husband, seemed relieved." She had never said that to another living soul before. Had she even said it to herself? The words were tumbling out now.

"He said 'I'm not sure I was ready for a baby.' He hadn't wanted to try again. What he'd wanted was for me to get over it. He didn't understand how you could grieve for something that had never breathed." She paused, and said so softly maybe she just said it to herself, "But my dreams breathed."

Dylan swore under his breath. One word. Not a word anyone else had said, except maybe her in the darkness of night when she had found herself so alone with a heart full of misery.

And Dylan meant it. And she knew he was a man

who would never be relieved if something happened to his unborn baby. Never.

The yearning leaped in her, clawed at her, told her, *Take a chance on him.*

On him? That was craziness! She had looked after his flowers. She knew better. Except what she had seen in his eyes just now was like a beacon that called the ships lost at sea home to safe harbor.

"If Tara's your sister," she asked, suddenly, "who's Sarah?"

He slid her a look, smiled crookedly. "PR manager."

"Margot?"

"Receptionist at my office."

"Janet?"

He sighed. "It's Sister Janet."

"I think," she decided out loud, "I'll move to another country." Was it even possible to outdistance what was unfolding within her? How far would she have to run to escape the *hope* that was unfurling inside of her?

"Katie, my lady," he said, "Oh, Katie, my lady."

Katie, my lady. Just a teasing phrase, not something that was intended to increase the yearning within her. But spoken with such tenderness, from his heart, that's exactly what it did. And it made her decide she wasn't going anywhere. Not just yet.

And then he took his hand in hers, and he kissed the top of it, and sighed, a man who would rewrite the past for her if he could.

But what would he write on her future?

The baby, who had been slurping contentedly, suddenly popped his thumb from his mouth and roared, "JAAAKE."

She laughed, startled and delighted.

"We're working on volume control," Dylan said affectionately. "He only has one setting, loud. And if I put him on the ground, he only has one speed."

"Let me guess. Fast."

"How did you guess?"

"Um. I can tell this is one acorn that didn't fall too far from the McKinnon family tree."

"Mr. McKinnon?" a nurse called. "Can you come with me for a minute?"

Dylan studied Katie. "Do you want me to leave Jake with you or take him with me?"

Katie struggled to keep her face composed. Yearning, sweet and tantalizing, burned through her. What she wanted to do was bury her face in the sweetness of that baby's scent and never come up for air again.

"Leave him with me," she whispered.

"Hey, stinker," Dylan warned his nephew sternly, "don't live up to your reputation." And then he turned and followed the nurse down the hallway.

Katie watched him go, and even though she knew better, even though she was trying so hard not to get any more entangled with a man who could exercise so much power over her—without any awareness of that power on his part—she felt her treacherous heart go right down the hall with him.

Dylan found his sister. She was being prepped for surgery and needed to give him some instructions, but he was having trouble focusing on her completely.

He wanted to kill somebody, or at least hurt them badly. He wanted to kill a man he'd never met before. He wanted to kill the man who had been so self-centered he'd left Katie all alone with her grief for that unborn child. What had she said? Her husband had been *relieved.*

Dylan couldn't believe a man could look into those eyes and not find it in himself to be there, one hundred per cent for her. Not *want* to be there for her.

"No chocolate, candy, choking-size hazards, hamburgers or steak and lobster," his sister said.

Dylan focused on Tara. Sheesh. She had been given something to control pain until her surgery. "What are you talking about?" he asked her.

She sighed elaborately. "Earth calling Dylan. I'm trying to tell you how to take care of a baby."

"Me?" he said. Katie's face faded from his mind and he focused on his sister. "I'm not looking after Jake. Where's Sam?"

"San Francisco. Fogged in. So unless you want your favorite nephew to go to foster care, time to step up to the plate." She giggled helplessly. "Step up to the plate. Get it? That's priceless, given your old career."

"Ha, ha," he said without an ounce of humor. "When's Sam going to get in?"

"Dylan, I have no gift for predicting the weather even when I'm not on drugs."

After getting a ton more of unhelpful advice from his sister, Dylan went back down the hall to the emergency waiting room. Katie had found a box of toys, and was now sitting on the floor with his nephew, unmindful of getting her outfit dirty; though of course that was, one would assume, why you wore an outfit like that. You wouldn't worry about wrecking it, you'd hope you could! Thank goodness, she had lost the babushka somewhere.

Or maybe not. Because without it, her hair fell like a shining wave to the slenderness of her shoulder.

As always happened, it felt as if it was not the outfit he saw at all. It was the look on her face, the sweet curve of her smile.

He realized why he had been so anxious to focus on the killing of her ex-husband. Because to focus on her was to threaten what remained of his tattered control after he had seen her do her spontaneous little dance over the Tac Revol tickets, after he had tasted the clear-brook sweetness of her kiss.

There was a look on her face as she studied Jake that was rapt, even more beautiful than when she had danced. She looked serene, almost like a Madonna.

A decent girl. A wholesome girl. A smart girl. *A girl absolutely born to be a mother.*

He was well aware that there on the cold hospital floor sat a woman he'd offered everything to: he'd offered to wine and dine her, escort her to the most-sought-after functions, take her on his motorcycle, give her dreams carved in ice.

She'd said no to each of his invitations without even a moment's hesitation. And then when he'd finally done something genuinely nice—as accidental as it may have been that she thought those tickets were for her mother—then it had been her turn to issue the invitation.

That was what Katie was doing even now, sitting on the floor, playing with the baby, shining with an inner light that was nearly blinding. She was issuing him an invitation to a life he had turned his back on when his mother had gotten ill. A life that he had decided was too full of foibles, too unpredictable, that extracted too great a cost.

That's why he had avoided her ever since she had ever so tentatively extended her invitation for coffee.

He was not unaware of a feeling of the universe conspiring against him. He'd decided, after seeing her dance with the Tac Revol tickets, after her kissing him, that the game was up. Over. The stakes had become a little too high for his tastes. And yet here he was, tangled with her again.

"Thanks, Katie," he said, coming up to her.

"Is your sister okay?"

"Whacked out on drugs. She seems to think I'd be a good candidate to look after Jake."

"Aren't you?"

What had he ever done to deserve the look of trust on her face?

"No."

"Haven't you ever looked after Jake before?"

"I've taken him out a couple of times by myself. To the mall. And the park. The little devil is a chick magnet. And the man-with-baby thing is unbelievable. The women are all over me when I have Jake." He knew exactly what he was trying to do. Put back the barrier that had been so conveniently provided by names of women she didn't know. Tara. Sarah. Janet. Margot.

"Trust you to see a baby as useful for that reason!"

"His usefulness is limited," Dylan said. It was working. She looked justifiably horrified. Part of him was thinking, *Katie, my lady, please see me in a bad light. You make the decision to not have anything to do with me. Because I can't seem to follow through when I make that decision about you.*

"The baby's usefulness is limited?" she asked, indignant.

"Oh, sure, he's cute, but he's basically a poop machine. Just when things have the potential to get interesting, he fills his pants. He actually leaked on me once. I thought I was going to hurl."

"Daredevil Dylan McKinnon was going to throw up over a little baby leak?" She started to laugh.

"Don't be so damned sanctimonious. You weren't there. The horror was unimaginable, even for someone like you, who probably has a fairly good imagination. Have you ever had to deal with a situation like that?"

"I used to babysit in high school. I wouldn't let a baby leak scare me!"

He snorted. "That's like a soldier who has never been in a combat zone saying bullets don't scare him."

"It's not quite the same thing," she said dryly.

"Yeah, well, baby leaks scare me, and I'm man enough to admit it."

"I appreciate your vulnerability," she said, tongue-in-cheek.

"Don't tell anybody. I'd be ruined. And don't you start smiling!"

Really, her smile was becoming the hardest thing to handle. It lit something in her. Had he known, right from the beginning, in some place he'd been afraid to go within himself, that her smile would be like this? *Worth it. Worth everything. Even the uncertainty of his own soul. Even coming face-to-face with all his own fears.*

"Why does everyone think me being tortured is funny?" he asked. He was asking the universe as much as her!

"Oh, Dylan, it's not exactly you being tortured that's funny. It's you being terrified of something so darling as a little baby."

That showed what she knew! "You won't think he's such a little darling when his forehead wrinkles up, he holds his breath and starts turning red."

He could see way too clearly that he was playing with something far too big now, something he might not be able to control. He'd never be able to forget the beauty he discovered, all her hopes and dreams in her face.

Wasn't that at the heart of this whole thing? Some instinct had told him she was beautiful, and he had wanted her to look beautiful again, had wanted to see those hopes and dreams shining in her face, had *needed* to know that some precious part of her had not been destroyed by whatever she had been through.

Proof his plan was working—there she sat on the floor in her Maria Von Trapp outfit, playing with baby toys, radiating absolute and extremely worrisome beauty.

"Hey," she said, looking up at him, wrinkling her nose. "Don't look so worried."

He had that sensation, watching her play building blocks with his nephew, that Katie could know him in ways he had never allowed people to know him. No one in the world ever guessed when he was feeling pressure, when he was rattled, when he was scared. Not even when he'd been posed at the door of that airplane waiting to jump had he betrayed how truly frightened he was. He'd made some wisecrack remark that had made everyone laugh.

But if she had been there he had the uneasy feeling she would have known, just as she had known to take those car keys from his hand a half an hour ago.

And Dylan McKinnon wasn't quite sure if it felt good or bad to be quite so transparent to another human being.

"So, what's the battle plan?" she asked him, brushing off her skirt/short fashion disaster and getting to her feet.

"The same as any battle plan," he told her. "Survival." And he was not sure he was referring to looking after a baby, either!

She looked askance at him. "Battle plans aren't about survival," she pointed out. "They're about victory. Winning."

Now, if anyone should know that, it should be him. He did know that. He'd had a battle plan all along, prove a decent girl would go out with him, give her the gift of hope in return and then, mission accomplished, withdraw. Now his battle plan was wavering before him like a mirage of an oasis on a blistering desert afternoon.

But now he saw it differently. Survival. His.

"I can take it from here," he said bravely. "I'll take him over to my sister's. I have her key. The place is babyproofed and supplied."

Something flitted across her face. Relief? But it was quickly replaced by another look. Determination. "You don't think I'm leaving you alone with this baby, do you?"

"I can manage a baby."

She rolled her eyes. "No, you can't."

He should have felt insulted, but he didn't. He felt relieved. And, oddly enough, not relieved at the very same time. As confused as he had ever felt. Before, even if she had been saying no, he'd felt as if he was in control. Now he didn't. And he was pretty sure Dylan McKinnon out of control was not going to be a good thing.

"Really," he said, a bit more forcefully, "I can manage it. I make million-dollar decisions every day. Forty-two people work for me. I'm the honorary spokesperson for three different charitable organizations. What is one twenty-pound baby in comparison to all that?"

She looked entirely unimpressed. "Dylan McKinnon, have you ever kept a plant alive for more than three weeks?"

"What kind of plant?" he hedged.

"Any kind. A garden flower? A houseplant?"

Mental pictures of a sordid history that included many dead, dead plants formed in his mind's eye.

"Anything *green?*" she asked, as if she was relaxing her standards to give him a chance.

"Bath towels?"

She shook her head. "Living green."

He lived in a condo. He didn't even have to remember to water the lawn! "The fact that plants, er, fail to thrive around me is irrelevant."

"Hmm. How about a puppy? Or a kitten?" She looked at him, shook her head. "A goldfish? Guppies?"

He scowled at her. "My lifestyle has never allowed for pets."

"Precisely my point. You don't know how to care for things."

"I travel! I know how to care for things! My car is cared for! That's diamond finish on the wax job in case you didn't notice."

"Living things," she amended.

Her chin was getting a stubborn set to it. A smart man would have been running. But he was in charge of a baby now, and it was hard to run with twenty pounds of squirming baby under your arm, and plus, he was thinking he kind of liked her chin pointed at him like that.

"Speaking of cars," she said, "do you have a car seat?"

And that clinched it. Dylan McKinnon knew, that whether he wanted to or not, he needed Katie Pritchard right now. Only a girl like her could be trusted to think of something as all important to his nephew's well-being as a car seat.

The baby did that wrinkly thing with his forehead, held his breath and started to turn a very unbecoming shade of red.

How humiliating. Dylan didn't just need Katie. He needed her *desperately.*

CHAPTER SIX

KATIE stared at Dylan with absolute astonishment. Here was a man who had jumped out of airplanes, bungee jumped, raced motorcycles. Here was a man who, as he had just pointed out, made million-dollar decisions, was responsible for employees, ran a company.

And yet there was an unmistakable bead of sweat on his forehead as he gazed at his nephew. His gorgeous blue eyes had a glint of pure fear in them. He was drumming his fingers nervously against the muscle of his thigh.

And all because his adorable nephew had stopped all activity—building block suddenly frozen in midair—a look of fierce concentration on his now reddening chubby face.

"Is he," Katie asked, uncertainly, "you know?"

But Dylan didn't have to answer. They were enveloped in a stench that seemed as if it could not possibly have been produced by the adorable little cherub in front of them. The look of concentration evaporated from Jake's face, he gurgled with what would seem to be self-satisfaction and returned to his blocks.

"Now what?" the president and CEO of Daredevils asked her in an undertone.

"I don't have a clue," she said.

She recognized how absurd this was. It was a baby. And it had two full-grown adults almost completely tied up in knots.

She couldn't help it. She started to laugh. When Dylan glared at her, mistakenly thinking she was laughing at his weakness instead of her own, she laughed harder. Finally, her howls of laughter petered down to sputters. She hoped she wouldn't snort. Of course she snorted.

Dylan was looking at her intently, as if he had never seen her before. More absurdity: she might have dreamed such a look over wine and dinner, with her hair upswept, diamonds sparkling at her ears, lips painted a beguiling shade of red. Such a look should be reserved for a woman wearing the perfect little black dress. But over baby poop? In hideous daisy-printed culottes? Right after she had snorted? *Welcome to your life, Katie Pritchard.* She licked her lips uncomfortably.

"You should do that more often," he decided, then looked away, as if he had said too much, revealed too much.

"What should I do more often?" she breathed, feeling her stomach drop out at the way his eyes had fastened, with searing heat, on her mouth. She might have dreamed such a look to be appropriate right before a man leaned forward to take his true love's lips with his own.

"Laugh."

Part of her had hoped he meant lick her lips!

"Okay, Mr. Daredevil," she said, "I'm waiting for the plan."

"You're the one who knows how to keep plants alive!"

A nurse came by, gray haired, very efficient looking. “If you check at the reception desk before you leave, we can lend you a car seat to take the baby home.”

Dylan turned up the full wattage of his smile. Katie guessed he was going to put his charm to good use and get that diaper looked after for them.

Instead he surprised her by saying to the nurse, “Uh, we have two rank amateurs here who don’t know the first thing about a messy diaper. Or maybe I should say two messy amateurs who don’t know anything about a rank diaper. Could you find somebody to give us a quick lesson, before we take him home?”

The nurse smiled at him. Was nobody immune to this man’s charms? “ I’d be happy to show you how to change a diaper.”

A few minutes later they were in a little room, the nurse not as charmed by Dylan as Katie had thought. She made him change the diaper!

Katie was not unaware, as she watched, that this was something she had thought she would be doing with her husband one day. She had looked forward to every little thing about that baby coming. Foolishly, the day she had found out she was pregnant, she had even begun to buy diapers, pajamas with feet in them, soothers, stuffed crib toys.

Now, in a room with *reality,* she wondered if Marcus ever would have tackled a mess like that! She had not allowed herself to think much about *what if.* But now she did wonder. What if they had stayed together? Would she have felt as alone with parenting as she had started to feel in their marriage?

Certainly, she could not imagine Marcus bending

over such an arduous task with such a look of grim determination on his face.

Dylan shot a look at her. "I don't have anything on me, do I?" he whispered.

"Such as?" she whispered back.

He glared at her, then at the baby. "Such as *brown.*"

"You look like you're okay. So far."

The baby gurgled happily and wagged his legs.

"I wish he wouldn't do that," Dylan said grimly.

"Me, too," she admitted.

They both laughed, and the nurse joined in. The impromptu diaper changing class was a strangely intimate moment. A mommy-and-daddy kind of moment that made Katie feel that stab of longing for the life she did not have, a life that had been snatched from her by a cruel twist of fate.

That's what she needed to remember as she was admiring the confidence with which Dylan was taking on this task. She need to remind herself that life had cruel twists and turns that she had no hope of controlling. That she had withdrawn from the race for a *reason.* It could hurt too much to run.

But standing in this little room, almost shoulder to shoulder with Dylan, the pain of *not* running the race could compete with the pain of running with all your heart.

"Just hold his feet in one hand, lift him up and swab," the nurse suggested helpfully.

For a man who had made his living being a professional athlete, Dylan suddenly seemed hopelessly uncoordinated. But determined. "You take his feet," he told Katie. A small thing, but it somehow solidified them as a team.

Gingerly she did. Jake tried to kick free.

Dylan scowled at the baby as if he were a puzzle that needed to be solved, then took a deep breath and did what needed to be done.

That, Katie thought, was the kind of man he was. He wanted people to believe it was all fun and frolic about him, but that was not the truth at all. She felt as if she could see the truth about Dylan.

"You don't shirk from the hard stuff do you?" she said. That was why he was such a success at business

Dylan cast a glance at her.

"You just dig in and get the job done."

"I don't think *dig in* is exactly what I want to hear right now," he said lightly, but rather than looking pleased at her assessment, Dylan looked pensive. "That's not what my sister would tell you," he said. "She thinks I shirk from the hard stuff."

"Like what?" Katie asked, incredulous.

But he was engrossed in his task, and didn't answer. Several wrecked diapers later—the tabs would not stick once his hands were slippery with baby oil and powder—the job was done. Dylan, unaware he was dusted from head to toe with baby powder himself, looked very pleased as he lifted his nephew off the table.

"Next time, your turn."

But it seemed to her maybe next time wasn't such a good idea. She was looking for excuses to hang on to him, to hang on to the intimacy of this little mommy-daddy experience.

But really, if he could change a diaper, he was good to go.

Without her.

"My sister says that it's different when it's your own baby," he said with an easy grin. "Not so nauseating."

Your own baby.

"Are you planning your own baby?" she asked him. She said it ever so casually. Just conversation. Pathetic that she was holding her breath waiting for his answer.

"I thought that's what I wanted once, but," he suddenly looked uncomfortable, "lately I don't seem to know what I want."

There. His answer.

And yet, even though it was not what she wanted to hear, Katie appreciated Dylan was giving her something that he rarely gave. He presented himself to the world as an extremely confident man. A man who jumped out of airplanes, no hesitation. A daredevil.

And so, his showing her his doubt was a gift.

Seeing him with his nephew had brought her yearnings sharply to the surface, and sharply into focus. It had made her contemplate entering the race all over again, like a person drawn to the mystery of Everest, Mountain of Tragedy.

He didn't know what he wanted. And she felt shadows of doubt on what she wanted. A month ago her flower shop, her quiet life had been enough. Now it wasn't.

Like lightning, fear struck her. What if she lost another baby? Could she survive that kind of loss again?

Was it completely delusional to think being with a man like him would somehow make the burden of that loss a shared one?

She recognized the insanity of her own thoughts. She had never even had a cup of coffee with this man.

Really, she knew less about him than what was printed on the back of his baseball cards. And here she was weaving a fantasy that he was at the center of! *Her own baby. A home to call her own. A man like this one.*

This was precisely why she had immersed herself in her business. This was why she had made a simple life for herself: reading, her cats, taking her mother on outings. This was precisely why she had done a voluntary exit from the whole man/woman game. She wasn't strong enough to play again, to run the race again. Not yet, and maybe not ever. She reminded herself she *liked* her safe, predictable world.

Or had liked it. But maybe a small dissatisfaction had been stirring from the very moment she had given in to the temptation to watch a glorious man run.

She made the mistake of looking at the baby and his uncle.

Jake was nestled into Dylan's chest, sucking sleepily on his thumb. The picture they made caused her heart to ache. Dylan's strength and self-assurance in stark contrast to the baby's helplessness and need. Dylan was all hard lines and taut muscle, a warrior, the baby was like a little puddle of warmth and softness, the one the warrior was sworn to protect.

And yet the tenderness that glowed in Dylan's eyes when he looked at his nephew, that softened the masculine assuredness of his face, made him seem more attractive to Katie than he ever had.

And he had always seemed plenty attractive!

All her weeks of successfully resisting Dylan McKinnon were going straight down the tubes. Worse, at the moment she was feeling raw and vulnerable after the strange intimacy of the encounter in the bathroom, her confessions, his reassurances.

Katie recognized she was doing exactly what Dylan expected every single woman to do around him. She was capitulating to his charms!

It had to stop. There had to be one woman in the world who would not throw herself at his feet, and it had to be her!

And yet here she was, so taken with him she felt weak-kneed and dry-mouthed, and like she wanted to spend the rest of her life contemplating the sensual fullness of his bottom lip! Here she was, practically floating, feeling a strange and glorious little fire in her bosom because of the way Dylan's eyes rested on her, for just a touch too long, when he looked over his nephew's head.

Katie needed to remember that charm came as naturally to him as hunting came to the lion. And his charm probably fell in the same category—self-serving and predatory.

The thing to do before she was any more helplessly overwhelmed by his attractiveness, his playfulness, his allure, would be, obviously, to remove herself from this situation.

She knew she had to do it without it *seeming* as if she had to get away from him. There was nothing that would trigger a predator's instincts like prey in full flight!

A nurse came and set down a car seat beside them.

"Dylan," Katie said firmly "you take the baby home. I'll grab a cab."

Dylan glanced from her to the baby. Then back at her. That adorable doubt was playing across his normally self-assured features. "I thought I couldn't even be trusted with a houseplant," he reminded her.

"Well, you can't. But help is a phone call away, if you need it."

"Yeah," he muttered, "911." He juggled the baby and picked up the car seat.

"Here. I'll take one of those as far as your car."

"Thanks." He handed her Jake. She was glad. One more small chance to hold his warm little body, to smell the baby shampoo in his hair, to fill her senses with him.

Before she let go.

They crossed the parking lot, and she watched as Dylan struggled to fit the car seat into his nearly non-existent back seat.

"Okay," she said, "ready." Ready to let go. Ready to go back to her old life. Ready to forget the smell of babies and the look in a man's eyes.

Liar. Out loud she said, "You can call from your sister's if you need anything else from me."

There. Didn't she sound cool and composed, totally collected? She felt she had very successfully disguised the fact that she was a woman who could be wooed into a helpless, spineless jellyfish by a man with a baby in his arms!

Dylan reached for the baby. Jake whimpered.

"Come on, little man, you're coming with your favorite unkie." Dylan glared at Katie. "Don't ever tell a single soul about that."

"What?"

"Unkie," he whispered.

She juggled the baby, held up her two fingers, Scout's honor style.

"Come on, Jake," Dylan said.

The baby nestled in tight against her, sidled a look at his uncle. "NO!"

She tried to help by detaching him from her, but as Dylan reached around his tummy to take him, she found a chunky hand wrapped in her hair. Dylan's hand was brushing her breast. She felt the burn of it. Her eyes met his. He jerked his hand away.

"NO YOU," the baby informed him, taking a tighter wrap on her hair. *"SHE."*

"Jake," he said firmly, CEO of a million-dollar company, "You are coming with me. Let go."

"NO, NO, NO," little Jakie shrieked. A passerby gave them a curious look.

"Shhh, little man," Dylan said. His voice, roughened with tenderness, sent shivers of new appreciation up and down Katie's spine.

The baby, however, was unimpressed. He wrapped his free arm around her neck. When Dylan reached for him again, he loosed it just long enough to slug his unkie in the ear.

"Hey, Jakie, calm down." Dylan enveloped the small fist in the strength of his own hand, and she felt another shiver of raw appreciation at how gently he leashed his strength to control the baby.

However, Jake could give her a lesson or two in being immune to the charm of Dylan McKinnon. The baby shrieked and pulled his solid little body in even closer to her. When Dylan tried one more time to pull him away, the baby busted him one in the chops.

"Here," Katie said, her maternal instincts feeling

nothing but sympathy for the poor distraught baby. "Give it up before you get seriously hurt."

"If he's going to hurt anyone it's going to be me," Dylan said with such furious protectiveness *of her* that her tummy did the roller-coaster ride down to the bottom of her stomach.

"Just see if he'll calm down."

Reluctantly Dylan moved back a step. The baby eyed him warily. Then he went limp, his fight over. Jake gave his uncle a baleful glare and settled himself against Katie's chest. After a moment, he put one thumb back in his mouth, but kept the chubby fingers of his other hand curled possessively through her hair and closed his eyes. He hiccupped sadly.

"And you've never even snuck him chocolate or taken him to the park!" Dylan said wryly. And then with satisfaction, "He's getting drool on your shirt."

"A little drool never hurt—"

But Dylan had lifted the hem of his own shirt, reached up with it, giving her a glimpse of a belly so hard and muscled her fingers actually tingled from wanting to touch. He wiped Jake's face and let the hem of his shirt drop back down.

Dangerous thoughts crowded her mind, at least partially triggered by that glimpse of Dylan's gorgeous flat belly, the very kind of thoughts she had been trying so desperately to get away from. What if this could be her real life? Her real man? Babies and baby seats, and glimpses of things that made your heart race on an ordinary afternoon. It might even be worth the diaper part.

While she was living dangerously, she stole another look at Dylan's lips, allowed herself to remember what they tasted like, allowed herself to think of the secret and sacred things that occurred between a man and a woman to make a baby.

"You try and put him in the seat," Dylan whispered.

She was dreadfully reluctant to give up the baby, but she knew this was a dangerous game she was playing. She untangled his chubby fist from her hair.

The baby's eyes popped open, he eyed his uncle with grave suspicion.

"Hey, great imitation of Chucky."

"Who?"

"Chucky. A demented doll that comes to life. Horror movie. It goes without saying that you wouldn't like it."

"Did you like it?" she asked. Surely a full-grown man wouldn't like such nonsense? A feeble excuse to find him flawed, but she was a desperate woman.

"Of course I liked Chucky. It's a classic!" He noticed the baby was relaxed, and he reached for him.

But when Dylan touched him, Jake screamed. Dylan jerked back his hand as if he'd been burned, Jake became silent. Dylan's lips twitched. He reached out. This time he didn't even have to touch the baby. Jake screamed long and loud.

Katie tucked the baby's head in close. "How do you *expect* him to behave toward someone who liked Chucky? And just for your information *Jane Eyre* is a classic."

"He doesn't know the difference between Chuck and Jane. He's not even two!"

"Babies are sensitive to vibes," she said, and as if to confirm it the baby blew some indignant spit bubbles his uncle's way and regarded him with silent challenge.

"The little devil," Dylan muttered. "He's playing a game with me. What's worse, he's winning!"

It was a rather funny thing to see one of the world's most competitive men losing a battle of will with a baby!

Finally Dylan shoved his hands in his pockets and glared at his nephew. "I've never done anything to him, honest!"

He regarded Katie and the baby thoughtfully, then grinned. "Oh, I get it. Vibes aside, you're nice and soft in all the right places."

As if to confirm, the baby snuggled deeper against her breast.

It occurred to her that Dylan was now studying her chest with grave interest. She began to blush, and then was astounded when he did, too!

Dylan backed away from her hurriedly. Katie managed to get the baby's uncooperative limbs into his car seat. Jake contemplated this development suspiciously, and Katie wondered how well Dylan was going to drive when his nephew figured out they were leaving *SHE* behind.

"Katie, hop in. Just for a few minutes. I know how the male mind works. Easily distracted. Our first stop will be Bill's Wild Toy Store. I'll get Jakie one of those windup buffalos they advertise on TV, and then, Katie, we can release you to your flower store."

Step into the car, or let him handle it himself? This was not her life, not her man, not her baby. This was not a man she would ever be making babies with. This was a man who had just given her fair warning how his mind worked.

How the male mind worked. They were a breed easily distracted. Everyone could be replaced with something or someone more entertaining, more interesting.

Even knowing that, she got in the car. She told herself it was just for Jakie's sake, not because she was reluctant to say goodbye to the little adventure life had dropped in her lap.

At Bill's Wild Toy Store, the funniest thing happened. Once inside the building, arguably every child's fantasy, Jake clung to her more tenaciously than ever. He was not trading up: he could not be wooed away from her with a three-foot-tall ride-on buffalo, foam footballs, red wagons or beach balls. Jake's lack of enthusiasm did not prevent Dylan from loading two shopping carts full of toys, one which he shoved ahead of him, and one which he dragged behind to the checkout.

How could you spend an hour shopping for toys with Dylan and keep your guard up? How could you watch him put on a passable juggling act with beanie babies and not come a whole lot closer to being in love with him? How could you watch him crashing remote control cars into the doll display with fiendish enthusiasm and not forgive him his easily distracted male mind?

The 50-per-cent-off, spring-fling sale was in full swing, and the famous toy store was full of women. Young women, old women, mom women, single women, pretty women, plain women.

To Katie, every single one of them seemed to slide Dylan the most appreciative of glances, and he seemed way more distracted by the toys than by any of those glances. He didn't even seem to notice that he was on the receiving end of rapt gazes, some that were shy, some that were openly inviting.

Some of those women looked at him as if he were a piece of art, to be admired but not touched, others let the heat of their thoughts right into their eyes, the sudden sway of their hips. It reminded her that he was the playboy and she was the plain Jane. That she was allowing herself to be sucked into a fantasy, to entertain the illusion that she and Dylan and Jake were just an ordinary little family, out shopping for toys.

For a man who had claimed to be easily distracted, he didn't even seem notice the female kafuffle he was generating. He seemed seriously and sincerely engrossed in trying out the remote-control helicopter, punching the bounce-back rubber clown, tossing the foam basketballs through the hoop that had been set up. At the basketball hoops, she was almost certain he was showing off for *her.*

She was overtaken by a feeling of *wanting* to let her guard down and just give in to liking him, enjoying him, feeling compatible with him. Within moments he had her laughing, and feeling light inside. She had seen his most secret side. She had seen the side of him that tempered his phenomenal strength with equally phenomenal tenderness, she had seen the part of him that was patient, she had seen the part that was laughter filled and joyous.

Back in the car now stuffed with their purchases, Dylan contemplated his nephew's indifference to the toys, and the new sumo wrestler hold he had on Katie.

"SHE," Jake announced, as she strapped him into the car seat. He watched the two adults on the curb.

"He's getting ready to throw himself into a prize-winning tantrum if you leave," Dylan deduced.

"You're going to have to deal with that sooner or later," she said firmly, though she didn't think in his car, dealing with the steadily building rush hour traffic, would be a good place for him to do it.

"A puppy!" Dylan announced with a snap of his fingers. "I'll get him a puppy. And then drive you back to work."

"Dylan, we have already established the fact that you cannot even be trusted with a plant. A puppy?"

"I'll bet once he has a puppy he won't even notice you're gone."

And would Dylan notice she was gone once *he* had a puppy to engage himself? Probably not.

She slid him a look. Was he trying to get rid of her? Did he sense, as she did, something deepening around them, a force gathering, beckoning, whispering?

Follow me. Come.

Her heart was calling. It was an ancient calling, not so much words as feeling, *instinct,* drive. But following the voice of the heart was no matter to be taken lightly. Some choices were momentous, they had the potential to change everything, forever. Was he feeling that, too? Could he feel that they were standing on the precipice of choosing heart over logic, over mind? Was he trying to get away from that choice?

As if to answer her, Dylan began fishing through one of his shopping bags. He found and unwrapped a ping-pong ball attached to a paddle, and began to play with it, trying to distract Jake. He appeared to be the man least likely to be listening for the ancient language of the heart.

"Let's go to your sister's house," she suggested, resigned. "I'm sure he'll settle more quickly in his own surroundings. He must be ready for a nap. When he goes down, I'll slide out the door. He can wake up to that remote-control helicopter. He won't even know I'm gone."

"Thanks, Katie, my lady."

He wanted her to stay with them.

She glanced at her watch. "I'll call Mrs. Abercrombie and tell her to lock up the store," she said.

"You'll never regret it."

But she already did, because she knew she was getting herself deeper and deeper into this path of the heart. It felt easy and peaceful like a forest walk on a Sunday afternoon, but she wondered how quickly it could turn treacherous, like an encounter with quicksand. Lulled in too far, would she be in real trouble before she realized there was no way to get back out?

"We could still get a puppy," Dylan said wistfully, his expression chasing away her sinister thought of quicksand and danger. He opened the car door for her and she slid in.

Jake crowed, *"SHE!"*

Dylan got in the other side and pulled smoothly into traffic.

"You know what?" Katie said. "Your nephew is not yet two, and he's trying to teach you something."

"Such as?"

"You cannot replace people with things. He wants his *m-o-m,* you can't buy him out of feeling like that. Not with a thousand dollars worth of toys, and not with a puppy."

Dylan shook his head with mock regret. "I hate it when you're right, Katie."

"So, it appears since he can't have his *m-o-m,* he's chosen me as the next best thing. You're stuck with me, Dylan, for the time being. Take me home."

Dylan sighed with satisfaction. "I've been waiting a long time to hear those words from you, Katie, my lady."

"Well, don't get your hopes up. I don't plan to be on the receiving end of a bouquet number two from you."

"I didn't particularly like the bouquet of his number two, either," Dylan said defensively. And then she couldn't help it. She was laughing. And the baby was laughing, and Dylan was laughing, and it felt as if life had handed her the most delightful of gifts when she least expected it. And a woman could not harden her heart against this kind of gift forever.

"I wish we could starve him," Dylan said to Katie, glared at his nephew, and said, "Choo-choo." Jake's mouth remained firmly shut to the spoonful of butterscotch pudding.

They were into day three of looking after Jake. San Francisco was in the soup. His sister was scheduled for yet more surgery. Dylan had resigned himself to the fact his brother-in-law was never coming home, and his sister *liked* the hospital.

No wonder, since her son was a monster.

On the other hand Dylan was aware he had started to hope this funny little escapade he was sharing with Katie could last forever.

Who could have guessed spending time with Katie could be so good? She had tried to leave several times, but Jake had a radar! As soon as the door closed behind Katie, he started to scream and he didn't stop.

The first night, after Jake had awoken in the night to find his beloved mother and his beloved SHE missing, the baby had begun to give his lungs a no-holds-barred workout. Dylan had tried everything. Diaper changes. Cookies. New toys. Bottles. If there had been a place to get a puppy in the middle of the night, he would have tried that, too.

Finally, he had sat outside on the front steps but he had still been able to hear the howls of the baby. When the neighbors' lights started coming on, Dylan had surrendered and called her. He knew he didn't really have to call her. He knew lots of ladies. But he only knew one he trusted so completely. He did not even know quite when or how in the last year of knowing her that Katie had snuck so completely into that zone of trust.

"Hello?" she'd said, her voice soft with sleep. He imagined her all tousled and warm, and suddenly didn't want to get her up, felt as if he was face-to-face with how selfish he really was.

"Sorry, I shouldn't have called."

"Dylan? What's wrong? Is that the baby crying in the background?"

Her voice felt like a life line. "I can't make him stop. Katie, I'm three steps from suicidal."

She laughed.

"Listen to this," he said and held up the phone. Then he'd put it back to his mouth. "Can SHE come?"

Katie had come within minutes, rocked the distraught baby to sleep, sung him some lovely little song that felt as if it would haunt Dylan's heart forever. But every time she tried to put Jake down, he woke, whimpered, wrapped his fist in her hair. Finally, she fell asleep in the rocking chair beside his crib.

When Dylan crept in and covered her with a blanket, he was not prepared for the welling of emotion he felt as he looked into the gentle beauty of her face.

He knew people—people like him—could look at a girl like her and miss all the things that were most important in human nature: it wasn't about being able to stop traffic or your beauty, or the perfect red-carpet twirl. It was about surviving your sorrows and allowing them to make you better instead of worse. He could learn something from her, from how her gentle spirit had remained intact. Guarded to be sure, but intact nonetheless. Katie was still willing to risk *giving,* and living, a kind of quiet courage about her that was incredibly beautiful.

The next day, while Jake napped, she had left for long enough to pack a little overnight bag and come back. She was now set up in his sister's guest room.

Dylan had done some of the most exciting things a man could do. He had been attracted to speed and to adrenaline his entire life.

So how was it, playing in the backyard, digging in a flowerbed, introducing Jake to the joy of worms and watching Katie brush dirt off his nephew's face, could be more satisfying than that?

Dylan had been to some of the world's most enviable parties. He had schmoozed with the Oscar winners, the rock stars, the Olympians.

So how was it, having a quiet glass of wine with her, when Jake finally surrendered to sleep was better than that? How was it that to hear her tell him a story about a customer at the flower shop was funnier and better than hearing a famous comedian's hilarious rendition of his week in treatment?

He had run marathons and accepted trophies, but when he had gotten on a bike attached to a little baby carrier on wheels, and Katie had ridden beside him, deliberately hitting every puddle at full speed, shining with light and laughter, it was then that he had felt completely fulfilled.

Now this. A silly moment with butterscotch pudding and a baby and her, better than the five-star meals he'd had in some of the best restaurants in the world.

"Try the airplane," Katie said.

Despite all his best cajoling, Jake's mouth remained stubbornly shut to him. Jake swatted crankily at the spoon and it added to the butterscotch pudding in his hair, on his ears and down the front of his shirt. And there was some on the baby, too!

Dylan surrendered the spoon to Katie, and Jake opened his mouth eagerly, like a greedy little bird.

"Everything you put in there has to come out the other end," Dylan reminded her.

"Dylan, stop it. You're being gross."

"Realistic," he argued, even though the truth was he took a rather fiendish delight grossing her out. It was so easy to do, and it played havoc with her carefully erected barricades. "Hopefully by recycling time, Sam will be home."

"Hopefully," she agreed weakly, and he knew she dreaded Sam coming home as much as he did. "Though, really, Dylan we should clean up the house before he comes home."

Over the last few days, Dylan had opened every toy he had bought. His sister's house was littered with toys: jack-in-the-box, foam rubber footballs, stuffed animals, building blocks. They'd crashed remote control cars into his sister's furniture and got finger-paint on her couch. Dylan was unabashed in the fact he was enjoying the toys far more than the baby who seemed to have a fascination with the boxes they came in.

"Since my sister likes to address all my complaints about the position I have been forced into with 'Suck it up, buttercup,' I am not cleaning up her house."

Katie laughed.

"And the next time she asks me to get Sam tickets to a Blue Jays game, you know what she's getting? 'Outta luck, pickup truck.'"

He liked making Katie laugh. And grossing her out. He liked teasing her. He even had to admit he liked showing off for her. The bottom line was he liked sharing this experience with her.

Somewhere he remembered hearing that dogs and babies were true judges of character, and he could clearly see that was true in the way Jake had taken to Kate.

Not just taken to her, but was possessive of her, unwilling to share. Tonight he was wondering if the baby was ever going to go to sleep so he could have Katie to himself. It had become such a wonderful part of his day. Katie relaxed on the couch beside him, sipping wine.

It occurred to him he should have a plan. That he wanted things to move forward. Sooner or later that baby was going down. Then what? Ah, maybe the baby had judged the nefariousness of his own character a little too well!

You had to be careful with a girl like Katie. Things he would do with another woman, almost without a thought, would have repercussions with her.

Still, could he kiss her? Just one little brush of his lips

against hers? That kind of kiss a guy gave a girl that meant thank you? That expressed "I don't know how I could have done this without you."

The problem was he'd had very little practice at that kind of kiss. When he kissed a girl it was a prelude to the main show.

And Katie wasn't that kind of girl. Kissing her would complicate both their worlds unbearably. It would be a dumb, dumb thing to do.

So of course he did it. Right in between his nephew gulping down bites of butterscotch pudding, not even waiting for the right moment, he leaned over and surrendered to the utter temptation of her plump lips. He kissed her.

She tasted of something he was not sure he had ever tasted before. Given her understated look, her mouth tasted wild and clean, like rain-soaked mist over an untamed mountain.

There were a thousand things she could have done, and he was aware that he was prepared for each of them: for her lips to remain prudish underneath his, for her to hit him, throw pudding on him, get up and run—

But Katie's lips parted under his, warm and delicious, as if she had known her whole life this moment would come, as if she had waited, a desert flower opening for the rain.

Her kiss was not the predatory kiss of Heather, nor the promising kiss of a thousand other girls he had kissed. It was not reckless or abandoned.

Her lips on his were faintly thoughtful, curious, undeniably sensual in the loveliest of ways, like having silk drawn over freshly bathed skin.

He reeled back from her, stunned by what he had discovered.

And what he had known all along.

He had known all along that beneath that demure exterior, she was something special, that her treasures were hidden. No, there were no gaudy displays for the entire world to see, a man had to go deeper, trust his heart to lead him, follow his instincts to the place where her true beauty would be unveiled.

What he'd discovered was that he wanted to be a guy who was worthy of discovering her deepest secrets, her treasure. What he discovered in that single tantalizing kiss was that he was tired of shallow people and superficial relationships, he was weary to the bone of the games he had played. They had emptied him, and something about her moist mouth under his promised to do the exact opposite.

To fill the emptiness within him until he overflowed.

He wanted what he had tasted: depth, mystery, complexity, companionship, integrity. It seemed impossible that her mouth, in that brief encounter that had left him hungry for more, had told him each of those things, but it had.

Or maybe he had seen each of those things in the gorgeous depths of those ever-changing eyes, one second green, the next gold, for as long as he could remember.

And maybe he had always known he was afraid his sister had been right that day. That he had gone so far down a wrong road that he could not be worthy of a girl like Katie. Just like her ex-husband had not been worthy.

But even thinking of that, he knew he was not anything like her ex had been. Because he *wanted* to be the one who was there for her when life turned unexpectedly sour, when she needed someone strong to lean on. It felt like the job he'd been born to do.

Oh sure, he had played the field and availed himself of every perk that came with his career and fame and money. But he had never, ever pretended with anyone.

He had never claimed he would be more than he was. He had never said he was ready for commitment. He had always been totally honest about where each and every relationship was going: nowhere.

But in her lips he had tasted somewhere. And it was a somewhere he had never been. A place where the loneliness he had somehow come to live with promised to disappear like mist under a gentle sun, a place that invited him to be more, better, deeper, truer.

A place that invited him to know another person for the pleasure and richness of knowing them to their soul, not for whatever use they might be to him.

He leaped back from all the things he had tasted in her lips so swiftly he knocked over the kitchen chair. He couldn't be trusted with anything as precious, as real, as Katie Pritchard. As she'd already pointed out he couldn't even be trusted with a houseplant!

On the other hand, he'd just been trusted with a baby. Maybe there was more to him than he'd ever given himself credit for.

"Dylan," she said primly, "I don't think you should do that again."

"No kidding," he muttered, and went and busied himself assembling the wagon he had bought earlier. He liked things that came with instructions. Even things that appeared to people to be daredevil like skydiving or riding motorcycles really weren't.

They came with a complete set of rigid rules. If you followed those rules exactly, you got an exact result. Problems only resulted when the rules were broken, modified, stretched.

All his life people had seen him as a daredevil.

And there was some truth to that. He liked the rush of adrenaline that came from pushing the envelope. He liked the adventure of trying new things. He liked how activity could make a man feel full to the top.

And then one tiny little kiss toppled the whole thing, and made him feel empty and look into the face an uncomfortable truth.

He wasn't fearless at all.

He had filled all the spaces around him with things, successes, activities. He had tried to fill up every hole inside of him, to plug the leaks in his soul. To run from the fact that he had become afraid of the one thing that could truly fill him up.

Dylan McKinnon was fearful of love.

He had believed in it once. He had always thought one day he would be done living fast and having fun and he would find *the* girl to settle down with. He had assumed he would have a wonderful relationship, like the one his mother and father had enjoyed. Theirs had been a relationship of complete respect. Of laughter. Of companionship. You could not be in the same room as them and not sense the connection: the tender brush of hands, the meeting of eyes.

And then his mother had become ill. It had seemed innocuous at first, maybe even funny: her curling iron in the fridge, her saying bum when she meant bun. But it had deteriorated at a horrifying speed, stove burners left on, wandering through the neighborhood in the dead of night. Dylan remembered the day he'd known it was never going to be the same. He'd been in her car with her, and she'd looked at him, called him by his father's name, and announced calmly she couldn't remember the difference between the gas pedal and the brake.

Still, even though at some level he understood his father could not cope with it, and that it was no longer safe for him to try, he felt furious when his father made the decision to put her in the nursing home, a fury that deepened when his father became reluctant to visit her.

This had been his model for love, his model *for better or worse,* and it had fallen apart when the *worse* arrived.

Dylan felt as if he grieved a mother who was not yet dead, and a dream—his own dream—of a relationship that had never been born.

Katie was the best of things, because a little seedling of hope came to life inside him around her. And she was the worst of things, because a little seedling of hope came to life inside of him around her.

She required him to look at the thing he most wanted to deny. Dylan McKinnon, daredevil, fearless, was being ruled by fear. He was afraid to love.

He had achieved it all. He had money, success, fame. Until he'd met Katie he'd been able to outrun the fact that for all that, he was empty.

Because he had rejected and run from that one thing that made a man truly rich.

Love.

CHAPTER SEVEN

THERE were probably words, moments, that people regretted to their graves, Katie decided. And she knew exactly which ones she would be contemplating with deep remorse on her death bed. After that spontaneous kiss over butterscotch pudding had she really said, "Dylan, I don't think you should do that again"?

Katie sighed. She really had. And he hadn't even attempted to do it again. Which was annoying, because it was just a little late in life for Dylan McKinnon to start being a gentleman! She knew he wanted to kiss her again.

They had been in this house together, manning the baby battle stations with Jake for days. The house itself filled her with yearning, not because it was a beautiful house, though it was. But because she could feel the love of the family that lived here.

It was in the wedding pictures proudly displayed, in the baby pictures of the three of them. It was in the funny little notes Sam and Tara left on the fridge for each other, it was in the flowers that he'd sent her while he was away on business.

There was one photo in particular, of just Sam and Tara, and Sam was looking at his wife with such pride and delight and hunger that it felt like spying to even look at it.

Katie was well aware that Dylan watched her when he thought she wasn't looking, and she was astounded that his look was not that different than the look of his brother-in-law looking at his wife.

She was well aware of the carefully masked heat in Dylan's eyes when he looked at her lips. She was well aware of how his hand brushed hers far more than was necessary, lingering. She was well aware of the beat of her own heart, her own secret looks at him, the roller-coaster rush in her stomach that seemed to be permanent.

She was exhausted with tension, in his sister's guest bedroom, wide awake, despite the late hour and the fact they had had an absolutely unbelievable day with Jake. Who knew a tiny little baby took so much energy?

Who knew everything about a baby was hard? From bathing him, to trying to get him into his cute little clothes? Who knew a baby could cry without stopping until his eyes ran dry and just the howls remained?

And who knew that same baby could cause your heart to feel as if it would burst it was so filled with tenderness? Who knew that a tiny little scrap of humanity, one who didn't even have words, could be so funny you could hurt from laughing so hard?

Who knew that a baby could show you everything that was real about a man's heart? The baby could show you how a man could be in a situation totally alien to him, frustrating, challenging, aggravating, and remain patient, strong, capable, good-humored. Dylan's disguise was that he was a playboy. In reality, the man was a natural-born daddy.

Katie was seeing him through that filter, and it filled her with the most terrifying longing. That longing had only been intensified by his kiss.

His kiss, in the wildly unromantic atmosphere of butterscotch pudding, had taken her completely by surprise. It had come out of nowhere. One second she'd been feeding the baby, the next she had been falling into the unknown abyss that was love.

But wasn't that where most life-altering events came from? Seemingly from nowhere? Deciding to go one place instead of another, meeting a stranger's eyes on the bus, answering an email, saying yes to the friend who had been bugging you about the blind date. An ordinary life, suddenly on an intercept course with destiny.

Destiny.

She was twenty-six years old and she had found out something brand-new. When you kissed a person, there was an exchange of energy: some mysterious force leapt from them to you, and you saw or felt things you had never seen or felt before.

This had not been the case with her ex-husband, which she now realized, had she been more experienced, she would have read as a warning. The fact that Marcus's kiss had been so unrevealing should have been a big red stop sign.

Because when Dylan's lips had touched hers she had known things about him: felt his strength, his heart, his soul. And she had felt her own destiny.

The thing was, a person always had choices. Destiny was a road with many branches off it. You didn't have to take each one that beckoned. You could choose the safe road, predictable, pleasantly scenic, well marked, the destination clear.

Who wouldn't choose that one, rather than the barely discernible path that climbed steeply upward, through forests that undoubtedly held monsters, hazards, messy places that were terribly hard to traverse, if they could be traversed at all?

Who would choose a path that's only promise was that you would be challenged, tossed and turned, your comfort zone a distant memory? Who would choose the path that made your heart race with fear and discovery and exertion? Who would choose the path that made you feel as though you had lost your map, your direction, your compass? Who would choose such a way?

But only one way rewarded the intrepid soul who had chosen it with the pure exhilaration of the mountaintop, and that was never going to be the safe road.

The safe road led her where she had already been.

The sad truth was, when she had married Marcus, Katie had known somewhere in herself, she was *settling,* taking less than she deserved, so much less than what she wanted. She had been so desperate to make all her dreams come true, that she had become determined to make her husband fit *her* dream. She had thought once they had the baby it would all start to work out. She had ignored the clues he had given her that they didn't want the same things. Marcus had wanted career and financial success, a family had been secondary to him. She had missed that until it was too late.

Had life given her another chance? Or was she deluding herself that a man like Dylan, confident, successful, gorgeous, charming could ever care for a girl like her, plain and ordinary? No, not *care.* It was more than obvious he *cared.* And she could *settle* again, try to make that enough. Or she could take the chance to find out if he could *love* her.

But if sending his flowers was any indication, Dylan didn't have a particularly good track record.

On the other hand, neither did she.

And if she did not want to spend her last moment on earth filled with regret, wondering what could have been if she had just showed a little more courage, a touch more spunk, she was going to have to do something.

Opportunity knocked. They were in this house together now. Sam and Tara could arrive home at any time.

Their adventure would be over.

How did she want it to end? Could she prevent it from ending? The thoughts were so audacious it frightened her to think about them, let alone to contemplate acting on them. But to be with Dylan, she was going to have to find out if she could be as fearless as he could.

Taking a deep breath, she got up, opened her door, crept down the hall to where he slept in the master bedroom.

Her hand went to the doorknob, and she almost fainted at what she was thinking of doing. Quickly she scurried down the hall to the kitchen, turned on the light. She would make cocoa. She would think this through before she did anything drastic, irreversible.

She looked down at herself and groaned. She had made one quick trip home to pick up her car, check on the store, gather a few items of clothing and toiletries. What had she been thinking when she had chosen these pajamas? Not of seduction, obviously.

They were her spring pajamas: drawstring pants, too

large button-down shirt, embossed flowers, bells of Ireland, which stood for good luck. Which, she realized with a sigh, was very different than getting lucky.

Good luck said with a certain intonation could even mean the exact opposite, a sarcastic prediction of failure.

She was not sexy. She could not do lingerie and lace with any degree of comfort. Lace *scratched* for goodness' sake.

Though at the moment she would have made the sacrifice if it would have given her the confidence to open that closed bedroom door, go through it, whisper Dylan awake with a kiss on his whisker-roughened face.

She opened a cupboard in search of cocoa, sadly aware this could be her life, past, present and future: sleepless nights with cocoa as her only companion.

"Hi, there."

She dropped the cocoa on the floor, spun to look at him.

Life was so unfair.

He was wearing drawstring pajama bottoms, plaid, not so unlike the unisex models she sported. But on him they were absolutely tantalizing. They rode low, stretched over his hips to show the tautness of his belly. His chest was bare, and so beautiful it made her feel almost faint with wanting: to touch him, to hold him, to *have* him.

All this time she'd been resisting. If only he'd known the only thing he had to do was take off his shirt and she would have succumbed. He stooped and picked up the dropped cocoa, set it on the counter, as if he was afraid to hand it to her, afraid to touch her.

It seemed *trashy* to her, to be feeling this way, and at the same time she was aware of the wonderful freedom of not caring about labels, about what anyone thought.

She was aware of *liking* the compelling feeling inside her, wanting to follow it where it led.

To take the pathway, uncharted, that led to the mountaintop.

"Hi," she stammered, turning back to the open cupboard, pretending to study its contents, when in fact she didn't know if she was looking at peanut butter or marshmallows. And didn't care, either. "I couldn't sleep."

"Me, neither. Funny, because I'm exhausted."

She sneaked another look at him. Her heart thudded wildly. What had she thought she was going to do when she'd had her hand on the doorknob? She licked her lips.

"Don't do that, Katie, my lady."

"What?" she stammered.

"Lick your lips. Please don't do that." His voice was hoarse.

She should just say okay, but she was in the grip of something bigger than the logic that had controlled her for her entire life. She was on the mountain path. So instead she said, surprised at how sultry her voice was, "Why not?"

He ran a hand through the tousled locks of his dark hair. "Because it makes you look so sexy it hurts."

She stared at him. No lace. No lingerie.

It washed over her unexpectedly. Pure courage. A desire to take the other path, no matter how treacherous it was, no matter how many surprises it held.

She went to him.

His eyes never left her. She stopped in front of him, closed her eyes, breathed in the deep glorious scent of the mountaintop. She put her hand on his chest, and he covered it with his own and then placed the other one on the small of her back and propelled her into him.

His body was lean, strong, his naked skin the texture of silk. She sighed against him. It felt as though her whole life she had waited for this exact moment. It was a moment of pure homecoming, her body pressed so close to his that she absorbed the beat of his heart through her skin, and it drummed her own life song.

She hadn't just reached the mountaintop. She *belonged* on it. She was worthy of soaring with eagles.

She tilted her head up, and he took his hand that had been on the small of her back, caressed her cheek, looked at her with a wonder that reflected her own. He scraped his thumb across her lips, exploring, the look of wonder deepening in his eyes.

She nuzzled his thumb, then nipped it, watched the surprise and then the welcome darken his eyes. They sparked with the dangerous and absolutely delightful light of desire.

She knew he sincerely did not know she was in the world's ugliest pajamas. When he looked at her like that, she felt as if he saw her, she felt as if it was the first time anyone had truly seen her.

"You told me not to do this again," he said hoarsely.

"I know. And I meant it."

"Tease," he choked out.

"No. It's my turn. I'm going to do the kissing this time, Dylan."

She reached up and took his lips with her own. She tasted, she explored, she delighted, she discovered. He held back, pliant, letting her have her moment, surrendering to her female power.

And then he held back no longer. With a moan of suppressed desire, he tangled his hands in her hair, drew her lips more aggressively to his own. He tasted her back, his hunger fierce, his desire unleashed.

His kiss took her to her own fullness. It returned to the wild call in her that had been tamed, it set unlocked what had been captive. It brought her to the place where she was, finally, free: no thought, no plan, no predictions and especially no fear.

She was the eagle, soaring, proud, hungry, fierce, independent, majestic.

As her lips drank him, her hands explored, greedy with wanting to know every ripple of muscle, every hard plain of skin, every hair on his arms and chest. She felt a delicious sense of the sacred: that she was obeying the ancient call.

It was the voice that called without words. It commanded one man and one woman to be together. Only a union so intense and so intimate and so powerful was worthy of what it produced, the life force being celebrated, honored, passed from one generation to the next. This was the ancient call that guaranteed the survival of something so frail and so flawed as the human race.

Katie wanted it. She wanted the mountaintop. And in this moment she had no care what it cost her to get there. Like a climber on Everest, her focus had narrowed to one thing, the price of having it was no longer of consequence.

When he scooped her up in his arms, she felt his strength, knew he had committed just as she had. And she was glad.

* * *

Dylan McKinnon had probably kissed a thousand women, so many that the experiences blurred together, a casual coming together of human beings to meet a mutual need.

Now he was aware of being in the grip of something so powerful and so sacred that it made him ashamed of what he had accepted before.

This thing with Katie was physical, and yet it was more than that, her spirit rushing out to meet his in a way that was all encompassing, that promised to bring him to a place he had never been before.

Kissing Katie made him feel as if he was a man who had crossed the desert, finding oasis after oasis, only to know now each had been a mirage, each had given the illusion of a thirst slaked, but each illusion had actually made his thirst grow.

It was not a thirst for sex.

It was a thirst for connection.

It was a thirst for completion.

He lifted her into his arms and felt her slightness, felt how wonderfully she fit with him, felt something in her open, her cautiousness gone, and behind the wall of it, an oasis, a garden so full of vibrant life and delight, that a man could satisfy his thirst there forever.

He carried her down the hall and through the door of the guest bedroom. He laid her on the bed, stood above her and marveled at the fullness of her lips, the hooded desire in her eyes, the way her hair scattered across the pillow.

Her eyes never leaving his, she found her top button and undid it, and then the next and the next.

He wanted to ask her if she was sure, but he was

afraid words might break the spell, the enchantment, they were both in. Instead he lay down beside her, stilled her hand, undid the last two buttons himself.

But he did not open her shirt. Instead he thought of the tremendous gift she was giving him. Instead he wondered if he was worthy.

And suddenly he knew a terrible truth.

It was absolutely the wrong time to think of his mother. And yet he knew a simple and wondrous thing, even if the timing was awful. His mother, as he had known her, was gone. But what she had taught him was not gone. Who she had been—a woman of absolute integrity, would be with him forever.

That was how she would go on, and that was how he could honor the memory of the strong incredible woman she had been.

By doing the right thing. The thing she would have approved of. The thing she would have been proud of him for. The thing his sister had called *decent.*

If he took Katie like this, he was not the man his mother had always hoped he would be. Not even close. If he took the way he had been taking this past year, he was desecrating the life lessons his mother had given him, and even worse desecrating what Katie offered.

His mother would go on *through* him, through how he lived, the choices he made. And that choice had to be to live with honor, no matter how hard that was.

And in this moment it was plenty hard.

He had always entered into liaisons thoughtlessly. No thought of the future, no thought of what it meant, certainly no thought of the damage he might cause another person.

But to damage Katie?

To take her greatest gift without thinking what it meant to him? And to her? And to them? To enter into this most sacred of unions with her and not have a plan for tomorrow and the next day and the day beyond that.

He groaned out loud.

"What's wrong?"

"Katie, nothing. Everything."

"You have a look on your face," she said tentatively. "I've seen it before."

He reached to her, and began doing the buttons back up.

"Dylan," she said, her voice a whimper of wanting that nearly killed him, that threatened to overcome the discipline it was taking to do her shirt back up.

Lust had undone her buttons. Love did them back up.

Love. He loved her. And he hated it that he loved her. What, of all the nebulous things in the universe, was more unpredictable than that? Harder to control?

"That's where I've seen that look before," she said softly. "Sadness. It's when you choose that bouquet of flowers every Friday."

The flowers he brought to his mother.

"Who are the flowers for?" she whispered.

This was not what he wanted to give Katie. His baggage, his burdens. If they ever made love he wanted it to be free and joyous.

His sister had kept warning him to deal with his "stuff." Naturally, he had thought she should mind her own business, and felt that dealing with "stuff" was for wimps who had not perfected the art of shutting down their feelings by pursuing manly arts like drinking beer, chasing girls and riding motorcycles.

Now, though, that stuff had come back to bite him. The door was open, and thoughts of his mother and father crept through. He had always thought it was never ending.

And then his mother slipping into what they would later learn was early onset Alzheimer's. And his father giving up. Putting her in a home. Meeting Dylan's fury with resignation and stubbornness.

Dylan took his mother flowers every week, looked for some sign that she recognized him, cared. When it was obvious she had nothing left to give him, he tried to think of things to give her. He read her the poetry she had so enjoyed when he was young. He bought her movies and magazines. But not a spark of recognition, not a hint of who she used to be. He was not even sure his father went to see her anymore.

In fact, last time he had gone by his father's he had seen a brochure for a cruise lying open on the kitchen table. A cruise. His suspicions that his father was seeing someone else had deepened, but not been discussed.

Now, looking at Katie, for the first time he felt the smallest glimmer of understanding for his father. To see those eyes, in this moment so filled with love, staring at him blankly, without recognition, that would be a kind of death in itself.

To remember a woman who'd ridden her bike through puddles, and tackled diaper changes and butterscotch pudding, whose laughter could put the sun to shame, while looking at a shell, would be the most devastating kind of pain.

He didn't want to understand his father!

And maybe, really, he had no desire to understand himself, either. Or at least not the part that would be weak instead of strong.

What if he had inherited the gene that brought on his mother's illness? What if asking Katie to share a future with him meant that someday she would be looking at him and no longer knowing who he was? What if it meant she would have to make some of those hard, hard choices that his father had made?

Was that what love did? Asked people to make choices so hard they could tear the heart right out of them? Love could change cruelly and without warning, so was it better to not risk it at all?

He looked at Katie, kissed her finger, put it to his lips. God, he'd been playing a game with her all along.

All he'd had to say, from the very beginning, was he was sorry life had delivered her some blows she did not deserve. No, instead of keeping it simple he'd had to make everything complicated, play with her, kid himself about his motivations. He'd allowed himself to be driven to prove his own decency, now he wondered if he had not proved the exact opposite instead.

What was decent about a man trying to make love to a woman he had offered no commitment to? Especially if that woman was like Katie?

"I can't do this," he said softly. "I'm sorry." The decent thing after all.

But she didn't react with any appreciation for his sacrifice or his decency!

She gave him one killing look, scrambled out of the bed and turned and marched out of the room. Apparently uncaring that she was in her pajamas and her feet were bare, she went out the front door of his sister's house, slammed the door behind her. He heard her car start up and pull away.

He lay there for a long time with his eyes open. They felt like they were burning. He tried to choke back whatever emotion he was feeling. He was glad he had not told her he bought that weekly bouquet for his mother. There was no point in feeling even more vulnerable than he did.

He resented Katie. Nothing with her ever went the way he planned it. Not wooing her, not making love to her, not apologizing to her, nothing.

Having a relationship with her would be a constant challenge. He would have to make a habit of being thoughtful and nice, completely honest, *giving*. He had obviously pulled back just in the nick of time.

But if that was true why did he feel so sick inside? No, not just sick, bereft, as if he was suddenly being swamped by every single feeling he'd ever refused to have.

But if there was one thing Daredevil Dylan McKinnon had become it was an absolute expert at outrunning feelings.

CHAPTER EIGHT

THE DOOR to her shop opened, and Katie jumped, whirled to see who was coming in her door. She had to quit doing that. It wasn't going to be Dylan. Two weeks had passed since that night they had almost made love.

She tried to stop hoping he was coming, tried to stop hoping that one of these days he would breeze in, and say, "Katie, my lady, what do you think of the jacket?"

Or "Katie, my lady, come and swim with me and the dolphins."

Maybe he would drop by on Friday, the day he had always come in to choose the blossoms for his special bouquet?

On the verge of intimacy, she reminded herself, she had asked him about that bouquet. And he had kept his secret. A man with secrets was *always* a bad thing.

She was divorced, and she had not missed her ex-husband the way she missed Dylan. In fact, underneath the shame of failing at marriage, she had been relieved to leave the tension and uncertainty and loneliness of sharing a life with Marcus far behind her.

Still, she was tense and uncertain now! It was a blessing that things had not gone further between her and Dylan, that he had come to his senses that night. Because if she could feel like this over absolutely nothing—which is what had gone on between them—how would she feel if anything more had happened?

How would she feel if she had said yes to motorcycle rides and dinners for two and skating through the park? Much worse. Yes, she had been very wise to beat off his advances.

Maybe, a little voice chided her, *had she said yes she would feel as though she had lived, as if she would be one of those lucky few people, who on their deathbeds, had no regrets.*

Maybe she was hoping for a second chance to live, maybe that's why she could not stop her heart from leaping every time the door opened, from turning to look, hope nearly strangling her, just wanting to see him and hear his voice.

Not that that was going to be enough anymore. Not now that she had tasted his lips, not now that she had touched his skin; not now that she had unbuttoned her blouse to him.

Katie watched the door squeak open. A strikingly lovely woman struggled through in a wheelchair, one leg, plaster-encased from toe to hip, stretched out in front of her. Katie would have come out from behind the counter to assist her, except she recognized her from the photographs at Tara and Sam's house. This was Jake's mother. This was Dylan's sister.

Her first horrible thought was that something had happened to Dylan. That's why she hadn't seen him. That's why he was no longer running at one o'clock every day. As upset about the foibles of love as Katie herself, he'd wrapped his motorcycle around a telephone pole. They'd found Katie's name on some papers on his desk. No! They were coming to order the flowers for—

Katie cut herself off sharply. The face she was looking at was not the face of a woman planning a funeral. Tara's face was cheerful and filled with warmth.

She rolled up to the counter, put out her hand. Katie leaned across and took it, aware she was being regarded with interest that was more than casual.

"I found some of your things at my place," Tara said, and passed Katie a bag.

Katie grabbed the bag, peeked in it at some of her most personal items and stuffed it behind the counter. She was reminded she had left in a hurry.

"It's not what you think!" she squeaked.

"What do I think?" Tara asked mildly.

"That Dylan and I—" She could feel herself blushing scarlet.

"Of course I don't think that!" Tara said kindly. "I could believe it of my brother, but not of you. I can tell by looking at you, you aren't that kind of girl."

Katie found herself being studied intently.

"Decent," Tara proclaimed happily, as if that compliment rated right up there with *beautiful*.

Kate decided it would not be in her best interest to point out she had very nearly not been a decent girl at all.

But looking at Tara, she decided what Dylan's sister meant, but was too kind to say, was that Katie Pritchard was not Dylan's kind of girl.

As in a candidate for a professional football team's cheerleading squad.

"I just wanted to thank you for all you did for Dylan

and Jakie when I had my accident. The thought of Dylan with Jake by himself…" She shook her head, and rolled her eyes.

"Dylan's actually very good with the baby," Katie said, and then could have kicked herself for defending him, especially when the light of interest in his sister's eyes deepened even further.

"Oh, I know he's good with Jake," Tara said. "I just don't know if the house would have still been standing if he'd been left entirely to his own devices. As it was, I had to give three boxes of toys away, and have been scraping butterscotch pudding off the cabinets since I got home."

Katie had meant to look after the butterscotch pudding. She was reminded again that she had left in a hurry.

"Who liked the toys more," Tara asked, "Dylan or Jake?"

"Dylan," Katie said without hesitation, and then found herself chuckling along with Tara. It was the first time in two weeks she'd laughed.

"I bet that ridiculous remote control helicopter was his favorite. It's my husband, Sam's favorite, too. Or was. I can't tell you how overjoyed I was when Sam got it stuck in that high chandelier above the stairwell."

She smiled with indulgence for her husband that revealed such love that Katie felt a pang of envy. She had seen that love, *felt* it in their home.

"I wanted to send flowers to thank you, but when Dylan said not to bother, that you had a flower shop, I decided to come see if you wanted to go for lunch instead. I left Jake at Dylan's office. Just for revenge I loaded up his baby pack with butterscotch pudding and the fire engine with the extra loud siren."

Katie found herself laughing again. Truly, she wanted to say no. What was the point of tangling her life with his any more than she already had? It would just make life awkward for him. On the other hand, he had said not to bother sending her flowers? Jerk! What did she care if life was awkward for him?

When she was busy mooning over imagined conversations about jacket sleeves and dolphin swimming she'd do well to remember this side of him.

Besides, Katie felt herself liking his sister. She had laughed more in the past two minutes than she had in the past two weeks. Why not go for lunch? Friendships with women were so wonderfully *safe.*

"I'd love to have lunch with you," she decided impulsively. "Let me just leave a few instructions with Mrs. Abercrombie and we can go."

As they passed his office, Katie pushing the wheelchair, she saw Dylan standing at the window with Jake. He scowled when he saw his sister with her. Tara stuck out her tongue at him, while Katie looked determinedly straight ahead. Still, even through the windows, they could hear Jake's excited shouts of *SHE.*

Once they were past the obstacle of the window, though, Katie noticed the weather was beautiful, a fact Katie had not even registered about the day until now. Given the gorgeous sunshine they chose a little café with an outdoor eating area just down the block from the flower shop and Dylan's office. They ordered wraps, sipped chai tea and basked in the warmth.

"Have you noticed Dylan seems a little, um, cranky?" Tara said, when her food had arrived.

"I haven't seen Dylan," Katie said proudly.

"You haven't?"

"No. Him standing at the window is the closest I've been to him in two weeks."

"But why?"

"Surely you know your brother well enough to know his—" she tried to think of a word, and said carefully "—his dalliances are temporary."

"You are not a dalliance!"

Almost. Katie had almost been a dalliance. Ashamed to admit, even to herself, how she wished she had been, even if he had secrets. Even if it did last only one night. Surely she couldn't hurt more than she did right now. And then she would have had that experience to cradle in her lonely bed at night.

Anyway, being a dalliance would have been much easier to handle than being rejected right at the moment of truth!

"Did you have a fight?" Tara asked. "I wondered if you'd left my place on bad terms. You left so many things there."

"We didn't have a fight." *He rejected me.* A knock-down, drag-'em-out screaming match seemed as if it would have been preferable.

"Hmm. Well, something's eating him. He's gone into overdrive. Given that what most people would consider overdrive is his normal, his overdrive is maniacal."

"What do you mean?"

"Let's see—he's taking up rock climbing, just on the wall for now, he tells me, but planning a trip to the Rockies this summer. Then I saw him drive by with a kayak on top of his car, he invited us to watch him in a motorcycle race this past weekend and I heard on the news last night he's leaving for a camel trek across the Sahara in a few days. On Friday."

"A camel trek?" Katie said, incredulous.

"I tried to ask him about it this morning, but he just growled at me that he'd send a postcard. Where on earth do you send a postcard from in the Sahara?"

"The Desert Oasis and Belly-Dancing Emporium," Katie guessed cynically.

"Strangely, as far as I can tell, he doesn't have one of his bimbos on his arm right now."

Katie tried to keep her relief from her face. It was none of her business who he had or didn't have on his arm. She just had to pray when he did have a new object of his interest, he wasn't going to send that nice-to-meet-you bouquet through her!

If he did, she'd have no choice but to use yellow carnations to express her disappointment and disdain. And maybe a little monkshood to warn the poor girl a deadly foe was near.

Tara looked troubled. "I don't know about this playboy thing he does. He was never like that before Mom got sick."

"Your mom is sick?" Katie asked slowly. His mother was sick? "I'm sorry. I thought she had passed on."

Why had he let her believe that? But when she thought back on it, he had never said his mother was dead.

"Dylan told me she was gone."

Tara nodded sadly. "She is gone. Alzheimer's. My dad made a decision to put her in a care facility. It's the best, Highlands, over on the Westside, but there's still no mistaking it's an institution. Dylan was against it, to put it mildly. He offered to hire a nurse to care for her at home. But the thought of someone else living in their home twenty-four hours a day did not sit well with Dad. It's not just that he's a very private person.

"I think having Mom at home, in the shape she was in, was like being stabbed in the heart over and over again for Dad. She was becoming a stranger, not the woman he had loved for thirty-five years.

"Those last months when she was at home were absolutely frightening. She was leaving the stove on, breaking things. Sometimes she'd go out at night and wander around the neighborhood in her nightgown. She even found a hidden set of car keys one day and went for a drive. The police brought her home. Thank God she didn't kill someone or get lost somewhere where she might have been in danger."

"Oh, I'm so sorry," Katie said. "I can't imagine how dreadful that must be for your whole family." Dylan hadn't told her. He had not trusted her with the wound to his own heart.

It seemed that little secret hope she had been harboring, that he would come around, that there might be something there, was shriveling up inside her and dying. He had not shown her anything about him that *mattered* after all.

Or maybe in a way he had. Every week, coming in, faithfully choosing the most beautiful flowers, his secret bouquet.

Katie knew suddenly, who they were for, remembered the sadness in his face as he had chosen them. Then she remembered that same sadness marring his handsome features when he had been about to surrender to her.

And then pulled back.

"It's been hard on everyone. Dylan is all stiff upper lip, but he's been terribly unforgiving of my father. Then, to make everything worse, one of the neighbors, a friend of Mom's, has been really there for Dad. I suspect it's been platonic, but they were planning to go on a cruise together, and Dylan got wind of it. Poor Dad canceled the cruise, but Dylan still won't take his calls.

"Anyway, Dylan's gone-wild-with-girls thing seemed to have coincided with my mother's hospitalization. Not to mention the other craziness. I thought bungee jumping was the worst of it. Oh, no, he has to one-up himself and ride a camel across the desert!"

Katie saw Tara's very real love and concern for her brother. And she began to see his pulling away from her that night might not have been about her at all. It hadn't been about any of the things she had tormented herself with in the last weeks.

It had not been because she was not beautiful enough. It had not been because she had said or done the wrong thing at the wrong time. It had not been because she was divorced, *flawed.* Those were her own insecurities.

It wasn't her he'd been afraid to surrender to; it was love. Love, the beautiful rose with the terrible thorns.

"When did your mother become ill?" Katie asked softly.

"It started about three years ago, it's been about a year now since she went to Highlands."

Katie could have guessed that, without Tara confirming it. A year ago, just when she had opened The Flower Girl. His girl-a-month campaign just getting under way.

"Dylan," his sister said, "has always been popular, to be sure. But when he was playing ball he had a singleness of focus that was unreal. No relationships then, or at least nothing serious. It was the same when he started the business. He's always been very intensely focused on his career. There was no time for romance. I used to nag him about it. I wanted so badly for him to meet the right girl, have a family. He's such a great guy. I didn't want him to miss everything that was best in life. Though, after watching him perform this year it's been a case of 'Be careful what you wish for.' My goodness, I have never seen such an aggravating line-up of empty-headed bimbos in my whole life."

But Katie got it. *Women who required nothing of him.*

And when he had met one who had required more of him, he had backed away.

And Katie had to admit, even at the height of Dylan's girl-a-month campaign, there was nothing sneaky about him, unless she counted the fact he had tried—almost desperately—to make her believe he was a worse person than he was. He had done what he had done but without pretense, without leading anyone on, without making any promises.

She knew all that, because she had said it all for him with flowers.

It was probably a mark of her own weakness that Katie was seeing that as a kind of honor system.

"I think he's decided superficial is the way to go if you don't want to get hurt," Tara mused.

All this time, Katie thought, she had made it about her. And suddenly she could clearly see it was not about her at all. It was about a man who was trying desperately to show the world how fearless he was, when really the truth was he was afraid of the very same thing every other person on the face of the earth was afraid of.

He was afraid of getting hurt. Not physically. Anyone who had ever had a broken bone knew it could not hold a candle to a broken heart.

The topics moved on to other things. By the time lunch was done, wisely or not, Katie knew she and Tara were going to be the best of friends.

On Friday, knowing Dylan was gone to trek with camels in one more desperate effort to ward off the things that could really hurt him, Katie chose the flowers herself. She chose the flowers she had seen Dylan choose for his mother, the flowers he had chosen even when he didn't know they had meaning. She chose white chrysanthemums for truth, and she chose daisies for purity and loyal love.

Then she began to add her own touches, white heather for protection, and day lilies for motherhood. Finally she mixed in the last of her spring tulips, with their message of perfect love. She wove her heart into the bouquet for Dylan's mother, and she felt the sweetness of the flowers begin to weave healing into her.

She loved him.

And she loved him so intensely it did not matter if there was nothing in it for her. While he was in the Sahara she would let the love come out, once a week, in these bouquets for his mother.

The bouquet finished, she stood back from it. It radiated something so pure it took her breath away. It radiated love that gave instead of took, it had captured the essence of love at its best and purest. Katie closed her shop doors for the day and drove to Highlands.

An hour later she found Dylan's mother in her room. Dylan's mother was a handsome woman, her strong face dignified, her carriage regal. Her gray hair was coiffed perfectly, and she had on a lovely suit. But when she turned blue eyes exactly like Dylan's to her visitor, there was a sad blankness in them.

"Hello, Mrs. McKinnon." She saw Mrs. McKinnon looking at her anxiously, trying to figure out who she was, searching a memory filled with gaping spaces.

"You don't know me," Katie assured her gently. "I brought you some flowers."

His mother looked at the bouquet, smiled sweetly, touched each of the blossoms with trembling hands, seemed to forget Katie was there. The message of the flowers seemed to reach through her fog. For a moment, the blue of her eyes sharpened with clarity. She put her nose to them, and sighed with such contentment that Katie understood perfectly why Dylan had been so loyal about bringing them.

A care giver came in loaded with fresh towels. "Oh, the flowers!" she said. "Mrs. McKinnon's son usually brings them. And reads to her, shows her pictures from albums, brings videos of old home movies. I understand he's been away or is away right now, though."

The care giver admired the flowers and chatted while she replaced the towels about what a nice boy that Mr. McKinnon was, how loyal to his mother.

"She doesn't even know he's come, of course, poor dear," the aide said, and then left.

Katie looked around the room. There were remnants of the other bouquets he had sent. And other things. Poetry books, framed pictures, photo albums. There was a signed baseball, a TV over in the corner, with a video machine underneath it.

This was the side he'd always kept hidden. This was how much a man could love. So much that it could hurt him, drain him dry, take more than he had to give, especially if he was shouldering his burdens alone.

Katie picked up one of the poetry books, and went and sat on the edge of the bed, facing his mother's chair. She began to read.

Yellow sunlight, soft as a lover's kiss,
Touches the face, wrinkled now,
Of the one he loved in youth.
He does not see the age-glazed eyes,
Or the hair as silver as a frost-painted morn,
For he sees her through the lens of memory
Where she forever dances with whirling skirts
And flying hair
His heart remains unchanged
Denying a world that has faded.

Katie looked up from the book, and *felt* the love and courage and hope that had been poured into this room. She looked at Dylan's mother, and saw not the bewildered look of dementia, but instead the woman who had once been.

She saw the love this woman must have felt in her lifetime, the love that she had been at the heart of. It was love that had produced two wonderful children, a legacy that went on in that grandson that she probably didn't even recognize.

When Dylan's mother's soft hand crept tentatively into hers, Katie began to cry.

Dylan sat glumly in the airport terminal, baseball cap pulled low over his eyes so he wouldn't be recognized. His neck hurt from the tumble he'd taken off the climbing wall, and the thought of spending three weeks on a camel was about as appealing as having his toenails pulled out one at time.

It had always worked before! The relentless activity, the adrenaline rushes, had always been a balm and a distraction in the past.

But this time it wasn't working.

He was missing Katie so badly it hurt worse than his neck. How had she gotten such a hold on him? Why couldn't he just turn off the way he was feeling?

And then he knew.

Love wasn't a faucet that could be turned on and off at will. He loved her, and he could go wander around in the Sahara for the rest of his life, and it wasn't going to change that.

He'd been kidding himself about how *full* his life was. How *gratifying.*

An afternoon with Katie and a baby beat the hell out of jumping out of airplanes. Climbing rock walls.

It sure beat the hell out of riding camels.

His flight was called. He got up, took a few steps toward the life he no longer wanted and then stopped.

It was Friday. He didn't need to be going to the Sahara. He needed to go see his mother.

Suddenly, there under the harsh glare of the airport lights he got it: life's message wasn't that love changed so never risk it. The message was that everything changed, so grab the gifts you were offered when you were offered them; to treasure the time you were given with those gifts, because time was short. He realized he didn't want to waste a minute.

Dylan McKinnon had played baseball all his life. But suddenly he knew exactly what it meant to step up to the plate.

It meant to do the hard thing, even when you weren't ready, even when you didn't want to.

When he stepped out of the airport and raised his hand for a cab, he was stunned to discover that for the first time in a long, long time he felt like a free man. A man who was all done running.

Dylan paused in the doorway of his mother's room. He'd thought of stopping at a neighborhood grocery and picking up a bouquet, but somehow he wasn't going to be able to ever do flowers again without thinking of Katie.

Besides, he seemed to know a thing or two about flowers now. Not about their meanings, but about quality, how the petals should look on open flowers, how the buds should hold the promise of light inside of them.

When he saw the young woman sitting on the bed, his mother's hand in hers, her shoulders trembling with tears, he lurched to a halt.

Katie.

Seeing her filled him. The persistent ache that had been in him for two weeks quieted. That feeling of *needing* to do something stopped. Her shoulders were shaking. He realized she was crying.

Once upon a time, a woman crying would have sent him running the other way. Instead he walked in quietly, sank down on the bed beside her.

She looked up, startled, and for a moment there was something panicked in her face, and it stabbed him that he had caused her to feel like that. She looked as if she was going to get up and bolt, but he took her hand, kissed the top of it, drew her head onto his shoulder.

He saw the flowers. He had been buying flowers from Katie for a year. Her flowers were spectacular. And yet even he, self-acknowledged cretin that he was, knew this bouquet was different. It shone with a light from within.

And then he saw his mother was looking at him. A sudden smile lit her face, and he knew whatever light shone from those flowers, was shining from him, too. His mother, befuddled as she was, still recognized love, *unfaded,* as that poem he had read to her so many times had promised.

Katie pulled away from his shoulder, but not away from him.

"I thought you were riding camels in the Sahara," she said defensively.

"In the end I decided it sounded boring."

"God forbid you should ever be bored," she said, and then she did pull away from him.

"Are you angry at me?"

"That would imply I cared about you."

"Oh, Katie, my lady, we both know you care about me."

Her defenses crumpled and she started to cry again. He didn't feel the least bit impatient with her tears. He didn't feel annoyed. He didn't feel as if he needed to stop them.

"I wish you had told me," Katie finally said, "I wish you had felt you could trust me with this."

And it really said it all. His gift: never saying the things that needed to be said.

Hiding in quips and business and games, in adrenaline rushes and stupid new conquests.

"I haven't talked about it to anyone," he said. "It hurts too much."

"Sometimes things hurt less when you share them."

"It wasn't you I didn't trust, it was myself. What if I'm like my father? What if I can't be trusted to do the right thing when the going gets tough?"

"Hasn't the going gotten tough?" she whispered. She held up the book of poetry to him. "Haven't you done the right thing?"

"He doesn't come to see her, you know." It was as if he was making one last-ditch attempt to be right.

But Katie was never going to be the girl who saw him in the way he wanted to be seen. She was always going to be the girl who saw him as he really was.

Katie looked at his mother and then at him. "I think," she decided softly, "what she'd want more than anything else is for your father to be happy. That's what I'd want if—"

She stopped abruptly.

"If what?" he asked her.

She tossed her head and looked at him bravely. "That's what I'd want if it was you and me."

"He's abandoned her. She didn't deserve that. Oh, Katie, you should have seen her. It was always about everyone else. If there was one piece of cake left, she never had it. If there was money for a new sink in the bathroom or a bike for me I always got the bike."

"See? I'm right, then," Katie said firmly. "She's in that chair. The last thing she would want is for everyone to be trapped there with her. Love isn't a prison. Love wants people to be free."

He realized that's what love did. Real love. It set people free. It didn't take hostages, hold captives, demand great demonstrations, or gifts.

He remembered that sensation of freedom he'd felt at the airport when he chose the road that led back to her, to Katie, instead of the one that would have led him even further into the desert.

"And what if it was the one you loved in that chair?" he asked gruffly. If he'd inherited that gene from his mother, it could be him in this place someday. "Then what?"

"Are you worried it could be you?" she guessed softly.

The old Dylan would have scoffed at the word *worry.* But he nodded.

"If you're truly worried about ending up like this, maybe you should stop jumping out of airplanes. Off bridges." But then she smiled. "No, I'm kidding. I love that about you. That you live fully. That's what you teach me."

"And so, if I ended up like this?"

"Why then," she said, without hesitation, "I would bring flowers and read poetry. I would go through the photo albums, and I would show the old family movies. I would do exactly what you have done, Dylan."

"A captive?" he asked gruffly.

"A captive?" She looked askance at him. "Of course not. It wouldn't be a chore to me, or a duty. It would be an act of grace."

He looked at the flowers she had arranged, and felt the love brimming out of them. He looked at her face, and what he saw was a truth about himself being reflected back to him.

When he had started coming here to do things for his mother, it had been the first time in his life that he had really done something for anyone else with absolutely nothing in it for him. Most of the time his mother had not even known who he was. And yet still he had come, giving the gift of his time and his heart, doing things that did not come naturally to him, like reading her poetry, combing her hair. He had not recognized it for what it was.

But Katie was right.

It had been an act of grace, of the purest love.

And something more: a rite of passage. When a man was capable of doing something, finally, for another, with no thought for himself, with no thought for his own rewards, or his own comfort, then he was ready.

Ready to quit riding camels and throwing himself off bridges.

Ready to acknowledge his true heart and his true courage. He was ready to be trusted with houseplants and goldfish and maybe a puppy.

Most of all, he was ready to love Katie Pritchard.

His mother's hand was on his cheek, and when he looked in her eyes he saw recognition. Not of him, maybe. But of love, certainly.

"I usually take Mom down to the dining hall for supper," he said gruffly. "Do you want to come with us?"

"Of course," she said.

At the front door to the dining hall, he paid the three-dollar charge for visitors for his and Katie's meals. They sat down with heavy plastic plates. The entrée was shredded beef. It came with mashed potatoes and peas. Three delightful old ladies sang vigorous tunes, and his mother forgot her meal and clapped her hands.

Dylan sighed and met Katie's eye.

"Somehow," he said, "I'd pictured something a little different than this for our first official date."

"Is that what this is?" Katie asked, and she looked delighted.

He nodded.

"Really," she said, "what would be better than having dinner with a guy and his mother?"

And he knew she meant it. And he knew something else. He loved her beyond words.

CHAPTER NINE

DYLAN knocked on the front door of his childhood home. He had a pizza in one hand and a half sack of beer in the other. The flowerbeds had gone to seed. An old newspaper was caught in a dead shrub. Maybe some weekend soon, he'd come and clean them out. He knew it was the kind of thing Katie would like to do with him.

He liked the mental picture of them digging together in dirt. What he was learning about Katie, ever since that first "official" date six weeks ago, was that she loved the small everyday pleasures. Coffee at the outdoor café down the street from their businesses, holding hands in the park, watching the sun go down over the lake with a bottle of wine and a bag of potato chips.

But she was full of surprises, too. The first time he'd taken her on his motorbike she had wrapped her arms around him and screeched, "Faster. Go faster!" She had beat him to the top of the rock-climbing wall three times out of four, and looked down at him grinning fearlessly.

Oh, yeah, she was giving brand-new meaning to the word *fearless.*

And that was what brought him here.

He was ready to go to the next level with Katie, but

he had some of his own "stuff" that needed dealing with first. You could not come to a girl like Katie with blackness in your heart.

His dad opened the door, and Dylan saw that time did not stand still. His mother's illness had taken a toll on everyone. His father looked tired, his military bearing stooped, his hair thinner.

Dylan saw, not the man who had betrayed his mother, but the man who had thrown baseballs for him until it was so dark he could barely see the white of the ball coming out of the night. He saw the man who had hung a tire in a tree for him to practice pitching his fastball. He saw the man who had come to every single Little League game, the man who had cried like a child when Dylan had been signed to the Jays, the man who had told him it didn't matter, when his career had ended as suddenly as it had begun.

"I brought some supper," Dylan said.

His father looked so happy to see him, but wary, too. "I thought you were doing some damn fool thing with a camel," he said gruffly, holding open the door. "Damn shame to hear what your son's up to on the local news at five."

His dad was right. It was shame-on-him, that his father did not even know he had never gone on the camel trip. "Ah, I decided I could live life without adding the title of camel jockey to my résumé."

They ate pizza in front of the TV, watched sports, sipped cold beer. Dylan realized, his dad, just like him, and maybe all men, had trouble with emotion, with communication.

It would be so easy to not even speak of the rift that

had been between them, to just pretend it had never happened, to let the pizza and beer and his presence be apology enough.

But Dylan wasn't just here for himself. He was here to be a man big enough to acknowledge his own errors, big enough to forgive those others had made.

He was here to prove he was a man with enough heart and soul and ordinary garden variety guts to live up to the love of a woman like Katie Pritchard.

During a commercial, he took a deep breath, reached for the Mute on the remote control, and he cleared his throat. "Dad, I wanted to let you know I'm sorry. I know it was a hard enough decision for you, without me making it harder."

His father made a harrumphing noise that could have meant "Shut up" or "Go on," so Dylan charged on. "I know what Mom would want more than anything else is for you to be happy. For all of us to be happy. For the family to always be a family, even without her.

"I know we've lost her. I know she isn't ever going to be the way she was before, but, Dad, if we lose the lessons she gave us, that would be the real tragedy. She taught me what love means, and I feel really bad that I forgot that for a while."

His father put his head in his hands. "Okay," he said, and then he looked up, tears shining in his eyes. His tone was defensive. "She doesn't even know whether I go or not, Dylan."

"I know."

"It's not that I don't love her. You understand that, don't you?"

"Yeah."

"It's that I love her so much. It's not just that I don't want to see her like that, it's that I feel she wouldn't want me to see her like that. She put so much stock in this thing she called dignity. What would she think of me seeing her stripped of hers?

"We used to talk about what we'd do if one of us was on life support, with no hope. We both agreed that would be the gift we'd give the other one. We'd pull the plug. We both agreed that once the spirit was gone…" His voice faded. "It was supposed to be me, you know? That's how selfish I can be. I wanted to die first so I would never have to live without her. This is even worse, living without her, even though she lives."

They were silent, but the silence was without tension, two men contemplating the unpredictable twists and turns of life.

"Ah, maybe its time for you to go on that cruise, Dad."

"Maybe it is," his father said, and took the remote and turned the TV back up.

Dylan reached in his pocket and pulled out tickets. Two tickets. "For you and a friend," he said. "I'm going to be in Cabo San Lucas on these dates. Swimming with dolphins. I was kind of hoping you might like to meet me there."

When he left his father that night he went home and turned on his computer. Now he was worthy.

Now it was time to woo his woman. For real this time. Not part of a game, not with no clearly defined goal. Dylan knew exactly what he wanted. And he was pretty sure he knew how to get there.

He thought for a moment and then typed a phrase into the Internet search engine. He typed in *the secret meaning of flowers.*

Katie left work early, aware of feeling tense. What was going on with Dylan? For weeks now he had called her every day, wooed her, made her fall so far in love with him she couldn't believe such depths existed. She knew what it was to wake feeling as if you were walking on air, and to go to sleep with such a feeling of fullness, even if all you had to eat was potato chips and wine. Her life was more than she had ever dreamed it could be.

He'd called yesterday, but he'd seemed distracted, like a man with a great deal on his mind. He'd said something about visiting his father. She was aware of the estrangement, she had always known in her heart who he was, and that he would do the right thing. No matter what Tara thought, Dylan was no shirker when it came to the hard things.

So, instead of focusing on him, she had gone to see her own mom, and felt such a deep sense of appreciation for her, loved every minute with her. Her mother showed her the outfit she had bought to wear to the Tac Revol reading—a hideous black-and-white sweater suit embossed from head to hem with cats.

Katie had the horrible feeling she might have inherited her mother's fashion sense. But if she also had her joie de vivre, it was all good.

Now, the teeniest little doubt. Had he tired of her, returned to his old pattern? But here was the difference between loving Dylan and every other love she had ever experienced: if it ended it would leave her feeling richer and deeper and better than she had felt before, not depleted, not lacking, not as if there was something wrong with her. Loving Dylan had taught her life's most glorious secret: real love did not make a person feel afraid. No, it made them fearless, exhilarated, *exactly* what she felt when she reached the top of the climbing wall and looked down at Dylan.

She had seen herself through his eyes now. And she knew a delicious truth about herself. She was beautiful. She was deserving. She was worthy of this thing called love.

She unlocked her car door and went to slide in. She stopped, stepped back out and picked up a bouquet off the seat.

Dandelions! She glanced around. No one in sight. How had her door gotten unlocked?

Then she turned her attention back to her bright yellow bouquet, and allowed herself to feel the pure delight of the unexpected gift.

It was put together so carefully, so that it looked like a gigantic pom-pom, the stems tied with a ribbon, and wrapped with wet towel, then wrapped again in plastic.

Katie knew of only one man in the whole world with enough confidence, with enough of a sense of fun to leave a bouquet of dandelions!

And of course she knew, as few others would, in the old days, before there were flower shops, a man could pick his girl a bouquet of these anytime from spring to fall, reminding her that he would always be faithful, that her happiness meant everything to him.

Her eyes filled with tears. So, things had gone well with his father. Dylan was ready to embrace everything that love meant, including the hardest thing of all. Forgiveness.

Still mulling over her unexpected gift, she got home to find another. There on her small front porch stood a potted shrub. Dogwood, in full bloom. *Love undiminished.*

She gathered it up in her arms, and put it and the dandelions right in the middle of her kitchen table. And then she picked up Motley and, ignoring his shrill meows of protest, she waltzed him around her whole house. Should she call Dylan? Thank him?

No, it was his show. But even so, she could barely sleep that night. She was so restless the cats got up in protest and left her bedroom. She had a funny feeling the cats were going to have to get used to not sleeping with her soon, anyway.

She woke up Sunday morning to a knock on her door, but despite barely a wink of sleep she leaped from that bed like Cinderella going out the door to her awaiting carriage.

On her porch was an orange tree, heavy with blossom. The fragrance was absolutely heavenly, which went rather well with the traditional message of orange blossom.

Eternal love.

The tree was really much too heavy to lug in the house, but she could not bear to leave it outside. Her tiny house was soon filled with the scent of eternal love.

Nervous, she sat by the phone and chewed her fingernails, guarded her precious orange tree from the cats, who thought they should climb it. But as the day progressed, it occurred to her she had to do something productive with her time. She couldn't just wait around as if she was pathetic. She was more than that now! She was determined never to think of herself as pathetic again. That's what love did.

Katie went to her closet and threw out every single item of clothing that was not worthy of a woman totally, breathlessly in love. Then she lugged the orange tree into the bathroom and shut the door to protect it from the cats.

She went shopping and bought the wardrobe she had always wanted to have. It wasn't the sophisticated, glamorous wardrobe she had purchased for her life with Marcus. But it wasn't the wardrobe of a crazy cat lady, either.

It was the wardrobe of a woman filled to the brim with the confidence that being admired brought—flirty skirts and snug jeans, beaded blouses, sexy necklines, pajamas made of real silk.

She had just arrived home when the orchids were delivered. Like her other gifts there was no card, but then, she didn't need a card, because she had always known that flowers had a language of their own. Orchids spoke of love and beauty.

"How on earth did he get orchids delivered on a Sunday?" she asked the delivery boy.

"Hey, what would you do for tickets to a Jays game?" the boy said.

Again, despite a luxurious bath in her orange-blossom-scented bathroom, Katie had a sleepless night. She got up in the morning to find a sunflower on her porch. Bartholomew took an instant dislike to it, and she had to put it in the bathroom with her orange tree.

All the way to work she contemplated the meaning of sunflowers. They held in their sunny petals promises of devotion, reminders of sunshine even on days when the skies had turned gray.

That morning Katie had dressed more carefully than

she ever had in her life: a rich-chocolate embroidered skirt, tight, a matching jacket that dipped at her chest, hugged her curves. She dressed like a woman who knew she was beautiful, and worthy of all she was receiving. She dressed like a woman who tingled with the life force.

And then she arrived at work, opened her flower shop to find a single full-bloom rose, pink, on the counter. A single full-bloom always meant *I love you.*

Pink stood for perfect happiness. For all that this was wonderfully romantic, more than she ever could have dreamed for herself, Katie knew perfect happiness would be when he came forward, when he held her, when he took her lips with his own.

When they took up where they had left off that night at his sister's. But Dylan was surprising her by being the most patient of men, by wooing her with all the slow deliberation of those gents of Victorian times who knew the secret meaning of flowers and who knew a courtship was as much about anticipation as it was about anything else.

The onslaught continued over the next few days: he sent red camellias, which meant she was a flame in his heart, and red roses that meant he loved passionately.

But, even though she dressed every day as if she would see him, dressed in a way that was guaranteed to make his eyes pop nearly out of his head, she saw not one hint of Dylan anywhere. When the white violet arrived, she decided she'd had enough. Her patience was at an end. She called his office, and was put through immediately.

But when she heard his voice, she felt suddenly shy, tongue-tied. "Okay," she finally blurted out, and repeated the message of the white violet. "Let's take a chance."

"How big a chance?" he answered back.

"You're the daredevil. You tell me."

"All right. I will."

Within ten minutes a box arrived. She opened it, and saw a departure from the flowers. Inside it was a hooded, sleeveless running jacket, with the Daredevils emblem on it. She put it on.

It looked absolutely dreadful, the bright red clashing with the soft bronze of her full skirt, and her high heels. Uncaring her look was now somewhat comic, Katie admired herself in the mirror, and felt more attractive than she had ever felt. After she was done admiring herself, she found a note inside the pocket:

"Pull the tab on the shoulder."

She did. A sleeve, light as silk, flowed down her arm like an accordion expanding. She laughed out loud, and pulled the tab at the other shoulder. Another sleeve, and this time another note:

"See Mrs. Abercrombie."

She went into her back workroom. She should have known he had a accomplice. Mrs. Abercrombie was not scheduled to work today.

"I thought you didn't like him," she said to her stalwart assistant.

"Well, I didn't. Not until I found out his intentions were honorable." Mrs. Abercrombie looked at her employer and smiled. "Finally," she said, "the rose blooms within you. Here, he said to give you this."

From underneath a curtained sink, she produced a plant. Smiling, she handed it to Katie, who began to tremble.

Ivy.

"I…I…I seem to have forgotten what ivy means," she said, but the truth was she had not forgotten at all, but was afraid to believe.

"Ah, well," Mrs. Abercrombie said, looking over her shoulder and slipping on her jacket, heading out the back door, "maybe it will come to you."

The door closed behind her, and she was shaking like a leaf. And then he cleared his throat, and she turned and looked at him.

How could he be even more beautiful than her memory had painted him? He was wearing a jacket identical to hers and was leaning against the doorjamb, a picture of male confidence. Except, maybe in the blue of his eyes was the tiniest bit of doubt, of concern.

"An ivy stands for wedded love," he told her. "For fidelity." Was his voice shaking ever so slightly, this daredevil, this man without fear?

"Yes," she said, amazed by her own sudden calm, "it does."

"The jacket looks great," he decided, changing the subject. "One of the nicer things I've seen you wear." He stopped, "Though I've got to say that skirt is phenomenal."

He'd noticed what she was wearing! He never noticed what she was wearing!

"It's a beautiful jacket," she agreed, "I love the sleeves."

"An old cyclist's trick. If you approve of the design, they're going into production next week."

"I love the jacket," she said again. What she meant was *I love the man who gave me the jacket.* "Could we get back to the ivy?"

"Oh, sure. You should look in the leaves," he said.

She found a small envelope. Inside was a necklace with

two diamond-encrusted dolphins jumping together. She was not sure she had ever seen a piece of jewelry so lovely.

"This is what I thought," he said. "You've already had the white-wedding thing. Do you want to do that again?"

She shook her head no. Somehow she had pictured a quiet beach and a setting sun, maybe some champagne and potato chips, bare feet in warm sand.

"This time I want it to be just for you. And me."

The tears were beginning to come and she could not stop them.

"I thought maybe we could go swim with the dolphins," he told her softly. "And, you know. Maybe get married at the same time. On the beach at a place called Land's End. Land's End. Love's beginning. After we get married, our families could join us for a holiday." He looked at her closely. "You aren't going to faint, are you, Katie, my lady?"

But he wasn't taking any chances. He came and scooped her up into his arms, twirled her around the whole flower shop, her dress whirling around them until they were laughing breathlessly.

"I've been wanting to do that ever since you took those stupid tickets for a dance instead of me," he confessed to her.

"Are you trembling?" she asked him.

"Yes."

"Are you afraid?"

"I was," he admitted, "before I heard your answer. I'm not afraid now. I think sometimes a person trembles when they are in the presence of something greater than they are. I am in the presence of love, and I have waited my whole life to stand here.

"I looked for it in so many places, places where I could not hope to find it, and I mistook so many imitations for this. But now that I have felt the real thing, I'm never going back, Katie." He whispered in her ear, "Like that poem my mother likes, you will never fade for me, Katie, my lady. My heart will remain unchanged. That is my vow to you."

In that moment Katie knew a truth about herself. She had come to doubt her instincts, but now she saw they had always been good. Her instincts—her heart—had spotted this man when he was just an anonymous guy in a track suit. No, her instincts were very good. It was when she did not listen to them that she got herself in all kinds of trouble.

Dylan McKinnon had shown her the way—fearlessly—back to herself.

Her instinct now was to kiss him.

And she did. She tasted the whole world in his lips, and part of heaven, too. She tasted the past that had led them to this place, and the future that was beckoning. She tasted the strength and joy that would bring them through hardship, the faith that would welcome their children to the world, the hope that all things could be healed.

And on his lips she caught the faintest taste of roses, and why not? For all time those flowers, more than any other, had brought the messages of men's hearts: desire, excitement, happiness, unity, passion, worthiness, gratitude.

Her soul opened like a rose, and her heart knew every secret a flower had ever told.

[illegible] many, many places where I [illegible]

[illegible]

[illegible] a truth [illegible] She [illegible]

[illegible] when he was [illegible]

[illegible] instincts were always good. It was when she did not listen to them that she got herself in [illegible]

[illegible] had shown her the way—[illegible] ready—[illegible]

Her instinct now was to trust him.

And [illegible] the whole [illegible] She missed the [illegible] that had led [illegible] she was becoming. She [illegible]

[illegible] the world [illegible] all things could be healed.

[illegible]

[illegible]

THE LONER'S GUARDED HEART

BY
MICHELLE DOUGLAS

For Greg

CHAPTER ONE

'HELLO?'

Josie Peterson bent down and called her greeting into the half-open window before knocking on the door again.

No movement. No sound. Nothing.

Chewing her lip, she stepped back and surveyed the front of the cottage—weatherboard, neatly painted white. A serviceable grey-checked gingham curtain hung at the windows.

Grey? A sigh rose up through her. She was tired of grey. She wanted frills. And colour. She wanted fun and fanciful.

She could feel the grey try to settle over her shoulders.

She shook herself and swung away, took in the view about her. The paths were swept, the lawns were cared for, but there wasn't a single garden bed to soften the uniformity. Not even a pot plant. At the moment, Josie would kill for the sight of a single cheerful gerbera, let alone a whole row of them.

Six wooden cabins marched down the slope away from the cottage. Nothing moved. No signs of habitation greeted her. No cars, no towels drying on verandas, no pushbikes or cricket bats leant against the walls.

No people.

Fun and fanciful weren't the first descriptions that came

to mind. The grass around the cabins, though, was green and clipped short. Someone took the trouble to maintain it all.

If only she could find that person.

Or people. She prayed for people.

The view spread before her was a glorious patchwork of golden grasses, khaki gum trees and a flash of silver river, all haloed and in soft focus from the late-afternoon sunshine. Josie had to fight back the absurd desire to cry.

What on earth had Marty and Frank been thinking?

You were the one who said you wanted some peace and quiet, she reminded herself, collapsing on the top step and propping her chin in her hands.

Yes, but there was peace and quiet and then there was this.

From the front veranda of the cottage, there wasn't another habitation in sight. She hid her face in her hands. Marty and Frank knew her well enough to know she hadn't meant this, didn't they?

Her insides clenched and she pulled her hands away. She didn't want the kind of peace and quiet that landed a person so far from civilisation they couldn't get a signal on their cell-phone.

She wanted people. She wanted to lie back, close her eyes and hear people laughing and living. She wanted to watch people laughing and living. She wanted—

Enough already! This was the one nice thing Marty and Frank had done for her in…

She tried to remember, but her mind went blank. OK, so maybe they weren't the most demonstrative of brothers, but sending her on holiday was a nice thing. Did she intend spoiling it with criticisms and rank ingratitude?

Some people would kill to be in her position. Lots of people would love to spend a month in the gorgeous

Upper Hunter Valley of rural New South Wales with nothing to do.

She gazed about her wistfully. She wished all those people were lining the hills of this valley right now.

She dusted off her hands and pushed to her feet. She'd make the best of it. According to her map there was a town a few kilometres further on. She could drive in there whenever she wanted. She'd make friends. She was tired. That was all. It had taken too long to get here, which was probably why her landlord had given up on her.

She wondered what kind of people would live out here all on their own. Hopefully the kind of people who took a solitary soul under their wing, introduced them around and enthusiastically outlined all the local activities available. Hopefully they'd love a chat over a cup of tea and a biscuit.

Josie would provide the biscuits.

Impatience shifted through her. She rolled her shoulders, stamped her feet and gulped in a breath of late-afternoon air. She didn't recognise the dry, dusty scents she pulled into her lungs, so different from the humid, salt-laden air of Buchanan's Point on the coast, her home. Her stomach clenched up again at the unfamiliarity.

She didn't belong here.

'Nonsense.' She tried to laugh away the fanciful notion, but a great yearning for home welled inside her. The greyness settled more securely around her. She hastened down the three steps and back along the gravel path, hoping movement would give her thoughts new direction. She swung one way then another. She could check around the back, she supposed. Her landlord could be working in a…shed or vegetable plot or something.

In her hunger to clap eyes on a friendly face, Josie rushed around the side of the house to open the gate. Her fingers fumbled with the latch. Need ballooned inside her, a need for companionship, a need to connect with someone. The gate finally swung back to reveal a neat garden. Again, no flower beds or pots broke the austerity, but the lawn here too was clipped and short, the edges so precise they looked as if they'd been trimmed using a set square.

The fence was painted white to match the house and the obligatory rotary clothes-line sat smack-bang in the middle of it all. An old-fashioned steel one like the one Josie had at home. Its prosaic familiarity reassured her. She stared at the faded jeans, blue chambray shirt and navy boxer shorts hanging from it and decided her landlord must be male.

Why hadn't she found out his name from Marty or Frank? Although everything had moved so fast. They'd popped this surprise on her last night and had insisted on seeing her off at the crack of dawn this morning. Mrs Pengilly's bad turn, though, had put paid to an early start. Josie bit her lip. Maybe she should've stayed and—

A low, vicious growl halted her in her tracks. Icy fingers shot down her back and across her scalp.

Please God, no.

There hadn't been a 'Beware of the Dog' sign on the gate. She'd have seen it. She paid attention to those things. Close attention.

The growl came again, followed by the owner of the growl, and Josie's heart slugged so hard against her ribs she thought it might dash itself to pieces before the dog got anywhere near her. Her knees started to shake.

'Nice doggy,' she tried, but her tongue stuck to the

roof of her mouth, slurring her words and making them unintelligible.

The dog growled in answer. Nuh-uh, it wasn't a nice doggy and, although it wasn't as large as a Rottweiler or a Dobermann, it was heavy-set and its teeth, when bared, looked as vicious as if it were. She could imagine how easily those teeth would tear flesh.

She took a step back. The dog took a step forward.

She stopped. It stopped.

Her heart pounded so hard it hurt. She wanted to buckle over but she refused to drop her eyes from the dog's glare. It lowered its head and showed its teeth again. All the hackles on its back lifted.

Ooh. Not a good sign. Everything inside Josie strained towards the gate and freedom, but she knew she wouldn't make it. The dog would be on her before she was halfway there. And those teeth…

Swallowing, she took another step back. The dog stayed put.

Another step. The dog didn't move. Its hackles didn't lower.

With a half-sob, Josie flung herself sideways and somehow managed to half climb, half pull her way up until she was sitting on top of the rotary clothes-line.

'Help!' she hollered at the top of her voice.

Something tickled her face. She lifted a hand to brush it away. Spider web! She tried to claw it off but it stuck with clammy tentacles to her face and neck. It was the last straw. Josie burst into tears.

The dog took up position directly beneath her. Lifting its head, it howled. It made Josie cry harder.

'What the devil—?'

A person. 'Thank you, God.' Finally, a friendly face. She swung towards the voice, almost falling off the clothes-line in relief.

She stared.

Her heart all but stopped.

Then it dropped clean out of her chest to lie gasping and flailing on the ground like a dying fish. *This was her friendly face?*

No!

Fresh sobs shook her. The dog started up its mournful howl again.

'For the love of…'

The man glared at her, shifted his feet, hands on hips. Nice lean hips she couldn't help noticing.

'Why in the dickens are you crying?'

She'd give up the sight of those lean hips and taut male thighs for a single smile.

He didn't smile. She stared at the hard, rocky crags of his face and doubted this man could do friendly. He didn't have a single friendly feature on his face. Not one. Not even a tiny little one. The flint of his eyes didn't hold a speck of softness or warmth. She bet dickens wasn't the term he wanted to use either.

Heaven help her. This wasn't the kind of man who'd take her under his wing. A hysterical bubble rose in her throat. 'You're my landlord?'

His eyes narrowed. 'Are you Josephine Peterson?'

She nodded.

'Yes.' He scowled. 'I'm Kent Black.'

He didn't offer his hand, which she had to admit might be difficult considering she was stuck up his clothes-line.

'I asked why you were crying.'

Coming from another person the question would've been sympathetic, but not from Kent Black. Anyway, she'd have thought a more pressing question was 'What the dickens are you doing in my clothes-line?'

'Well?' He shifted again on those long, lean legs.

An hysterical bubble burst right out of her mouth. 'Why am I crying?' She bet he thought she was a madwoman.

'Yes.' His lips cracked open to issue the one curt word then closed over again.

'Why am I crying?' Her voice rose an octave. 'I'll tell you why I'm crying. I'm crying because, well look at this place.' She lifted her hands. 'It's the end of the earth,' She fixed him with a glare. It was the only thing that stopped her from crying again. 'How could Marty and Frank think I'd want to come here, huh?'

'Look, Ms Peterson, I think you ought to calm—'

'Oh, no, you don't. You asked the question and demanded an answer so you can darn well listen to it.' She pointed her finger at him as if he was personally responsible for everything that had gone wrong today.

'Not only am I stuck here at the end of the earth but…but I'm stuck in a clothes-line at the end of the earth. And to rub salt into the wound, I got lost trying to find this rotten place and ended up in Timbuktu, where I got a flat tyre. Then your dog chased me up this rotten clothes-line and there's spider web everywhere!'

Her voice rose with each word in a way that appalled her, but she couldn't rein it back the way she normally did. 'And Mrs Pengilly took a bad turn this morning and I had to call an ambulance and…and I buried my father a fortnight ago and…'

Her anger ran out. Just like that. She closed her eyes and

dropped her head. 'And I miss him,' she finished on a whisper so soft she hardly heard it herself.

Darn it. She reluctantly opened one eye and found him staring at her as if she was a madwoman. She opened the other eye and straightened. Then smoothed down her hair. She wasn't a madwoman. And despite her outburst she didn't feel much like apologising either. He didn't have the kind of face that invited apologies. She pulled in a breath and met his gaze.

'You're afraid of my dog?'

She raised an eyebrow. Did he think she sat in clotheslines for the fun of it? 'Even at the end of the earth you should put signs up on your gates warning people about vicious dogs.'

He continued to survey her with that flinty gaze and she felt herself redden beneath it. With a sigh, she lifted her T-shirt. She didn't need to glance down to see the jagged white scar that ran the length of her right side and across her stomach. She could trace it in her dreams. To do him credit, though, he hardly blinked.

'How old were you?'

'Twelve.'

'And you're afraid of Molly here?'

Wasn't that obvious?

She glanced at the dog. Molly? The name wasn't right up there with Killer or Slasher or Crusher, was it? And with Kent Black standing beside her the dog didn't look anywhere near as formidable as it had a moment ago. Josie gulped. 'She's a girl?'

'Yep.'

The dog that had attacked her had been a big male Dobermann. 'She growled at me.'

'You frightened her.'

'Me?' She nearly fell out of the clothes-line.

'If you'd clapped your hands and said boo she'd have run away.'

Now she really didn't believe him.

His lips twisted, but not into a smile. 'Moll.' The dog wagged her tail and shuffled across to him. He scratched her behind the ears. 'Roll over, girl.'

His voice was low and gentle and it snagged at Josie's insides. Molly rolled onto her back and a part of Josie didn't blame her. If he spoke to her like that she'd roll over too.

Oh, don't be so ridiculous, she ordered. She focused her attention back on Kent. He parted the fur on the dog's belly. He had large, weathered hands. Even from her perch in the clothes-line she could see the calluses that lined his fingers.

'Look,' he ordered.

She did, and saw a mirror image of her own scar etched in the dog's flesh. An ugly white raised scar that jagged across Molly's stomach and ribs.

'A man with a piece of four-by-two studded with nails did that to her.'

Sympathy and horror pounded through Josie in equal measure. How could someone hurt a defenceless animal like that? It was inhuman.

She scrambled down out of the clothes-line, dropped to her knees at its base and held out her arms. 'You poor thing.'

Molly walked straight into them.

Kent had never seen anything like it in all his thirty-two years. Molly hid from strangers. When someone surprised her, like Josephine Peterson here obviously had, she'd try and bluff her way out of it by growling and stalking off.

Then she'd hide. The one thing she didn't do was let strangers pet her. She sure as hell didn't let them hug her.

For the first time in a long time Kent found himself wanting to smile. Then he remembered Josephine Peterson's blood-curdling cry for help and he went cold all over again. He didn't need a woman like her at Eagle Reach.

A woman who couldn't look after herself.

He'd bet each and every one of his grass-fed steers that Josephine Peterson didn't have a self-sufficient bone in her body. And he'd be blowed if he'd take on the role of her protector.

His lip curled. She was a mouse. She had mousy brown hair, mousy brown eyes and a mouse-thin body that looked as if it'd bow under the weight of an armload of firewood. Even her smile was all mousiness—timid and tentative. She aimed it at him now, but he refused to return it.

It trembled right off her lips. Guilt slugged him in the guts. He bit back an oath.

She rose and cast a fearful glance at the back of the house. 'Do…do you have any other dogs?'

'No.' The memory of her scarred abdomen rushed on him again. His hands clenched to fists. When she'd lifted her shirt, shown him her scar, it wasn't tenderness or desire that had surged through him. He had a feeling, though, that it was something closely related, something partway between the two, something he didn't have a name for.

What he did know was he didn't want Josephine Peterson here on his hill. She didn't belong here. She was a townie, a city girl. For Pete's sake, look at her fingernails. Long and perfectly painted in a shimmery pink. They were squared off at the tips with such uniformity he knew they had to be fake. This wasn't fake-fingernail country.

It was roughing-it country.

He hadn't seen anyone less likely to want to rough it than Josephine Peterson.

When he glanced at her again she tried another smile. 'Do you have a wife?'

Her soft question slammed into him with more force than it had any right to. She needn't look to him for that either!

He glanced into her hopeful face and despite his best intentions desire fired along his nerve-endings, quickening his blood, reminding him of everything he'd turned his back on. Now that she stood directly in front of him, rather than perched up in his clothes-line or on her knees with her face buried in Molly's fur, he could see the gold flecks inside the melt-in-your-mouth chocolate of her iris. That didn't look too mousy.

Get a grip! Whatever the colour of her eyes, it didn't change the fact she wasn't the kind of woman he went for. He'd been stuck up this hill too long. He liked tall, curvy blondes who were out for a good time and nothing more. Josephine Peterson wasn't tall, curvy or blonde. And she looked too earnest for the kind of no-strings affairs he occasionally indulged in.

She continued to gaze at him hopefully. 'No,' he bit out. 'I don't have a wife.' And he had no intention of landing himself with one either. The sooner this woman realised that the better.

Rather than light up with interest, with calculation, her face fell. Kent did a double take.

'That's a shame. It would've been nice to have a woman around to talk to.'

He'd have laughed out loud at his mistake only he'd lost his funny bone.

'Is there anyone else here besides you?'

'No.' He snapped the word out. 'I'll get the key to your cabin.'

She blinked at his abruptness. 'Which one is mine?'

'They're all empty.' He strode around to the back of his house. She had to run to keep up with him. With a supreme effort he slowed his stride. 'You can have your pick.'

'I'll take that one.'

She pointed to the nearest cabin and Kent found himself biting back another oath. Damn and blast. Why hadn't he put her in the furthest one and been done with it? He disappeared inside, seized the key then strode back outside and thrust it at her.

'Thank…thank you. Umm…' She shuffled from one foot to the other. 'Does the cabin have a phone?'

His lip curled. He despised city folk. They came here mouthing clichés proclaiming they wanted to get away from it all, get back to nature, but all hell broke loose when they discovered they had to do without their little luxuries. It made him sick.

Granted, though, Josephine Peterson looked as though she wanted to be at Eagle Reach about as much as he wanted her here. Her earlier words came back to him and a laugh scraped out of his throat. 'This is the end of the earth, remember? What do you think?'

She eyed him warily. The gold in her eyes glittered. 'I'm guessing that's a no.'

'You're guessing right.'

She wouldn't last a month. At this rate she'd be lucky to last two days. What on earth had possessed her to book a cabin for four whole weeks? The advertisement he'd placed in the local tourism rag made no false promises. It sure as hell wasn't the kind of advert designed to attract the attention of the likes of her.

'Look, Ms Peterson, this obviously isn't your cup of tea. Why don't you go on into Gloucester? It's only half an hour further on. You'll find accommodation more suited to your tastes there.' Behind his back he crossed his fingers. 'I'll even return your deposit.'

'Please, call me Josie.'

She paused as if waiting for him to return the favour and tell her to call him Kent, but he had no intention of making any friendly overtures. He wanted her out of here.

When he remained silent, she sighed. 'I have to stay. My brothers organised all this as a treat.'

He recalled her rant whilst she'd clung to his clothes-line. Marty and Frank, wasn't it? His eyes narrowed. 'Are they practical jokers?'

'Heavens, no.' For a moment she looked as if she might laugh. It faded quickly. 'Which is why I have to stay. I wouldn't hurt their feelings for the world. And they would be hurt if they found out I'd stayed some-where else.'

Fabulous.

She smiled then. He recognised the effort behind it, and its simple courage did strange things to his insides. He wanted to resist it. Instinct warned him against befriend-ing this woman.

'Is Gloucester where I'll find the nearest phone? It's just...I'm not getting a signal on my mobile.'

Which was one of the reasons he loved this hill.

'And I'd really like to check on my neighbour, Mrs Pengilly.'

For a mouse she could sure make him feel like a heel.

'There's a phone in there.' He hitched his head in the direction of the house.

Josie's face lit up. 'May I…?'

'It's in the kitchen.'

She raced inside as if afraid he'd take his offer back. He collapsed onto the top step, shoulders sagging, and tried not to overhear her conversation, tried not to hear how she assured whoever answered the phone that the Gloucester Valley was beautiful, that the view from her cabin was glorious, that her cabin was wonderful.

He leapt up and started to pace. Two out of three wasn't bad. The Gloucester Valley *was* beautiful, and her view *was* glorious. He had a feeling she'd give up both for the wonderful cabin.

He blinked when she reappeared moments later. He'd expected her to be on the phone for hours. It was what women did, wasn't it?

She tripped down the back steps. 'Thank you, I…' She made as if to clasp his arm then stepped back as though she'd thought better of it. 'Thank you.'

His pulse quickened. 'How's your Mrs Pengilly?'

He couldn't believe he'd asked. Maybe it was time he had a holiday.

A smile lit her face. 'Her son Jacob came down from Brisbane and he says she's going to be OK. Apparently she has late-onset diabetes.'

'Once they've stabilised her blood sugar and organised her medication she'll be fine.' The words rolled out of him with an ease that was disconcerting.

'Yes.' The gold of her eyes glittered with curiosity. 'You sound like you know all about it.'

'I do.' But he wasn't volunteering any more information.

He'd already given enough away. He reached across and plucked the key from her fingers. 'Let's get you settled.'

To Josie, Kent's words sounded more like 'Let's get you out of my hair'. Nope, not a friendly bone in his body.

He did have a nice body, though—broad-shouldered, lean-hipped, athletic. And he wasn't all bad. He had let her use his phone. And he'd asked after Mrs Pengilly.

She trotted to keep up with him. She glanced at him from the corner of her eye and noted the uncompromising line of his mouth. Maybe he was just out of practice. Living here all on his own, he wouldn't get much chance at personable conversation. Anyhow, she was determined to give him the benefit of the doubt because the alternative was too bleak for words—stuck out in the middle of nowhere with a man who wouldn't give her the time of day.

No. No. She bit back a rising tide of panic. Beneath his gruffness Kent had a kind heart.

On what proof are you basing such an assumption? a disbelieving voice at the back of her head demanded.

She swallowed. He'd asked after an old lady. And… And he had a dog.

Not much though, is it? the same voice pointed out with maddening logic.

No, she guessed not. The panic rose through her again. 'Did you nurse Molly back to health?'

'Yes.'

One uncompromising word, but it lifted the weight settling across her shoulders. See? He did have a kind heart. For dogs.

It was a start.

Kent leapt up onto the tiny veranda that fronted the

cabin and pushed the key into the door. Josie started after him then swallowed. The cabins all looked really tiny. She'd hoped…

The door swung open and she gulped back a surge of disappointment. When Marty and Frank had said 'cabin' she'd thought… Well, she hadn't expected five-star luxury or anything, but she had hoped for three-star comfort.

She was landed with one-star basic. And that was being charitable.

Kent's shoulders stiffened as if he sensed her judgement and resented it. 'It has everything you need.' He pointed. 'The sofa pulls out into a bed.'

Uh-huh. She took a tentative step into the room and glanced around. Where were the flowers? The bowl of fruit? The welcoming bottle of bubbly? There wasn't a single rug on the floor or print on the wall. No colourful throw on the sofa either. In fact, there wasn't a throw full stop, grey or otherwise.

Admittedly, everything looked clean, scrubbed to within an inch of its life. By the light of the single overhead bulb—no light shade—the table and two chairs gleamed dully. Would it really have been such an effort to toss over a tablecloth and tie on chair pads?

'The kitchen is fully equipped.'

It was. It had an oven and hotplates, a toaster and kettle. But it didn't have any complimentary sachets of tea or coffee. It didn't have a dishwasher. She hadn't wanted the world, but—

An awful thought struck her. 'Is there a bathroom?'

Without a word, Kent strode forward and opened a door she hadn't noticed in the far wall. She wasn't sure she wanted to look.

She ordered her legs forward, glanced through the door and released the breath she held. There was a flushable toilet. And a shower.

But no bathtub.

So much for the aromatherapy candles and scented bath oils she'd packed.

'What do you think?'

Josie gaped at him. The question seemed so out of character she found herself blurting out her first impression without restraint. 'It's awful.'

He stiffened as if she'd slapped him.

'I'm sorry, I don't mean to offend you, but it's a dog kennel.' In fact, she bet Molly's quarters surpassed this. 'It's… Do all the cabins have the same colour scheme?'

The pulse at the base of his jaw jerked. 'What's wrong with the colour scheme?'

'It's grey!' Couldn't he see that? Did he seriously think grey made for a homely, inspiring atmosphere? A holiday atmosphere?

He folded his arms. His eyes glittered. 'All the cabins are identical.'

So she was stuck with it, then.

'Look, I know this probably isn't up to your usual standard,' he unfolded his arms, 'but I only promised basic accommodation and—'

'It doesn't matter.' Tiredness surged through her. Was this all Marty and Frank thought she was worth? She gulped back the lump in her throat.

'Like you said, it has everything I need.' The greyness settled behind her eyelids.

CHAPTER TWO

KENT strode off into the lengthening shadows of the afternoon, his back stiff, his jaw clenched. For once he didn't notice the purple-green goldness of the approaching sunset. He skidded to a halt, spun around and slapped a hand to his thigh. 'C'mon, Moll.'

Molly pricked her ears forward, thumped her tail against the rough-hewn boards of the cabin's veranda, but she didn't move from her post by Josie's door.

Oh, great. Just great.

'See if I care,' he muttered, stalking back off. Solitude was his preferred state of affairs. Josie Peterson was welcome to his dog for all the good it would do her. Molly wouldn't say boo to a fly.

Birds of a feather…

Up on the ridge a kookaburra started its boisterous cry and in the next moment the hills were ringing with answering laughter. Kent ground to a halt. He swung back in frustration, hands on hips.

These cabins weren't meant for the likes of her. They were meant for men like him. And for men who lived in cities and hungered to get away occasionally, even if only for a long weekend. Men who wanted to leave the stench of car exhaust fumes and smog and crowds and endless traffic behind. Men who wanted nothing more than to see the sky above their heads, breathe fresh air into their lungs, and feel grass rather than concrete beneath their feet. Men happy to live on toast and tea and beer for three days.

Josie didn't want that. She'd want spa baths and water-beds. She'd want seafood platters and racks of lamb and soft, woody chardonnays.

And he didn't blame her. If she'd just lost her father she probably deserved some pampering, a treat, not this rugged emptiness. Her brothers had to be certifiable idiots.

He kicked at a stone. He couldn't give her spa baths and seafood platters.

A vivid image of mousy Josie Peterson lying back in a bubble-filled spa rose up through him and his skin went tight. She didn't look too mousy in that fantasy.

He scratched a hand through his hair. Idiot. The kookaburras continued to laugh. Their derision itched through him. He surveyed the cabin, hands on hips. Not a sign of movement. His earlier vision gave way to one of her lying face down on the sofa, sobbing. He took a step towards the cabin.

He ground to a halt.

He didn't do crying women. Not any more.

A month. *A whole month.*

His gaze flicked to her car. He wasn't a blasted porter either, but that didn't stop him from stalking over to it and removing two suitcases and a box of groceries. Or from stalking back to the house, grabbing a bottle of chardonnay and shoving it in an ice bucket and adding that to the items piled up by her front door.

He bent down and scratched Molly's ears. 'Keep an eye

on her, girl.' That would have to do. Common decency demanded he check on her in the morning, then his neighbourly duty was done.

If she hadn't already had a crying jag when perched in the clothes-line, Josie would've had one now. But she decided one a day was enough.

A whole month. She was stuck out here for a whole month. *On her own.*

She tried to repress a shudder. She tried to force herself to smile as she glanced around the interior of the cabin again. She'd read somewhere that if you smiled it actually helped lift your spirits.

Ha! Not working.

She scrubbed her hands down her face. Oh, well, she supposed if nothing else she at least had plenty of time to sort out what she was going to do with the rest of her life. And that was the point of this holiday after all.

Things inside her cringed and burned. She wrapped her arms around her waist. She wasn't qualified to do anything other than look after sick people. And she didn't want to do that any more.

Familiar doubts and worries crowded in on her. She pushed them away. Later. She'd deal with them later.

With a sigh, she collapsed onto the sofa. Then groaned. It was as rock-hard as Kent Black. That didn't bode well. She twisted against it, trying to get comfortable. It didn't take a brain surgeon to work out Kent didn't want her here. As far as she could see, he didn't have an ounce of sympathy in that big, broad body of his for weakness of any kind.

She had to admit it was a nice, broad body though, with scrummy shoulders. If a girl disregarded that scowl she could get all sorts of ideas in her head and—

No, she couldn't! Besides, Josie could never disregard that scowl. Kent didn't think she belonged out here and he was one hundred per cent right.

A whole month.

'Stop it!'

Her voice echoed eerily in the cabin, reminding her how alone she was. She suppressed another shudder. She was just tired, that was all, and sitting around wallowing in self-pity wasn't going to help. A shower, that was what she needed. That'd pep her up. Then she'd unpack the car and make a cup of tea. Things always looked better over a cup of tea.

The shower did help. She emerged into the main room of the cabin, vigorously drying her hair. Then froze.

Something was on her veranda!

There it was again. A scuffling, creaking, snorting noise right outside her front door. She hadn't locked it!

Josie's mouth went dry. She held the towel to her face. Oh, please. Whatever was out there she prayed it didn't have an opposable thumb, that it couldn't reach out and open door handles.

And that it didn't have the kind of bulk that barged through flimsy wooden doors.

Just clap your hands and say boo!

Kent's earlier advice almost made her laugh out loud. Not funny ha-ha, but losing it big-time ha-ha. She retreated to the bathroom door. She doubted she could manage much of a boo at the moment.

'Kent?' Maybe he was out there. Maybe he'd come back for… She couldn't think of any conceivable reason why he'd come back. He hadn't been able to get away fast enough, horrible, unfriendly man.

She'd give anything for it to be him out there now, though.

'Mr Black?'

A low whine answered her, followed by scratching at her door and a bark.

'Molly.' With her heart hammering in her throat, Josie stumbled forward, wrenched the door open and dropped to her knees to hug the dog. 'You scared me half out of my wits,' she scolded. Molly licked her face in response.

Thank heavens Kent hadn't been here to witness her panic. He'd have laughed his head off then curled his lip in scorn. She'd have died on the spot.

She glanced out into the darkness and gulped. Night had fallen in full force. She couldn't remember a night so dark. Not a single streetlight pierced the blackness. Her cabin faced away from Kent's house, so not a single house light penetrated it either. The moon hadn't risen yet, but a multitude of stars arced across the sky in a display that hitched the breath in her throat.

She should've unpacked her car whilst it was light. She didn't fancy stumbling around in the dark. Dragging her eyes from the glory of the night sky, she turned and found her suitcases lined up neatly on the end of her veranda. Her jaw dropped. Kent had unpacked her car for her?

That was nice. Friendly. In fact—she struggled to her feet—it was almost…sweet?

No, you couldn't describe Kent as sweet.

She reached for the nearest bag then stilled. She adjusted her reach to the right and picked up an ice bucket, complete with a bottle of wine.

She blinked madly and hugged it to her chest. Now, that *was* friendly.

And sweet. Most definitely sweet.

* * *

Josie groaned and pulled a pillow over her head in an effort to drown out the cacophony of noise. Molly whined and scratched to be let out. She'd spent the night sleeping on the end of the sofa bed, and Josie had welcomed the company. Molly's presence had made her feel less alone. Last night she'd needed that.

Now she needed sleep.

Molly whined again. Groaning, Josie reached for her watch. Six o'clock! She crawled out of bed and opened the door. Kookaburras laughed as if the sight of her filled them with hilarity and, overhead, white cockatoos screeched, three crows adding their raucous caws. And that wasn't counting all the other cheeps and peeps and twitters she didn't recognise in the general riot. Magpies started warbling in a nearby gum tree. For heaven's sake, what was this place—a bird sanctuary?

Flashes of red and green passed directly in front of her to settle in a row of nearby grevillias, twittering happily as they supped on red-flowered nectar. Rosellas. Ooh. She loved rosellas.

Racing back inside, she clicked on the kettle, pulled on her jeans, threw on a shirt then dashed back out to her veranda with a steaming mug of coffee to watch as the world woke up around her.

OK. So maybe Eagle Reach was at the end of the earth, but she couldn't deny its beauty. To her left, the row of grevillias, still covered in rosellas, merged into a forest of gums and banksias. To her right, the five other cabins stretched away down the slope. Directly in front of her the hill fell away in gentle folds, the grassy slopes golden in the early-morning sunlight, dazzled with dew.

She blinked at its brightness, the freshness. Moist earth

and sun-warmed grasses and the faint tang of eucalyptus scented the air. She gulped it in greedily.

In the distance the River Gloucester, lined with river gums and weeping willows, wound its way along the base of the hill to disappear behind a neighbouring slope. Josie knew that if she followed the river she would eventually come to the little township of Martin's Gully, and then, further along, the larger township of Gloucester itself.

As one, the rosellas lifted from the bushes and took flight and, just like that, Josie found herself alone again. She swallowed. What would she find to do all day? Especially in light of the resolution she'd made last night.

She chafed her hands. She'd think of something. She'd stay at Eagle Reach for the whole day if it killed her. She would not drive into either Martin's Gully or Gloucester. Kent Black would expect her to do exactly that. And for some reason she found herself wanting to smash his expectations.

She found herself aching for just an ounce of his strength too.

By eight o'clock Josie wondered again at the sense of such a resolution. She'd breakfasted, tidied the cabin and now…

Nothing.

She made another coffee and sat back out on the veranda. She checked her watch. Five past eight. Even if she went to bed disgustingly early she still had at least twelve hours to kill. Her shoulders started to sag and her spine lost its early-morning buoyancy, the greyness of grief descending over her again.

She shouldn't have come here. It was too soon for a holiday. Any holiday. She'd buried her father a fortnight ago. She should be at home. She should be with her friends, her family. Maybe, right at this very minute, she could be forging closer bonds with Marty and Frank. Surely that was more important than—

'Good morning!'

Josie jumped out of her skin. Coffee sloshed over the side of her cup and onto her feet. Kent Black. Her heart hammered, though she told herself it was the effect of her fright. Not the fact that his big, broad body looked superb in a pair of faded jeans and a navy T-shirt that fitted him in a way that highlighted bulging arm muscles.

'Sorry. Didn't mean to startle you.'

He didn't look the least bit sorry. And if he didn't mean to startle people he shouldn't bark out good-mornings like a sergeant major springing a surprise inspection.

'Not a problem.' She tried to smile. 'Good morning.'

He didn't step any closer, he didn't come and sit with her on the veranda. She quelled her disappointment and tried to tell herself she didn't care.

'How'd you sleep?' The words scraped out of a throat that sounded rusty with disuse.

'Like a top,' she lied. She decided she'd been rude enough about the amenities—or lack of amenities—last night. She couldn't start back in on him today. Yesterday at least she could plead the excuse of tiredness. 'I'm sorry about my lack of enthusiasm last night. It had been a long day and, like you said, the cabin is perfectly adequate.'

He blinked. His eyes narrowed. Up close she could see they were the most startling shade of blue, almost navy. Still, it didn't mean she wanted them practically dissecting her.

'How was the wine?'

A smile spread through her. He could look as unfriendly and unapproachable as he liked, but actions spoke louder than words. Last night, over her first glass of wine, she'd decided Kent Black had a kind heart. He'd just forgotten how to show it, that was all. 'The wine was lovely.'

Really lovely. So lovely she'd drunk half the bottle before she'd realised it. Once she had, she'd hastily shoved the rest of the bottle in the tiny bar fridge. Quaffing copious quantities of wine when she was stuck out here all on her own might not be the wisest of ideas.

'It was a really thoughtful gesture. Thank you, Mr Black.' She waited for him to tell her to call him Kent. She bit back a sigh when he didn't.

He touched the brim of his hat in what she took to be a kind of farewell salute and panic spiked through her. She didn't want to be left all alone again. Not yet.

Molly nudged Josie's arm with her nose, forcing her to lift it so she could sidle in close. 'I, umm… Molly is a lovely dog. Really lovely. I was wrong about her too.' Ugh, she should be ashamed of such inane babble. 'I… She spent the night with me.'

He spun back, hands on hips. 'I noticed.'

Oh, dear. She should've let him leave. Her fingers curled into Molly's fur. She didn't want to give Molly up. 'I… Do you want me to shoo her home in future?'

'She's all yours.'

Relief chugged through her and she swore his eyes softened. Then he turned away again and she knew she must've imagined it. 'Are any of the other cabins booked over the next few weeks?' She crossed her fingers.

His impatience, when he turned back, made her want to cringe.

'No.'

The single syllable rang a death knell through her last

forlorn hope. All alone. For a month. 'Then…what do people do out here?'

'Do?' One eyebrow lifted. 'Nothing. That's the point.'

Dread fizzed through her. 'Would you like a cup of tea?' Surely he'd like a cup of tea. Kind hearts and cups of tea went together and—

'No.'

She gulped. Couldn't he have at least added a thank-you to his refusal? She tried to dredge up indignation, but her loneliness overrode it.

'Some of us actually have work to do.'

Work? 'What kind of work?' Could she help? She knew she was grasping at straws, but she couldn't stop herself. She knew she'd die a thousand deaths when she went back over this conversation later.

'I run cattle on this hill, Ms Peterson.'

'Josie,' she whispered, a hand fluttering to her throat. 'Please call me Josie.'

He pulled the brim of his hat down low over his eyes. 'Bushwalking.'

'I beg your pardon?'

'People who come here. They like to bushwalk.'

'Oh. OK.' She liked walking. She walked on the beach back home. She didn't know her way around here, though. What if she got lost? Who'd know she was missing? She didn't trust Kent Black to notice.

'There are some pretty trails through there.' He pointed at the forest of gums. 'They lead down to the river.'

Trails? She brightened. She could follow a path without getting lost.

'Take Molly with you.'

'OK. Thank you,' she called out after him, but she

doubted he'd heard. His long legs had already put an alarming amount of distance between them in a seriously short space of time.

She turned her gaze to the shadowed depths of the eucalypt forest and made out the beginnings of a path. A walk? She leapt up, glad to have a purpose.

Kent swung around as an almighty screech pierced the forest. Birds lifted from trees and fluttered away. He glanced at his watch and shook his head. Fifteen minutes. She'd lasted fifteen minutes. Not that he'd deliberately followed her, of course. He hadn't. He'd just taken note of when she'd set off and down which path, that was all.

He'd chosen a different path, an adjacent one, and it wasn't as if he was keeping an eye on her or anything. He had business down this way.

Yeah, but not until later this afternoon, a voice in his head jeered

He ignored it.

No more screams or screeches or shrieks for help followed. She'd probably walked into a spider's web or something. But then Molly started up her low, mournful howl. Kent folded his arms and glared. With a muttered curse, he unfolded his arms, cut through the undergrowth and set off towards the noise.

He almost laughed out loud when he reached them. Josie clung to a branch of a nearby gum and a goanna clung to the main trunk of the same tree, effectively cutting off her escape. Molly sat beneath it all, howling for all she was worth. He chuckled then realised what he'd done.

'Enjoying your walk I hope, Ms Peterson?'

She swung her head around to glare at him over her

shoulder. The branch swayed precariously. He readied himself to catch her if she overbalanced.

'What do you think?' she snapped.

'I think you enjoy scaring all the wildlife on my side of the hill.'

'Scaring? Me?' Her mouth opened and closed but no sound came out. She pointed an accusing finger at the goanna then clutched the branch again as it started to sway. 'Move it.'

He glanced at it. 'Nope, not touching it.'

'So, you're scared of it too?' she hissed.

'Let's just say I like to treat our native wildlife with a great deal of respect.'

'Oh, that's just great. Of all the wildlife in this God-forsaken place I had to get a…a dinosaur rather than a cute, cuddly koala, huh? Any wildlife wrestlers in the neighbourhood by any chance?'

'Not much call for them out here.'

'How am I going to get down?'

Behind her bluff he could see she was scared. He had a feeling she hadn't stopped being scared since she'd scrambled out of his clothes-line yesterday. 'Jump,' he ordered. 'I'll catch you.' She wasn't that high up. In fact, if she hung from that branch by her hands, she'd only be four or five feet from the ground. He knew it would look vastly different from her perspective, though.

He wished she wasn't so cute.

The thought flitted in and out of his head in the time it took to blink. 'Cut out the racket, Molly,' he growled. The dog had kept right on howling all this time. Like most of the females of his experience, Molly loved the sound of her own voice.

Josie bit her lip and glanced at the goanna. 'Is it going to jump too? Or chase me?'

'Nope. This is his tree. It's where he feels safe.'

She glared at him again. 'So, of all the trees in the forest I had to pick his?'

'Yep.'

'I'm so happy.'

He guessed from the way she gritted her teeth together as she said it, she didn't mean it.

Without any more prompting on his part, Josie shifted her weight from her behind to her stomach then tried to take her full weight with her arms to lower herself to the ground. Kent leapt forward and wrapped his arms around the tops of her thighs.

'I don't need—'

The rest of her words were lost when her hands slipped and she landed against him with a muffled, 'Oomph.'

Kent couldn't manage much either as the top half of her body slumped over him and he found his face mashed between her breasts. Then a long, delicious slide as her body slipped down his.

They were both breathing hard when her feet finally touched the ground.

They paused then sprang apart.

'Thank you,' Josie babbled, smoothing down her hair. 'I, umm… It probably wasn't necessary to jump to my rescue like that, but, umm…thank you all the same.'

'Are you going to make a habit of that?' he snapped. He darn well hoped not. His body wouldn't cope with it. Even now he had to fight down a rising tide of raw desire. He didn't need this.

'It's not part of my plans.'

He wanted her off his mountain. Fast. He flung his arms out. 'Doesn't this prove how unsuited you are to this place?'

Her chin shot up although her shoulders stayed hunched around her ears. 'Because I'm frightened of goannas?'

'Because you're frightened of everything.'

'I'm not afraid of Molly. Not now,' she pointed out reasonably enough. 'I just didn't know what to do when that thing started running at me.'

'Run away at right angles to it,' he answered automatically.

'I'll remember that.'

He didn't want her remembering. He wanted her gone. 'You don't know how to protect yourself out here.'

'Well…I'm not dead yet.'

'What would you do if some big, burly guy jumped out at you, huh?' To prove his point, he lunged at her.

The next moment he was lying on his back, and staring up through the leaves of the trees at the clear blue of the sky. With no idea how he had got there.

Josie's face hovered into view as she leaned over him. 'Does that answer your question?'

She'd thrown him? He deserved that smug little smile. For some reason he wanted to laugh again.

He scowled. No, he didn't. He wanted her off his mountain.

'I might be hopeless, but I'm not completely helpless, you know. Men I can defend myself against. It's the dogs and goannas that I have trouble with.'

He rolled over onto his stomach to watch her saunter away. He really wished he didn't notice how sweetly she filled out a pair of jeans. Molly licked his face, as if in sympathy, then trotted after her new-found friend.

CHAPTER THREE

JOSIE was back at her cabin by ten o'clock.

So, now she only had ten hours to kill.

She wished she'd learnt how to draw or paint. Or knit.

A craft project, that was what she needed. She made a mental note to hunt out a craft shop when she went into Gloucester. Tomorrow.

Still, what would it hurt if she went in today and—?

Kent's scornful lips flashed through her mind. No! She'd manage to stick it out here for a whole day. Somehow.

Books. She'd buy some books. And a radio. Tomorrow.

She rearranged her grocery supplies on the kitchen shelves. That took less than ten minutes. She made a shopping list. For tomorrow. That took another ten minutes, but only because she dallied over it. She glanced around, clapped her hands together and wondered what she could do next.

'Oh, for heaven's sake!' she growled out loud, suddenly impatient. Seizing a pen and notepad, she plonked herself down at the table. If she'd just work out what she wanted to do with the rest of her life instead of putting it off, then she could get on with living that life and leave this awful place behind. Marty and Frank would forgive her for curtailing her holiday if she came up with a plan.

At the top of the page she wrote: 'What do I want to do with my life?' Her mind went blank, so she added an exclamation mark, in brackets.

Familiar doubts and worries flitted about her. She swallowed and tried not to panic. She was looking at this all wrong. She should break it down into smaller, more manageable bits. Skills. She should list her skills.

1—Assistant in Nursing certificate. 2—She could give bed baths. 3—She could measure out medicines. 4—She could coax a difficult patient to eat. 5—

No. No. No.

She slammed the pen to the table. She didn't want to do those things any more. There had to be other things she could do. She had to have at least one talent that could steer her towards a new vocation. Take her brothers. Frank had a great head for figures, which made him a successful accountant. Marty had great spatial abilities, which was why he was an architect. She had…?

Nothing.

Her shoulders sagged. She couldn't think of one single thing she had a talent for. Except looking after sick people, dying people. Fear clogged her throat. She couldn't do that. Not any more. She'd loved her father dearly, missed him terribly, and she didn't regret one single day she'd spent looking after him. But…

She couldn't take on another dementia patient. She couldn't watch another person die.

She leapt up and started to pace. The grey drabness of the cabin pressed in against her. The only splashes of colour were the labels on her groceries. Her gaze drifted across them, paused on the packet cake mix that, for some reason, she'd thrown in. What? Did she think she'd be giving tea parties? Her laugh held an edge that earned her a low bark from Molly.

She'd love to give a tea party. A sigh welled up inside her. She chewed her bottom lip and cast another glance at the cake mix. She could cook it up for Kent.

As a thank-you for last night's bottle of wine.

Maybe he'd even invite her to stay and share it. She chewed her bottom lip some more. She wanted to find out what made him tick, what made him so strong. She wanted to be more like that. She put her list away and reached for a mixing bowl.

Kent rubbed his hands together as he waited for the tea to brew. With his chores done, he could kick back and enjoy the fading golden light of the afternoon, his favourite time of day.

The cattle were fed and watered. He ran a herd small enough to manage on his own. And between them, the cattle and the cabins, they kept him busy enough through the days.

The nights, though…

The nights nothing!

A knock sounded on his back door. He swung around. Josie?

It had to be. He rarely had visitors out here, which was the way he liked it. He wasn't a sociable man. He thought he'd made that plain to her this morning.

Guilt wormed through him. He scowled at the teapot.

Maybe she'd come to return the key and tell him she was leaving? His jaw clenched. Good. She could drive off into the sunset. He didn't care. No skin off his nose.

'Kent?' She knocked again.

He bit back a string of curses and strode out to answer the door. The sharp remark on his lips died when he found her standing on the bottom step with a frosted chocolate cake in her hands and a hopeful expression in her gold-flecked eyes.

Damn.

'Hello.' She smiled, or at least her lips gave the tiniest of upward lifts.

He grunted in reply. Things inside him shuffled about and refused to settle into place.

She'd recently showered and damp hair curled around her shoulders. It gleamed in the last shaft of sunlight that touched his house for the afternoon, and he could pick out more shades of brown than he thought possible for one person to possess. Everything from light honeyed brown all the way through to rich walnut.

And not a mouse in sight.

She smelled fresh and fruity. Not run-of-the-mill apples and oranges either, but something more exotic. Like pineapple and…cucumber? She smelt like summer nights on the beach.

He couldn't remember the last time he'd sat on a beach. Or when he'd last wanted to. He couldn't remember the last time he'd eaten chocolate cake either. He tried to stop his mouth from watering.

She thrust the cake towards him. 'This is for you.'

He had no option but to take it. 'Why?' His eyes narrowed. He didn't trust the sensations pounding through him and he didn't trust her either.

Her gaze darted behind him into the house. She moistened her lips when she met his gaze again. 'I, umm—'

'You want to use the phone again?' Typical woman. Couldn't be without—

'No.' She drew herself up. 'It's a thank-you for last night's bottle of wine.'

He'd known he'd end up regretting that bottle of wine. He stared at her. She had a pointy little chin that stuck out when indignant. He wanted to reach out a finger and trace the fine line of her jaw.

He darn well didn't! He shoved the cake back at her. 'I don't want it.'

She took a step back and blinked. Then amazingly she laughed. 'Wrong answer, Mr Black; you're supposed to say thank you.'

Shame bore down on him. There was a world of difference between unsociable and downright rude. Jeez. 'You're right.' He dragged his free hand down his face. 'I'm sorry.' He pulled in a breath and tried to gulp back hasty words clamouring for release. 'You better call me Kent.'

He couldn't grind back the rest of his words either.

'I've just made a pot of tea. Would you like to join me?'

The gold flecks in her eyes lit up. 'Yes, please.'

Josie wanted to run from Kent's scowl. Then she remembered the only place she could run to was her cabin. Her bleak, lonely cabin. She gulped back her trepidation and followed him into the kitchen.

She wrinkled her nose as she glanced around. Definitely a bachelor's pad—no frills, no colour, next to no comfort. A woman wouldn't put up with this.

She glanced at Kent. She had a feeling he wouldn't give two hoots what a woman thought.

A large wooden table dominated the room. That was about all she'd taken in yesterday when she'd made her quick phone call. She wondered if there was a separate dining room, then dismissed the idea. The house wasn't large enough.

She glanced through the doorway leading through to the rest of the house. It looked like a typical gun-barrel miner's cottage. The next room along would be the living room then a short hallway would lead to two bedrooms at the front of the house.

She also guessed she'd never make it past this kitchen.

Heat suddenly flamed through her. Not that she wanted to make it as far as the bedroom with Kent Black, of course. Good lord. She couldn't imagine him unbending his stiff upper lip long enough to kiss a woman, let alone—

Are you so sure? a wicked voice asked.

Umm…

She slammed a lid on that thought, swung away and found herself confronted with the hard, lean lines of Kent's back…and backside, as he reached into a cupboard above the sink for two mugs.

Oh, dear. She fanned her face and swung around another ninety degrees. She didn't want to ogle his, uh, assets. In fact, it probably wasn't a good idea to ogle any man's assets until she'd sorted out what she was going to do with the rest of her life.

The rest of her life? What was she going to do with the next ten minutes?

Arghh. She scanned the room, searching for distraction. Her eyes landed on a chess set. A beautiful hand-carved chess set.

At her indrawn breath, audible in the silence of the room, Kent spun to face her. 'What?' He glanced around as if searching for a spider or lizard, some creepy-crawly that may have frightened her.

'I…' She pointed. 'Did you make that?'

He grunted and shrugged.

'It's beautiful.' She stared at him, trying to recognise the creator of the work of art in the hard stern man in front of her. 'It's one of the most beautiful things I've ever seen.'

'Then you need to get out more.'

She'd have laughed at his response if she hadn't been so engrossed in admiring the individual chess pieces. Each one was intricately carved into the shape of a tree. The skill and workmanship that had gone into each piece took her breath away. The kings were mighty oaks, the queens graceful weeping willows and the bishops upright poplars. Talk about a craft project!

She held her breath and reached out to pick up a pawn—a miniature banksia—and marvelled at the detail. She could see each cylindrical flower on the delicate branches. How on earth had he managed that?

'Do you play?'

She jumped, startled by his closeness. His breath disturbed the hair at her temple as he leant over to survey the piece she held. 'I…'

He took a step back and she found she could breathe again.

'Not really.' She placed the pawn back on the board and sadness pierced her. She tried to smile. 'My father was teaching me before he fell ill.'

The rest of Kent Black could look as hard as stone, but his eyes could soften from a winter gale to a spring breeze in the time it took to draw breath. Josie's heart started to pound.

'I'm sorry about your father, Josie.'

'Thank you.' *He'd called her Josie.*

'I'm sorry he never had a chance to finish teaching you how to play.'

'Me too.' She couldn't look away.

'I'll give you lessons if you like.'

She wondered if she looked as surprised by the offer as he did. She had no intention of letting him off the hook, though. 'I'd like that very much.'

He grunted and took a step back. With one blink his eyes became as carved-from-rock hard as the rest of him.

'When?' she persisted. 'Now?'

'No.' He strode back to the table. 'Monday afternoons,' he said after a pause. 'At about this time.'

It was Tuesday now. Monday was six whole days away. He'd done that on purpose, she was sure of it. She'd missed out one lesson already if you counted yesterday.

She wanted to stamp a foot in frustration. The glint in his eye told her he knew it too. She forced her lips into a smile instead. 'I'll look forward to it.' Beggars couldn't be choosers, and she now only had six afternoons a week to fill. She didn't want him retracting the offer.

She wondered if she could talk him into two afternoons a week? One look at his face told her to leave it for now.

'Why don't we have our tea outside?' He lifted a tray holding their tea things and Josie had no choice but to follow him back out into the sunshine.

She cut large wedges of cake whilst he poured out mugs of tea. He made no attempt at conversation and, strangely, Josie didn't mind. She watched him instead. He devoured his slice of chocolate cake with the kind of hunger that did strange things to her insides.

Warm, fuzzy things.

She had to glance away when he licked the frosting from his fingers. She cut him another slice then cleared her throat. 'Did you grow up around here?'

'No.'

He physically drew back in his seat, his face shuttered,

and disappointment filtered through her. He didn't want her prying into his background. Though at least she now knew his unique brand of strength wasn't something born and bred into him because he'd grown up out here on Eagle Reach. There was hope for her yet.

He eyed her warily. She smiled back. 'It's only a packet mix.' She motioned to the cake. 'I make a much better one from scratch.'

'It's good.'

His manners were improving, but the wariness didn't leave his eyes. It made her feel…wrong. She couldn't remember making anyone feel wary before. She didn't like the sensation. She searched for something deliberately inconsequential to say. She stared at the cake. Her lips twitched. 'I was sorry I didn't pack hundreds and thousands to sprinkle on top.'

Kent choked.

'But then I figured you probably weren't a hundreds and thousands kind of guy. A chocolate-sprinkle kind of guy maybe, but not hundreds and thousands.'

Kent stared at her. Then his wariness fled. He threw his head back and laughed. It changed him utterly, and it stole Josie's breath.

One thing became brilliantly and dazzlingly clear. She could certainly imagine this incarnation of Kent kissing a woman. She saw it in bright Technicolor vividness.

Seeing it, though, didn't mean she wanted it.

It didn't.

Kent rolled his shoulders, stretching out the aches in his muscles. He'd spent most of the day fixing a broken fence and he was dying for his afternoon cup of tea.

And the rest of that chocolate cake Josie had baked yesterday. He couldn't remember the last time he'd eaten anything quite so satisfying. His stomach grumbled low and long. His mouth watered. He reached out to unlatch the back gate then froze.

'Kent?'

Josie.

He peered over the palings and found her standing on the top step of his house, hand raised to knock on his back door. In her other hand she held a plate of what looked suspiciously like freshly baked biscuits.

His stomach growled again. His mouth watered some more. In the sunlight her hair glowed all the hues of a varnished piece of sandalwood and his stomach clenched. He couldn't believe he'd ever thought it mousy. Anticipation leapt to life in his chest. He reached out to unlatch the gate again when reality crashed around him.

This couldn't happen. He didn't do afternoon tea parties.

You don't do chess lessons either, a wry voice in his head pointed out.

Yeah, well, as soon as he found a way to get out of those you could bet your life he would.

'Kent?'

Her soft contralto voice tugged at him. She turned to survey the surrounding area and with a muffled oath he ducked down behind the fence.

Grown men don't hide behind fences, he told himself. For Pete's sake, what would it hurt to have another cup of tea with her? Yesterday's hadn't killed him.

A scowl shuffled through him. He knew exactly how it would hurt. He'd recognised the loneliness in her eyes. If he had a cup of tea again with her today it'd become a habit. A daily thing. She'd start to rely on him. He scowled down at his work-roughened hands. He wasn't going to let that happen.

He'd seen the flash of awareness in her eyes yesterday. He knew exactly where that would lead, because in the space of a heartbeat desire had thrummed through him in unequivocal response. He'd be an idiot to ignore it.

If he met with Josie Peterson for afternoon tea today, she'd be in his bed by the end of the week.

His skin went hard and tight at the thought.

But he knew women like Josie didn't indulge in affairs.

And men like him didn't offer anything more.

He edged away from the fence and stole back the way he'd come, throbbing with a mixture of guilt and desire. He tried to tell himself this was best for both of them. Somehow, though, the sentiment rang hollow.

A spurt of anger shot through him, lending speed to his feet. Darn her for invading his space. Darn her for invading his refuge.

CHAPTER FOUR

JOSIE woke on Thursday morning to rain. She sat on her tiny veranda in the gaily patterned camp chair she'd bought on her trip into Gloucester yesterday, her hands curled around her morning coffee, and stared out into the greyness. Given half a chance she feared that greyness would invade her.

She dropped a hand to Molly's head. 'It doesn't look like we'll get a walk in today.' That had been the plan—a big hike. Especially since Kent had assured her goannas weren't ferocious carnivores.

The rain put paid to that.

She wondered if the rain affected Kent's work. She wondered if he'd be home if she knocked at his back door with muffins this afternoon.

Was he even OK? She hadn't clapped eyes on him since Tuesday afternoon. What if he'd fallen in some gully and broken his leg? What if a brown snake had bitten him? What if—?

Stop it! He'd lived at Eagle Reach for heaven only knew how many years. He wasn't going to start breaking legs or getting bitten by snakes because she'd shown up. Besides,

Molly would know if something was wrong. Josie glanced down at the dog and bit her lip. She would, wouldn't she?

Face it. Kent just didn't need people the way she did. Yesterday she'd sat in two different cafés in Gloucester's main street, lapping up the noise and bustle along with her coffee. In a few days, when the isolation became too much, she'd do it again.

Not today, though. Today she'd start one of her craft projects—the embroidered cushion, or the latch-hook wall hanging, or the candle-making. Or she could finish reading the newspapers. She'd seized every available paper yesterday and wasn't halfway through them yet. Or she could start reading one of the novels she'd bought. She'd bought six.

She drained her coffee and strode inside, determined to make a decision, but the drab bleakness of the cabin's interior sucked all the energy out of her. It really was horrible. Ugly.

Yesterday, when she hadn't found Kent home, she'd come back here, collapsed into a chair and stared at a wall until the dark had gathered about her and she couldn't see her surroundings any more.

It had frightened her when she finally came back to herself. She didn't want that happening again.

'You know what, Molly?' Molly's tail thumped against the bare floorboards in instant response. 'If I want to stay sane for the next month we're going to have to spend today making this place fit to live in.'

She threw open her suitcase and rifled through its contents, searching for inspiration. Suddenly, she laughed. Sarongs! She'd packed her sarongs.

That was when she'd imagined cabins to mean pretty little cabanas set in lush gardens, encircling a lagoon-style swimming pool. Back when she'd pictured banana loungers and exotic drinks in coconut shells with colourful paper umbrellas sticking out of them at jaunty angles.

She'd pictured comfort and ease. Relaxation. Not bare, lonely landscapes that stretched as wide as the empty places inside her.

She pulled the sarongs out in a hasty rush then switched on her brand-new transistor radio. She tuned it to one of those ubiquitous radio stations that played cheerful, inane pop, twenty-four-seven. She'd push back the greyness. Somehow. And cheerful and inane would do very nicely at the moment, thank you.

'OK.' Josie pulled in a breath. 'Are you ready for the big test?'

Molly wagged her tail.

Josie drank the last of her tea, crossed her fingers and leapt to her feet. She'd worked on the interior of the cabin for hours. Now came the test—to walk through the door and see if it still sucked the lifeblood from her.

Without giving herself any more time to think, Josie strode across the threshold and into the cabin. She held her breath and completed a slow circle. With a sigh of relief, almost a sob, she dropped to her knees and hugged Molly hard. 'Now this is a place I can live in for the next month. What do you say?'

Molly's answer was a wet lick up the side of her face. Laughing, Josie jumped up. OK, what to do for the rest of the day?

Her eyes fell on the notepad on the table. The what-am-I-going-to-do-with-the-rest-of-my-life-and-what-skills-do-I-have? notepad. Her heart dropped, her shoulders sagged. She gulped back a hard ball of panic.

'Muffins.' Her voice held a high edge that stopped

Molly's tail mid-wag. 'Which would your master prefer, do you think? Date and walnut or apple and cinnamon?'

Kent swore when the knock sounded on his back door. He set down the chess piece he was carving and glanced at his watch. Two o'clock.

Four o'clock on Tuesday. Three o'clock yesterday. She wouldn't last the week at this rate.

Good. He clenched his jaw. Josie Peterson was getting as pesky as a darn mosquito. And as persistent. He rubbed the back of his neck. He could always sneak out the front way. She'd never know.

No. She wasn't chasing him out of his house. Another knock sounded. He gritted his teeth. She wasn't worming her way into it either. The sooner he set the ground rules the easier the next month would be. He stormed to the back door and flung it open. As he expected, Josie stood there. The rain had stopped, the sun hadn't come out, but her hair still gleamed like burnished sandalwood, which for some reason irritated him.

'What?' he barked. No pretence at friendliness, no pretence at politeness.

Josie's face fell. He hardened his heart and hated himself for it.

'I, umm…' She moistened her lips. 'I've been baking and I've made too much for one. It seems a shame to waste it all, though. I thought you might like some.'

The aroma of freshly baked muffins mingled with her fresh, fruity fragrance and ploughed straight into his gut. He couldn't remember the last time he'd faced so much temptation. 'You thought wrong,' he snapped.

Strong. He had to stay strong.

Darn it! Those muffins looked good. Dangerously good. Just like her. He had a feeling he could get used to her cooking. If the truth be told, he had a feeling he could get used to her, and that couldn't happen. He'd let her down. The way he'd let—

The gold flecks in her eyes suddenly flashed. 'You didn't mind the chocolate cake the other day.' Her chin quivered when she stuck it out. 'We had a very pleasant half an hour over that cake.'

Precisely. Which was why it wasn't going to happen again. 'Look, Ms Peterson—'

'Josie.'

'I am not your nursemaid. I am not your friend. I am the man you've rented a cabin from for a month and that's as far as our association goes, got it?'

Her eyes widened at his bluntness. Her mouth worked. 'Don't you get lonely?' she finally blurted out.

'Nope.' Not any more. Not most of the time anyway.

'So how do you do it?' She lifted the plate of muffins as if they could provide an answer. 'How do you manage to live out here all on your own and not mind?'

He could see it wasn't idle curiosity. She wanted to know. Needed to know, maybe. He supposed he'd started off much the same way she was now.

Not the searching out of human contact. He'd shunned that from the start. But he'd carved and whittled wood the way she baked. He'd kept himself busy with cattle and cabins and carving until the days had taken on a shape of their own.

So he didn't need the likes of her coming around here now and disrupting it. Making him ache for things that couldn't be.

She shook her head. 'You can't be human.'

He wished that were true.

'We all need people.'

'Believe me, some needy fly-by-night is not essential to my well-being.'

She paled at his words and he loathed himself all the more. His resolve started to waver and weaken. 'What do you see happening between us?' he snapped out. 'You'll be gone in a month.' Probably less. That thought steeled his determination again.

'Friends?' she whispered.

He laughed, a harsh sound that scraped out of his throat leaving it raw. He had to get rid of her. She could capture a man with those sad, gold-flecked eyes and the soft curve of her lips. It'd all end in tears. Her tears. Then he'd really hate himself.

She took one step back, then another, her face white. 'You are a piece of work, you know that?'

Yep. It wasn't news to him. But Josie wasn't cut out for all this. 'Try the general store in Martin's Gully.' He nodded at the plate in her hand. 'They might be interested in placing an order or two with you.'

Liz Perkins would take Josie under her ample, matronly wing. It'd do both of them the world of good. On that thought, he slammed the door in Josie's face before guilt got the better of him and he hauled her inside and tried to make amends.

Josie stalked back to her cabin, quivering all over with outrage. She ranted in incoherent half-sentences to Molly.

'Of all the arrogant assumptions! Needy fly-by-night? Who does he think he is?'

She slammed the plate to the kitchen bench and paced. Ha! At least she'd eradicated his grey presence from her cabin. Satisfaction shot through her when she surveyed the changes she'd made.

'And he needn't think I'm going to sit around here all afternoon and moon about it either.'

Molly whined and pushed her nose against Josie's hand. Josie dropped to her knees and scratched Molly's ears. 'I'm sorry, girl. It's not your fault. You're lovely and loyal and sweet and too good for the likes of him. It's not your fault you drew the short straw when it came to masters.'

Molly rolled onto her back and groaned with pleasure when Josie scratched her tummy. 'You're gorgeous and beautiful.'

Her fingers brushed the scar that zigzagged across Molly's abdomen and she stilled. 'I don't get him at all.' She meant to take his advice, though.

It took exactly twelve and a half minutes to reach the tiny township of Martin's Gully. It wasn't exactly a blink-and-miss town, but it wasn't far from it. It had, at the most, two-dozen houses, though it boasted its own tiny wooden church. Completing the picture was a post office that, according to the sign in its window, opened two and a half days a week, and Perkins' General Store.

Josie pushed through the door of the latter then waited for her eyes to adjust to the dimness. She blinked as the size of the interior came into focus. Bags of feed grain competed with tools for floor space on her left. Bolts of material lined the wall. On her right, shelves full of tinned food and every known grocery item arced away from her. Down the middle sat an old-fashioned freezer. The store smelt dry and dusty and good.

'Can I help you?' a thin, middle-aged woman hailed her from behind the counter at the rear of the room.

Someone with a smile. Josie hastened towards her. 'Hi, I'm Josie Peterson. I'm staying at Eagle Reach for the next few weeks.'

'Bridget Anderson.' Her eyes narrowed as she shook Josie's proffered hand. 'Ain't Eagle Reach Kent Black's place?'

Josie nodded. She'd have thought everyone in Martin's Gully would know everybody else's business. Maybe Kent Black maintained an unfriendly distance with the folk in town too?

As if reading her mind, the other woman leaned in closer. 'This is my sister's store. I'm helping out for a bit.'

Another newcomer? Fellow feeling rushed through Josie.

'Lizzie's husband, Ted, died back in November.'

'Oh, that's awful.'

'And she won't have a word said against Kent Black.'

Really? Josie tried to stop her eyebrows from shooting straight up into her hairline. So, Kent had at least one friend in town, did he?

Bridget's face darkened. 'Me, on the other hand…'

'He's very solitary,' Josie offered, she hoped tactfully.

Bridget snorted. 'Downright unfriendly if you ask me.'

She recalled Kent's black glare. Ooh, yes, she'd agree. Not that she had any intention of saying so, of course.

'Though a body can understand it, what with all that tragedy in his past and all.'

'Tragedy?' The word slipped out before she could help it.

'Aye. His father tried to murder the entire family in their beds as they slept. Set fire to the house in the wee hours of the morning. Kent was the only one that got out. It claimed his mother and sister, his father too.'

Josie's jaw dropped. The room spun. She gripped the

counter top for support. 'That's…that's one of the most awful things I've ever heard.'

'Aye. The father was a violent man, from all accounts.'

What accounts?

'You wanna hear the worst of it?'

No, she didn't. She'd heard enough. But she couldn't move to shake her head. She'd frozen to a block of ice.

'Kent had taken the mother and sister to live with him, to protect them. Didn't work out, though, did it?'

Bile rose in Josie's throat. No wonder Kent scowled and growled and hid away as he did. To lose his entire family in such an awful way.

She promptly forgave him every unfriendly scowl, each clipped word and all the times he'd turned away without so much as a backward glance. But was burying yourself away from the entire human race the answer? She remembered the way he'd tucked into her chocolate cake. She bet he was hungry for a whole lot more than flour and sugar.

Bridget opened her mouth to add what Josie imagined would be more lurid details, so she quickly peeled the lid off her container and held it out, hastily changing the subject. 'I was wondering if there'd be a market for any home-baked goodies around here at all?'

Bridget's nose quivered appreciatively. She reached in, seized a muffin and greedily devoured it. 'Mmm… We can see how they go, love.' She brushed crumbs off her fingers. 'You never know what'll happen once word gets around.' Her eyes narrowed. 'But if you're only here on holiday, what you doing cookin'?'

Josie gulped. She didn't want to be the latest object of Bridget's gossip. 'It's a hobby,' she lied. 'I wanted to try out some new recipes while I had the time, that's all.'

Bridget helped herself to another muffin. 'What are your other specialities?'

'What do you think would sell well?'

'Caramel slice, homemade shortbread, lemon meringue pie.'

She wondered if Bridget was merely reciting her own list of favourites.

'The church fête is on Sunday. We're always looking for goodies to sell. Why don't you make up a few batches of whatever you like and see how they go over?'

If Josie had ears like Molly they'd have immediately pricked forward. A church fête? This Sunday? That gave her something to do over the weekend. Time suddenly didn't hang quite so heavily about her. 'That sounds like fun.'

'Lizzie and me, we're manning our own stall. Would you like to join us, love?'

Would she what? 'It sounds lovely.'

'Have you ever made a Mars-bar slice? Give it a go,' she advised when Josie shook her head. 'It'll be a real winner.'

Josie's lips twitched as Bridget reached for a third muffin. From where she was standing, the feedback was already pretty positive. At this rate there wouldn't be any muffins left for the rest of Martin's Gully to sample.

That was OK. She'd bake more for Sunday.

But as she drove back to Eagle's Reach it wasn't church fêtes or muffin and slice recipes that wove through her mind, but the awful history Bridget had related about Kent. More than anything, she found herself wishing she could do something for him. Something more than chocolate cake.

CHAPTER FIVE

FRIDAY morning Josie drove into Gloucester, stocked up on supplies and bought a recipe book.

Friday afternoon she and Molly went for a big walk. Kent was right. The trails leading down to the river really were very pretty. Not that she had a chance to tell him. She didn't clap eyes on him.

Friday night she made toffee and rum balls.

Saturday morning she made muffins, caramel slice, a Mars-bar slice and cooked chocolate cake from scratch.

Saturday afternoon she found a tick at her waist.

She promptly sat, took a deep breath and tried to remember her first aid. She was an AIN, for heaven's sake, an Assistant in Nursing. She gulped, but her mind went blank. Her kind of nursing hadn't involved ticks. It had involved watching her father die.

She peeled back the waistband of her shorts and stared at the tick again. She must've picked it up on her walk yesterday. It wriggled. Ugh. She hastily folded the waistband back into place. What if there were more? What if she was covered in ticks?

The entire surface of her skin started to itch.

'Don't be ridiculous,' she said out loud. But panic and

adrenaline surged through her. Did adrenaline do anything to ticks? She gulped. It probably turned them into super-ticks or something.

'Oh, get a grip.'

Molly whined and rested her head on Josie's lap. Josie stared down at the trusting brown eyes and stiffened. What if Molly had ticks too? How did you get ticks off a dog? She surged to her feet. She'd have to ask Kent.

Josie was proud of herself for not racing as fast as she could for Kent's back door and pounding on it with both fists. She made herself walk at an even pace, a quick even pace, and when she reached his door she raised her hand and knocked twice. A quick rat-tat.

His frown was the first thing she registered. She raised her hand before he could say something sharp and cutting. 'I just want to ask a quick question, that's all. It won't take long, I swear.'

'Well?' he snapped when she paused.

'What…what is the treatment for ticks?'

Kent stared at her for a moment. The dark blue eyes did strange things to her insides as they roamed across her face. With a smothered oath, he seized her elbow and pulled her inside.

'Where?' he demanded, letting her go and planting his hands on his hips.

'Please check Molly first. She's smaller than me and I hear ticks can do nasty things to dogs.' Awful, terrible things like paralysis and…and worse.

'They can do nasty things to humans too.'

When Josie folded her hands flat against her stomach and said nothing, he raised his eyes to the ceiling. 'Molly will be fine. I give her a monthly tablet.'

Josie sagged. Relief pounded through her. 'Thank heavens. I'd thought…' The rest of her words dried up in her throat as Kent continued to stare at her.

'Where is this tick?'

She had a sudden vision of his strong, tanned fingers on her flesh and her pulse started to pound. 'If you, umm, just tell me what I should do I'll take care of it. I don't mean to put you out or anything.'

She didn't think she wanted Kent touching her. She had a feeling it'd be a whole lot safer for her peace of mind if he didn't. His lips twitched as if he knew exactly what she was thinking, and Josie's heart hammered all the way into her throat and back again.

'What you need to do, Josie, is point to the tick.'

Her name rolled off his tongue, thick and sweet like golden syrup. It turned her insides thick and syrupy too.

The twitch of his lips became a kind of half-grin. 'Trust me.' He waggled his fingers. 'I'm a doctor.'

'Yeah, right.' The one thing she did trust was that he wholly enjoyed her discomfort. She remembered what Bridget had said the day before yesterday and surrendered with a sigh. 'Here.' She peeled back the waistband of her shorts to show him.

He crouched down beside her, his fingers gentle on her skin as he turned her towards the light. Then he leapt up, grabbed a jar of Vaseline from beneath the sink, crouched down beside her again and swiped a generous glob of the ointment across the tick's body.

'Vaseline?' Her voice was breathy. She wondered if he felt the leap of her blood against his fingertips. Oh, boy. She'd known there were areas of her life she'd neglected in the last few months, but this was ridiculous.

'Ticks breathe through their rear-ends. It can't breathe through the Vaseline, so it'll work its way out. Then I'll pick it off with these.' He held up a pair of tweezers. 'It means there's little chance of the head breaking off.'

She gulped. 'Good.' She didn't want the tick leaving any of its body parts behind, thank you. She didn't want to know what would happen if it did either.

'Do you have any more?'

His words cut through a fog that seemed to have descended around her brain. 'More ticks?'

His lips twitched again. 'Yes.'

'Oh, umm.' She shrugged. 'I don't know.'

'Spin for me.'

She did. His finger trailed across the bare flesh of her waist as she turned, making her suck in a breath.

'All clear there, now sit.' He pushed her into a kitchen chair. 'Ticks, like most other living creatures, choose warm, protected places to live.'

'Uh-huh.' It was about as much as she could manage.

'Like behind the ears and at the nape of the neck.'

He brushed her hair to one side and it was all she could do not to melt against him as his fingers moved across said areas. Up this close his heat buffeted her. As did his hot man scent, a combination of wood and wood smoke and freshly cut grass. She wanted to breathe him in and never stop.

Crazy thought. Nerves skittered through her. 'Thank you for the tip about taking my muffins into the general store.' She knew she was about to start babbling, but she needed to distract herself somehow and babbling seemed relatively innocuous, given the alternatives racing through her mind.

'Did you meet Liz Perkins?'

She seized the question as a verbal lifeline and tried for all she was worth to erect some kind of metaphorical wall between them. 'Umm, no.'

The metaphorical-wall thing wasn't working. It did nothing to assuage the sensations that pounded through her when he swept her hair across the other side of her neck. She closed her eyes and bit back a groan.

'Liz wasn't there.' Concentrate, she ordered herself. 'I met her sister, Bridget.'

Kent's humph told her exactly what he thought of Bridget.

She didn't blame him. Not when she recalled how eager Bridget had been to impart her information. Guilt squirmed through her. She'd listened, hadn't she?

'I'm going to the church fête on Sunday,' she rushed on quickly. 'Tomorrow.' Sunday was tomorrow, she reminded herself. Though, with Kent standing this close, she wouldn't swear to it. She wouldn't swear which way was up.

His fingers stilled. 'Is that why you're cooking up a storm?'

'Uh-huh.' How'd he know she was cooking up a storm?

'The smells have been wafting up the hill,' he said as if she'd asked the question out loud. His fingers moved across her neck again. 'It smells good.'

'What's your favourite sweet treat?' If he told her she'd make it for him. As a thank-you, nothing more. She certainly wouldn't make the mistake of expecting him to share it or anything.

'Why?'

She winced at the sudden harsh note in his voice. 'No reason, just looking for inspiration,' she lied. 'Bridget asked me to make a Mars-bar slice.'

He finished checking her neck and she breathed a sigh of relief when he moved away, but only for a moment, as he almost immediately crouched down beside her to check the tick at her waist again.

'It needs a couple more minutes.'

He moved off abruptly to a chair opposite, and, contrarily, Josie missed the warmth of his hands, the touch of his breath against her flesh.

His eyes narrowed on her face. 'You feel OK? Any nausea or wooziness?'

'No.' Unbalanced by his touch, maybe, but she had a feeling that was not what he meant.

'So, Bridget has roped you into all that baking?'

'No.' She lifted her chin. Not everyone found her company abhorrent. 'She and Liz are manning a stall and I'm going to help.'

He gave a short laugh. 'She's an opportunist, that one. I'll give her that.'

'I wanted to do it.' But then she recalled how Bridget had said more muffins would go down a treat, not to mention a chocolate cake. And that if Josie had time, maybe she could come by early and help them set up the trestle table for the stall too.

She shook her head impatiently. It didn't matter. She wanted to help. It'd be fun. The knowing twist of his lips, though, irked her. 'Are you going?'

'Me? You're joking, right?'

'Why not?' She lifted her hands. 'This is a tiny community. You should support it.'

'By letting the Bridgets of the town get their claws into me? No, thank you very much. I've far better things to do on a Sunday than be hounded into helping set up stalls and manning the chocolate wheel.'

Like what? she wanted to ask. She didn't, though. She

didn't dare. 'I think it'll be fun. It's not like you'd have to do anything. Just…'

'Just what?' he mocked.

'Just take part,' she snapped back.

Then wished she hadn't as everything she'd found out about Kent yesterday rose up inside her. Her stomach burned acid. 'You're right. Bridget is a terrible gossip. But it doesn't necessarily follow that she's a bad person. And not everyone in Martin's Gully is like that, surely?'

His eyes darkened and narrowed in on her in the space of a heartbeat.

Josie flushed and twisted her hands together. She knew precisely how guilty she looked. 'Bridget told me what happened to your mother and sister,' she blurted out.

Kent reared back as if her words had slapped him. His face paled. Dark red slashed his cheekbones. 'She had no right—'

'No, she didn't,' Josie hastily agreed. 'No right at all.' She wanted to reach out and touch him, but was too afraid to. 'I'm sorry. What happened to them…' She lifted her hands again. 'It must've been the most awful thing in the world.' His eyes glittered dangerously. 'I'm sorry,' she repeated. She wanted to say so much more but didn't have the words for it.

He stared at her as if he didn't know what to say. She didn't know what to say either.

His gaze dropped to her waist. 'That tick should be ready to come out now.'

Before she was aware of it, he'd tweezered it out.

'Thank you.' Her breath hitched at his nearness. She rose and took a hasty step back. 'Would you like me to bring you anything from the fête?'

'Like?'

'I don't know.' She had an awful feeling she was babbling again. 'Maybe you have a secret yearning for Mrs Elwood's tomato chutney or Mr Smith's home-produced honey?'

'There aren't any Mrs Elwoods in Martin's Gully.'

'Any Mr Smiths?'

'Several, but none of them are beekeepers.'

She edged towards his back door. 'So, no tomato chutney or honey, then?'

'No, thank you.'

'OK.' She practically fell down the back steps. 'Goodnight, then.'

'Josie.'

She turned back, her heart thumping.

'I…'

She held her breath, but she hardly knew what she was waiting for.

'You need to shower. You need to check under your arms and behind your knees. Anywhere a tick might get.'

'OK.' She waited but when he didn't add anything else she gave a tiny wave then fled.

Josie left early the next morning. Kent knew because he watched. His lips drew back from his teeth in a grimace. So Bridget Anderson had roped Josie into setting up the stall, huh?

He remembered the way Josie had hugged Molly that first day. He remembered the feel of her curves pressed against him as she'd slid out of that tree and down his body. He shook his head and called himself every kind of idiot he could think of. Josie Peterson could look after herself. She wasn't his responsibility.

'Go check the cattle,' he growled out loud. At least they were something he was responsible for.

Not that checking the cattle required much effort. More a case of checking the levels in the water troughs, checking the fences, making sure the steers hadn't picked up an injury or were showing signs of disease.

Checking the cattle took less than an hour.

He wondered how Josie was finding the fête. He bet her goodies sold fast. He bet Bridget Anderson had her stuck behind that stall all day. He bet she wouldn't even get a chance to buy a ticket in the chocolate wheel.

Josie would like the chocolate wheel.

For Pete's sake! 'Go clean the cabins.'

He grabbed the bucket of cleaning supplies and an ancient wooden broom. He averted his gaze as he stalked past Josie's cabin. His nostrils flared, though, and he imagined, if he took a deep enough breath, her fresh, fruity fragrance would fill his lungs.

He held his breath and tried to banish her from his mind.

By lunchtime he'd finished cleaning the cabins. Every surface gleamed with fresh-scrubbed cleanliness. Just as they had before he'd started.

He averted his gaze as he stalked past her cabin again, but he remembered the way her eyes had filled with a soft light when she'd told him how sorry she was about his mother and sister. He couldn't doubt her sincerity. He'd wanted to rage and stamp and throw things, but that soft light in her eyes had held him still.

Nobody in Martin's Gully, not even Liz Perkins, had dared mention his past. He hadn't encouraged them to. He hadn't confided in a single soul. But they all knew what had happened and they skirted around the subject, skirted around him. Not Josie, though. He couldn't help but admire her honesty, her guts.

Her generosity.

A generosity he didn't doubt Bridget Anderson was taking advantage of right now.

He stowed away the broom and bucket then glanced around the kitchen. Darn it! He jammed his hat on his head and grabbed his car keys. He had a sudden craving for tomato chutney and honey. He refused to acknowledge any more than that.

Kent spotted Josie straight away, sitting all by herself at the far end of a row of trestle tables. Her hair gleamed, but her shoulders sagged. The rest of the town congregated on the opposite side of the field around a flatbed truck for the traditional auction. He bit back an oath, adjusted the brim of his hat and headed towards her.

Her eyes widened when he strode up. 'Kent! What are you doing here? I mean…' She glanced away then back again as if trying to moderate her surprise. 'I didn't think this was your thing.'

'I'm all out of tomato chutney and honey,' he muttered.

She smiled then, and it kicked him right in the gut. With a flourish, she waved her arm across the table. 'Can I tempt you with any of our goodies?'

Our? He recognised Liz's gramma pies and choko pickles, but he'd bet Josie had contributed the rest. 'How long have you been stuck behind there?'

Her smile slipped. 'It doesn't matter. I'm sure once the auction is over Bridget will be back and—'

'You haven't moved from there all morning, have you? You haven't even had a chance to look around yet?'

'There's still plenty of time.'

'Have you had lunch?' he barked.

She started to laugh. 'I'm being punished for skipping breakfast. Smell that,' she ordered. She pulled in a big breath and he practically saw her start to salivate. 'They've set up a sausage sizzle behind the church hall and all I can smell is frying onions. It's pure torture.'

He could tell she was only joking, but a surge of anger shot through him. Bloody Bridget. 'Where's Liz?'

'Sick.'

Sick of her sister, he'd bet.

Josie's skin was pale and he could see it starting to turn pink in the sun. She'd erected a canopy to shelter the food, but not one for herself.

'C'mon.' He waved a hand, practically ordering her out from behind the trestle table.

'I can't leave.'

'Why not? Everyone else has.'

'But…but I told Bridget I'd man the fort and…then there's the money tin and—'

'Give it to me.'

'But…'

He reached over and took it, placing it firmly in the middle of the table. 'Now seems to me you've done your share. If Bridget wants the stall manned, she'll come back when she sees it's empty. Right then, see that weeping willow down by the river?' He pointed and she nodded. 'Grab us something,' he nodded at the table, 'and meet me down there.'

'I can't just take something.'

'Why not? You cooked it.'

She drew herself up. 'It's for charity!'

He laughed at the outrage plastered across her face.

Josie Peterson made him feel light years younger. He fished out a twenty-dollar note from his pocket, held it out for her to see then put it into the money tin.

Her jaw dropped. 'That's too much.'

'It's for charity, isn't it?'

She stared then laughed, and it throbbed through him in all the places he shouldn't be thinking about.

'So, you're pretty hungry, huh?'

'Starved.' And it'd take a whole lot more than sugar to satisfy his cravings.

'The weeping willow?'

'The weeping willow,' he agreed.

With that he turned and headed straight across the field before he could pull Josie over the trestle table and kiss her.

When she reached the tree, Josie had to admit Kent had chosen a pretty spot for a picnic. The river slid by, silver and silent, meditative. It soothed the sore, bruised places inside her. She wondered if it did the same for Kent. Maybe that was why he chose to bury himself out here.

Settling on the grass beneath the tree, she welcomed the shade and the almost hypnotic sway of fronds in the breeze, and wondered about her unusual rescue. And her even more unusual rescuer.

Kent, carrying sausage sandwiches and cans of lemonade, appeared and Josie's hunger momentarily overrode her other concerns. 'Mmm.' She closed her eyes and savoured her first bite. 'This is fabulous.' When she opened them again she found Kent staring at her strangely. She suddenly remembered her manners. 'Thank you.'

'You're welcome.'

The faded blue of his chambray shirt highlighted the

brilliant blue of his eyes. The snug fit of his jeans highlighted the firmness of his thighs. The sudden shortness of Josie's breath highlighted her heretofore unknown partiality for firm thigh muscles encased in faded denim.

'I, umm…' She dragged her gaze upwards. 'Thank you for rescuing me…again.' That seemed to be becoming a habit.

'Not a problem.'

Oh, dear. She obviously had a partiality for firm lips and chiselled jaws too. She dragged her gaze to the river and tried to recreate the peace it had invoked in her only moments ago. She ate the rest of her sausage sandwich in silence.

Three ducks, small, brown and dappled, paddled by; bellbirds started up on the other bank. She pulled in a breath and her tension eased out of her, but her awareness for the man opposite didn't.

'When I look at all this,' she motioned to the river, 'I can see why you live out here. It's beautiful.'

'Yep.' A pause. 'You can't imagine living out here yourself?'

'No.' And she couldn't. Too much of it frightened her, even as she admired the starkness of its beauty.

'A city girl at heart?'

She glanced at him sharply, but no scorn or censure marred the perfect blue of his eyes. 'No, not a city girl.' Though she could more easily imagine living in a city than at Eagle Reach. 'I live in a sleepy little town on the coast about three hours north from here.' Her whole frame lightened when she thought of it. 'It's beautiful. Especially at this time of year.' When summer merged into autumn, the days still warm but the nights cool.

'If it's so pretty there, what are you doing here?'

Good question. Sadness and a thread of something

harsher—anger?—trickled through her. She quashed it. 'My father died. He'd suffered from dementia for a few years. I was his full-time carer. I needed to get away for a bit.'

But somewhere nice. Somewhere she could close her eyes and breathe more freely. Not somewhere that scared her half out of her wits in one instant then stole her breath with its beauty the next. And she hadn't wanted to be shipped off for a whole month. A week would've done.

She gulped. She was an ungrateful wretch.

Kent reached out and covered her hand with his. 'That must've been hard.'

She nodded, her throat thickening with unshed tears at the kindness reflected in the deep blue of his eyes. She could see he understood her grief.

Dear heavens above, of course he did!

She gazed back out at the river, determined not to cry, but as the warmth of his hand stole through her her heart started to pound. She glanced up at him and her mouth went dry. Did he feel it too?

As if in answer, his hand tightened over hers. Exhilaration sped through her when his eyes narrowed on her lips, then desire—hot and hard and relentless. Three feet separated them and she wanted that gap closed, fast. Needed it. She couldn't remember craving a man's touch so intently. She wanted to lose herself in him and not come up for air.

Gripped by forces greater than common sense, Josie swayed towards him, lips parted. Time freeze-framed and lost all meaning, except in the way it sharpened all her senses. Every single muscle ached to meld itself against him. Her fingers, her palm, hungered to caress the dark shading at his jaw. She wanted to breathe in his hot male scent, she wanted to wrap her arms around his neck and slide her fingers through the crisp darkness of his hair.

Hunger flared in his eyes. Her own blood quickened in response. Then, with a tiny shake of his head, he removed his hand and sat back, his mouth a grim line as he stared out at the river. Disappointment flooded her, filling her mouth with the acrid taste of its bitterness.

Embarrassment quickly followed. 'I, umm… Dessert?'

She seized the bag of goodies like a lifeline. 'I didn't know what you felt like so I grabbed a couple of pieces of caramel slice, half a dozen oatmeal biscuits and a slice each of lemon meringue pie and chocolate cake.'

As she named each item she pulled the appropriate paper plate out of the bag and lined them up between them. His twenty dollars deserved a whole lot more than this, but she couldn't have carried anything else. 'I mean, you could've had carrot cake or muffins,' she babbled on, scrunching the plastic carrier bag into a tiny ball and squeezing it. 'But if you'd prefer something else then I'm sure…'

He reached across and halted her movements. The rest of her words dried up in her throat. Her stupid pulse fluttered in her throat.

'It wouldn't have been a good idea.'

She knew he wasn't talking about cake. He was talking about kissing her. She nodded, her throat tight. 'I know.'

He drew back. 'What do you want?' He motioned to the plates.

She seized the oatmeal biscuits, more for something to do, than because she was hungry. Her hunger had fled.

Her hunger for food, that was.

Stop thinking about it!

She flung a glance over her shoulder, searching for

something, anything, and her jaw dropped at the size of the crowd milling in the field behind her. 'Where did they all come from?'

Kent glanced up then shrugged and stretched out on his side. 'I'd heard the fête took off in the afternoon. The folk of Gloucester have caught wind of it in the last few years.'

She glanced at him and tried not to notice how the lean angles of his body stretched out like an invitation. 'Why?'

'A couple of the local specialities have started making names for themselves,' he said, peeling plastic wrap from around the chocolate cake.

Her ears pricked up. 'Like?' She shuffled around on her knees to watch the crowd. Lots of people, lots of laughter—it loosened the knots inside her.

'You mean besides tomato chutney and honey?'

She glanced at him then laughed. So, scowling-don't-get-too-close-to-me Kent could crack a joke…and grin while he did it. She could grow to like this Kent. A lot. 'So, I was on the money with my guess, huh?'

'If you substitute the chutney for Liz's choko pickles then yes.'

His smile crinkled the lines around his eyes. Her stomach flip-flopped.

'They're famous and with some cause. Nothing beats a silverside and choko pickle sandwich.'

She filed that for future reference.

'Except maybe this!' His eyes bugged as he chewed chocolate cake. 'Jeez, Josie.' He stared at her, half in admiration, half in consternation. 'This is…'

'Good?'

'Better than good.'

'I told you I made a better one from scratch.'

He chuckled at the smug toss of her head and her stomach flip-flopped more.

'What else should I be on the look-out for?'

'Chloe Isaac's homemade soap. Popular opinion is divided between the granulated strawberry bar and the smooth lemon myrtle.'

'Ooh, yum. I'm getting both.' She pointed an accusing finger at him, but kept her eyes on the crowd. 'That's the sort of thing you should put in the cabins. People would love it.' She sent him a sly glance. 'What about the honey? Famous too?'

He polished off the rest of the cake with a grin. 'I'll introduce you to our local beekeeper, old Fraser Todd. He'll sell you a pot of honey fresh from the hive with a piece of the honeycomb still in it. You'll never taste anything like it,' he promised.

Her mouth watered. She pushed the plate of biscuits towards him. She'd better save her appetite.

'You think I need fattening up or something?'

'You were the one who said you were hungry. You've still a slice of lemon meringue pie and a couple of pieces of caramel slice to go yet.'

'I'll save them for later.' He nodded towards the stalls with their crowds clustered around them. 'Besides, I'd have thought you'd be eager to get us out amongst them, fighting for all the goodies before they're gone.'

She loved the way he said 'us'; it meant he intended to hang around for a bit. Her blood did a funny little dance through her veins, which she tried to ignore. She lifted a hand that encompassed the scene before her. 'I'm enjoying all this first.'

'Enjoying what?'

'Watching the people having fun, hearing them laugh. It's what I meant when I told Marty and Frank I wanted a break.'

Kent stilled, mid-munch. Carefully, he chewed and swallowed the rest of his biscuit. 'Don't you want to be a part of it?'

'Eventually.' She didn't take her eyes off the crowd, lapping it all up like a starving dog. 'But I'm happy to savour it all first. Ooh, an artist is setting up.'

'She's one of our best-kept secrets.'

Kent collected up the uneaten goodies and placed them back in the bag, then, with his face gentle, offered Josie his hand. 'C'mon, why don't I show you the cream of the town's offerings?'

Josie was more than happy to place her hand in Kent's tanned, capable one and be pulled to her feet, more than ready to become one with the laughing, happy crowd.

CHAPTER SIX

'YOU should be ashamed of yourself,' Josie chided a couple of hours later, collapsing at a picnic table.

'Ashamed of myself?'

What the...? He'd made a sterling effort to play the sociable companion to Josie over the afternoon. What was more, he thought he'd succeeded.

Not that it'd been an effort. No effort at all. It had earned him more than one speculative glance from more than one local, though. Not that he cared. Their gossip couldn't touch him and Josie would be gone in three weeks, so it couldn't hurt her either.

Three weeks. And don't you forget it, he warned himself. He eased his long legs beneath the table to sit opposite her when he had a feeling what he should be doing was getting to his feet and running in the opposite direction.

Fast.

He couldn't. When Josie had made her remarkable declaration about what she really wanted from her holiday—her eyes hungry on the crowd, those peculiarly restful hands of hers folded against her knees and a tendril of weeping willow playing across her shoulder and catching in her hair—he'd gained a sudden insight into all she'd given up when she'd taken on the role of carer to her father.

She didn't need a holiday stuck halfway up a mountain. She needed people, she needed to feel connected again. She needed images of life and laughter to help mitigate the recent images of sickness and death. He understood that. And he cursed her brothers for not seeing it.

He couldn't help that she was stuck halfway up a mountain, but he had taken it upon himself to make sure she enjoyed the fête today. And that no one, including that witch Bridget Anderson, took advantage of her generosity. Now here she was, telling him he should be ashamed of himself? So much for gratitude.

'Why?' he demanded, irked more than he wanted to admit.

She spread her arms wide and he found himself wanting to walk straight into them. He scowled. 'What?'

'Look at the wealth of all this local produce.'

He reckoned she'd bought just about every example of it too. That made him grin. Her delight in the smallest of things had touched him. 'And?'

'With all this available at your fingertips, how could you possibly make such a sorry job on those cabins?'

'Sorry job!' His jaw dropped. He jabbed the air between them with a finger. 'I know Eagle Reach isn't exactly the Ritz, but—'

Her snort cut him short. 'You can say that again.'

'Look, you're not my usual grade of clientele.'

She leaned forward. 'I know you keep saying the cabins attract the tough, rugged outdoor types, but really…' She leaned back, arms outspread again.

He wished she'd stop doing that. 'What?' He lifted a hand. 'What?' The cabins were perfectly…adequate.

'Would it really be such an effort to make them a little more inviting?'

She had to be joking, right?

'Even rough, rugged outdoor types like something nice to come home to after all that hiking and fishing or whatever it is rough, rugged outdoor types do.'

'So…so you want me to put strawberry-scented soap in the bathrooms,' he spluttered, 'and…and frangipani-scented candles in the living rooms?' It'd make him a laughing stock.

'Maybe not the strawberry soap,' she allowed. 'That might not be a big hit with your tough types, but what about the mint and eucalyptus soap, huh? It'd add a bit of local colour and wouldn't threaten anyone's masculinity. What's wrong with that? It's a nice touch.'

She folded her arms and glared at him. He folded his arms and glared back.

'A couple of Mrs Gower's rag rugs wouldn't go astray either.'

Rugs!

'Not to mention a painting or two.'

OK, so the cabins were bare. He'd admit that much.

'And I know you're not a fruit and flowers kind of guy—'

It was his turn to snort. 'You can say that again.'

'But,' she persisted, 'a jar of Mr Todd's honey and Liz's choko pickles would be a friendly gesture. To the town as well as the guests.'

He wished he could ignore the way the gold flecks in her eyes flashed when she got all fired up, or the way her pretty little chin pointed at him, angling her lips in a way that made his mouth water.

Not good. He shouldn't be thinking about kissing her. He clenched his hands beneath the table to stop from reaching out and grabbing that pretty little chin in his fingers and slanting his lips over hers. Heck, that'd get the gossips' tongues wagging.

'You know what?'

'What?' The word growled out of him from between teeth that were likewise clenched. Fortunately, or unfortunately, his gruffness didn't so much as make her blink any more.

'I think you're afraid of making those cabins too home-like.'

He jerked back.

'I think you're afraid to make any place too much like home.'

Something started to thud painfully in his chest. He tried to throw her words off, but found he couldn't. 'All this because I like simple and plain?' he snapped.

Not so much as a blink. 'Either that or you're afraid of making them so nice that you'll have to share your mountain with all of the repeat business you'd get.'

The thudding eased to an ache at her teasing.

'You could be on to something, lass. Our Kent here doesn't like to share his solitude.'

Kent jumped up, pleasure lighting through him at the sight of Clancy Whitehall's dancing dark eyes and thatch of white hair. He helped the elderly man to a seat. 'Clancy, this is Josie Peterson. She's staying at Eagle Reach for a few weeks.'

'A pleasure. Clancy Whitehall.' He introduced himself before Kent had a chance. His dark eyes danced across Josie's face as he shook her hand. 'I have the dubious distinction of being Martin's Gully's oldest resident.'

Josie broke into one of those grins that hit Kent square in the gut. 'Pleased to meet you, Mr Whitehall.'

'Call me Clancy, please. Mr Whitehall was my father.'

Josie laughed, her eyes darting to Kent's to share her delight. Kent could've groaned out loud when Clancy followed the movement. The old man was as sharp as all get out and Kent didn't like the speculation suddenly rife in the older man's eyes. Or the smile that curved his lips.

'Have you lived in Martin's Gully all your life, Clancy?'

'Aye, lass.'

'I bet you've some stories you could tell.'

Kent could see Josie would love to hear each and every one of them.

'That I could.' Clancy's gaze darted from Josie to Kent and back again. 'How are you finding the hospitality at Eagle Reach?'

Josie's lips twitched and her eyes met Kent's again. 'Improving.'

Great. Wonderful. He knew exactly what Clancy would make of that.

As expected, Clancy raised a telling eyebrow and Kent found himself leaping to his feet. He didn't care what the gossips like Bridget Anderson thought, but he did care what Clancy thought. And he wanted Clancy to unthink it right now.

'Kent?'

Josie's breathy whisper brought him back. 'It's time I was going.' He pulled the brim of his hat down low on his forehead. 'I want to check on Liz before I head back.'

'I hear she's poorly. Give her my love.'

Kent nodded then strode off, though he didn't know whose gaze burned through him the hotter—Clancy's or Josie's.

* * *

Josie pulled her gaze from Kent's rigid, rapidly retreating back and smiled at Clancy.

Clancy's eyes were knowing. He nodded after Kent. 'He's a good lad.'

Good? Lad? More like maddening man. Not that that did justice to the clamour Kent created inside her either, but she nodded all the same. Kent obviously looked out for Clancy and she had to give him credit for that. In fact, it was right neighbourly of him. 'He saved me from a day of servitude behind one of the stalls.' That was right neighbourly too.

Clancy chuckled. 'Bridget Anderson got her claws into you, did she? She's a managing kind of woman, that one. Likes to run things. She should've gone into politics.'

Josie laughed at the idea, but it was perfect. She wondered if Clancy could come up with a vocation as appropriate for her?

'How are you enjoying your holiday at Eagle Reach?'

Her hesitation betrayed her. 'I… It's a bit lonely.' She shrugged. 'I mean, it is beautiful—the bush, the river, and I've never seen night skies quite like it.' She didn't want Clancy thinking she didn't appreciate it. 'I just… I don't think I'm cut out for so much solitude.'

'Aye.' Clancy nodded. 'Neither is Kent.'

She sat back so fast she nearly fell off her seat. 'Are you serious?'

His eyes twinkled for a moment then they sobered. 'Aye, lass.'

'But…' She floundered with the idea. 'He's so rugged and strong and…hard. He doesn't look as if it bothers him at all.' She frowned. 'In fact, he seems jealous of it, doesn't want anything encroaching on it.' Especially her.

'Ahh…'

But Clancy didn't add anything and Josie refused to pry. The older man's eyes did watch her closely though, speculation rife in their depths, and she suddenly realised why Kent had left so abruptly. It made her want to laugh. Then it didn't.

Clancy was the one person she'd met in Martin's Gully who cared about Kent. Their mutual respect, their friendship, had been evident from the first moment. She reached across the table and touched the older man's hand. 'I'm only here for three more weeks. Kent thinks I'm a lame duck. Believe me, he'll be glad to see the back of me.'

Clancy chuckled. 'That's what he wants you to think.' He patted her hand. 'Now, why don't you come visit an old man next time you're in town?'

'I'd love to.'

'That's my place there.'

He nodded to a neat weatherboard house across the road and Josie beamed. The next three weeks were starting to look brighter and brighter.

Josie tried to slow her heart rate as she raised her hand and knocked on Kent's back door. 'Hi,' she said when he appeared. She tried to grin but found her lips had gone as rubbery as her knees.

He eyed her for a moment. 'Hi.'

No scowl, not even a frown, just a wary caution. Relief slugged through her. She hoped she'd seen the last of the prickly, unfriendly Kent. She much preferred the laughing, teasing one.

He glanced behind her. 'Is everything OK?'

'Yes, of course; I…'

He'd forgotten. She wanted to stamp her feet. She wanted to slap him. She wanted to cry with irrational disappointment. She'd looked forward to this all day, and…and he'd forgotten.

She didn't stamp her feet. She didn't slap him. She didn't cry. She kept right on trying to smile. 'It's Monday.'

His eyes narrowed and travelled over her face as if searching for signs of sunstroke. 'That's right,' he said slowly, as if agreeing with a child.

Which didn't help her eradicate those childish impulses. She pulled in a breath and counted to three. 'You said you'd give me a chess lesson.'

He slapped a hand to his forehead and scowled. Josie took two steps back. 'Don't do that,' she hollered, keeping a tight rein on feet that itched to stamp and hands that burned to slap.

His scowl deepened. 'Do what?'

'Look like that, turn back into Mr Hyde.' Pride lifted her chin. 'I know you're not my nursemaid, I know you're not even my friend, but we can at least be civil to each other and enjoy a game of chess, can't we?'

'Sure we can.'

'We had a nice time yesterday.'

'Yep.'

She wished he'd show a bit more enthusiasm.

He shuffled his feet. 'So, no chocolate cake?' He smiled, but it didn't reach his eyes.

'Umm, no.' She'd hummed and hawed over that for ages. Then she'd remembered his reaction the last time she'd brought afternoon tea. 'Didn't you have enough of it yesterday?'

'Not on your life.'

This time the smile made it all the way to his eyes and Josie found herself breathing easier. 'Next Monday,' she promised.

* * *

He should've found a way to get out of this.

Josie stood there in a pair of white cargo shorts and a jade-green tank-top and she looked better than chocolate cake. She looked better than anything he'd seen in a long, long time. He had the distinct feeling the less time he spent in her company, though, the better. She made him want things he'd forced himself to forget. But as he stared down into her half-hopeful, half-fearful face, he couldn't turn her away. He'd promised.

'Why don't we sit out here?' He nodded to the seating on his veranda. He didn't want to sit in the kitchen, didn't want her scent clogging up his senses and wafting through his house so the first thing he smelt when he woke in the morning was her.

With a shrug she took a seat, stared out at him from her gold-flecked eyes then crossed her legs. Jeez! She couldn't be more than a hundred and sixty centimetres, tops, but she had legs that went on forever. He turned and stumbled back into the house, tossed a critical glance around the kitchen then scowled. The real reason he didn't want her in here was so he didn't have to hear any more about his lack of homeliness. That still stung.

'Smile,' she ordered when he reappeared with the chess set, dimpling herself.

He did his best to tutor his face into a bland mask. Yesterday he'd found it too easy to smile with Josie, too easy to laugh. It wasn't a habit he intended to cultivate. Women like Josie were best protected from men like him.

Chess lesson. They'd concentrate on the chess lesson. 'How well can you play?' He sighed when she stared at him blankly. 'How much do you know?'

'I know how the pieces move.'

It was a starting point.

Forty minutes later, Kent came to the conclusion that Josie was a terrible chess player. She seemed to have a constitutional aversion to seizing her opponent's pieces. Or, for that matter, giving up any of her own. He attacked. She retreated, trying to find a way to save every single pawn. She didn't understand the concept of sacrificing a piece for the greater good. She didn't have an attacking bone in her body.

Nice body, though.

Stop it. Focus on the chess. Don't go noticing…other stuff.

Problem was, he'd spent the entire chess lesson noticing other stuff. Noticing how still her hands were between plays. How small and shapely they were. Noticing how she caught her bottom lip between her teeth as she attempted to decipher the complexities of the game. Noticing how her skin had started to take on a golden glow after a week of being out in the sun.

Her tank-top outlined a shape that had his hands clenching into fists beneath the table. He'd deliberately angled his chair so he couldn't see her legs. He knew they were there, though. He bet she'd feel like silk. Warm silk. He wondered if he could ask her to wear something long-sleeved and shapeless next time. And a bag over her head.

Get a grip. He'd lost his marbles. Too much time in her company had addled his brain.

He shifted in his chair. Fat lot of good it'd do him anyway. It wouldn't matter how many layers she wore, they couldn't hide the unconscious grace of her hand movements. Even when he closed his eyes against the tug of her body, he could still smell her.

She didn't even chatter away at him, which was a darn shame because inane chatter always got on his nerves.

And if she got on his nerves it might distract him from her more…from other things. But no, he wasn't to be given even that salve. She sat there, hands folded on the table, eyes intent on the game, perfectly relaxed, perfectly at ease. Perfectly happy to keep her mouth-watering lips curved in a smile without offering up so much as one inane remark.

With something midway between a sigh of frustration and a groan of relief, Kent moved his queen in front of her king. 'Checkmate.'

Very gently, Josie laid her oak-tree king on its side then looked at all her pieces lined up on Kent's side of the table. 'I may not know a great deal about chess, but you just smashed me, didn't you?'

'Yep.'

'I'm pretty terrible, aren't I?'

'Yep.' If he was lucky she might give it up as a bad joke. Especially if he didn't encourage her.

'I'll get better with practice.'

Damn.

She angled her cute little chin at him. Double damn.

She motioned to the chessboard. 'Do you want any help packing up?'

'No.'

'Well, thanks for the game.' She leapt up and, with a little wave, sauntered off. If Kent didn't know better he'd swear pique rather than relief needled through him. He opened his mouth to call something after her then snapped it shut.

Seizing the game board, he stomped inside, his shoulders as stiff and wooden as one of his chess pieces.

* * *

'Which way, Molly?'

Molly panted and pushed herself against Josie's legs when Josie paused at the juncture of the path, but didn't indicate which direction she'd prefer.

Josie pursed her lips. They'd explored downriver last week. So, should they cross the river or explore upstream? She lifted her face to the sun, revelling in its warmth, noted the shade on the other side of the river and promptly made her decision. 'Upriver today, Molly. What do you say?'

Molly's tail wagged harder, making Josie laugh. If anyone heard the way she spoke to the dog they'd think she was certifiable. She'd begun to look forward to her daily walks, though. They might have started out as a way to kill time, but she could feel her body reaping the benefits of regular exercise. Since she'd been practically housebound for the last few months, it felt good to work her muscles and drag fresh, clean air into her lungs. She'd continue the walks when she got home too.

And she'd get a dog.

She and Molly walked for about ten minutes before the trees started to thin and the river widened and grew shallow, creating a natural ford. Boulders dotted the river and both banks. The splashing of water and the glint of sun off mini-rapids and the pleasant browns and reds of the river stone created a scene that charmed her.

Until she heard a deeper splash immediately up ahead behind another group of boulders.

She didn't like big noises. That kind of splash indicated an animal at least as big as Molly. Were there wild pigs out here? She didn't know and didn't want to find out. She started to back up. 'C'mon, Molly, time to…'

She didn't get to finish her sentence because Molly,

with a bark, charged ahead. Oh, lord. Josie groaned and took off after her. What on earth would she say to Kent if anything happened to Molly?

No way was she skirting around the boulders as Molly had, though. Josie scrambled on top of them, hoping for a height advantage, readying herself to wave her arms and holler her lungs out in an effort to appear as big and scary as possible to whatever was below.

She wound up for her first holler when… 'Hello, Josie.'

Josie nearly fell into the river. 'Kent!'

Below her, Kent trod water in a natural pool formed by the boulders. Something midway between a scowl and a grimace darted across his face. Water glistened off his hair and his tanned, broad shoulders, and Josie's heart started to pound. She had a startlingly erotic image of licking those water droplets from his body, and the breath hitched in her throat. The water was clear, but the lower portion of his body was hidden by the shadow cast by the boulders.

Good thing!

When Josie didn't answer him Kent shaded his eyes and stared up at her. He must've noticed the colour in her cheeks, the way her eyes bugged, because a slow smile tilted one corner of his mouth. 'Earth to Josie.'

She started and rushed to cover her confusion. 'I, umm, heard a splash.'

'And you decided to investigate?'

'Umm, no.' She scrambled down from the boulder before she fell off. From the bank she couldn't see any part of Kent below the water line, but if she moved a little to her left and took a step forward—

Arghh! She hauled herself back and promptly sat on a

rock, and tried to quell the outrageous impulses coursing through her. She wrapped her arms around her knees to stop them trembling. 'No, umm…'

She grasped around for her train of thought, found it, and started to breathe easier once again. 'It sounded like a big splash, so I was going to slink back the way I'd come.' She sent him an apologetic grimace. 'Afraid I'm not interested in bumping into a hippopotamus or polar bear or anything.'

His smile became a grin. 'Last time I checked, they didn't do real well in the Australian wild.'

His grin was infectious. 'You know what I mean.' She grinned back. 'A wild pig or something.'

'You're pretty safe around here, but up a tree is a seriously good option if you ever do come across one. OK?'

'OK.' She filed the information away.

'So how come you decided to investigate?'

'Molly took off up here.'

'And you figured it was safe?'

She wanted to slap a hand to her forehead. Of course it was safe. Molly was a bigger scaredy cat than Josie. She must've smelt Kent or something. She wouldn't have gone racing off into danger. Josie suddenly felt like the biggest idiot on the planet. 'Umm,' she moistened her lips, 'that's right.'

Kent threw his head back and laughed. 'Liar. You thought Molly needed protecting, didn't you?'

She hitched up her chin. 'What's wrong with that?

He shook his head and grinned. 'Josie, you're a hopeless case, you know that?'

But he said it so nicely she didn't care. 'This is a lovely spot.' She lifted her face to the sun and glanced around with half-closed eyes, took in the clothes tossed on a nearby rock—shirt, jeans…underpants. Her eyes widened. 'Are you skinny-dipping, Mr Black?'

'I most certainly am, Ms Peterson.'

Warmth and wistfulness squirmed through her in equal measure. She bet it was lovely, the cool silk of water flowing over you without impediment. The freedom of it. 'I've never skinny-dipped in my life.'

He smiled challengingly and waggled his eyebrows. 'Wanna try it?'

He should do that more. Smile. It softened the craggy lines of his face and made him look like a man she could—

Nonsense! Crazy thought. She smiled and settled back on her sun-warmed rock. 'No, thank you.' Her smile widened. 'Though I might take it up as a spectator sport.'

Ooh, yes, definitely some ogling potential here. Not that she needed to see more than his shoulders and arms. He had biceps that could hurl a girl's heart rate right off the chart.

'If you don't stop looking at me like that I'm going to pull you in here to cool off.'

He practically growled the words at her and their former teasing banter vanished, replaced by a hot and heavy awareness. Heat surged through her…and not just in her cheeks. For one heart-stopping moment she was tempted to keep ogling and see what happened.

Another crazy thought. If he pulled her in there with him neither one of them would cool off. She tried to school her face. 'Sorry.'

'I'm going to get out now.'

Her mouth watered. 'Uh-huh.'

'Would you like to turn around?'

Her lips twitched at the gentleness of the question. 'Why, Kent Black, are you embarrassed?'

'No.' He held her gaze. 'But I thought you might be.'

He started to rise and with a squawk she leapt off her rock and spun around, heart pounding. His chuckle made it that much harder to keep from turning around. She could imagine what she'd see. All too vividly. She forced herself to take several paces upstream. Away from temptation. Or, at least, another couple of big rocks from it.

If only she was the kind of woman who could indulge in a holiday romance, in transitory affairs.

Her heart slapped against her ribcage. Her mind suddenly whirled. Well, why couldn't she? She was on holiday, wasn't she? She wanted to change her life, didn't she? Maybe that meant taking a few risks.

And if it meant seeing Kent naked…

She didn't think twice, she swung back to face him. Ooh…jockey shorts—navy blue—plastered to—

Oh, God! She couldn't drag her eyes away from the evidence of his arousal.

'What do you think you're doing?' Kent shouted at her, his eyes starting from his head.

She tried to stop her heart from thudding right out of her chest. Oh, dear lord. The man was beautiful. The air in front of her eyes shimmered with heat. He wanted her. That much was obvious. And exhilarating. It gave her the courage to hitch up her chin and meet his gaze. 'I've changed my mind.'

'About?'

'Seeing you naked.'

'You what?'

'So couldn't we take it from the top?' She took a step towards him. 'I'd love to try skinny-dipping.'

He stabbed a finger at her. He glared. 'You stay right where you are.'

His eyes darkened when she ignored him, when she moved in so close she could watch the pulse pounding at the base of his throat. She wanted to touch her tongue to it.

'You don't know what you're doing.' His voice rasped out of his throat. His chest rose and fell.

'I know exactly what I'm doing.' She reached out and placed her hand over his heart. He stiffened, but he didn't step back. His skin was cool and firm. The blood pounded beneath her palm, making her tremble.

'Think, Josie, think!' The words rapped out of him like stone on tin. 'You're not a holiday-fling kind of person. You couldn't stop it from meaning too much. I've met women like you before.'

Still…he didn't step away.

'You'd smother me, I'd fight for space,' his voice grew ragged, 'we'd argue, you'd cry.' He pulled in a breath. 'It'd get complicated and I don't do complicated.'

'Complicated? How?'

'You said you couldn't live out here and I can't live anywhere else.'

Can't or won't? But she let it pass. Beneath her hand his heart pounded hard and fast.

'Too complicated,' he repeated, but she noted the way his jaw clenched, the way his eyes flared with desire.

'On the contrary, it's remarkably simple.' She reached out and took his right hand, placed it between her breasts so he could feel her heart racing too. 'I want to touch you, and I want you to touch me.' The warmth of his hand pressed into her. She arched against it. Her lips parted. 'What's complicated about that?'

The words had barely left her when, with a wild oath, Kent swung an arm around her waist and his mouth crashed down on hers. His urgency, the hardness of his arousal against her stomach, fired her with an answering urgency, with a hunger she hadn't known she possessed, hadn't even known existed.

His tongue swept across her inner lips, enticed her to tangle her tongue with his, and turned everything topsy-turvy. The shoulders, the rock-hard body she clung to, though, stayed upright and held her fast, one hand at her hip, the other tangled in her hair, urging her closer.

He broke off to press hot kisses to her throat before claiming her mouth again. Their desire swept her along like a swollen current of the river, like gale-force winds that bent the tops of trees. She felt wild, free…cherished. She—

'No!'

Kent jerked back and glared. Through the haze of her desire she saw the torment in his eyes. His fingers bit into her shoulders and he shook her, but she had a feeling it was himself he wanted to shake. She made a move to reach out to him, to try and wipe away the pain that raked his face, but he dropped his hands and stepped back out of her reach.

'This is not going to happen,' he ground out.

Her arms felt bereft, cold. She gulped. Need lapped at her. 'Don't you want me?' she whispered. What had she done wrong?

A laugh scraped out of Kent's throat. He shoved his hands into opposite armpits and gripped for dear life. 'Don't play the ingénue. You can't be blind to the effect you have on men.'

The effect she had on…

What? Her? A smile suddenly zipped through her. Kent backed up as if he'd seen and recognised the glint in her eyes. He seized his jeans and shoved his legs into them bending over as he pulled on his boots.

'Nice butt,' she offered.

He glared, pushed his arms into his chambray shirt.

'Ditto for the shoulders.'

He growled but she couldn't make out what he said. It sounded like 'crazy thinking' and something about a mouse, which didn't make any sense at all.

He seized his hat, slapped it against his thigh and strode off without saying another word. Josie watched him until he disappeared into the trees then she dropped to her knees and buried her face in Molly's fur. 'He wants me,' she whispered. She couldn't temper the jubilation that rushed through her, didn't try to.

He wanted her. He just needed some time to get used to the idea. That was all.

CHAPTER SEVEN

JOSIE didn't clap eyes on Kent again till Friday. Three whole days since that kiss by the river. And it wasn't for lack of trying. She'd kept her eyes peeled for sight of him, whilst her imagination played any number of fantasies through her mind. Lovely, provocative fantasies.

Three days. She'd tried to keep a lid on her impatience, reminded herself he needed time.

Then on Friday, when she pulled up in her car after visiting Clancy, she glanced up to find Kent striding towards her cabin. He wore an expression of such single-minded determination that her heart started to hammer. Oh, man, had he finally come to his senses? She leapt out of her car, her knees barely holding her up.

Then she saw the bucket and broom in his hands and her heart plummeted. He wasn't looking for her. He wasn't heading for her cabin, but the one next door. He had no intention of sweeping her up in his arms and kissing her senseless.

Across a distance of twenty feet or so, they stopped and stared at each other like adversaries in an old-fashioned gun draw, each waiting for the other to make a move.

She swallowed back her disappointment…and impatience…brought their kiss to the forefront of her mind and grinned. Kent could act as aloof and distant as he wanted. She knew better. And she had no intention of making things easy for him. She sent him a cheery wave. 'Hey, Kent. Want a coffee?'

He tipped his hat in answer and bolted.

Her mouth dropped open and, unbidden, tears blurred her vision as a shaft of pain skewered her to the spot. In that moment she saw with startling clarity what she'd refused to see before. Kent had been right. If she couldn't stop a kiss from meaning too much, how would she cope with making love with him? She sagged against the bonnet of her car. How could she walk away at the end of her holiday if they made love?

She wouldn't, that was what. And Kent knew it. She'd cling; he'd rebel. She'd cry; he'd hate himself. A shudder racked through her. Dear lord, what had she been thinking?

Quite obviously she hadn't been thinking at all. But no matter how many times she listed all the reasons why it was a bad idea to make love with Kent, her wayward body went right on trying to imagine it anyway.

The last three days had created a gentle rhythm to Josie's days. She'd wake early, have her first cup of coffee on the veranda with Molly and the birds, then she'd bake up a batch of muffins and a cake, or some biscuits and a tart, and drive into Martin's Gully to the general store.

She'd met Liz on Monday, recovered from the worst of her flu, and had immediately warmed to the other woman. She understood why Kent held her in such high esteem. Liz Perkins had a kind heart and not a bad word for anybody. So, naturally, Josie, Liz and Bridget breakfasted together over muffins and a pot of tea.

Then it was home again to wash her pots and pans, tidy her cabin, and to read the day's paper. As soon as any disquieting thought popped into her head she'd quickly push it aside. She'd decided the question of what to do with the rest of her life could wait until the middle of next week. She'd have a go at sorting it all out then, but she'd resolved on at least two weeks of complete relaxation first.

Then it was back into Martin's Gully for lunch with Clancy, a habit she was hardly aware of forming, but one she enjoyed all the same. Once home again, she and Molly would go for their walk.

Most of the time, throughout the day, Josie could push thoughts of Kent from her mind. Mostly. Sure, it required the occasional concerted effort, but she managed it. The nights, though, were a different matter.

As soon as evening fell another woman seemed to inhabit her body. A reckless, wanton woman who wanted nothing more than to stride up to Kent's back door in something skimpy and seductive and demand entry. No number of craft projects, no amount of postcard writing could drive the ensuing images out of her mind.

When sleep finally claimed her, she tossed and turned and groaned until Molly's whine or bark woke her. Then she'd surge upright, erotic images branded on her brain, her skin fevered with need.

Molly took to sleeping on the floor rather than the foot of Josie's bed. Josie didn't blame her. She'd sleep on the floor too if she thought it'd help.

Saturday morning Josie woke with a cough and a pain behind her eyes. She ignored it and carried on as normal.

Sunday morning she dragged herself out of bed, pulled muffin ingredients off the shelves then remembered it was

Sunday and she didn't need to bake today. She let Molly out, crawled back into bed and pulled the covers over her head. Today she'd hibernate.

Kent woke at two o'clock in the morning to whining and scratching outside his bedroom window. Then Molly set up a howl. 'For Pete's sake!' He threw back the covers, muttering imprecations under his breath as he lurched to the front door and flung it open. Who'd ever heard of a dog afraid of the dark? 'C'mon, then,' he grumbled.

Molly didn't try to bowl him over with ecstatic wriggling and licks the way she normally did. She barked at him then turned her head in the direction of the cabins.

In the direction of Josie's cabin.

It might be two o'clock in the morning and he might be fuzzy-headed, but Kent didn't need a second signal. He jumped through the door, realised he was stark naked, raced back inside to pull on jeans and a shirt, dragged on his trainers and slammed out of the house to race after Molly.

Fear surged through him. His heart grew so large it pressed against his lungs, making him battle for every breath. Let her be OK. Let her be OK. The words pounded through him with each step.

Her cabin was all lit up and he didn't hesitate to catch his breath. He didn't hesitate for anything. He pounded on her door then tried it. Locked. He peered through the window but the curtains obscured his view. He pounded on the door again. 'Josie!' He rattled the handle. If she didn't answer he'd break the damn thing down. 'Josie!'

His shout should've woken the dead. From inside he heard a groan then a soft shuffling… The door opened. He took one look at her face and pity, tenderness and concern punched him. She looked terrible. She looked worse than terrible.

She blinked and clutched the doorframe, rested her head against it. 'What can I do for you?'

He could hardly make out the words as they rasped from her throat. Didn't she realise this wasn't a social call? That it was two o'clock in the morning? Another rush of tenderness took him off guard. 'Sweetheart, I think you'll find you're not well.'

She swayed and he leapt forward, slid an arm around her waist and moved her back to sit on the end of the sofa bed. She felt small and frail beneath his hands, her skin clammy and hot. She was burning up.

'Might be why I don't feel too good,' she slurred.

She went to lie back down but he stopped her, so she leaned into him instead. Even sick she still smelt good enough to eat. 'I promise to let you go back to sleep, as soon as you've answered a couple of questions.' She gave no indication she'd heard him, so he placed a finger beneath her chin and lifted her face towards him. 'Josie?'

'I'm wearing my silly, skimpy pyjamas.' Her mouth turned down. 'I should get my robe.'

He had a feeling she felt too tired and sick to care about the robe, but he wished she hadn't drawn attention to her nightwear. He'd done his best not to notice. Her pyjamas consisted of pale pink short shorts and a singlet top covered in fluffy white sheep jumping fences.

Corny. Cute. And in other circumstances downright sexy. He fought the bolt of need that shot through him. 'I promise to tease you about them when you're well again.' Her lips twitched into what he guessed was meant to be a smile. 'Now, tell me where it hurts most.'

'Chest,' she wheezed. 'It's hard to breathe.'

'Are you an asthmatic?'

She shook her head and leaned further into him until her head rested fully against his shoulder. Her face lifted towards his, her eyes closed.

'Josie.' He cupped her face and felt her glands. Swollen. 'I want you to open your mouth and stick out your tongue.'

She opened one eye then lifted one hand and waggled a finger at him. 'Trust me, right? I'm a doctor.'

He smiled. He couldn't help it. He couldn't believe she'd try and crack a joke when she obviously felt so bad. He fought the urge to kiss her forehead. 'That's the one.'

If only she knew.

None the less, she did as he asked. He angled her face to the light. He could smell the infection on her breath but a quick look at her throat confirmed it.

She had a throat and chest infection. And a fever. She needed antibiotics. She needed to keep hydrated. And she needed sleep. He helped her back under the covers. 'When did you last eat?'

But she'd drifted down under cover of sleep and he knew he wouldn't get any more from her tonight. He poured a glass of water, noticed the remains of a barely touched bowl of soup and drew his own conclusions. He made her drink several mouthfuls of the water.

'Stay,' he ordered Molly, who lay on a rug at the base of the sofa bed. Rug? He shook the thought away then strode back up to the house, seized a jar of broad-spectrum antibiotics from his bag, the night lamp from beside his bed then headed straight back down to the cabin.

He made her take two tablets and another couple of sips of water before cooling her forehead with a cold cloth.

Then he set the lamp up on the table, flicked off the overhead light and settled down to keep vigil.

Josie had that dream again. That lovely dream where Kent leaned over her, his face softened in concern, his hands gentle on her face and beautifully cool. This time the room was bathed in a gentle light rather than the harsh light above her head. She tried to smile at him, tried to say she thought him wonderful…and sexy, but her body felt mired in thick mud and she couldn't manage it.

Then a jag of coughing shook through her entire frame and each breath felt like broken glass and it took all her concentration to breathe through it. For a moment she swore a pair of strong arms lifted her and supported her, but then everything went black as a deeper sleep claimed her.

The next time Kent entered her dreams she wanted him to get right back out of them again. Why couldn't she dream what she wanted to dream? Why couldn't they be floating down a wide, slow river on a beautiful, cushion-strewn pontoon, or lying in a field of wild flowers with the sky blue above them, listening to the lazy hum of the bees?

Sure, he was still as sexy as ever with a smile made for sin, and he smelt better than any man had a right to, but he was also annoying. She didn't want to take tablets and drink water. Why wouldn't he stop making her? She couldn't avoid him, though. He wouldn't let her. His big hands and superior strength mocked her efforts to elude him.

The dream was all the more annoying because in it she was as weak as a kitten and her brain was too fuzzy to bring into play her self-defence tactics. By the time she remembered the right move, she found herself lying back down on the pillow with a gentle hand soothing her forehead and she couldn't remember what she'd wanted to fight against.

Dreams were like that.

Josie opened one eye, noticed the soft light pouring in at the windows and realised she'd slept later than she'd meant to or, at least, later than she normally did. She pulled a tentative breath into her lungs. Her chest still hurt, but the sharp, broken-glass pains had dulled to an ache. A definite improvement.

She pulled herself slowly upright, pushed her hair off her face then froze. Kent sat half-slumped in one of the hard chairs at the kitchen table, fast asleep. What was he doing here? Then she remembered fragments from her dreams and wondered if they'd been dreams at all. She frowned. She had the faintest recollection of opening her door to him at some stage last night.

Molly lumbered to her feet from her rug on the floor, stretched and yawned. When she saw Josie she gave a joyful bark. Kent was on his feet in seconds. Josie had never seen anyone move so fast in her life. Certainly not like that, from sleep to wakefulness in an instant.

He was at her side in seconds, his hand at her forehead, his eyes intent on her face. 'How do you feel?'

'Crappy,' she groaned.

He broke out into a huge grin.

'I'm glad you find it amusing,' she grumbled, throwing back the covers and reaching for her robe.

The smile slid right off his face. 'What do you think you're doing?'

'Gotta make the muffins,' she wheezed. Liz would be expecting them.

'No, you're not.'

He seized her feet and lifted them straight back into bed, and Josie found herself too weak to fight him. In fact, she found it took most of her energy just to breathe. He tucked the covers around her and sat on the edge of the bed. Luckily, she didn't have the energy to pull him down to kiss her either. She gripped her hands tightly in her lap all the same, just in case she found a sudden second wind.

'You're not getting out of bed at all today.'

'But—'

'Doctor's orders.'

She snapped her mouth shut. Then she frowned. 'The doctor's been to see me?'

He hesitated then nodded. 'Yep.'

She didn't remember that at all. 'Could you…?' She twisted her hands together. She hated putting him out like this. 'Could you ring Liz and explain that—?'

'Already taken care of.'

It was? She glanced at the light filtering through the curtains. 'But it can't even be eight o'clock yet.'

'Twenty to,' he confirmed with a glance at his watch.

'Heavens! What time did you call her?' A spurt of indignation shuffled through her. What right did he have to take matters into his own hands?

Then she remembered he was only following the doctor's orders. 'I… Thank you.'

A frown drew his brows low over the brilliant blue of his eyes, tightening then deepening the groove that ran from his nose to the side of his mouth. Her chest, already clenched, clenched up more until she realised he hadn't directed the frown at her, but at the wall behind her. 'What day of the week do you think it is?'

An awful premonition shook her. 'Monday, of course.' Though she suddenly realised there was no 'of course' about it. If she couldn't recall a visit from the doctor, then…

'You've been quite sick, Josie.'

'What kind of sick?'

He folded his arms and glared in the direction of the sink. As long as he didn't glare at her she didn't mind.

'You have a chest infection.'

Uh-huh. 'What day is it?'

He rubbed a hand across the back of his neck then glanced at her through the lock of hair that fell forward on his forehead. 'Thursday.'

'Thursday!' She surged upright, found it hard to breathe again and subsided back against the pillows. How could she have lost three days just like that? Another thought spiked through her. She didn't jump up and wring her hands, although she wanted to. Her mouth went dry. 'Have you been looking after me all that time?'

He nodded and she wanted to cover her face with her hands and curl up into a ball. 'I'm sorry.'

'No big deal.'

No big deal. He was joking, right? It was a huge deal.

Had he seen her naked? The thought spiked through her and she wanted to die. 'Serves you right for that crack you made last week about not being my nursemaid,' she suddenly snapped. 'You shouldn't tempt fate like that.'

He blinked then grinned. 'You're going to be one of those grumbling, sniping, griping patients, huh?'

She covered her mouth with her hand. 'I'm sorry.'

'Nah, it serves me right.'

It did?

She shook her head. 'I know how much you hate being… I mean, I'm sorry I've been such a nuisance. I wouldn't have put you to so much trouble for the world.'

He reached out and clasped her hand, his eyes gentle. 'I'm quite sure you'd have much preferred to stay healthy.'

He leaned back with that grin and her mouth watered. She suddenly found it hard to breathe leaning back against the pillows too.

'So, as penance, I have to spend the next three days playing chess with the worst chess player in the history of man.'

Josie stared then laughed. It ended in a fit of coughing. Kent's arms came around her and held her steady until it finished. Finally she drew back, just far enough to stare up into his face, to take in the lean, tempting line of his lips. He needed a shave and she wondered how it'd feel to run her palm along the length of his jaw.

Kent released her and shot to his feet, shoved his hands in his pockets. 'Time for you to rest.'

Then she remembered the way he'd raced away from her that day by the river, and how he'd avoided her ever since.

How he didn't want her on his mountain.

'Is that how long I have to stay in bed?' Is that what the doctor had ordered? 'Three days?'

'At the very least.'

She couldn't continue being such a drain on him for another three days, but she found it hard to focus that thought as her eyes fought against the sleep that suddenly wanted to claim her. 'I can't possibly stay here.'

'Sure you can.'

No, she couldn't. But her eyes closed and she found she didn't have the strength to push the words past her throat.

* * *

Fabulous. Wonderful.

Kent dragged a hand down his face. It'd been hard enough dealing with a Josie who was out of it. Having to touch her, hold her, whilst he administered antibiotics and made her sip water. Having to steel himself against the desire that coursed through him when he sponged her down, when he changed the sheets. Whenever he darn well looked at her. Having to fight the urge to kiss her when, in her delirium, she told him she dreamed of making love with him.

He despised himself for his weakness, for not being able to view her as just another patient. His lips twisted. So much for maintaining a professional distance.

He dragged a hand down his face. A sleeping Josie had strained all his reserves of self-control and discipline, but a waking one was that much more potent again. He didn't know how he'd get through the next few days.

'What about your cows?' Josie asked the next time he moved to sit on the edge of her bed.

'Steers,' he corrected. He hadn't realised she was awake. He hadn't wanted to wake her either, but it was time she ate something. She eased herself up into a sitting position. He propped the pillows behind her.

'Who's looking after them?'

He suppressed a grin. He should've known it wouldn't take her long to get around to that. 'Smiley McDonald. A neighbour. We have an arrangement.'

She eyed him doubtfully. 'You do?'

'Yep.' He slid a tray holding a bowl of soup and a couple of slices of toast onto her lap.

'Which is?'

When she didn't pick up her spoon and start eating, he

put the spoon into her hand. 'Smiley hangs his head over our boundary fence and checks on my cattle. If there's a problem he takes care of it, or calls the vet, or lets me know. I'm returning the favour next month when he attends his sister's wedding in Adelaide.'

'Oh.'

She started to eat and he moved to the hard chair by the table. When she finished he cleared the tray and returned with a glass of water and a pill. 'Antibiotics,' he said when she hesitated.

'Thank you.' She took it without a murmur. 'Thank you for lunch and thank you for taking such good care of me.'

She smiled and in that instant he swore it was all worthwhile. 'Not a problem.' He retreated to the sink, out of temptation's way. Or at least out of its reach for the moment.

'Yes, it is. You said it's three days before I can get back up.'

He swung around sharply, not liking the tone of her voice. 'You won't be able to do too much all at once.' He didn't want her overdoing it. 'You'll need to take it pretty easy for a couple of weeks.'

'But—'

'There are no buts. Not if you don't want a relapse.'

She huddled back against the pillows and bit her lip. He wanted to pull her into his arms and tell her it'd all be OK. She just needed to take it easy, that was all. He bet she wasn't used to taking it easy. He had a feeling that over the last few months she'd taken care of her father at the expense of her own health. He didn't like that thought. Why hadn't her brothers looked out for her? He straddled the chair and tried not to scowl. He'd make sure she took it easy.

'I can't trespass on your kindness for that long.'

'Sure you can.'

'It's not fair on you. You have your work and other responsibilities.'

No, he didn't. Not real responsibilities like making a sick person well again. He'd forgotten what that felt like…and he missed it. He shrugged the thought aside. He'd chosen his path. 'Lots of things aren't fair.' It wasn't fair she was stuck halfway up a mountain on a holiday she didn't even want.

'I'll have to go home.'

Her voice was flat, matter-of-fact, and the words jarred through him. He leapt out of his chair, but then didn't know what he meant to do. Concern spiked through him when the colour drained from her face.

He closed the distance in an instant and felt her forehead—cool and dry. Her fever hadn't returned. Relief flooded him. 'Josie, you're not strong enough to drive home just yet.'

She met his gaze then glanced down to where her fingers pleated the blanket. 'I know, but if you rang Marty and Frank then they could come collect me.'

Marty and Frank wouldn't look after her as well as he could. If they were such good brothers, why had they sent her out to this God-forsaken spot in the first place, huh? He didn't want to let Josie out of his sight until he was one hundred per cent sure she was well again.

'Will they be able to look after you?' he fired at her.

'Of course.'

'Properly?'

'Yes.' She laughed but he caught the strain behind it. 'I think it'd be for the best, don't you?'

Her soft words speared through him and he wanted to

say no. But damn it. What could he offer her other than a rustic cabin, huh?

And a hard bed.

And tinned soup.

She hadn't wanted to stay when she was well, why would she want to stay now she was sick? She deserved all the comforts of home and she wouldn't get those even if he moved her up into the house. She should be taken care of and made a fuss of by her family and friends, the people who loved her. A circle that didn't include him.

His hands clenched. If that was what she wanted he'd make sure it happened. 'I'll do whatever you need me to,' he promised. 'Are you sure you wouldn't rather stay?'

She smiled but it didn't reach her eyes. 'You're not my nursemaid, remember?'

She didn't say it in a mean way to make him eat his words or anything, and that only made it worse. 'But—'

'We both know I'm someone you just got lumped with.'

'Not true.' He wished he'd been friendlier in the first week of her stay. He shifted awkwardly. 'You'll be missed.'

She raised an eyebrow and he found himself shrugging. 'Liz enjoys her morning cuppa with you. And I haven't seen Clancy looking so dapper in a long time.'

'Oh.' She gave a wan smile.

'And I was looking forward to thrashing you some more at chess.'

She sent him an even thinner, sadder excuse for a smile. 'I don't believe you.'

If he kissed her she'd believe him.

For Pete's sake! She's sick, you jerk.

On second thoughts, it was probably a good idea if she went home. A scowl scuffed through him, but he kept his face bland and pleasant. No, not pleasant. He couldn't do pleasant if his life depended on it. He could just about manage polite if he concentrated really hard.

He concentrated really hard then seized a notepad and pen and thrust them at her. 'If you write down their phone numbers I'll get on to it.'

He swung away to lean in the doorway and stare out at the view. He wanted to get out of the close confines of the cabin. Now. He needed to stride out beneath a big sky and breathe in fresh air.

When he swung back, he found Josie pale and trembling. He was at her side in the space of a heartbeat, but she refused to relinquish the notepad when he tried to take it. 'Rest,' he ordered, cursing himself for not keeping a closer eye on her. 'We'll deal with this later.'

She scribbled down the numbers, tore off the top page and handed it to him. 'I'll rest while you get on to this.'

She hunkered back down under the covers and turned her back to him. He didn't even try to keep the scowl from his face as he strode from the cabin.

He glanced down at the scrap of paper. She'd scrawled four phone numbers—home and business for Marty, home and business for Frank. He wanted to scrunch it up into a ball and throw it away. When she woke he could tell her she'd dreamt the whole incident, and that she was staying put until she was well again.

But he knew it wouldn't work. Josie wasn't delirious any more. She knew fact from fiction. She knew what she wanted.

She wanted to go home.

He slammed into the house. It seemed strangely grey after the touches of colour Josie had added to her cabin. His scowl deepened. Without giving himself time to think, he pulled the phone towards him and punched in the first number—Marty, business.

Ten minutes later he slammed the phone down. The sound echoed in the sudden silence.

Of all the miserable low-lifes! Once he'd discovered she wasn't sick enough for hospital, Marty Peterson had claimed he couldn't possibly collect Josie before Tuesday next week at the earliest.

Tuesday. That was five days away.

And he was dreadfully sorry for the inconvenience, but he'd make sure Mr Black was amply reimbursed for all the bother.

Bother! Kent snorted. Josie didn't need some jerk throwing money around. She needed family and friends and some wildly overdue pampering. What she didn't need was a miserable excuse for a brother who couldn't come and collect her because he had *very important work* to do.

Kent would give him very important work. If he ever clapped eyes on Marty Peterson he'd knock him flat on his back.

He punched in the business number for the second brother, Frank. They couldn't both be low-life scum. Josie was a sweetheart. At least one of her brothers had to share some of the same personality traits, surely?

A busy signal greeted him. He gripped the receiver so hard by rights it should've cracked. He slammed it down and swore once, loudly. What was the bet crappy brother number one was on the phone warning crappy brother number two?

He paced. These were the guys whose feelings Josie had wanted to protect by staying here and not complaining?

It took him forty-seven minutes to get through, but he

had no intention of giving up. Finally a secretary answered and informed him *regretfully* that Mr Peterson was away on a business trip, and would he like to leave a message?

The kind of message he wanted to leave would've blistered her ears and peeled the paint clean off the kitchen wall. He reminded himself not to shoot the messenger. With a curt, 'No,' he hung up.

What the heck was he going to tell Josie?

He had vivid, satisfying visions of beating both men to a pulp. Immature, he admitted, but still satisfying. He rubbed the back of his neck, his mind working overtime. He could drive Josie home himself. A round trip would take the best part of a day. No drama. He could drive her car then hire another for the return journey. At least he'd know she'd arrived safely. Three hours there, a couple of hours to see her settled, then three hours back again.

But what would she be going home to? He couldn't count on her brothers with their *very important work* to look after her. And she had that sick neighbour. He couldn't count on Josie looking after herself properly if she thought somebody needed her.

Nope, he wasn't taking her home. He might only be able to offer her a rustic cabin, but he could make sure she got the care she needed. That at least was something he could do. He reached for the phone and made another two calls, both far more satisfying than the earlier two. He actually found himself smiling at the end of them.

CHAPTER EIGHT

JOSIE must've dozed because when she next opened her eyes the sun had moved across the sky and the shadows outside her cabin were lengthening. She reached for her watch.

'Nearly four o'clock,' Kent said.

She couldn't believe how much she'd slept. A thought that slid right out of her head when she sat up and gazed at him. He sat sprawled at the table with one of her crossword books and he looked so good her mouth started to water. It was pointless all this wistful sighing and mouth-watering, but she couldn't seem to stop it.

The sooner she left the better. For both their sakes. She gulped and tried to make herself believe it. 'Did you—?'

'What's a five-letter word for food seasoning? The fourth letter is M.'

She tried to visualise the word. 'A food seasoning? No other letters yet?'

'I think four down is "astonish", so that would give us H as the second letter.'

'Something—H—something—M—something? I don't like it.' She held her hand out for the book. 'I bet you've made a mistake.'

He handed it to her then stretched out along the foot of

her bed and looked so darn sexy her eyes crossed, making it impossible to decipher the puzzle in front of her.

'Well?' He yawned.

'I can't make it out.' Wasn't that the truth?

He yawned again and guilt speared through her. She wondered how much sleep he'd managed in the last few days. Not much in those hard chairs, she'd bet.

She wanted to curl into a ball again and hide. The hairs on her arms lifted and her skin prickled whenever she thought about it. She opened her mouth to ask when Marty and Frank would be here, and something a whole lot greyer than guilt shuffled through her at the thought of leaving.

'Thyme,' she suddenly blurted out. 'T-H-Y-M-E. A food seasoning.'

Kent beamed at her and some of the greyness lifted. She'd ask about Marty and Frank right after she and Kent finished the crossword. But once they'd finished it, Kent stood and stretched, glanced around the cabin and she knew he was surveying the changes she'd made.

'Do you like it?'

He didn't pretend to misunderstand her. 'What's not to like? You've totally transformed the place.'

She snorted. 'Nonsense.'

'You have,' he insisted. 'The atmosphere in here is completely different.' He glanced around again, his brow furrowed. ' I can't even figure out what it is you've done exactly.'

'I've done nothing more than thrown a rug on the floor, a tablecloth on the table, and hung something cheerful at the windows.'

'What about that?' He pointed.

She shrugged. 'I hung a picture. Hardly an earth-shattering change.'

'And those?'

'They're just some candles I bought. They're supposed to smell like chocolate when you burn them.'

He was silent for a moment. 'You know, you might be right. Maybe I should do something…more with these cabins.'

Her jaw dropped. She wanted to throw her arms around him.

Bad, bad idea. What she should really be doing was asking him if he'd spoken to Marty.

But she couldn't seem to push the words out and in the end it was Kent who raised the subject first. 'Are you close to your brothers, Josie?'

'Why?' Her chin shot up, her back stiffened and she slammed the crossword book closed. 'What makes you ask?'

He raised his hands and backed up. 'No reason.'

She ordered herself to act less defensive, less…touchy.

'But they sent you out here to the back of beyond, didn't they?'

His voice was light, teasing, as if trying to put her at ease, and it roused all of her suspicions. 'Why, what did they say? You have spoken to them, haven't you?'

He shrugged. 'Only Marty so far.'

'And what—?'

'Knock, knock.'

Clancy stood in the doorway, an enormous bunch of flowers in one hand, an assortment of odds and ends in the other.

'How are you feeling, lass?' He placed the flowers in her arms.

'Oh, Clancy, they're beautiful.'

'Knew you'd like them. They're a bribe.'

'A bribe?'

'If you can't come to me for lunch then I'll just have to come to you.' His dark eyes twinkled. 'If you can fit me into your schedule, that is.'

She didn't even know if she'd be here for lunch tomorrow. She could be on her way home. 'Oh, Clancy, I…'

Kent shook his head wildly behind Clancy's back and Josie swallowed the rest of her words and pasted on a smile. 'Why, that sounds lovely.'

Clancy beamed his delight and guilt trickled through her. And regret. She'd miss him when she left.

She made a silent promise to have lunch with him tomorrow, although Marty and Frank wouldn't like the delay if they were here by then. Her insides shrank. In fact, they'd hate it. She steeled herself against tomorrow's inevitable argument and forced her attention back to Clancy. 'Though you're a little late for lunch today.'

'Oh, aye,' he agreed, setting up a folding table by her bed then taking her flowers and handing them to Kent. 'Make yourself useful, lad. Put those in water.' He disappeared back outside. Kent looked so charmingly nonplussed Josie had to laugh. The flowers did nothing to take the edge off his masculinity, though.

'I wanted to get in early and make it a date for the rest of the week before someone else snapped you up,' Clancy said, trundling back into the cabin with her camp chair and setting it by the folding table. 'Those others,' he nodded to the wooden chairs by her table, 'are too hard for old bones like mine.'

He set about brewing a large pot of tea, as at home in

her cabin as if born there. Kent managed to distribute the flowers between a single vase and a couple of jugs. Their fresh, clean scent filled the cabin. 'Clancy, you don't need to bribe me to have lunch with you.'

'They're not for lunch, lass, but for this.' He held up a pack of dominoes. 'Been feeling kind of dull over the last couple of days. Need a game or two to liven me up.'

Nonsense. He wanted to liven her up, keep her from being bored. His kindness touched her. But even she couldn't deny the enjoyment that coloured his cheeks and enlivened his eyes as he poured cups of tea, sliced a Boston bun and set out the dominoes.

He lifted his eyebrow at Kent, who hovered near by. 'I'm perfectly capable of looking after the patient. Don't you have work or something to do?' He held out the plate of Boston bun. 'Take a slice and be off with you.'

Josie choked back a laugh. Kent grinned. 'I can take a hint.'

Clancy's white hair danced. 'Smart man.'

A part of Josie followed Kent right out the door, wanting to dog his footsteps as he left. A bigger part of her wanted to throw her arms around Clancy and thank him. Kent probably needed a break. The less of a strain she proved to be the better.

Clancy stayed for just over an hour and left with promises to return for lunch tomorrow. He even left his folding table and dominoes. She stared at them and gulped. She had to find out what arrangements Kent had made with her brothers.

As if her thoughts had conjured him up, Kent stuck his head around the door. 'Worn out?'

'I'm fine.' She pulled in a deep breath. 'Kent, what—?'

'That was kindly done.'

She blinked. 'Oh, you mean it was kind of Clancy to come and visit?' Her face cleared. 'Of course it was and—'

'I meant exactly what I said.'

He folded his arms and the material of his T-shirt strained across his shoulders and the muscles of his upper arms. A great sigh rose up through her.

'He has one living relative. A nephew in Scotland. He's lonely. Visiting you made him feel needed.'

Josie didn't know what to say. 'I…I enjoy his company,' she finally managed.

'Exactly.'

'That's not kind, it's human.'

Kent took a step back and frustration pulsed through her, though she couldn't have said why. 'Look, Kent, what—?'

'Hello?' Footsteps sounded outside on the veranda and Liz appeared in the doorway, basket in hand.

'Come in,' Josie urged when she hovered there, staring from one to the other.

'Are you sure? Am I interrupting anything?'

Josie snorted though she wasn't sure why she did that either. She was aware of Kent's narrow-eyed gaze, though. 'You're not interrupting and visitors are always welcome.' She refused to look at him.

Liz bustled in. 'To be honest with you, I needed to get away from Bridget for a bit. You know what I mean?'

Josie wasn't sure if she should nod or not, but it didn't matter. Liz, with a roll of her eyes, took Josie's agreement for granted. Josie blinked when Liz pulled out a casserole from her basket and popped it in the oven.

'I told Bridge I was eating out tonight. I hope you don't mind.'

Josie shook her head. 'Not at all.'

Liz settled herself in Clancy's camp chair. 'No offence, Kent, but my Hungarian beef stew is a whole lot tastier than your tinned soup.'

Kent straddled one of the hard chairs. 'None taken.'

As the rich aroma of the casserole filled the air, Josie's mouth started to water. From the furtive glances Kent sent towards the oven, she guessed his did too.

'It'll be ready in thirty to forty minutes.' Liz edged her chair closer to the bed. 'Just long enough for us to have a cosy, girly chat.'

Kent shot to his feet. 'I'll, umm, go do some stuff.'

Josie couldn't mistake the wistful glance he directed towards them, though. She remembered Clancy's comment the day of the fête, about how Kent wasn't cut out for all this solitude. She wanted to ask him what stuff he had to do.

She wanted to ask him to stay.

Then she remembered she was a millstone around his neck. It wasn't company he pined for. At least, not hers. It'd be the food. And it smelt so good she didn't blame him.

'I'll be serving up in forty minutes, so if you don't want to miss out…'

Kent grinned and it did the strangest things to Josie's insides. A grin like that should come with warning bells and flashing lights so a person had the chance to look away before it bammed them right between the eyes. So they had a chance to maintain at least a scrap of balance.

'I'll be back.' He settled his hat on his head, touched the brim in a farewell salute and swaggered out.

Josie couldn't help but admire the view as he left.

Liz leaned forward and touched Josie's arm. Josie could see the strain on her face. 'This is going to sound awful, but your getting sick is a godsend to me. Don't take it the wrong way, love.' She patted Josie's hand. 'I'm sorry you're feeling poorly.'

Josie didn't doubt it.

'But it does give me an excuse to get out of the house.'

Josie sat up a little straighter. 'Is it really that bad?'

Liz nodded. 'Your having breakfast with us helped me cope with her. Deflected her attention from me for a bit. She makes me feel like an invalid.' She paused. 'I loved Ted and I miss him terribly, but just because he's no longer here doesn't mean I can't look after myself.'

'Of course not.'

'But you try telling Bridge that.'

Bridget was pretty overbearing. 'She means well.'

'Oh, I know that, love. If she didn't I'd have turfed her out on her ear by now. But coming to see you not only gives me a break from her, but also makes me feel useful again.' She hitched herself up. 'I'm not ready to be put out to pasture just yet.'

Josie's throat started to thicken.

'I finally have a reason to cook dinner again if you know what I mean.'

Josie knew exactly what she meant. For the first week after her father had died, she hadn't seen much point in cooking for one. She hadn't felt much like eating either.

'So if you don't mind, I'd like to stretch your illness out for at least a week. Then I'll have to think of something else because I honestly don't know what I'm going to do once you leave.'

Josie gulped. A lie of omission was still a lie, and she couldn't do it. 'Liz, I might be going home as soon as tomorrow. I asked Kent,' insisted more like, 'to call my brothers to come and collect me.'

Liz stiffened. 'Get him to call them back and say you've changed your mind. You don't really want to cut your holiday short, do you?'

'I… But…I can't keep being such a burden on Kent.'

'Nonsense. You're good for him.'

She was? How?

Before she could ask, Liz had rushed on. 'How are you a burden? The worst is past. Kent doesn't need to sit up with you all night now, and you'll be right as rain after a bit of bed rest. What does he have to do? I'll cook you dinner in the evening and,' she folded her arms, 'I know how much Clancy is looking forward to taking care of your lunch. He dropped by the store as pleased as punch about it.'

Josie bit her lip.

'All Kent has to do is make you a piece of toast in the mornings and pop his head around the door a couple of times a day to check if you need anything.'

When it was put like that…

'In fact, he'll be gaining from the arrangement because he can have his dinner with us instead of cooking it for himself.'

That was true.

'And I need you to help me figure out what I'm going to do about Bridge.' Liz leaned across and clasped Josie's hand. 'Please?'

A great yearning opened up inside her. 'Well…if it's OK with Kent.'

Liz sat back and beamed. 'It'll be OK with Kent.'

'What'll be OK with me?' Kent said, sauntering into the cabin and pulling off his hat.

'If Josie changes her mind and stays on here after all.'

He swung around. 'Have you changed your mind?'

She nodded, unable for the moment to speak. But she

kept her gaze on his face. She couldn't have watched him any closer if she'd put him under a microscope, but no scowls, not even a fraction of a frown, appeared. His eyes didn't narrow, his shoulders didn't freeze into place and his mouth didn't tighten. In fact, he literally beamed at her.

'It's more than OK. It's great.'

It was?

'That is smelling seriously good.' He nodded towards the oven. 'How long—?'

'Long enough for you to go ring Josie's brothers and tell them she's staying on after all.'

'No problem.'

With a nod and a grin he left, and Josie found she couldn't work Kent Black out at all. 'The tennis club,' she said, dragging her attention back to Liz. At least Liz made sense. 'Bridget needs something else to organise other than you. Does she like tennis?'

'Yes!' The word whistled out between Kent's teeth as he strode up to the house. He wanted to punch the air in victory. Josie was staying.

Not for good, he reminded himself. Just until the end of next week, but long enough for him to get her well and strong again. He wanted to celebrate. He pulled open the fridge and seized the neck of a bottle of chardonnay then remembered Josie couldn't drink while taking medication. He pushed it back in and pulled out several cans of lemonade instead. They'd celebrate properly when she was well.

Not him and Josie on their own, though. No. An image of candlelight and champagne and Josie in those cute little PJs of hers and—

He went tight and hard, his thickness straining against the denim of his jeans. He bit back an oath and tried to replace the image with a different one—he, Liz and Clancy holding a little party to send Josie off. That could be fun.

Not as fun as the first image, though.

He pulled his mind back, seized the phone and punched in Marty's business number. 'This is Kent Black,' he barked at the answering machine. 'Josie will be staying till the end of next week as planned.' Then he hung up.

He hadn't told Liz about his conversation with Marty, just that Josie had asked him to contact her brothers to come and collect her. The depth of Liz and Clancy's horror at the idea had surprised him. They'd done a sterling job at convincing her to stay, at convincing her she was needed. At convincing her she was no trouble at all. He'd never have managed that on his own.

And the way they'd marched into her cabin with its bright splashes of colour and its easy laughter, its comforting cosiness…all at ease and with that lazy kind of energy that spoke of goodwill and friendship, had made him realise everything his own life lacked. It gave him a glimpse of what life with a woman like Josie would be like.

Liz and Clancy would miss her when she left.

There was no denying it: so would he. But a man like him had no right messing with a woman like Josie.

He pushed that thought away and seized the lemonades. It was time to go and enjoy dinner with Josie. And Liz; he hadn't forgotten Liz.

When Liz left, Kent tidied up. He thought Josie had dozed off, but when he turned he found her watching him. He rolled his shoulders, shifted his weight from the balls of his feet to his heels and back again. He wondered if she sensed his reluctance to leave the cosiness of her cabin. 'Not tired?'

'I feel pleasantly lazy. I'm glad you wouldn't let me help clean up.'

Her honesty made him grin, put him at ease.

She readjusted a pillow at her back. 'Tell me about your sister.'

It took a moment for the words to hit him, and when they did they stabbed through him with a ferocity that took his breath. He took a step back and went to shout an unthinking 'No!' but clamped down on his lips until he'd brought the impulse under control. The night was cool but that didn't account for the coldness that rushed through him. 'Why?' The word sounded sharp in the silence of the cabin but Josie seemed oblivious to his reaction, to the difficulty he had breathing.

'Because I always wanted a sister.'

He thought of her brothers, took in her wistful expression, and understood why.

'What was her name? What things did she like to do?'

For Josie's sake he tried to think past the pain. 'Her name was Rebecca. I always called her Beck. Everyone else called her Becky.' His words came out short and halting as a picture of Beck's face turning to laugh at him in her sailing boat rose in his mind.

'I've always liked that name.' She shaded her eyes against the brightness of the overhead light. 'Would it be OK if we turned on the lamp?'

He switched on the lamp, turned off the overhead light and a warm glow suffused the room. Josie patted the bed beside her, her lips curved in a soft smile he wanted to fall into. He sat in Clancy's camp chair instead. He couldn't trust himself any closer to her than that. Not when the dark beat at the windows, not when this room and this woman transported him away from his lonely mountain. If he was fanciful he'd say Josie's cabin was an Aladdin's cave where fairy tales came true.

Only he was too old to believe in fairy tales.

'Was Becky a girly girl or a tomboy?'

That made him laugh. 'In company butter wouldn't melt in her mouth. But when nobody was watching she'd try and out-rough and out-tumble me.'

Josie grinned. 'Did she succeed?'

'Not a chance.' He grinned too. 'She was two years younger and not much bigger than you.'

'What did she like to do?'

He told her about Beck's love of sailing, the job she'd had as a pathologist, her addiction to candied ginger, and about the time when she was fifteen and she'd dyed her hair such a deep purple they'd spent an entire Christmas calling her Miss Plum. And the more he talked the easier it became. Finally he stopped and he couldn't have said why, but he felt lighter.

'I envy you,' Josie sighed. 'Not losing Becky, of course. That's awful.'

Sadness swept through him, but the weight didn't press back down.

'But the relationship the two of you had… It was really lovely.'

He nodded. He'd been in danger of forgetting. He eyed Josie for a moment. 'It's not like that with you and your brothers?'

He waited for her to tense up, but she didn't. 'They're

over ten years older than me. We didn't grow up together. They're the children of my father's first marriage.'

A wealth of meaning emerged from her words. Kent suddenly saw the picture clearly—along with what he suspected was Marty and Frank's resentment and jealousy of their younger half-sibling.

'Their lives have been harder than mine,' she added as if she read his mind. 'They grew up with their mother and she was a bitter woman, hard.'

'That's not your fault,' he pointed out gently.

'No, but I want to build whatever bridges with them that I can. I promised my father I'd try.' She fixed him with a look. 'What did Marty say when you spoke to him?'

'I left a message on his answering machine,' he hedged.

'Not tonight, but earlier when you spoke to him.'

He didn't want her upset, but he didn't want to lie to her either. He wanted her on her guard around this Marty and Frank. 'He said he was snowed under with work and would find it difficult to get away before next Tuesday.'

'Oh.'

At the look on her face he wanted to smash Marty all over again.

'They're always so busy,' she sighed. 'I think they hide behind their work.' She pleated the blanket between her fingers. 'I think they're afraid to love me.'

'What kind of nonsense is that?' he exploded.

She met his gaze head-on. 'I'd say it was your kind of nonsense, Kent.'

He shot to his feet, rubbed the back of his nape. 'It's getting late. It's time you got some rest.'

'Scaredy cat,' she murmured, but she settled back without demur as he pulled the covers up around her shoulders.

'Goodnight, Josie.'

'Goodnight, Kent.'

He hovered for a moment, wanting to kiss her forehead, but he pulled back at the last moment. Her taunt followed him all the way back to the house and plagued his sleep like a stray dog that fed on his dreams.

On Friday afternoon after Clancy left, Josie finally grew sick of staring at four walls. Actually, she'd grown sick of it yesterday, but today her inactivity really started to pall. This morning she'd argued with Kent about exchanging her pyjamas for real clothes, and lost. Pulling her wrap more firmly about her and tying it at her waist, Josie folded the camp chair, took it out to the veranda, unfolded it again and collapsed into it, breathing hard. She hated how the smallest thing wore her out.

She'd hated arguing with Kent too.

She cringed when she remembered the things she'd shouted at him. She'd called him a tyrant. And a voyeur. She still couldn't believe she'd said that.

He'd laughed at her, and she'd wanted to stamp her feet—a near impossible feat when confined to bed.

She doubted he even saw her as a woman now. She scowled. Oh, yes, he gave her friendly concern, teasingly derided her chess skills and praised the excellence of her crossword-solving skills.

She knew she was sinking low when she clung to praise about crosswords.

Somehow he'd purged his desire for her and she wanted to know how. Though maybe he hadn't had all that much to begin with. Her scowl deepened. She just wasn't his kind of woman, was she? That new sense of closeness that had developed between them since they'd talked about their siblings had disappeared too. In some imperceptible way Kent was withdrawing from her. And she didn't know how to stop him.

She made an impatient noise in the back of her throat. She hadn't come on this holiday to obsess about a man. If he wanted to withdraw that was his business. She'd come to formulate a plan for the rest of her life, remember? She was no closer to doing that than when she'd arrived.

And she only had a week left. Marty and Frank would be expecting an answer to that particular question at the end of all this. She could practically see their serious half-frowns, hear their foot-tapping impatience.

Oh, for heaven's sake! What business was it of theirs? It was not as if they had to financially support her or…

They were her brothers. She chided herself for her lack of charity. Of course they worried about her. And now that her father was gone she hoped they might forge closer ties.

She scowled again. She was all for promoting closer ties, but they needn't think they could bully her.

'Heck! Whose blood are you after?'

Josie started then drooled. Kent. She swiped a hand across her chin.

'Still imagining skinning me alive after our spat this morning?'

His grin told her he didn't harbour any hard feelings and she found herself smiling back at him. 'No, though I find myself cringing every time I remember calling you a voyeur.'

He eased himself down onto the single step, his grin widening. 'Nah, don't feel bad about that. You've got me pegged. I'm waiting with bated breath for those cute little shortie pyjamas to make a comeback. Those fluffy sheep did strange things to me.'

His teasing fired the blood through her veins, although she knew he didn't mean it. 'Funny things?' She tried to ignore the burn of desire. 'Like falling all over the place laughing, right?'

'More like getting me hot and bothered when I imagine peeling them off your body.'

Josie gulped and the blood pumped through her so hard and hot she thought her fever had returned. Kent jerked back as if he couldn't believe he'd uttered the words. And just like that the tension coiled around them.

With a muttered curse, he leapt up and strode several feet away. Josie expected him to plunge straight into the cover of the trees and keep walking. Without a backward glance. When he didn't, her eyes, greedy for the sight of him, memorised every hard, lean angle of his body.

He always wore jeans and either a T-shirt or a long-sleeved chambray shirt, and she couldn't decide which did him the greater justice. The jeans, whether low-slung, stretch or bootleg, did strange things to her pulse. They also left her in little doubt of his, uh, assets.

And she literally drooled at the sight of thin cotton stretched across his shoulders and arms in those fitted T-shirts. But the faded blue chambray intensified the blue of his eyes and caught her up in fantasies of making love with him on long, lazy summer afternoons.

Oh, who was she kidding? It didn't matter what he wore for her to get caught up in those kinds of fantasies.

He swung back to face her and she could see him trying to fight a scowl. 'Sorry.' The word snapped out of him. 'You'd better forget I said that.'

She didn't want to forget. She wanted—

'We already decided that wouldn't be sensible.'

Had they? When? 'I'm tired of sensible,' she muttered.

His eyes darkened, then he grinned. 'Either way, Josephine Peterson, you're not physically up for an athletic bout of lovemaking. Besides, it's against doctor's orders.'

She knew he was right. If a shower wore her out, then how on earth…?

Pictures rose in her mind. Pictures that didn't help. She tried to push them away, far far away where they couldn't torment her.

'So, in the meantime,' he took his seat on the step again, 'why don't you tell me why you were glaring at this glorious view as if you meant to do it physical harm?'

CHAPTER NINE

JOSIE'S lips turned down and her shoulders sagged. Kent wanted to haul her into his lap, tuck her head under his chin and wrap his arms around her slight body until she stopped looking so glum.

Not a good idea.

He didn't do hugs. And he had no doubt that if he hugged Josie she'd get the wrong idea. He couldn't let that happen, couldn't let her rely on him in the long term.

A scowl shrugged through him. He shouldn't let her rely on him in the short term either.

If it wasn't for her darn brothers he wouldn't, but she needed someone to look out for her. She'd drawn the short straw in him, though maybe Clancy and Liz made up for it.

'Did Marty say anything else when you spoke to him? Has Frank called at all?'

Was she upset because of her brothers?

'Nope and nope.' He kept the snarl out of his voice. Just.

Her lips turned down more. 'I mean,' he added quickly, 'he was concerned about your health, of course. Relieved when I told him you'd be OK.' Because then he wouldn't be dragged away from his *oh-so-important work*.

Not that he'd rung in the last couple of days to check

on how she was doing. That knowledge hung in the silence between them. 'Why?'

She lifted one shoulder. 'No reason.'

'Are they why you looked fit to kill someone?' He understood that. In fact, he'd help her if she wanted.

'Oh, no.' She quickly shook her head and all the browns and russets and maples of her hair swished about her face before settling back around her shoulders. He wanted to reach out and touch it. He wanted to bury his face in it.

'But, you see, I haven't worked out what I'm going to do with the rest of my life yet and that's the reason for this holiday in the first place.'

The note of panic in her words hauled him back. He skewed around on the step to face her more fully. 'Let's back up a bit. Why can't you keep doing whatever it was you did before you came to Eagle Reach?' Had she been sacked or something?

She smiled, a sad smile that speared right through the centre of him. 'For the last two years I looked after my father. That job doesn't exist any more.'

Bile rose in his throat. 'I'm sorry I—'

'It's not your fault.' She waved his apology away. 'My father had dementia and I didn't want to place him in a nursing home so I completed an Assistant in Nursing course. I don't regret it. I cherish the time I spent with him.'

'But you don't want to do that any more?'

'No, I don't want to do that any more.' A shadow passed across her face. 'No. No more.'

He understood. Watching someone die was the hardest thing in the world. Especially when it was someone you loved.

'What did you do, Kent? Before your sea change and you came out here?'

The question caught him off guard. He'd known she hadn't believed him when he'd said it before. He hadn't bothered trying to set her straight and now it reeked of deceit. He rubbed the back of his neck.

'Kent?'

'I was a doctor.' Dedicated to saving people's lives. He'd removed himself from society pretty quick-smart once he realised he had a greater talent for destruction, though.

If he had an ounce of decency in him he'd leave Josie alone too.

'You're a doctor?' Josie shot forward so quickly she'd have fallen out of her chair if Kent hadn't reached out and steadied her. His fingers wrapped around her arm, warm and vibrant. More than anything, she wanted to fall into him. He removed his hand before she could do anything so stupid.

His close-lipped silence spoke volumes. 'I was a GP.'

It shouldn't have made sense, but in a strange way it did. She wanted to cry. 'And why—?'

She gulped back her words at his glare.

'I found I was unsuited to the profession.'

She didn't believe that for a moment. She refused to risk another soul-crushing glare by saying so, though. 'So, the doctor's orders I've been following have been yours?'

'Yes.'

It explained his professional detachment.

A wave of dizziness shook her. He hadn't stopped practising because of his mother and sister, had he?

'You're free to consult a second opinion, of course. Dr Jenkins does house calls. If you want I'll ring him and—'

'No.' She stared at him, horrified. 'I trust your judgement.' The scowl left his face but not his eyes. 'You made Molly well again, didn't you?'

At her name, Molly lifted her head and thumped her tail. She'd hardly left Josie's side since she'd been let back in after the worst of her illness had passed.

'And she was in way worse shape than me.'

His lips twisted into the wryest of smiles. 'I hate to point this out to you, Josie, but Molly is just a dog.'

'Molly isn't *just* anything. She's lovely and you made her well again, like you're making me well again. I don't think you're unsuited to the profession at all.' But she didn't want him to start scowling again so she didn't pursue that line further. She collapsed against the back of her chair. 'Not that it's doing me much good.'

His eyebrows shot up and she laughed, realising what she'd just said. 'I meant inspiration-wise. It won't help me sort out what to do with the rest of my life.' Marty and Frank's faces rose in front of her and her quick surge of humour evaporated in a puff that berated her for her frivolity.

One week. She glanced out at the view spread before her and couldn't hold back a sigh. Her eyes drifted to the man seated on the step.

'What did you do before you took on the care of your father?'

'I was halfway through a teaching degree.' He raised an eyebrow but she shook her head. 'The thought of study doesn't fill me with a great deal of enthusiasm. Besides, I don't want to leave Buchanan's Point and there aren't many opportunities for teachers in the local area.' It'd take years before she was posted there.

'Why don't you want to leave?'

'It's home.' It was that simple. 'It's where I belong. And then there's the house. It's been in the family for generations. I couldn't just leave it.'

'Couldn't your brothers look after it?'

Marty and Frank again. The sky became a little greyer, although there wasn't a cloud in it. 'The house belonged to my mother. Her family have lived in it since it was built over a hundred years ago.' And she wasn't selling it.

Kent stared at her for a moment then grinned as if eminently satisfied with something. 'If you've a house, Josie, then at least you've a roof over your head.'

'I have a home,' she corrected, which was more than Kent could boast out here at Eagle Reach, for all his cows and cabins.

His eyes gentled. 'Tell me about it.'

She shrugged. Where to start? But as she imagined her home her lips curved into a smile. 'It's beautiful. It's called Geraldine's Gardens and it's the only house on the bluff and it looks out over the town and beach. A little path winds down to a private beach. It's only tiny, but it is lovely.'

He sat up straighter. 'And the house?'

'It's beautiful too. Federation style, return verandas, fancy fretwork.' All of which took an enormous amount of upkeep. 'It is a little large for one person,' she admitted, 'but…but who knows what'll happen down the track?' She hoped to fill it with a family of her own one day.

'Too big?' His eyes narrowed. 'How many bedrooms?'

She hesitated. 'Eight.'

'Eight!' Kent shot to his feet. 'I…'

'Yeah, it's big.' And it took a lot of cleaning, but it was worth it. And she wasn't selling.

'Josie?'

She pulled her thoughts back. 'Hmm?'

'Marty and Frank are OK about the house?'

'Oh, no, they want me to sell it. They think it's too much for me.'

Kent's eyebrows knitted together.

'But the house is like a family heirloom.' She smiled up at him. Instinctively, she knew he'd understand. 'I need to preserve it to pass on to the next generation.'

He brushed the backs of his fingers across her cheek. 'I envy you your home, Josephine Peterson.'

Her heart thumped like a mad thing. 'Then you should come and visit some time. It's not like I don't have the room or anything. Next time you're passing through…' A pipedream, she knew. She also knew she was babbling.

He pulled his fingers back abruptly. 'Time you were back in bed.'

'But I'm not doing anything. I'm just sitting.'

Her argument died in her throat when he leaned down and picked her up. Her heart pounded so hard she swore there'd be bruises. 'I, umm…' Her tongue stuck to the roof of her mouth. She tried to unglue it. 'I can walk, you know?'

Not that she wanted to. She wanted to stay right here. She looped an arm around his shoulders, his broad, beautiful shoulders, and bit back a purr of pure pleasure.

His gaze met hers then flicked to her lips. She gulped. An insistent throb started up low, deep down in her abdomen. His lips opened and her breath stilled. Then he waggled those wicked eyebrows. 'I want you to conserve your energy. Doctor's orders.'

He made no move towards the door of the cabin, though. His hot male scent filled her nostrils, his hard body imprinted itself on hers and her heart continued to beat itself to a pulp.

'I, umm…' She wished she could speak properly. She gave a shaky laugh. 'I think I'd conserve a whole lot more energy if you put me down again.'

He grinned. 'Yeah?'

She loved his teasing. 'You do seriously wicked things to my pulse rate, Kent Black.'

He shook his head, mock serious. 'That's not good for conserving energy. You'll need to do something about that.'

Like what? All the images, ideas, suggestions flooding through her involved her expending a whole lot more energy, not conserving it. 'Doctor's orders, huh?'

'You bet.'

She trailed her fingers into the V of his shirt. Heat came off him in thick, drugging waves and she tugged gently at the hair there, revelling in its springiness, before tracing her hand back up his neck to his jaw. His breath caught when she ran her palm across the roughness of his half-day growth and hers quickened. The scrape of desire sparked from her palm to curl her toes.

His eyes turned a deep, dark navy. 'Josie.'

The single word growled out of his throat, but he made no move to set her down and a reckless triumph seized her. 'You know what?' She traced his lips with her fingers. 'I'm afraid of stray dogs and goannas and of the kind of solitude that means you don't clap eyes on another human being for three days straight, but I'm not afraid of this.'

She reached up and replaced her fingers with her lips. Kent's arms tightened around her and her whole body sang, but he held himself rigid, his lips refusing to respond as hers moved tentatively over his.

She'd never taken the initiative before. It part-appalled, part-thrilled her.

No, it wholly thrilled her. But Kent's lack of involvement sent a shock wave of frustration through her. Determination welled up, determination to draw out that response.

She traced the length of his bottom lip with her tongue, from left to right, slowly, savouring his taste and texture. 'Yum,' she murmured against the corner of his mouth when she reached it. Then she slipped her tongue inside to trace his inner lips, from right to left, and Kent jerked as if electrified.

Then he crushed her against him and his mouth devoured hers and she'd never known that so much feeling could go into a single kiss. She flung both her arms around his neck and kissed him back with everything inside her, a fury of need pulsing through her veins as his tongue teased and tangled with hers.

Both his arms went around her waist and the lower half of her body slid down his until the tips of her toes touched the ground. Pulled flush against him, the most sensitive part of her pressed against the hard length straining through the denim of his jeans, teasing her until nothing made sense except her overwhelming need for him. With an inarticulate moan, her head dropped back and Josie lost herself in sensation.

Kent branded her neck with kisses. One hand curved around her bottom to keep her planted hard up against him, the other tangled in the hair at her nape to draw her mouth back to his. He claimed drugging kiss after drugging kiss until she was a trembling, sobbing mass of need.

Then a fit of coughing claimed her.

She leaned against him after it finished, trying to get her

breath back, trying to draw strength into limbs that shook. His hands curved around her shoulders, steadying her, supporting her, but she sensed his withdrawal. Still…

What a kiss! She couldn't curb the exhilaration coursing through her body.

She wondered how soon they could do that again.

One look at Kent's face told her there'd be no repeat performances today. And from the look of that scowl, probably not tomorrow either.

Oh, well. It'd give her a chance to get her strength back. With a sigh of regret she pushed away from him. 'Well,' she started brightly, 'that was…'

The words died in her throat for the second time when he swept her up in his arms and strode inside with her. Being held by Kent felt like coming home.

And she was homesick. Big time.

His face might be grim, but he laid her on the bed with a gentleness normally reserved for priceless artworks. She blinked furiously when he took a hasty step away, bit back a moan of loss.

He glared as she nestled down against the pillows. 'That was—'

'Heavenly,' she announced. 'When can we do it again?'

His jaw dropped then he swung away and stalked straight back out of the cabin.

'Kent Black,' she murmured, her eyes fluttering closed. 'You are one sexy man.'

She wondered if he'd ever stop running.

'Checkmate.'

Josie pushed the chessboard away with a sigh. 'I'm not improving.'

'You don't concentrate,' Kent chided.

How on earth was a girl supposed to concentrate when Kent's lips hovered just there across the chessboard and created all kinds of tempting fantasies inside her, huh?

Fantasies that were way more exciting than beating him at chess.

It was Sunday. Two whole days since their kiss. But for the past two days that kiss was all Josie could think about. She'd completed her three days of prescribed bed rest, but she could tell Kent didn't think her recovered enough for more kissing.

'What about catering?'

His words momentarily dragged her away from thoughts of kissing. 'Umm…' What had she missed?

'You could start up your own catering company.'

Oh, they were back to that. Still, it was better than nothing, she supposed. She'd expected him to bolt out of here as soon as he'd annihilated her at chess. As he had yesterday. As if afraid she'd try and kiss him again.

She wasn't going to kiss him again until she'd recovered her full strength. She had no intention of letting a little cough get in her way next time.

'I can't go into catering.' She'd already considered the idea and dismissed it.

'Why not?'

'Suzanna de Freits has the market cornered in Buchanan's Point, not to mention the surrounding seaside villages of Crescent Beach and Diamond Head.'

'Afraid of a little competition?'

She grinned at the rallying note in his voice. He obviously thought she needed a pep talk. 'Her savouries are better than mine.'

'I bet her chocolate cake doesn't come close.'

Bless his heart. He actually looked as if he meant that. Thoughts of kissing rose up through her again. She shook her head. 'Suzanna is a single mother of three school-age children.' And a friend. 'She works hard. I'm not poaching her customers.'

'Not even to save your house…home?'

'People are more important than bricks and mortar.' Even when those bricks and mortar made up Geraldine's Gardens. 'I'd rather take on another dementia patient than do that.' Maybe it wouldn't be so bad if she wasn't nursing her father? Her stomach curdled at the thought all the same.

'Don't do that.'

She may not have any choice. Frustration shot through her. She should've spent the last two days searching for a solution to this particular problem rather than obsessing about kissing Kent.

'Ooh, humungous huntsman.' She shrank in her chair and pointed to the kitchen wall.

With an exaggerated sigh, Kent climbed to his feet, rolled up yesterday's newspaper and advanced on the hapless spider. Josie scampered after him and snatched the paper out of his hands. 'What do you think you're doing?'

He stared at her. 'I'm going to squash it.'

Her eyes widened. 'But you're like a hundred million times bigger than it.' She whacked him on the arm with the rolled-up newspaper. 'It's only a spider.'

'You were the one that said—'

'I didn't say kill it!' She whacked him again. 'And just because I'm female doesn't mean I run yelling and screaming from a spider.'

'You do from dogs and goannas.'

'I'm going to pretend I didn't hear that.' She glared at him. 'Out of my way.'

Josie unrolled the newspaper, folded it in half then eased in under the spider's legs—slowly, slowly—until the spider sat on the end of the newspaper. Without taking her eyes off it, she walked across the room and outside.

She was halfway between her cabin and the nearest stand of trees when the spider rose up on all of its eight legs and raced the length of the newspaper towards her. She dropped the newspaper with a squeal and jumped back.

Kent laughed so hard from his vantage point on the veranda he had to sit down. 'I didn't say I wanted it on me!'

She glared at him, but he only laughed harder. 'I've found your new career, Josie.'

'This should be good,' she muttered, but her lips started to twitch.

'Stand-up comedy.'

'Oh, ha-ha, very funny.' She rolled her eyes and collapsed onto the veranda beside him. Then glanced around warily. 'Where did it go?'

'Not scared of spiders, huh?'

She lifted her chin. 'Not scared enough to kill them.'

He grinned down at her, shook his head, went to turn away then swung back and kissed her, hard. Once.

Her eyes glazed over. When they finally cleared she could see him already regretting the impulsive act.

'Wow!' She swore she'd keep it light if it was the last thing she did. 'With that kind of positive reinforcement I'll never be afraid of spiders again. Though,' some imp made her add, 'I'll need another two or three sessions of that same therapy before I'm fully cured.'

His grin, when it came, was one of those long, slow,

crooked ones that made her heart go boom. Desire slowly burned through her.

'You're impossible, you know that?'

She shrugged. 'If stand-up comedy is my thing then I'd best get in some practice.' But the stand-up comedy thing was just a joke. They both knew that. Her smile dipped as her original problem bore down on her again.

Kent nudged her shoulder. 'Earth to Josie.'

She shook herself. 'What are you up to for the next hour or so?'

His eyes narrowed. 'Why?'

She leaned back and raised an eyebrow. 'You know, that question just begs for a suggestive comeback.' She took pity on him when he dragged a hand down his face. 'I feel like making chocolate cake.'

She went to jump up but his hand on her arm stopped her. 'You're supposed to be taking it easy.'

'Don't worry.' She shot him a cheeky grin. 'You'll be the one doing all the hard work.'

Kent didn't know how Josie managed it, but she made baking a cake fun. He'd tried to tell himself he'd only hung around to prevent her from overdoing it, but that was a lie. He'd stayed because he couldn't stay away. In fact, if he could've eased her suffering and his own worry, Josie's illness was probably the highlight of the last year.

He cut that thought off, angry with himself. But then Josie smiled and the tightness inside him eased. He enjoyed watching her deft hands measuring out ingredients. He enjoyed her teasing his ineptness with a wooden spoon. He enjoyed watching the colour bloom back into her cheeks.

Josie popped the cake in the oven then swiped a finger

along the inside rim of the mixing bowl, gathering as much cake mix as she could, then popped the finger in her mouth and closed her eyes in bliss. He enjoyed that too.

'Yum.' As if aware of his gaze she opened her eyes and held out the wooden spoon for him. 'Go on,' she urged when he hesitated. 'I bet you and Becky fought over the wooden spoon when you were kids and your mum baked a cake.'

He jerked back, waiting for acid to fill his stomach at the mention of his family. It didn't come, so he reached for the spoon. 'She wasn't much of a one for baking cakes. Soup was her thing.' Big, rich pots of simmering goodness. In winter he'd rush home from school, his mouth watering with the knowledge of what awaited him when he got there.

He hadn't thought of that in a long time.

'Soup.' Josie stared at him in mock indignation. 'Your mum cooked the most scrumptious homemade soup ever, and don't tell me she didn't because I can tell from the expression on your face that she did. Yet you had the gall to feed me tinned stuff?'

He grinned, but he wished he had cooked her up a big pot of soup. 'To be honest, I didn't think you'd much notice…or care.'

'To be honest,' she leaned in close as if confiding a secret, 'you'd be right.'

He wanted to kiss her again, so he retreated to the table and set about licking the spoon clean. Josie had made this cabin the cosiest darn place on this side of the mountain. On second thoughts, probably the cosiest place on the whole mountain. He'd never set foot inside Smiley McDonald's house, but he'd bet Mrs Smiley McDonald didn't have the same knack Josie did. The knack of creating a home from nothing.

It'd started him thinking too. He could make improvements to all these cabins. The way Josie had done. And up at the house too. His mind fizzed with new possibilities.

Maybe she should go into interior decorating. He wondered if a person needed qualifications or whether they—

He jerked in his seat as the solution to Josie's problem slapped him on the head. 'How many bedrooms did you say you had at Geraldine's Gardens?'

'Eight.' She didn't turn from washing the dishes.

'And how many living areas?'

She tossed a glance over her shoulder then shrugged and went back to the dishes. 'There's the formal and informal lounge rooms, the family room, the sunroom, the breakfast room and the library. Oh, and there's a ballroom.'

How big was this place? 'Josie,' he tried to keep his tone measured, tried to keep the excitement out of his voice, 'why don't you turn Geraldine's Gardens into a bed and breakfast?'

She dropped the bowl she was washing and swung to face him. Soapsuds dripped to her bare toes. Her mouth formed a perfect O and Kent found himself wanting to kiss it.

Again.

Josie couldn't contain her excitement. She raced over to the table, plonked herself down and gripped his hands. 'Do you really think I could do that?'

'Sure you could.'

He squeezed her hands before gently detaching them and leaning back to survey her. She wanted to wriggle beneath his scrutiny, but she didn't. She stared back, held her breath and hoped he liked what he saw.

'I mean, look at what you've done with this place.'

She knew her grin must be ridiculously wide. Kent had the kind of rugged good looks that could make her pulse perform a tango, but it was more than that. He possessed a kindness, a generosity, and, no matter how hard he tried to hide it, it always seemed to find a way to the surface.

She knew now what Clancy meant. Kent didn't suit this solitude any more than she did. Burying himself out here like this was a crime.

And none of your business, a voice intoned inside her.

Pooh. What did she care about that? She'd poke her nose in where it wasn't wanted if she thought it'd do any good. But it wouldn't. Kent wouldn't listen to her. He'd scowl and become a stranger and be glad to see the back of her.

'If you can manage all this here,' he continued, 'how much more could you achieve at Geraldine's Gardens?'

Excitement shifted through her.

'I bet there are plenty of local handicrafts in Buchanan's Point you could feature.'

She could theme the rooms. And she could get in tourist brochures for areas of local interest. Maybe even arrange the odd tour or two to the near by vineyards or the recreated colonial town less than an hour away.

'And you could showcase local produce.'

Ooh, yes. Suzanna made the most fabulous preserved fruit, and someone from the women's institute would be happy to provide her with pickles and jam.

Kent leaned forward. 'More to the point, you're great with people, Josie. You'd make a wonderful hostess.'

She found herself starting to choke up…then she sat back, her shoulders sagging. 'There are hundreds of little seaside towns all along the coast of New South Wales identical to Buchanan's Point. Not to mention the larger centres that offer nightlife and restaurants and attractions galore. How on earth do I compete with them? What can I offer except a stay in a lovely house?'

'You need a selling point.' Kent drummed his fingers against the table. 'How much did you hate the nursing aspects of looking after your father?'

She gazed at him blankly.

'I mean the bathing and feeding, making sure he took his medication et cetera?'

'Oh, I didn't mind that at all.' It was the watching him die that she'd hated.

'Then why don't you tailor your b & b for invalids and their carers? There's a rapidly expanding aged population in this country. There's a market out there, Josie, just waiting to be tapped into. Your qualifications are an added bonus, especially if you can offer the carers a couple of hours' free time for themselves each day.'

Her jaw dropped. There'd been days when she'd have killed for a couple of hours off. Not for anything special, just a haircut or to browse in the local library, or even just to sit over a cup of coffee she hadn't made herself. It would've helped. Marty and Frank had always been too busy to sit with their father much. And she wouldn't have dreamed of asking anyone else except in an emergency.

'Have you any savings?'

'Some. Why?'

'Because you'll need something to tide you over until the money starts coming in.'

Good point. She did a quick calculation in her head. If she was frugal she'd have enough for a few months.

'Advertising will be your major expense.'

Oops, she hadn't factored that in. She wondered if the bank would give her a loan.

'Let me invest in the project, Josie.'

Her jaw dropped.

'Don't worry, I'm not being altruistic.' His grin said otherwise. 'I have plenty of money stashed away, and I have a feeling I'll be seeing quite a return on that money.'

Did he really have that much faith in her? The blue of his eyes held such an earnest appeal Josie almost said yes. She dragged her eyes from his and forced herself to think the idea through.

Her heart sank. She tried to swallow the bile that rose in her throat. 'No,' she croaked.

He sat back as if she'd struck him. 'Why not?'

Because he'd made it clear he wasn't interested in any kind of personal commitment. If he invested in her project he'd be hovering in the background of her life for heaven only knew how long, kissing her then running away. She wouldn't be able to stop herself from building larger-scale fantasies around him.

She'd never move on.

She stared at the rugged, lean lines of his face and her mouth went dry. Some time over the last three weeks she'd gone and done the stupidest thing in the world. She'd fallen in love with Kent Black.

When? While he nursed her through the worst of her fever? Or earlier…when he rescued her from the goanna, perhaps, or the first time they'd played chess? Maybe it was the day of the church fête, or the time she'd caught him skinny-dipping down at the river or—

Enough already!

He'd never love her back. Panic pounded through her.

She was afraid of dogs and goannas and ticks and spiders. She was even a bit afraid of Bridget Anderson. He could never love a woman who was like that.

Numbness settled over the surface of her skin. Even if by some miracle he grew fond of her, she could never live out here with him in all his isolation. It went against everything she was.

And he would never give it up.

Stalemate.

Kent leaned across the table, took her chin in his hand and studied her face closely. 'You're pale. You need to rest. We'll talk about this later.'

Josie wanted to laugh, not because she found it funny but because her heart was breaking and Kent's concern over a mere chest infection seemed suddenly trivial.

Nevertheless, she made no murmur of protest, but climbed onto the sofa bed and buried her face in a pillow.

The minutes seemed like hours as she waited for Kent to finish washing the last of the dishes, to dry them then take the cake out of the oven when the timer rang. She could've groaned out loud when he started tidying the cabin. She sensed him hovering over her, but she refused to turn around, refused to unbury her face from the pillow.

Only when she heard him tiptoe out did she let the hot tears slide down her cheeks.

CHAPTER TEN

'WHY won't you let me invest in your b & b?'

It was Monday afternoon and Clancy had just left. Since yesterday, she and Kent had circled around each other very carefully—with the emphasis on the very. Super-polite. Extremely wary.

Josie didn't know how she'd get through the next week if things remained like this. She didn't know how she'd get through it if they didn't. The one thing she did know—she didn't want to have this conversation.

Kent straddled one of the hard chairs and folded his arms along its back. They bulged in his fitted T-shirt, each muscle clearly delineated in pale blue cotton. Josie curled herself into a corner of the sofa and tried not to drool. She might not want to have this conversation, but she didn't want to stop ogling him either.

That probably made her a female chauvinist pig. She cleared her throat and dragged her gaze away from his tempting arms, his tempting lips. She doubted she could look at him and talk at the same time.

She hated confrontations. Wherever possible she avoided them. Kent's body language, though, told her she wasn't going to avoid this one. They could keep this pleasant and polite. She pulled in a breath. It didn't have to descend into an argument or a fight.

'Why are you refusing my money?'

'I really appreciate your offer, Kent, but I'm not going to risk your money when I don't know if I can pull this off.'

'You'll succeed. I know you will.'

His smile almost undid her. Of course they could keep this pleasant. They were adults, weren't they?

'If I invest in your project, I know I'll get a good return for my money.'

She couldn't let him go on thinking he could change her mind. 'What do you want with more money? It's not like you have anything to spend it on out here.'

His jaw dropped and she hated herself, but she ploughed on all the same. 'What kind of input would you expect to have at Geraldine's Gardens if you did invest, huh?'

'None. All the business decisions would be yours.'

He meant it too. She could see that. A lump lodged in her throat and refused to budge. 'I don't want your charity,' she finally managed.

He leaned forward. 'Where will you get the money for the initial outlay, then?'

At least she could answer that. She'd lain awake last night pondering that exact same question. She forced her smile to widen. 'From Marty and Frank. This is just the kind of project designed to bring us closer.'

They were family. They'd help. This scheme was perfect. She crossed her fingers and prayed she was right, because she had a feeling she'd need their support when she returned home. In more ways than one.

Kent leapt up, his chair crashing to the floor. 'Marty and Frank!'

She hunched her shoulders up around her ears. What on earth…? They were supposed to be keeping this pleasant.

'Are you mad?'

No, but he was. Hopping mad. And she didn't get it. 'They're family. They're who I should turn to.' And if it all went to plan it'd be perfect.

Perfect except Kent wouldn't be in her life.

He wouldn't be in her life if he did invest in her b & b anyway, not in the way she wanted, so it was a moot point.

It didn't feel like a moot point.

'Do you seriously think they'll help you?'

He stared at her the same way she'd stared at that tick as it had burrowed into her flesh. Her chin shot up, though her shoulders stayed hunched. 'Why wouldn't they?'

They would. Of course they would.

'They sent you out here, didn't they?'

'Which just goes to show how thoughtful and—'

'Garbage. It just goes to show how little they know you.'

She hated the thread of truth that wove its way through his words. She resisted it. Her brothers had sent her on this holiday because they knew she'd needed it.

'For Pete's sake,' he glared at her, 'this is your idea of the holiday from hell.'

Had been—past tense. She'd come back. To visit Clancy and Liz. She wouldn't stay at Eagle Reach, though. She had a feeling she wouldn't be welcome. 'It's turned out all right,' she argued.

'You got sick!'

'That could've happened anywhere.'

He swung away, raked his hands through his hair then swung back. 'You can't trust them.'

She gaped at him. She couldn't believe he'd just said

that, couldn't believe he'd try and dash all her hopes in one fell blow. They were the only hopes she had left.

She leapt up, trembling. 'You don't even know my brothers. You've spoken to Marty on the phone for all of two minutes and…'

A horrible thought struck her. 'Unless you haven't told me everything. Is there something I should know?'

What on earth could Marty have said to make Kent react like this? Her mouth went dry. For one craven moment she wished she could call that question back.

Kent stared at her. He rolled his shoulders then shoved his hands in his pockets and glanced away. 'No.'

Her shoulders sagged until her thoughts caught up with her relief. *You can't trust them!* 'Then…' Her mouth worked but for a moment no sound would come out. 'Then you're basing your assumption on what you know of me. You think they'll take advantage of me, because I can't look after myself. You think I can be manipulated just like that.' She took two steps forward and clicked her fingers under his nose. 'You don't think I have a backbone.' Which was why he would never love her.

'You won't get any arguments from me on that score.'

She swallowed back her sudden nausea and wished she'd never seen herself through his eyes. Frustration rose up and engulfed her in a red mist. She'd give him backbone! 'Where on earth do you get off, lecturing me about backbone when you're the one who's burying himself out here in the back of beyond like some scared kid?'

The silence that echoed in the room after her hasty words made her take a step back. Oh, dear lord. She gulped. Then she hitched up her chin and held her ground. In for a penny… 'I don't care how responsible you think you are for your mother's and sister's deaths. You weren't.'

'Don't you…'

He didn't finish the sentence. He shoved a finger under her nose instead, but she batted it away. 'You weren't the one who lit the match and torched the house. You're doing penance for a crime that's not yours.'

His head snapped back. 'It was my job to keep them safe.'

But even as his eyes blazed their fury, Josie saw the desolation in their depths. She had to bite her lip to keep from crying out.

'I should've known what he'd do.' The words wrenched out of him, harsh and merciless.

Josie wanted to cry. And she wanted to drag his head down to her shoulder and hold him. Neither would help, so she gulped back the impulses and glared at him. 'Why?' she demanded. 'Why should you be gifted as a mind-reader when the rest of us aren't? Why should you have known what he'd do when neither your mother nor sister guessed either?'

He blinked.

'I know you'd have saved them if you could've. I know you'd swap places with them if you could. But you can't.'

The lines around his mouth tightened, stark in the tanned lines of his face, then that colour too seemed to leach away, leaving him grey. Her heart ached so hard her knees threatened to buckle.

'You blame yourself and hide out here because it's easier than risking all and learning how to live again.' Anger flashed in his eyes but, curiously, she wasn't afraid of it. 'So until you're prepared to rejoin the land of the living, Kent Black, don't lecture me about backbone.'

Then she had to sit.

His lip curled. 'You can do what you damn well please, but don't tell me how to live my life.'

The anger in his eyes chilled over with the iciness of his withdrawal and Josie hated it. 'What? That's a right you reserve for yourself, is it?' She wanted him angry again. 'Trust me, Josie, but don't trust your brothers?'

If possible, his eyes became colder. She gave a shaky laugh. 'You know as well as I do you should be out there being a doctor and saving what lives you can. It's what you want to do, what you were born to do.'

She watched him close himself up, become the stranger she'd met on her first day here at Eagle Reach, and there wasn't anything she could do about it. She had no words left with which to reach him. Except childish words like 'Grow up', or 'Please love me'.

She couldn't tell him she loved him. He'd hate that worst of all. She glanced up and met his gaze. 'I'll accept your help for my b & b if you go back to being a doctor.'

The pulse at his jaw worked. 'No deal.'

Her heart slumped at his coldness. The last of her hope keeled over and died. She hadn't helped him at all. She'd just raked up painful memories and made him relive them. He was right not to love her.

But before she could apologise, find some way to make amends, Kent spun around and stalked out of the cabin. Even though Josie recovered more of her strength every day, she knew she'd never keep up with him.

Molly whined and poked her head out from her hidey-hole behind the sofa. 'I screwed up, Molly,' Josie sighed. Molly crept out and rested her head on Josie's knee. 'Not only will he never love me, but he'll probably never speak to me again.'

So much for one final week of treasured memories. She had about as much hope of Kent kissing her again as she did of sprouting feathers and laying an egg.

Josie didn't see Kent for the rest of the day. Or the next. Or the day after that either. She and Molly took short forays down to the river, where Josie sat on the bank and lifted her face to the sun, but it never seemed to penetrate to the chill around her heart. She skimmed stones and prayed for a glimpse of Kent.

The stones sank. Kent stayed away.

She'd return in time to have lunch with Clancy. And a game of dominoes. She baked in the afternoons, or read. She did the crossword. Alone.

She ate dinner with Liz, and as soon as Liz left she climbed into bed and pulled the covers over her head.

Was this what the rest of her life entailed—missing Kent? She tried to harden herself to it. During the days it almost worked.

At night the pretence fell away.

She didn't notice the changing greens of the landscape any more, or the silver flash of the river. She didn't see the fat, ice-cream whiteness of the clouds in the bright blue of the sky. Each day dawned grey, no matter how hard the sun shone.

On Thursday she returned from her walk with Molly to find a note pinned to her door. She recognised Kent's strong, masculine scrawl and her stupid heart leapt. She snatched it up. Unfolded it.

'Jacob Pengilly rang. Asked if you'd return his call.'

That was it. No *Dear Josie*. No *Regards, Kent*. Nothing.

Her stupid heart kept leaping about in her chest though, because it knew that this was the perfect excuse to go and see him. Clutching the note, she set off towards his house. She didn't wait to pull in a breath before she knocked on his back screen door. She deliberately turned round to peer at the lush greenness of the forest beyond his back fence. Colour started to intrude itself on the periphery of her consciousness again.

She knew the exact moment he stood behind her because she could smell him. That unique combination of wood smoke and hot man. She closed her eyes and breathed him in before she turned. The screen door partially obscured him, thankfully. Her heart thump-thumped hard enough as it was.

'Hi.' She tried for a smile.

He didn't return her greeting.

She lifted the note. 'I got the message. Thank you.'

Still nothing. Not a word. Not even a flicker of recognition. Certainly no interest.

She blew a strand of hair out of her eyes. 'May I use your phone?'

She waited for him to tell her to go to blazes.

One…two…three fraught seconds went by. Just as she was about to give up and walk away, he pushed the screen door open. Josie, afraid he'd change his mind, squeezed past him in double-quick time then berated herself for not making more of it, for not slowing it down and relishing the brush of her breasts against his chest, her arm against his arm.

Kent, silent still, waved her towards the phone.

She made for it, stopped then spun back. 'Are you all right?' She marched back to peer up into his face. 'Are you sick or anything?'

'No, why?'

Because he was so darn silent, that was why. 'No reason.' She backed off towards the phone. It wasn't a good idea to get too close to Kent. Whenever she did she found she wanted to plaster herself against the hot lines of his body.

Could you imagine the look on his face if she did? If she'd had a sense of humour left she'd have laughed.

He continued to stare at her and she shrugged. 'I haven't seen you around for a few days. It suddenly occurred to me that you might've caught whatever I had.'

'Nope.'

'That's good.' She edged closer to the phone, but wondered what he'd do if he did get sick. How long would it be before someone found him? She wanted to ask if he had a plan in case that happened, but she knew if she did he really would tell her to go to blazes. So she didn't. She picked up the phone instead.

Then dropped the receiver back in the cradle. She'd so busily analysed the note for a clue to Kent she hadn't given a moment's thought to what it might mean.

More proof of an addled brain.

'Something wrong?'

'No.' She bit her lip and stared at the note. 'I just don't know why Jacob would call me.' Unless there was an emergency.

'Who is he?'

'A neighbour.' She shook her head. 'Actually he's my neighbour's son. The neighbour that fell ill, you remember?'

'I remember. You had to call her.' His lips lost some of their tightness. 'Once I got you out of the clothes-line.'

'He works in Brisbane now. Oh, I hope his mum is OK. I hope nothing has happened at Geraldine's Gardens. I hope…'

If there was an emergency Marty or Frank would ring her, surely. Unless the emergency was about Marty or Frank!

With a muttered oath, Kent strode over. 'There's only one way to find out.' He took the note and punched in the number scrawled along its base. 'Ask him.' He pushed the receiver into her hand.

His curt tone had the desired effect and, before she could go off into another disaster scenario, Jacob had picked up the phone at the other end of the line. 'Hello?'

'Jacob, it's Josie Peterson. I got your message.' She abandoned pleasantries. 'Please tell me everyone is OK.'

'Sure they are. I didn't mean to worry you, Josie.'

She clutched her chest and sent Kent a smile. He shook his head, but his lips twitched. 'That's good news. Is your mum recovering?'

'Yes, she is. Look, Josie, I didn't know if I should call you or not, it's just…'

'Yes?'

'Marty and Frank have had a team of surveyors in at Geraldine's Gardens.'

She blinked. They had? She searched her mind for a plausible reason. Maybe there was some kind of mine subsidence in the area or… Her mind went blank.

'They've also had in a fancy property developer from the city.'

Her jaw dropped. She could feel Kent angle in on that straight away, so she hauled it back up. 'Uh-huh.' She couldn't manage much more for the moment.

'I don't know what they're up to, but I don't like it. I think you should come home and find out what's going on.'

So did she. 'I'll leave this afternoon.'

'Good.'

'Thanks for letting me know, Jacob.'

'It's the least I could do after everything you've done for Mum. If there's anything else we can do…'

'Thank you, but I'm sure it's nothing to worry about.'

Marty and Frank were her brothers. There'd be a perfectly logical explanation.

But then again…

You can't trust them. Kent's accusation pounded through her.

'Problem?'

After what he'd said about her and her brothers she had no intention of confiding in him. Not that he'd want her to, of course. 'Nothing I can't handle.' She pressed her hands tightly together. 'Though I'm afraid I have to cut my holiday short.'

'I heard.'

She swallowed. 'I guess it's only by three days.'

She wanted him to say something, anything. He shrugged and turned away. With a heart that flapped like a floundering fish, Josie stepped around him and left.

She was ready to leave in under two hours. That was, her bags were packed and she'd driven into Martin's Gully to say goodbye to Clancy and Liz. And Bridget. Bridget had been busy on tennis-club business but Liz had promised to pass on Josie's goodbyes.

They'd made her promise to ring and tell them she'd arrived home safely. They'd made her promise to return for a visit. Her heart ached, but she'd smiled brightly and promised on both counts.

Now all that was left was to take her bags out to the car, hand the cabin key back to Kent and hug Molly goodbye.

She didn't want to do any of those things. She wanted

to unfold the sofa bed and dive beneath its covers. She didn't. If Jacob had spotted surveyors and property developers at Geraldine's Gardens then so had the rest of Buchanan's Point. And those who hadn't would've been filled in by those who had. Speculation would be rife. Not that she could blame them for that. Her own mind seethed with it too.

What on earth were Marty and Frank up to?

A property developer? She gulped. The townsfolk of Buchanan's Point wouldn't want their seaside village turned into the latest tourist destination, with all its associated high-rises and traffic. They were happy just to meet the passing trade from the nearby hotspots.

At least the deeds to Geraldine's Gardens were in her name, so Marty and Frank couldn't sell it out from under her. And they couldn't force her to sign anything against her will either.

Molly whined and pressed against her legs. Josie dropped to her knees and buried her face in Molly's fur. 'At least you'll miss me,' she whispered. From the moment Josie had hauled out her suitcases, Molly had done her level best to get underfoot. Josie was grateful to her for it.

But she couldn't delay any longer. Not if she wanted to be home before dark.

Who cared about the dark?

Heaving a sigh, she pushed herself upright and shuffled over to her bags. She heaved them up then, dragging her feet, teetered to the door and dumped them outside. Kent jumped up from his seat at the end of the veranda.

How long had he been there? Josie gulped and gasped and coughed and found it near impossible to breathe. 'I, umm...'

He kind of half scowled, his nose curling up at one

corner. He scuffed the toe of a work boot in a patch of dirt. 'Thought you might need a hand with your bags.'

Great. Was he escorting her off the premises? She bet he had his cleaning equipment out before her car reached the end of the driveway. She bet he couldn't wait to erase all evidence of her stay here. After her rant at him on Monday, she didn't much blame him. If she hadn't attacked him like some shrill fishwife then this goodbye scene might be a whole lot—

She slammed a halt to that thought.

Still, it didn't seem right for things to end like this.

'Thank you. I'd appreciate that.' She didn't smile. She couldn't. Not that it mattered. Kent didn't so much as glance at her as he seized both bags and strode off towards her car. Trademark Kent—no backward glances.

His lean denim-encased legs ate up the distance. She wished she could freeze-frame time and drink in her fill. Not just of him, but of Eagle Reach too. She wanted to feast her eyes on Eagle Reach, and Molly, but mostly on him. She wanted to feast her eyes on him, unimpeded, and fix him in her mind forever.

He's already there.

She spun away and stumbled back into the cabin, tripping over Molly in the process. 'Sorry, girl.' She patted Molly's head, drawing comfort from her warmth. She scanned the single room one final time. Her eyes stung. Resolutely ignoring them, she swung her handbag over her shoulder, shoved the key to the cabin in her pocket and picked up her box of groceries.

'C'mon, Molly.' She tried to do a Kent—no backward glances—but she couldn't quite manage it. She glanced longingly around the room once more before she shut the door behind her.

Kent's shadow fell across her as she turned away from the cabin. She stopped and stared at his chest and wished his physical body would follow, wrap around her completely. For one heart-stopping moment she thought it would, but he'd only moved in to take the box from her arms.

Swallowing, she headed for her car. He kept easy pace beside her. The scent of wood and smoke and man swirled around her. She wanted it to last forever.

It lasted until they reached her hatchback.

She didn't even try to avert her gaze when he bent down and placed the box on the back seat. He straightened and Molly started to bark and whine, circling around Josie's legs, pressing against them. It jolted her out of herself. Dropping to her knees, she hugged her, hard. Then drew back to scratch her ears. 'I'm going to miss you.' Molly licked her and tried to climb into her lap. Josie shot to her feet before she disgraced herself and began to cry.

Kent's eyes had darkened to that peculiar shade of navy. She could've groaned at the way it contrasted against the chambray of his shirt. She fished out the key from the pocket of her jeans and dropped it into his hand. 'Thank you.'

He stared at the key for a moment then his fingers closed round it, forming a fist. 'You're welcome.'

She held her breath and prayed he'd sweep her up in his arms and kiss her until her blood sang. Hot, moist killer-kisses. She wasn't stupid enough to dream of a happy-ever-after. She just wanted a big, smoochy, full-body slam.

Wasn't going to happen. But her breath hitched at the thought all the same.

She jolted back to reality when he handed her a business card, his gaze not quite meeting hers. She glanced down at the line drawing of a quaint cottage on the front of the card overlaid with the name: The Station Café.

'"Drive. Revive. Survive."' He quoted a popular driver safety campaign and stared at a point above her head. 'You'll like this place. They do great cake and coffee. It's about halfway between here and Buchanan's Point. A good place to break your journey.'

She nodded and tried for a light, 'Doctor's orders, huh?' but it didn't quite come off. How glad would he be to see the back of her, huh?

His jaw tightened for a moment. 'Promise you'll stop. It's important not to overdo it.'

She tapped the card against her fingers and ordered herself not to cringe. 'I will. Thanks.'

So, this was it?

She dropped her handbag on the passenger seat and closed the door, wiped suddenly damp palms down the front of her jeans. There was still time for Kent to sweep her up…

He strode around the car and opened the driver's door for her and there was nothing for it but to follow him. Disappointment hit her so hard she felt she was wading through fast-drying concrete. Molly started up a long, mournful whine. Josie ducked into the car then got back out. 'This is horrible,' she blurted, motioning to Molly.

There was still time for a kiss. She'd settle for a solitary kiss with the car door between them. She'd—

'I'll look after her.'

Of course he would. She stared at the rigid set of his jaw and told herself to stop living in Cloud Cuckoo Land. It was just… 'I'm sorry we had a falling-out.' She reached up and kissed his cheek, breathed him in one last time. 'Goodbye, Kent.'

This time when she ducked into the car she didn't back out. He closed the door. She started the ignition. Without glancing at him, she wound down the window. He leaned in, brushed the backs of his fingers across her cheek. 'Have a safe journey, Josie.' Then he stepped away.

Josie gulped down the lump in her throat but another one replaced it. She nodded dumbly. When she set off down the drive, this time she didn't look back.

Kent ignored the kick in his stomach as Josie manoeuvred her car down the gravel drive. His chest gave an even bigger kick but he ignored that too. He did lift a hand, though, when she turned out of his driveway and onto the road, but she didn't wave back.

Or toot her horn.

Nothing.

Not that he deserved anything after the way he'd treated her since that ridiculous blow-up. Her sweet, fruity scent lingered around him. The touch of her lips still on his cheek. Bloody idiot to get up on his high horse like that and not come down until it was too damn late.

Too late for what?

Friends, he wanted to shout to the disbelieving voice in his head. They could've been friends.

What use did he have for friends?

He scowled. She was better off without him. And he was better off without her as a distraction. Tempting him with a life he'd promised never to return to.

He released Molly's collar and she bolted down to the end of the drive, but Josie's car had already disappeared. Molly whined then jumped up and down on the spot as if searching for one last glimpse of Josie. When that didn't work she turned and gazed at him, her head low, and he suddenly understood where the term 'hangdog' came from.

He understood exactly how she felt too. 'C'mon, Molly.' He patted his thigh but she ignored him and slunk off to Josie's cabin. He turned and headed back towards the house, then, with a bitten-off curse, swerved to followed her.

He found her laid across the doorway, head on paws and her big, liquid eyes downcast. 'She misses you too, Moll.'

Molly's tail didn't give even the tiniest of thumps. Kent had an unaccountable urge to lie down beside her.

Don't be such a bloody fool. He had cattle that needed attending to.

He didn't leave, though. He didn't lie down either. He pushed open Josie's door and stared at the room behind it.

The cabin was spotless. Its blankness reproached him. Not a scrap of litter, no accidentally abandoned socks, not even the newspaper. Nothing of Josie remained except the tang of her scent in the air.

Molly barrelled straight into the room and climbed up onto the sofa as if that would somehow connect her to Josie. He didn't have the heart to drag her off again. He sat down in the hard chair and pulled in great lungfuls of the sweet air.

CHAPTER ELEVEN

MARTY and Frank's cars lined the circular drive when Josie finally turned in at the gates to Geraldine's Gardens. Her heart didn't lift at the sight of her home. The evening seemed grey, lacking colour, although light spilled from the house. As if expecting her, Marty and Frank burst out of the front door then came to startled halts.

At the same time.

Climbing out of her car, she felt herself moving through that quick-setting concrete again. Behind her a large van turned in at the drive, its headlights temporarily blinding her as it pulled in behind her hatchback.

Marty and Frank skulked on the veranda, shoulders slightly hunched. Neither came forward, so Josie found herself greeting the man who stepped down from the cabin of the truck. 'May I help you?' Her throat felt strangely dry.

'Ted O'Leary from O'Leary's Removals,' he said cheerfully, sticking out his hand.

Josie shook it. 'I think there's been some mistake.'

He consulted his clipboard. 'This Geraldine's Gardens?'

'It is.' She couldn't believe how normal her voice sounded.

'Then no mistake, miss. We have instructions from a Mr Marty Peterson to have the house cleared by morning.'

'With instructions to take it where?'

He checked his clipboard again. 'Into storage.'

Marty finally jogged down the steps to join them. He smiled brightly, but perspiration gleamed on his upper lip. 'It was going to be a surprise for you, Josie.'

His fake jovial tone had her bile rising. She swallowed it back. 'It's certainly that.' Again the calm, measured tone. 'I think you'd better tell Mr O'Leary you've wasted his time and that his services will not be required today.'

Without another word she turned and walked up the three tessellated-tile steps to the ornate wrap-around veranda and started for the door. Frank stepped in front of her. 'There's no need to take on like this,' he blustered, though she noticed his hands shook. 'You need to at least hear—'

She stepped around him, ignoring the drone of his voice. 'Tomorrow,' she said firmly, cutting across him. 'I'll speak to you both tomorrow.'

Then she closed the door in his startled face.

Molly refused to budge from Josie's cabin. Unless Kent wanted to physically pick her up, Molly was staying put.

He didn't want to physically pick her up. He didn't want to do much of anything.

Molly wouldn't touch her food either. Kent didn't have much of an appetite himself. In the end, neither one of them ate. In the end they both slept in Josie's cabin.

Kent pulled out the sofa bed, grabbed a blanket and he and Molly lay side by side…on Josie's bed. It wasn't even dark yet. He stared at the ceiling and wondered if she'd arrived home yet, if she'd got home safe.

Why hadn't he asked her to ring him?

Molly whined. He scratched her ears. The light behind

the curtains had almost completely faded now, but there was still enough light for him to miss the colour Josie had created in here. And taken away with her when she left.

He wanted bright lengths of material draped at the windows. He wanted rag rugs on the floor. He wanted prints on the walls.

Tomorrow. He'd drive into Martin's Gully tomorrow and buy lengths of bright material at Liz's store. Maybe Liz would've heard from Josie. He'd order rag rugs from Thelma Gower; hopefully she'd have a couple to go. He'd stop by Rachel Stanton's studio and check out her water colours.

Then he'd lunch with Clancy. Josie would definitely have rung Clancy because Clancy would've made her promise to.

Kent scowled at the ceiling. Clancy was a smart man.

Josie opened the door. 'Heavens, that was quick. I'm really sorry to call you out like this, Steve.'

Having made it inside her house, Josie had found she was lucky to do so when she saw the shiny new locks in place. If she'd arrived when Marty and Frank weren't here she'd have been unable to get in.

'Not a problem, Josie.' He set his tools by the front door and sent her a shrewd glance. 'When it's a question of security and a woman at home alone then we locksmiths don't care what time of the day or night it is.'

She grinned. 'You guys take a professional vow in locksmith school or something? Like the doctors' Hippocratic oath?' She wished she hadn't said that, the doctor bit; it reminded her of Kent.

'You bet.' He glanced up. 'I'm glad you're home, Josie. The town's been worried.'

'I know. Jacob rang me.'

Steve wielded his screwdriver. 'Town took a vote and told him he had to.' He set about removing the lock.

That news didn't surprise her. Buchanan's Point was a close-knit community. Marty and Frank had never been a part of it. They were known as townies.

Steve was the only locksmith in Buchanan's Point. She'd gone to school with him. Had played spin the bottle in primary school. She could trust him. 'Did you change the locks at Marty and Frank's request?'

'Nope.'

Darn it. She wanted to know what excuse they'd given. She knew Steve would've asked for one. Which might be why they hadn't used him for the job.

'They hired a mate of mine from Diamond Head.' He winked. 'We went to locksmith school together. He told them I was closer and would be cheaper. But they insisted he do the job anyway. That made him suspicious, like, so he rang me.'

It made her suspicious too. She crouched down beside him. 'Did he find out why they wanted the locks changed?'

'The elder one, what's his name?'

'Marty.'

'He said he'd lost his spare key and rather than risk someone finding it and using it to break in, he thought he'd get the locks changed.'

She bit her lip again. 'He could be telling the truth.'

'Aye, he could be.'

But she could tell Steve didn't believe Marty's story. She didn't either. She jumped to her feet and started to pace. Kent had warned her about this.

She wondered if she rang him and told him he'd been right, if she apologised, if he'd hang up on her.

* * *

Josie glanced at the clock. One o'clock. She picked up the phone and hit redial.

'Mr Peterson's office.'

'Hi, Rita, it's Josie again.'

'I'm sorry, Josie.' Rita clicked her tongue in sympathy. 'He's still in a meeting with a client.'

'This is the fifth time I've called.' She'd rung on the hour, every hour, since nine o'clock this morning.

'I know. I'm sorry.'

She swallowed back her frustration. It wasn't Rita's fault Marty wouldn't return her calls.

'He swears he'll ring you tonight…or, at the very latest, tomorrow.'

Not satisfactory.

Josie didn't say that, though. She said, 'Thank you,' and rang off.

She drummed her fingers against the arm of her chair then picked up the phone and punched in a second number.

'I'm sorry,' a recorded voice started, 'this phone is temporarily out of range or—'

She hung up in disgust. She suspected Frank had turned his cell-phone off deliberately so she couldn't contact him. She massaged her temples. Perhaps if she'd slept better last night she'd feel more able to cope with this. But every time she'd closed her eyes Kent's image had risen up in front of her. Sleep had proven impossible.

She pleated the hem of her blouse with her fingers and wished Kent had asked her to ring him, as Clancy and Liz had done. A longing to hear his voice gripped her again. She'd lost count of the number of times she'd picked up the phone to call him and tell him she'd arrived safely, to tell him he'd been right about her brothers. At the last moment she'd chicken out. He'd have only given one of those derisive laughs and said, 'So what?'

In all fairness, he probably wouldn't, but she'd bet he'd want to. She didn't want that.

What she wanted was impossible.

Kent stepped back to admire his handiwork. Then swore. The material he'd twined around the curtain rods refused to hang in the same soft folds that Josie had created. He'd tossed a tablecloth across the table, he'd shoved flowers haphazardly in a vase and discovered the haphazard-flowers-in-a-vase-look required more skill than his fingers possessed. He'd scattered scatter cushions, he'd hung water colours, he'd thrown rag rugs across bare floorboards and yet it still wasn't working.

It didn't look cosy and inviting. It looked wrong.

Then he got mad. He shooed Molly off the sofa bed and folded it up with one hard shove. He shooed her right outside and slammed the door behind them. But Molly wouldn't budge further than the veranda. 'What's the point?' he shouted at her. 'She's gone.' And she wasn't coming back.

At least he knew she'd arrived home safely. She'd rung both Liz and Clancy. He scowled. And somewhere between yesterday and today the last trace of her fragrance had vanished. Gone. Just like that. He couldn't believe how much he missed it. That fact only fuelled his anger. He started to stride away then swung back to face his dog. 'And if you don't start eating again by tomorrow I'm taking you to the vet.'

At any mention of the vet, Molly usually bolted straight

under the house. This time her ears didn't so much as twitch. With a snort of disgust, Kent strode off.

That evening, however, he carried Molly up to the house and tried to coax her to eat. She lapped at her water, a half-hearted effort, but she still refused to touch her food. At bedtime he carried her into his bedroom and laid her on her usual blanket. At least, it had been her usual blanket before Josie came to Eagle Reach.

Molly spent the night scratching at his door and howling. He wanted to join her. At midnight he relented and let her out. He wondered if a dog could die of a broken heart? Then he called himself an idiot.

By Saturday lunchtime he finally realised Molly was no longer his dog but Josie's. Josie and Molly had connected from the very first moment.

Almost the very first moment, he amended, grinning when he remembered Josie perched in his clothes-line.

With a strange sense of relief he packed an overnight case, made a quick call to Smiley McDonald then bundled Molly into his car and drove into Martin's Gully.

He leapt out at Liz's store. Clancy and Liz stood side by side at the cash register in close conference. Kent didn't waste any time. 'I'm heading for Josie's. Just wanted to let you two know.'

'Good.' Clancy pointed to a case on the floor. 'You can give me a lift.'

'Me too.' Liz hoisted her bag onto her shoulder.

He stared at them and his stomach clenched up so tight he found it hard to breathe. 'Why?' he barked. Had something happened? 'Is she OK?' He wanted to punch something.

'She's fine.' Liz walked around the counter and took his arm. 'We'll explain on the way.'

He didn't say anything more, just grabbed their cases and shot them in the back of his four-wheel-drive, his face grim as he waited for them to climb into the car.

Josie removed Mrs Pengilly's cup and saucer from the arm of her chair as the elderly woman's head began to nod. The doorbell sounded, twice in quick succession. She darted a glance at her guest then padded down the hallway in her bare feet. 'Shh.' She opened the door, finger to lips, then drew back and folded her arms.

Marty pointed a shaking finger at her, his face red. 'You…you had the locks changed.'

'Yes, I did. As neither of you,' she took in Frank with her glance, 'left me a spare key or would answer my calls yesterday, I had no choice.'

'No choice? Nonsense,' Frank snapped, pushing past her.

'I had errands to run. I can't leave a place like Geraldine's Gardens unlocked and unattended.'

'But…but…' Marty followed her down the hall.

'Yes?' She lifted an eyebrow, careful to keep a pleasant smile on her face.

He eyed her warily then pasted on a smile and pulled her to a stop, fake jovial again. 'We have great news.'

She couldn't help feeling he was getting cues over her shoulder from Frank.

She turned. Frank sent her a huge smile too.

'Good news?' she asked. They both nodded eagerly. 'Good.' She rubbed her hands together. 'I love good news. You'd best come into the formal lounge.' It was the room they preferred anyway. 'Mrs Pengilly is dozing in the family room.'

Marty's smile fled. 'What's she doing here?'

'She's my friend. That's what she's doing here.' She closed the door to the formal lounge and prayed Mrs Pengilly was a sound sleeper. 'Do you have a problem with that?'

'No, no.' He backed down and made straight for her father's chair.

'Damn Nosy Parker, though,' Frank muttered, throwing himself into the one opposite. The one she normally used.

She perched on the edge of the sofa. 'It's what I love about this place. Everyone looks out for everyone else.'

Marty and Frank exchanged glances and Josie's heart sank. She just knew she wasn't going to like their good news.

They wanted her to sell her house.

Oh, that news didn't surprise her. They'd been telling her for years that the place was too big for her, too much to keep up with. Part of her agreed, but it didn't mean…

Given time she'd fill it with people. Somehow.

But they had a buyer already lined up, a property developer. And they had a contract ready for her to sign.

Marty pushed his solid silver and gold plated pen, the one he normally guarded with his life, into her hand and pointed. 'Sign there and there.'

'But I want to think about it first.'

Both men started talking at her at once, gesturing wildly, pacing up and down in front of her. Panic spiked through her. Her shoulders edged up towards her ears as walls started to close in around her.

'This is a once-in-a-lifetime chance, Josie.' Marty slapped a hand to the contract. 'You'll never be offered such a good price again.'

He was probably right. The amount offered was obscene.

'And you won't have to work again either if you don't want to,' Frank added. 'And you'll be helping the town.'

'Exactly.' Marty thumped another hand to the contract. 'At the moment it's dying a slow death.'

Her head shot up at that. 'Nonsense.'

'This will make sure it doesn't,' Frank rushed in with a warning glare at Marty.

She bit her lip. He might have a point. They weren't proposing to knock down Geraldine's Gardens and build a high-rise in its place. They were talking about a very exclusive, understated resort. Very swish, with the house and grounds of Geraldine's Gardens incorporated into the overall design. They'd shown her the projected plans. She couldn't deny the tastefulness of the enterprise. But…

'It'll be good for you, it'll be good for the community and it'll be good for us.'

'Good for you how?'

'For a start, we'll have peace of mind knowing you're taken care of. You deserve that after the way you looked after Dad.'

Frank's words hit the sore, needy part of her heart right at its very centre.

Marty patted her hand. 'You're our little sister. We want to see you settled.'

She gulped. She just needed to sign the contract and then…'What was the moving van about?'

'The buyer wants to start work immediately. We wanted to clear the way for things to move as quickly as they could once you got back and signed the contract.' Marty spread out his hands. He still clutched the contract in one of them.

'We didn't think you'd have any objections. We're just looking out for you, Jose.'

The only person in the world to call her Jose had been her father. She leapt up and thrust Marty's pen at him. 'Mrs Pengilly is due for her medication.'

And she fled. She leaned against the wall outside the door of the room, fingers steepled over her nose as she drew in several breaths. All she had to do was sign then she, Marty and Frank would all be one big, happy family.

Somehow the picture didn't quite fit.

When had they arranged all this? Before her holiday?

For the hundredth time that day she wished Kent were here. Not for any other reason than to rest her eyes on him, to breathe in his wood-smoke scent.

Mrs Pengilly's medication. She roused herself, pasted on a bright smile and breezed into the family room to find Mrs Pengilly's chair empty. The doorbell rang.

'Hope you don't mind,' Mrs Pengilly called out when Josie appeared at the end of the hallway, 'but I called for reinforcements.'

Mrs Pengilly opened the door and Josie's jaw dropped as she watched a substantial cross-section of the townsfolk of Buchanan's Point file past her and into the formal lounge. She followed in their wake, dazed.

'What the…? This is a private matter,' Marty shouted. 'What do you think you're doing?'

Jacob sent Josie an encouraging smile. 'We just want to make sure Josie has all the facts she needs to make an informed decision, that's all.'

'And it is our town,' Mr Piper called from the back of the group. 'Josie's decision will affect all of us.'

'Josie!' Marty hollered. 'You have to get rid—'

'They're my friends, Marty. I want them here.' She didn't wait for a reply but turned to the assembled crowd. 'Are you all aware of the proposal?'

Jacob nodded. 'Yes.'

It didn't surprise her. Someone's cousin's uncle would be on a board somewhere. 'It's not a high-rise,' she said anyway, just so they knew, 'but a very tasteful and exclusive resort.'

Jacob kind of shrugged. He didn't look very comfortable thrust into the role of town spokesperson. 'Town opinion is split. That's not the point.'

'Ooh, you should hear Josie's idea for a b & b,' Mrs Pengilly gushed. 'It's fabulous.'

'B & b?' Frank rounded on her.

'It was just an idea and—'

'We're getting off the track,' Jacob inserted quickly. 'What you decide to do with Geraldine's Gardens is up to you, Josie. It belongs to you. What we want is for you to know *all* the facts.'

That was the second time he'd said that. 'What facts?'

'That Marty's firm is guaranteed this buyer's business if the deal goes through. And Frank's firm will get the building contract.'

'That's not a secret.' Frank rounded on them. 'We were just telling Josie about all the advantages if the project goes ahead.'

Ha! She should've known. But she couldn't help wondering if Frank had meant to be as honest with her as he now claimed.

Marty swung to her. 'It guarantees Frank and I make partnerships with our firms.'

Weariness descended over her. For some reason she had

never been able to fathom, Marty and Frank had always felt they'd lost out to her financially. They'd both worked hard to achieve partnerships. She couldn't deny that. Did she really have the heart to stand in their way now? If she signed the contract, would they finally feel she'd squared things up?

'Josie?' Jacob prompted.

'I…' She didn't know what to say.

'What do you want?' he persisted.

She didn't get a chance to answer. At that moment an excited dog burst through the door and knocked her off her feet.

'Molly!' She hugged the squirming bundle of fur. She glanced up and her weariness fled. 'Kent!'

'Sorry, she got away from me.' He stopped dead when he saw the crowd assembled in the room. Clancy and Liz peeped around from behind Kent's back and waved to her. Josie hugged Molly and grinned like an idiot.

'Who the hell is this?' Marty shouted in sudden frustration and Josie came back to herself, even though she couldn't seem to quite catch her breath.

She jumped up. 'Everyone, these are my friends from Martin's Gully. Kent, Clancy and Liz. Umm,' she waved her arm at the assembled crowd, 'this is everyone.'

Her mind whirled. Murmurs of greeting sounded around her, but she couldn't make sense of anything. One thing suddenly became crystal-clear. 'Marty and Frank,' she turned to her brothers, 'I can't make a decision on this tonight.'

Her brothers' jaws dropped. Marty's face went so red she swore he'd burst a blood vessel. 'This is all because I wouldn't come and pick you up from that God-forsaken place, isn't it?' he yelled. 'It's some kind of payback.'

She didn't know how many volts of electricity it took

to snap someone to full attention, but his words ensured he had hers.

Completely.

Her voice, though, was surprisingly calm. 'You knew it was a God-forsaken place?'

'Of course I knew,' he spat. 'What do you think I am? Stupid?'

No, but she was. Anger hit her then in thick red waves. Not only had they set all this up so that she was out of the way while they tried to seal their deal, but in their measly selfishness they hadn't even been able to provide her with a decent holiday.

'So you played me for a sucker?' Neither brother said anything. 'And you prettied it all up by feigning concern for me?'

Marty stared at the floor, Frank at the ceiling.

'Oh, and I fell for it, hook, line and sinker, didn't I? What an idiot you must think I am.'

She waited for them to protest, to tell her they really had appreciated the way she'd taken care of their father, that they really did love her.

Nothing.

'Out.' She picked up the contract and slapped it to Marty's chest. 'You too,' she shouted at Frank. 'Take your contracts and your measly, selfish minds and get out. I don't want to see either of you again.'

Marty blanched. 'You can't mean that.'

'But you're our sister,' Frank started, visibly shaken.

Marty took a step towards her, but to Josie's astonishment Molly bustled up between them, hackles raised. Then she drew back her lips to display every single one of her teeth as she growled. Josie pointed to the door. 'Go.'

* * *

Kent stared at Josie and couldn't remember being prouder of anyone than he was of her at that moment. He wanted to grab her up in his arms and swing her around. He wanted to kiss her. He wanted to drag her off to the bedroom and—

He wanted to stay!

The realisation slugged him straight in the gut. But it didn't knock him off his feet. Instead it surged through him and lent him a strange kind of strength. He wanted to stay and it had nothing to do with Molly, or Clancy and Liz, or sticking up for Josie against her brothers.

It had everything to do with him…and her. It was why he'd come, even if he had tried to hide behind all those other reasons.

He shoved his hands in his pockets and studied her as surreptitiously as was possible with a roomful of people studying him too. The sandalwood highlights of her hair gleamed beneath the overhead lights. Her lips, lush and inviting, hinted at exotic delights. Her eyes still blazed from her sudden flash of temper. He'd never seen anything more desirable in his life.

But what if she didn't want him here? His hands curled into fists. What if she didn't want him?

Then he'd become the kind of man she bloody well did want, that was what.

Josie shook herself, tried to unscramble her mind. She turned to Kent, Clancy and Liz. 'What are you all doing here?' She couldn't believe how good it was to see them.

She tried not to feast her eyes too obviously on Kent. Liz and Clancy both burst forward to hug her. She hugged them back. Kent stayed where he was—hands in pockets, glaring moodily at the floor—and her heart burned.

'We were worried what those no-good brothers of yours were up to, lass.'

Liz's eyes twinkled. 'But it appears you didn't need the cavalry after all.'

'No.' Josie gave a shaky laugh. Her audacity in telling her brothers exactly what she thought and sticking up for herself still shocked her. She glanced at Kent. Had he come riding to her rescue too?

He shuffled his feet, rolled his shoulders. 'Since you left, Molly has refused to eat. She's going to have to live with you.'

Her jaw dropped.

He scowled. 'She misses you.'

She hauled it back up. What wouldn't she give to hear him say those self-same words to her?

'We all miss you,' Liz said. 'And I was thinking, if you start up this b & b of yours you're going to need a hand. Since Ted died I've been looking for a change, and I'm a very good cook, you know.'

Clancy shuffled in closer. 'And I know I'm getting on in years, but I'm still handy in the garden.'

Liz folded her arms. 'You'll need a cook.'

Clancy set his jaw. 'You'll need a gardener.'

A huge lump blocked her throat. She glanced at Kent. He stared at Liz and Clancy as if they'd just lost their minds.

His scowl redirected itself to her. 'And you'll need a husband!'

His words knocked the lump clean out of her throat. All conversation in the room stopped.

'What?' She gaped at him.

His scowl deepened as he glanced around the now silent room, at all the avid, curious faces. He rolled his shoulders again. 'Need probably isn't the right word,' he muttered.

'You don't *need* a husband. You probably don't *need* anyone, but I…'

He glanced around the room again and bit back an oath. Grabbing her hand, he dragged her out of the room, out of the front door and around the side of the house. Then he let her go and continued to glare at her.

Josie shook her head. She couldn't have heard him right. He couldn't have said husband. It wasn't possible.

'Doctor,' she babbled. 'I need a doctor.'

'OK, I'll be that too.'

She wanted to throw herself into his arms. So she massaged her temples instead. 'Did you say I needed a husband?'

'Yes.'

'Is this all about me needing someone to look after me and stuff?'

'I took back the word need.'

Another surge of temper and hope shot through her. 'Did you have someone particular in mind?' She wanted to scratch his eyes out. She—

Then he did something she could never have imagined—he dropped to his knees, wrapped his arms around her waist and buried his face in her stomach with a groan. 'I love you, Josie. Me and Molly, we don't function without you.' His arms tightened. 'I miss your laugh. I miss your smell. I miss you.'

He lifted his head and stared deep into her eyes. 'I didn't see at first that there's more strength in your way. There's more strength in a community, in helping people, in building bridges. I want to build that community with you.'

She brushed the hair off his forehead in wonder, traced

the strong planes of his face with her fingertips. This wonderful man loved her? Her vision blurred. 'You love me? Really?'

Everything inside her sang at his nod. 'And you can't function without me?'

He shook his head. 'No.'

Ooh, she knew how that felt. 'I'll let you in on a little secret: I can't function without you either.'

Kent surged to his feet with a whoop and swung her around. She wrapped her arms around his neck and laughed for the sheer joy of it. When he set her back on her feet she reached up and touched his face. 'I love you, Kent Black. I can't imagine anything more perfect than being your wife.'

He dropped a kiss to the corner of her mouth. 'Say that again.'

Heat started to pump through her. She wanted to melt into him and forget the rest of the world. 'I, umm…'

Her breath caught as he trailed a path of kisses down her throat. He lazily trailed the kisses back up again to nuzzle her ear. 'You taste divine, Josie Peterson.'

If he didn't kiss her properly soon she'd die.

She drew back to catch her breath. 'I love you.' He'd doubted it. She could see it in his face. 'I love you,' she repeated. She'd never tire of saying it.

His hands came up to cradle her face. 'I thought I'd destroyed any chance I had with you. I thought I'd chased you so far away that… And by the time I realised I loved you so much I couldn't live without you I—'

She reached up and pressed her fingers against his lips, stemming the flood of words, needing to drive the demons from his eyes. 'I love you, Kent. Forever.'

'Forever.' He breathed the word against her fingers.

She nodded then removed her hand and as his lips descended she lifted hers and met him in a kiss that sealed their promise.

MOONLIGHT AND ROSES

BY
JACKIE BRAUN

Jackie Braun worked as an award-winning editorial writer before leaving her job at a daily newspaper to write romance. She is a two-time RITA® Award finalist, a three-time National Readers' Choice Award finalist and a past winner of the Rising Star Award in traditional romance. She lives in Michigan with her husband and son, and can be reached through her website, www.jackiebraun.com.

For my good friend, Tina Haas, who didn't complain one bit when I asked her to help me research a winery in Leelanau County. And to the staff at Black Star Farms, who made our stay there an incredible experience. Any errors I made or liberties I took in writing this book bear no reflection on their winemaking knowledge and skill.

PROLOGUE

JAYE MONROE didn't consider herself the sort of woman to swoon, but as she sat with her stepmother in the stuffy office, listening to the lawyer read the contents of Frank Monroe's will, she definitely felt light-headed.

Not only was her beloved father gone, but he'd left their Leelanau County vineyard, along with its winery and tasting room, in the sole possession of his second wife of seven years rather the daughter who had toiled by his side for the past nine to help make the Medallion label an up-and-coming success.

Upon hearing this, Margaret sent Jaye a spiteful grin, but the older woman's glee didn't last long.

The lawyer was saying, "As for the house, the collection of original eighteenth-century artwork and all of the antique furnishings with the exception of those found in the master bedroom suite, Frank wanted you to have those, Jaye."

"What?" both women shouted simultaneously.

Jaye straightened in her seat. Her stepmother slumped sideways.

"Mrs. Monroe?" the lawyer said, rising partway from his chair. "Are you all right?"

Jaye knew Margaret wasn't the sort to swoon, either, but the older woman certainly enjoyed attention and had a flair for the dramatic.

"Water," Margaret murmured, her heavily made-up eyelids flickering. "I need water."

"What about you, Miss Monroe?" the lawyer asked. "Can I get you anything?"

Jaye considered requesting a shot of something potent to numb the pain and outrage she was experiencing, but she shook her head.

When he returned, she said in as steady a voice as she could manage, "This can't be right, Mr. Danielson. You must have read that part backward. Dad wouldn't leave the vineyard to Margaret. She doesn't want it any more than I want a house filled with old paintings and gaudy antiques."

"I paid good money for those old paintings and gaudy antiques," Margaret snapped, apparently having recovered from her near collapse.

"Yes, you enjoyed spending *my* father's money on anything that caught your eye."

"He was *my* husband, so it was *my* money to spend," the older woman retorted. Then she slumped back in her seat again. "I loved that man. What will I do without him?"

"Ladies, please." Jonas Danielson raised a bony hand to silence them. "I'm sorry, Miss Monroe, Mrs. Monroe.

I know this must come as a shock to both of you, but this is what Frank stipulated in the will he had drawn up just prior to his death last month."

"It doesn't make any sense," Jaye persisted. "I have my own house, my own furniture." All of which leaned toward the contemporary. "Dad and I built Medallion together. He can't have intended to pull the rug out from under me this way."

Mr. Danielson retrieved a couple of papers from a folder and handed one to Jaye and one to Margaret. "Perhaps this will help clarify the matter for you."

It was the photocopy of a letter. Jaye recognized her father's scratchy cursive immediately, and her heart began to race. The letter began: "Dear Margaret and Juliet."

Juliet. Her father only used Jaye's given name when she was in trouble, and boy was she ever, she realized, as she continued to read the words he'd penned.

> I know that the two of you have never been close, which is a pity since neither of you really has anyone else. I want the two women I love the most in this world to look after each other and to work together after I'm gone. I think this is a good way to ensure that you will.
>
> Juliet, Margaret will need help with Medallion's daily operations. Margaret, I know you've never taken an interest in the vineyard, but you are a bright and capable woman. I think you will be an asset. In the meantime, I'm sure Juliet will allow you to reside in the house as always, and I

ask that you allow Juliet to continue as head vintner at the winery. There's no one I trust more to ensure the label's quality and success.

I love you both and it saddens me to leave you. My only comfort is in knowing that you will have each other to lean on. Please, be good to each other.

Jaye traced his signature at the bottom of the page and then glanced over at Margaret, who was still busy reading, if the movement of her lips was any indication.

Be good to each other.

Jaye bit the inside of her cheek to keep from laughing. He might as well have asked them to flap their arms and fly. The two women had never been friends. Oh, they could manage to be cordial when the circumstances required it. On holidays, for instance, they sat together at the dinner table and exchanged polite small talk. But when it came right down to it, Jaye found the older woman vacuous and self-centered. Margaret was no fonder of Jaye, whom she'd often labeled as outspoken and a tomboy.

No, the women were not friends. They had tolerated each other for Frank's sake. Now that he was gone so was all pretense, as Margaret's next words made clear.

"I'm hiring my own lawyer. This is ridiculous." She stood, crumpled up the letter and tossed it onto the lawyer's desk. "*Everything* should be mine! I'm sure a judge will agree. I was his wife."

"Of seven years." Jaye stood as well. "I'm his daughter of nearly thirty. Yes, I can see how giving you everything, even the vineyard that you've never stepped foot in, would be fair."

Margaret's eyes narrowed. "He loved me. That still kills you, doesn't it?"

Jaye ignored the question, partly because it was true. Of all the women in the world for her father to marry, why did it have to be a silly bit of arm candy like Margaret?

"I'll hire a lawyer, too," she vowed. "We'll see who ends up with what."

"Ladies, ladies," Mr. Danielson pleaded. "Are you sure that's what you want to do? Litigation could take months, years. It will be draining emotionally, not to mention financially. Why not compromise? The solution in this matter seems obvious. If you don't want the vineyard," he said to Margaret, "and you don't want the house and its furnishings," his gaze moved to Jaye, "then perhaps you can make arrangements to transfer ownership?"

"That sounds reasonable," Jaye allowed.

But Margaret was shaking her head, her expression far more shrewd than vacuous now. "I don't know," she said slowly. "All of that acreage would fetch a pretty price in this real estate market, especially without a bunch of damned grapes growing on it."

Jaye knew a moment of true horror. She wouldn't put it past her stepmother to sell the vineyard's prime property to the highest bidder. "I'll give you everything my father left me, plus a fair sum."

"Will you now?" Margaret's smile bloomed.

"Yes. This was Dad's dream, Margaret. The vineyard represents all of his years of hard work." And mine, Jaye thought. And mine. "Promise me that you won't sell Medallion to a developer."

Margaret studied Jaye for a long moment before finally nodding. Still, Jaye didn't quite trust the gleam in her eye. "Okay, Jaye. You're right. This was Frank's dream. So, I promise you that I won't sell it to a developer."

And she didn't. Five months later, after Jaye had accepted an offer for her beachfront home and was busily scraping together the rest of the down payment for the vineyard, Margaret sold the Medallion Winery to a California vintner.

CHAPTER ONE

JAYE stood on the upstairs balcony of the house her father had left to her and watched the silver convertible shoot up the paved road that led to Medallion's winery, tasting room and business offices. She caught a glimpse of sandy hair, ruddy cheeks and a cocky smile. The car's top was down despite the fact that the outside temperature was flirting with fifty.

If it were later in the day, she might wonder if the fool driving had already imbibed a bit too freely at one of the area's many other wineries. Since it was just past eight in the morning she doubted that was the case. Besides, she figured she knew exactly who was driving that fancy foreign number.

Zackary Holland.

Even thinking his name had her lip curling. The man had pulled up stakes at his family's century-old Napa Valley vineyard and bought Medallion from Margaret before Jaye even had known a deal was in the works.

Jaye hadn't met Zack yet, although it looked like she

was going to have the privilege today. She wasn't looking forward to it, even if she was anxious to get it over with and find out where things stood. Where *she* stood. She wanted Medallion back, and eventually she would have it. A man who would slough off his birthright surely could be talked into parting with this vineyard. In the meantime, she wanted to keep her job as head vintner.

Usually, Jaye wasn't one given to snap judgments, but she doubted she would find she liked Zack very much and not just because he owned what by right should have been hers. Having traveled in wine circles, she figured she knew his type. She'd met more than one pompous, pedigreed vineyard heir who considered substandard any American wine produced east of the West Coast, a couple of New England vintages excepted.

As a child, Jaye had led a comfortable life thanks to her father's keen knack for investment, but after college she'd earned her own way, putting in fifty hours or more each week at the vineyard to draw a paycheck. The Zack Hollands of the world didn't earn their way. Some of them never bothered to learn more about the making of wine than how to assess their family's finished product from pricy stemware.

She surveyed the acres of terraced grapevines that were spread out like the quaint pattern of a quilt on the surrounding hillsides. Cabernet, chardonnay, and pinot were among the varieties she'd helped her father graft and plant. In the distance beyond them, the maples and oaks were starting to change color, sprinkling the horizon with splashes of red and gold that heralded fall as surely as the crisp air that turned her breath white.

It was nearly harvest time and this year promised one of the best yields yet at Medallion. Jaye and her father had spent the past nine years toiling and sweating, first to establish the vineyard and then to earn recognition for their wines. Finally they were succeeding. She swallowed around the lump in her throat. All of that hard work, and her father hadn't lived to see the fruits of their labor.

She swiped at the tears that streaked her face, irritated to find them there. Again. She wasn't one to cry, although she'd done her fair share in recent months. She didn't like it. After all, what was the point of crying? What had railing against fate ever changed for her in the past? Her mother hadn't come back. Her father couldn't. The vineyard? Time would tell.

She returned inside, plaited her heavy hair into its usual no-nonsense braid and dressed for work. Unless—or until—the new owner told her to clear out her desk and leave, she had a job to do.

Zack parked his car and got out. Then he stood, feet planted shoulder width apart, and grinned as wide as his wind-numbed face would allow. His previous visit to the vineyard hadn't prepared him for the beauty to come. Oh, the area had been pretty in late summer with all of those shades of blue and green, but decked out in the bold hues of autumn it simply dazzled.

He'd arrived in Michigan late the evening before,

taking a suite of rooms at a hotel in nearby Traverse City. Until he found a permanent home, he would be living there. When he'd awakened this morning, he'd felt like a child on Christmas, too keyed up to choke down more than a couple bites of toast before he'd hopped in his car and followed the highway that bordered the aquamarine waters of Traverse Bay. Halfway to the vineyard, he'd stopped to put down the top on his Mercedes. He'd wanted an unrestricted view of his surroundings.

He rubbed his stiff fingers before stuffing his hands into the pockets of his jeans. He was paying for his impulsiveness now, but he didn't care. He felt more alive than he had in years. Anticipation hummed inside him as he entered the tasting room at Medallion. This winery was his and his alone. He would set its course, decide its future, and call all of the shots. He wouldn't have to run his ideas past anyone else for approval that ultimately would be denied. No. He was in charge.

He revised his opinion half an hour later when a woman stalked through the main doors of the tasting room. He pegged her age at about thirty and her mood as supremely agitated if the stiff set of her shoulders and grim line of her mouth were any indication.

She was tall, only a few inches shorter than his six-foot-two, and lean. What he could see of her figure beneath a bulky wool sweater and loose-fitting carpenter jeans might best be described as willowy. She certainly commanded attention, though. The workers stopped what they were doing, glancing around nervously. An unnatural silence fell, and even though no one moved, Zack got the distinct impression sides had been taken.

Hers had more.

"You must be Juliet Monroe." No introduction was necessary, but he made one anyway. He believed in confronting awkwardness head-on. And so he extended a hand as he crossed to where she stood. "I've heard a lot about you. I'm Zack Holland."

Up close he realized her eyes were green and that the hair she'd scraped back into an unflattering braid was the color of freshly ground cinnamon. Something about her tugged at him, although he couldn't figure out why. She wasn't beautiful, at least not in the classical sense, or even in the chic sense like his former fiancée, Mira, who had turned heads wherever they'd gone.

Given Jaye's prominent cheekbones, slightly flared nose and wide-set eyes, the best word to describe her would be *striking*.

Her mouth was on the broad side, too, and her lips might have been full, although at the moment it was hard to tell as they were compressed into a frown. They loosened slightly, but only so she could tell him, "I don't care to be called Juliet."

Zack managed to keep his smile in place despite her clipped tone. This meeting had to be difficult for her, and he didn't mind letting her save face in front of the workers—as long as it didn't come at his expense. Everyone needed to understand and accept that he was in charge now, Juliet Monroe perhaps most of all.

"What *do* you care to be called?"

"Jaye. I go by Jaye." Her grip was firm to the point of being painful when she finally shook his hand. He half expected her to challenge him to a thumb war.

"Jaye." He nodded once. The short, boyish name fit her, since there was little about her that seemed soft or overtly feminine, except maybe the long hair. What would it look like…? He tamped down his curiosity. "It's nice to meet you."

She nodded but didn't actually return the sentiment. Instead she got right down to business. "I'd like to know what your plans are for Medallion." She spread her hand out to encompass the room's wide-eyed occupants. "And for its workers, of course."

Around them people shuffled their feet and murmured. Zack cleared his throat. He hadn't expected to be put on the spot. Nor was he used to being challenged by an employee.

"I'm going to hold a staff meeting at the end of the week to go over the particulars, once I've had a good look around. I have some changes in mind," he said, being purposefully vague.

"Such as?"

The woman was tenacious; he'd give her that. Under other circumstances, he might have admired the quality. At the moment, though, he found it insolent and annoying.

"They'll keep. But if you've got a minute, I'd like to talk to you."

He was well aware that everyone was watching

them and cataloging Zack and Jaye's every word, glance and gesture.

"I'm at your disposal," she drawled.

Right, he thought. When she made no effort to move, he added, "Why don't we go to my office?"

Jaye let Zack lead the way, even though she knew every step by heart. The business offices were located up a flight of stairs just off the tasting room. The biggest one was at the end of the hall. It made sense that it would be the one he'd claim as his own. Still, when the door closed behind them, Jaye felt her heart squeeze. The office, with its grand, panoramic view of the vineyard, had been her father's.

Nothing of Frank Monroe's belongings remained. She'd cleared out every last note card and paperclip after her stepmother announced the vineyard's sale. But she could still feel him here. She could smell the tangy tobacco he'd smoked in his pipe, and it took no effort at all to envision his bulky frame sitting behind a cluttered desk wearing his usual uniform of wrinkled khaki trousers, a Greek fisherman's cap and a navy button-down shirt, the breast pocket of which bulged from his glasses case and assorted other personal effects. Jaye swore her father carried more things in his pockets than most women did in their purses.

"Everything okay?" Zack asked.

The image dissolved. She glanced over to find Medallion's new owner standing beside her. She'd forgotten all about him for a moment as she'd stared at the empty desk and remembered…mourned. Her father had been gone nearly six months, but the ache had not lessened. If anything, it seemed to grow worse as the reality of never seeing him again set in and festered like an infected sore.

She felt too raw, too exposed, to answer Zack's question, so she asked one of her own. "What did you want to see me about?"

Zack leaned one hip on the edge of the desk. "I thought that would be obvious."

She swallowed as a lead weight settled in her stomach. "You're letting me go."

"No," he said slowly, hardly sounding decisive.

Jaye crossed her arms. "You mean, not yet."

He ran a hand over the back of his neck and chuckled, but he sounded more frustrated than amused when he said, "You don't like to make things easy, do you?"

She'd lost her father, their vineyard, and now her livelihood was on the line. "In my experience, nothing worth having comes easily."

She meant Medallion, recalling the backbreaking hours she and her father had spent grafting vines to root stock, fixing trellises, warding off pests and praying for just the right mix of sunshine and rain to produce a good crop.

To her surprise, Zack nodded, as if he understood completely. But what could have been difficult for Mr. Silver Spoon to attain?

"I'd appreciate your cooperation, Jaye. This transition is difficult for everyone, perhaps you most of all, but it won't become any easier if Medallion's workers feel they have to choose between us."

"I'm not asking them to choose."

"No?" His brows rose.

"I care about them," she insisted. "They're good workers, good people. They have families to feed. I don't want to see them strung along."

"I won't string anyone along. But I didn't appreciate being put on the spot down there." He waved a hand in the direction of the door.

"I'm sorry." She tried to sound sincere, but she couldn't resist adding, "If you felt that's what I was doing."

Zack inhaled deeply, but apparently decided to drop the matter because he changed the subject. "I'm impressed with the operation here. It's well run, and the finished product shows incredible potential. I understand from the workers that you're largely responsible for making this a first-class facility."

She wasn't comfortable with the compliment. "I played a small role. It was my father's doing. He loved Medallion and liked nothing better than seeing it succeed against bigger and supposedly better wineries both here and around the world."

"I'm sorry for your loss. I understand that he died this past spring."

"Yes." The pain of hearing those words still surprised her, but she managed a polite nod. "Thank you."

"I met your father once."

This news had her full attention. "You did? When was that?"

"A few years back at a wine competition in San

Diego. It must have been the first year Medallion entered. Your chardonnay did well as I recall."

Jaye wrinkled her nose. "Honorable mention. I thought it had a shot at silver. Bronze at the very least."

"It was pretty good," he said, as if he really remembered.

"Holland Farms took the gold."

"Yes." She thought he might gloat over his family's win, but he didn't. Instead he said, "I liked your father. We had dinner one night. Frank Monroe listened to some ideas I had." His expression turned thoughtful. "He was a really good listener."

Her throat ached too much to speak, so she merely nodded. She and her father had spent many afternoons in this very room, talking, and not all of their conversations had centered on wine.

"I don't recall seeing you there," Zack said.

"San Diego?"

"Uh-huh."

Jaye wasn't one to get dolled up, let alone mix and mingle. She was more comfortable in casual pants and loafers than in cocktail dresses and high heels. What's more she'd never understood the point of making small talk with strangers or chatting about the weather—unless, of course, the local forecast was calling for something that might harm the grapes.

Frank Monroe had often bemoaned the fact that he'd turned his only daughter into a tomboy, so much so that as an adult she was more interested in grafting vines than going out on dates. But Jaye had no regrets. Oh, she liked men and she did date, ending things amiably when her suitors turned serious. She wasn't commitmentphobic, as her best friend, Corey Worth, claimed. Jaye just didn't see the point in settling down and starting a family. To her way of thinking, it was better to know now that she wasn't the wife and mother type than to do what her mom had done: marry, have a child and then take off for parts unknown with nary a look back.

"I'm not a very memorable person," she told Zack.

He surprised her by replying, "I don't know about that. You make quite an impression."

His gaze was direct and it made her oddly uncomfortable. For the first time in memory, Jaye felt self-conscious and wished she'd taken a little more care with her appearance. What exactly she would have done differently, she wasn't sure. She only knew that compared to Zack, who stood before her in tailored trousers and a designer shirt that screamed expensive, she felt drab and outdated.

She noticed other things about him then. What filled out his clothes wasn't bad, either. He had broad shoulders, long limbs and narrow hips. He appeared fit, as if he might work out regularly. But he wasn't overly muscled.

While his body was definitely a prime specimen, it was his face that could make a woman forget her name. Paul Newman–blue eyes peaked out from beneath a slash of brows that were a good two shades darker than the sandy hair on his head. The hair had a nice wave to it, the kind women paid big money to achieve. And he wore it longer than most professional men did. Not quite long enough to pull into a ponytail, but it brushed his shirt's collar in the back and gave him a slightly dangerous look that was in stark contrast to his otherwise tidy appearance.

Jaye resisted the urge to fiddle with the end of her braid. "Actually, I didn't go with my dad that time. I stayed behind to look after things at the vineyard."

"That explains it then," Zack said. "I never forget a face."

"I never forget a wine. Your chardonnay was exceptional that year." It was a relief to return to the subject of grapes. She always felt on firm footing when the discussion centered on business.

"Yes, Holland's was," he said. Again, he seemed to distance himself from taking any credit. "I think Medallion's has the potential to be even better."

"Really?" she asked, too intrigued to act blasé.

"I wouldn't have bought this vineyard if I felt otherwise," he replied.

The reminder of the winery's change in ownership tempered her enthusiasm. "I see."

"I was disappointed I didn't get a chance to meet you when I toured Medallion before making my initial offer," Zack said.

"I was out of the country at the time."

He nodded. "A buying trip. France, I believe your mother told me."

"Margaret is my *step*mother." She snapped out the correction. "I was not informed of your visit until well after my return. In fact, I wasn't informed that the vineyard had changed hands until after the deal was done."

He blinked in surprise. "I…I didn't realize."

Jaye saw no point in beating around the bush. "Medallion should have been mine."

"But your father didn't leave it to you."

His equally blunt statement had her bristling. "Dad thought he could micromanage a peace treaty between his second wife and me from the grave. He was wrong."

"I'm sorry."

"I don't want your pity," she replied.

"Actually, that was an expression of sympathy," he said, making her feel small.

Jaye paced to the window in an effort to regroup. Her anger, justified as it was, was of no use here. So she moderated her tone and said evenly, "I want the vineyard, Mr. Holland. I'm prepared to offer you what you paid plus a little something extra for your trouble."

"Why don't you call me Zack? And it looks like we have a problem." He joined her at the window. "I want Medallion, too. I'm not interested in selling."

His reply was nothing less than Jaye had expected. After all, she had made the same offer to Margaret without success. Yet the disappointment of hearing him say the words nearly leveled her.

"Is that going to be an issue for you?" he asked.

She swallowed her outrage along with a good helping of pride. "I don't have much choice but to accept that you'll be the one calling the shots from now on."

To her surprise, he laughed out loud. "Gee, that sounds convincing."

"I said I would *accept* it. I didn't say anything about liking it."

"Ah. Thanks for the clarification."

While Zack appeared amused, Jaye was dead serious when she said, "I'm very good at my job. I…I would appreciate it if you would allow me to stay on."

He nodded. "I'd like that. You know the local people, not to mention the regional quirks of the Great Lakes growing season, far better than I do at this point. I'd like you to manage things."

"But I'm the head vintner. Tom Worley manages Medallion's operation."

"Not anymore. He'll be reassigned or offered a compensation package. Think you can handle it?"

She bristled at his tone. "There's not a job at Medallion I haven't done at one time or another. My father thought it was important to know the business inside and out. He didn't believe you could be an effective leader without understanding the jobs of the people you were leading."

"Is that a subtle barb?" he asked.

"Of course not." Before she could censor the thought, she added, "I wasn't trying to be subtle."

She expected him to be annoyed, perhaps angry. Instead he laughed.

"Do you think I've never worked a harvest or shoveled grapes into a crusher?"

"Have you?" Jaye asked.

"Yes. But I don't think I have to work every job to understand its demands or to appreciate the people I pay to perform it."

"Fair enough. So, if I'm no longer head vintner, who'll be in charge of winemaking?" she asked.

Zack only smiled.

"You?" Her tone was incredulous, so much so it bordered on insulting.

"No need to look so shocked. I have some prior experience," he informed her.

Jaye wasn't impressed by his claim. All she could see was that she would have her hands full in the coming months, likely pulling double duty while he dabbled. She cleared her throat. "I believe in being honest."

"That's good to know," he said slowly.

"I'll stay on, managing and assisting with the winemaking when necessary—"

"You're already assuming I'll need your help?"

"I said I believe in being honest."

"Yes, but what about tactful?" he asked wryly.

"I'll work on it."

"Fair enough," he replied.

"As I said, I'll stay on, but I won't be doing it for you or even for the paycheck."

His eyes narrowed. "Go on."

"I've got an investment here that goes well beyond money. Your name might be on the deed now, but make no mistake, Mr. Holland—"

"Zack," he said, for the first time sounding truly annoyed. "My name is Zack."

"Fine. Zack. I want Medallion. And I plan to keep making you fair offers for its sale until you finally accept one. I don't give up easily."

"So I've noticed." Then his expression turned oddly grim. "Do you love it that much?"

"Love it?" Jaye shook her head, not surprised in the least that someone who could walk away from his family's land would fail to understand the attachment she had to hers. "This vineyard is everything to me."

"Everything? It's just a place. It's not…people."

"No. It's more reliable than people." She hadn't meant to say that. Thankfully, he didn't understand her meaning.

"It's dirt and vines. It's real estate, an investment," he countered, blue eyes glittering like ice.

"Is that all it is to you?"

Zack didn't say anything, although for a moment she thought she saw something contradictory flicker in his expression. Then it was gone.

"Well, that's not all it is to me." She glanced back out the window. Her voice was low, her tone reverent when she added, "My dad and I built Medallion from nothing. It's…it's my life."

CHAPTER TWO

ZACK spent the following week getting acquainted with the winery's day-to-day operations and the people who performed them. As he'd told Jaye on the first day, other than the manager and the vintner, he didn't have any immediate plans to let people go, change their duties or make new hires, but neither did he intend to maintain the status quo. He saw potential at Medallion for greater profit, just as he saw potential for a superior product. He planned to achieve both.

Zack had something to prove.

He was sitting at his desk late Friday going through invoices when the telephone rang. It was his mother.

"I thought I'd call since you haven't." Judith Holland's tone held teasing censure as well as a little hurt. He regretted that. It wasn't his intention to wound her.

"Sorry. It's been a busy couple weeks. The harvest is beginning," he said.

"Here, too." It was her subtle way of saying she didn't buy his excuse.

"How is it looking?" he couldn't help asking. Hearing her voice had made him a little homesick for California and the vineyard he'd left behind. Winemaking was in his blood. It had been in the Holland blood for three generations.

"Good," she said. "Ross says it will be a better yield than last year, especially for the Sangioveses."

"That must please Dad." The Italian varietal was one of his father's personal favorites.

"It does. Phillip thinks we should expand that section of the vineyard and increase our production, given the rise in popularity of the wine."

"Of course he does." Zack's mood soured. He'd suggested the very same thing to his father two years ago without success, but only because Phillip had been against it at the time.

Phillip was Zack's cousin but the two men were more like brothers. They had been raised together after a car accident had left a four-year-old Phillip orphaned. Zack had been two at the time. Over the years the pair had butted heads often, enjoying what his mother termed sibling rivalry. It had run deeper than that. Now as adults, Holland Farms and their opposing visions for it posed the biggest source of friction.

No matter what innovations or changes Zack proposed, to make the staid winery stand out in a changing and ever more competitive marketplace, his cousin effectively vetoed them. It wasn't that Phillip had any more say or power than Zack did. No, what he had was more damning. He had Zack's father's ear. He'd *always* had his father's ear.

"How is old Phil these days?" Zack drawled. "Still sitting to the right hand of the father?"

"Zackary." Judith's tone sounded more weary than scolding.

"Sorry." And he was. He hadn't meant to put his mother in the middle.

She seemed satisfied with the apology. "Your cousin is well."

"And Mira?"

"She's well, too." The words came out slowly.

"They're still together then?" he asked.

Zack's fiancée's affections had soured quickly when he began talking about selling off his share of Holland Farms and shopping for his own vineyard. Soon after ending things with Zack, she'd turned up on Phillip's arm at his family's annual charity ball. It had been a hell of blow to his ego to learn that she'd considered the vineyard to be Zack's most appealing attribute.

"Yes." Judith cleared her throat before continuing. "In fact, she and Phillip recently became engaged."

It wasn't heartache he felt. He'd moved beyond that. What was left was bitterness. "Proof that one Holland is as good as the next as long as he comes with a stake in the land," he sneered.

"Zackary, please. It's been nearly a year. Don't be like that."

"Like what, Mother? Honest?" He snorted. "Apparently I'm the only one so afflicted in our family.

Everyone else just tiptoes around the fact that my cousin has always taken what belongs to me."

She didn't dispute that. Instead, she said, "They love one another."

"They love Holland and the lifestyle it affords them," Zack countered.

"You used to love Holland, too."

"Yes. I loved it enough to want to see it evolve." He let out a sigh. "It's not worth getting into again. Not over the phone and not with you, Mom." She'd always been in his corner. "I know you supported my ideas."

"I did and I still do. I know you'll do well." There was a hitch in her voice when she said, "I just wish Michigan weren't so far away."

"It's just a plane ride," he said lightly.

"Yes, just a plane ride," she repeated. Then, "Are you upset about Mira?"

"Not the way you think."

"Good. Mira is a nice young woman, but she wasn't right for you, Zack. You never would have been happy married to her," Judith said.

"That much we can agree on. So, when are they planning to make it official?"

"In the spring." She hesitated a moment before asking, "You'll come home for the wedding, won't you?"

"What and ruin my black sheep image?" His laughter held no humor. "Sorry, Mom. I think I'll send my regrets."

"There will always be a place for you here." Judith's voice was low, broken.

"I know that's how you feel, Mom, and I appreciate it. Really, I do." Left unsaid was that his father and cousin had long made him feel like an outsider. Mira's defection had been the final straw. There would be no going back, at least not until he'd achieved some of the ambitious goals he'd set for himself.

"Are you happy?" his mother asked quietly.

"I'm getting there." The reply wasn't only for her benefit. Zack meant it.

"That's good. I want you to be happy even more than I want you here. I love you."

"I love you, too, Mom."

After hanging up, he decided to call it a day. The sun had set already, and he was tired and not likely to get much more done—especially now. He felt too unsettled, too restless to sit behind his desk and sift through papers. His stomach rumbled noisily and he realized he was also hungry.

When he stepped out of his office, he noticed that Jaye was still in hers. Through the open door, he could see her hunched at her desk, reading a report. Her hair was in its usual utilitarian braid and she wore a flannel shirt that looked to be at least a couple of sizes too large. A bottle of spring water sat open next to her elbow, and she was munching on a granola bar.

He stopped at her door. "Please tell me that's not your dinner," he said.

Jaye glanced up at the sound of his voice and blinked as if trying to focus. In the past week Zack had learned one thing about her: she was no slacker. The woman put in long hours and gave everything she worked on her undivided attention.

"Sorry? What did you say?" she asked.

He motioned toward the bar of rolled oats and raisins she held in one hand. "I was just wondering if that was your dinner."

"Oh?" She shook her head. "A late lunch, actually."

"It's going on seven."

She glanced in the direction of the window, as if just realizing it was dark outside. "A *really* late lunch, then," she said.

He leaned against the doorjamb. "I can see how you manage to stay so slim. Got something against real food?"

"This *is* real food, but to answer your question, no. I just didn't have time to stop for a meal today."

He nodded and straightened, intending to be on his way. But he found himself saying, "I was thinking about grabbing a bite to eat before I head back to my hotel. Would you like to join me?"

Jaye eyed him the way a scientist might study an acutely contagious test subject and said nothing.

"You know, you're hell on a man's ego," Zack drawled, snorting out a laugh afterward.

"Sorry. I just…I just don't think that we should—"

"What?" He cocked one eyebrow in challenge. "Be friendly? I'm not asking you out, Jaye." Thinking of Mira and all of the pain and disillusionment she'd caused, he added with great feeling, "Believe me, I'm not interested."

"And you have the nerve to say I'm hell on the ego," she replied dryly.

He closed his eyes, rubbed them and sighed. “Sorry. That came out wrong.”

“Bad day?”

Zack shook his head. “Just a long one. A long week, for that matter.” Now the weekend yawned before him. More than likely he would spend it in his office. Better there than alone in a hotel room with nothing to do. “Well, I’ll leave you to your late lunch. See you Monday.”

He was turning to go when Jaye said, “Friday is pizza night.”

He angled back. “Pardon?”

“It’s Geneva’s night off. She’s my housekeeper. She plays bridge with her friends on Fridays, so I make pizza.”

“From scratch?” He was having a hard time picturing Jaye puttering around in a kitchen. She didn’t appear to be the domestic sort, given her affinity for men’s shirts and steel-toed work boots.

She shrugged. “It’s not like it’s rocket science. Besides, I buy the dough already made from a pizzeria in Sutton’s Bay. Saves me time.”

“I see.” He motioned with one hand. “So, are you extending an invitation to me or are you just sharing information?”

His ego took another beating when she took her time answering. “I’m extending an invitation, one coworker to another.”

He decided not to point out that technically he was her boss. “Gee, glad we have that straight.”

Jaye tossed the uneaten portion of her granola bar into the trash. "Give me five minutes to finish up here."

"Okay. I'll meet you downstairs."

Jaye didn't know what had possessed her to invite Zack to dinner, and at her house no less. She didn't want him in her home, invading more of her space. But there was no use wasting time regretting it now. The deed was done, and unless she planned to uninvite him, which she didn't, she was going to be spending the next couple of hours in his company.

The idea wasn't completely without appeal. She told herself that was because they had winemaking in common, which meant at the very least the conversation would be easy and interesting. Besides, what was that saying? Keep your friends close and your enemies closer. Zack wasn't her enemy exactly, but under the circumstances, neither was he her friend.

Downstairs, the tasting room had closed a couple of hours earlier and all of the employees had long since gone home. Stemmed glasses had been washed and put up, the hardwood surface of the large circular bar had been wiped down, and any opened bottles of wine properly stored. The security lights glowed softly, giving the large space with its vaulted ceiling and exposed oak beams a more intimate feel.

"Zack?" she called out.

"Over here." He stepped from behind a display of bottles that had been stacked on their sides to keep the corks moist.

"What are you doing?" she asked.

"My mom told me never to show up at someone's home empty-handed, so I'm looking for a little something to go with our dinner." He flashed an engaging grin that, along with the reference to his mother, made him appear far younger than the midthirties she knew him to be.

Jaye pointed to the next shelf over. "How about the house red?"

"It's good." He scratched his chin. "But I was thinking of something a little more…elegant."

"To go with pizza?"

Zack shrugged. "Is there a rule against that?"

"I guess not."

"Good. Besides, I feel like celebrating."

"Let me guess. Ownership of the vineyard?" Her tone was tight.

To her surprise he shook his head. "I was thinking more along the lines of freedom."

His lips twisted on the last word, as if it had left a foul taste in his mouth. Jaye didn't press him, even though the cryptic answer certainly made her curious. Freedom from what? Or the more intriguing question: Freedom from whom?

It was none of her business, though. So she asked instead, "If it's a celebration you have in mind, then how about our 2004 pinot noir?"

"Ah. Now you're talking."

He grinned again. This time there was nothing remotely boyish about the way he looked. He was all man, fully grown and way too easy on the eyes. Jaye swallowed. Friend? Enemy? For a moment her traitorous libido seemed interested in drafting an entirely different classification. She chalked it up to long work days and a virtually nonexistent social life, especially when it came to members of the opposite sex.

"I'll wait for you outside," she told him, and hastily retreated, happy to stand alone in the frigid moonlight while her pulse returned to normal.

Jaye was leaning against his car when Zack finished locking up the building's main doors. Unless she had appointments that took her away from the vineyard during the day, he'd noted that she walked the short distance from the house to work.

"Car's unlocked," he called. "I should have thought to give you the keys so you could start it up and get the heater going."

The air held an extra bite tonight, but she didn't look cold. In fact, her jacket remained unzipped.

"That's okay. I was just enjoying the peace."

"It's like this at night back home, too," he commented as he drew closer.

"Like what?"

He motioned with the bottle of wine to encompass the dark countryside beyond the lighted parking lot. "Isolated and quiet. It's easy to forget the rest of the world exists beyond the vineyard once the visitors go home for the day and the sun sets."

"My dad used to claim I did that even when it was light outside."

"A bit of a homebody?" Zack asked as he joined her on the passenger side of the car.

"I date." She sounded slightly defensive.

"I don't believe I said otherwise, Jaye." He opened her door. The basic courtesy that was so common on the dates she claimed to go on had her brows lifting. Still, she said nothing as she folded those long legs of hers inside his Mercedes. He wasn't sure how, but she managed to look graceful even wearing oversize cotton, abused denim and a pair of muddy boots. He took a moment to thank providence for the rubber floor mats he'd installed just the week before.

"It's just that I work a lot of hours," she was saying.

"Same here."

"It's hard to get out."

"At times." Mira, of course, had enjoyed spending time with him at Holland. He frowned.

"Not everyone understands the kind of commitment a vineyard requires."

"No. Not everyone does," he agreed. "Of course, there's a fine line between commitment and obsession." He moved to close the door, but she put a hand out to stop him.

"Which are you, Zack? Committed or obsessed?"

"I'm…driven," he replied, deciding there was a difference. This time she let him close the door, but the conversation wasn't over.

When he settled in behind the wheel, she said, "So, you straddle the line between the two."

Straddle? "I…no."

"Come on. Isn't that what driven is? Half obsession, half commitment?"

He wasn't sure how she'd managed to put him on the defensive, but he felt the need to explain himself. "I want to make a superior product. I want to prove—" He broke off abruptly. He wanted to prove to his father, to Phillip, come to that, to Mira, that his ideas had merit, that *he* had worth.

"What do you want to prove?"

"Nothing."

"You know what I want? I want another Judgment in Paris this time with Michigan wines, specifically Medallion wines, taking top honors," she said, referring to the 1976 blind tasting of California wines by French judges in which they won in every category against French wines.

"You aim high."

"Anything wrong with that?" she asked.

"Not a thing."

Zack started the engine. They arrived at her home barely a minute later. Thanks to moonlight and clever landscape lighting, he was able to admire the architecture inspired by Frank Lloyd Wright, with its wealth of rectangular windows and geometric motifs.

"I've got to tell you, this is a great house." Zack switched off the ignition and pocketed the keys.

"Dad liked it."

"But not you?" he asked.

"It's…big."

Something about the way she said it made him think the word was synonymous for lonely.

"It has seven bedrooms," she was saying. "My housekeeper is livid. My house only had three."

"I'm not following you."

"I owned a house on the water, a three-bedroom bungalow with an incredible view of the bay. I sold it and moved in here after…after I inherited the place. I don't really need all of this space." She blew out a breath. "But it's mine now."

"I like the way it takes advantage of its setting." The lower level and a three-car garage protruded from the side of a gently sloped hill. Rocky, terraced flowerbeds lit with small hanging lanterns angled sharply up to a wide, L-shaped porch that was braced with intermittently spaced square columns. "I bet these gardens are something in the summer."

"My dad's doing. He had a real green thumb, whether it was with grapes or herbs or black-eyed Susans."

That made twice she'd mentioned Frank. This time, Zack heard the sorrow in her voice. He envied the closeness they'd obviously enjoyed, even if he didn't envy her grief. Before he could think of something suitable to say, though, she was opening her door and getting out of the car.

He followed her up the steps to the porch.

"This is a Craftsman, right?" He'd always been a fan of that style of architecture with its solid look and angular lines.

"Yes. My dad had it built the year we moved here from the Detroit area."

"It's a very masculine design," he said.

"I manage to like it, anyway," she remarked dryly.

"It suits you."

"Oh?"

"No offense," he said quickly. "It's just that you're not, well, you're not a…"

"A what?" she asked.

He cleared his throat. "A frilly sort. And neither is the house."

"You only say that because you haven't been inside yet."

"Pardon?"

"You'll see."

Jaye opened the front door, ushered him inside, and Zack understood exactly what she'd meant.

Beyond the foyer he could see into the formal dining room. Busy floral wallpaper and a cabbage-rose area rug obscured the dark plank flooring and high wood baseboards. Not that either design element had much of a chance to shine in a room that had been stuffed with so much furniture. In addition to a mahogany sideboard and matching server, a massive curved-leg table stood surrounded by a dozen ornately carved, high-back chairs.

"The decor is very…unexpected," he managed when he recovered the power of speech.

"Unexpected? I call it hideous."

He let out a discreet sigh of relief. "I was trying to be tactful."

"No need. I'm not the one responsible for cluttering up the house's clean lines with all of these spindly legged antiques. I detest the stuff." She sloughed off her coat and tossed it over the scrolled arm of the English mahogany hall chair for emphasis.

"So, the entire place is decorated this way?" Zack hung his on the brass coatrack that stood next to the chair.

"Every room except the kitchen. Margaret wasn't much of a cook."

"You know, with the right furniture, this house would be a real showplace." He offered it as a casual observation even as an idea formed and excitement bubbled beneath the surface of his calm facade.

"Yeah, well, my stuff is in storage at the moment. Once I sell off all of Margaret's flea-market finds and auction-house antiques, the place will be decorated in a style more suited to its contemporary look."

"So you plan to continue living here?" he inquired. "I thought perhaps you would sell it since you don't need all the room."

"I'd like to sell, but I can't really bring myself to do it. It's so close to Medallion. It wouldn't be right to have someone else living here and enjoying the view."

He made a little humming noise as he processed her response. It wasn't what he'd hoped to hear, but he was relieved it wasn't an outright no. He glanced toward the stairs. "And you said it has seven bedrooms?"

"Actually, eight. Margaret turned one into a showroom for her dolls. She collects the kind that have eyes that open and close. Thankfully, she took all 212 of them with her when she left. The things gave me the creeps." Jaye shuddered.

Zack was only half listening. It just kept getting better and better. Jaye's house was perfect, absolutely perfect, for his plans to add a sumptuous, spa-style bed and breakfast to the winery.

He'd tried to convince his family to do something similar with the century-old mansion that had belonged to his great-grandparents. The massive Italian Renaissance–style structure at the southern edge of the vineyard had sat empty for the better part of three decades. It was in need of major repairs and renovations to make it habitable. With a little more investment, though, Zack saw it as a profitable venture. When he pitched the idea of an inn to his father and cousin, though, they'd shot it down quickly.

"We're winemakers, Zack, not innkeepers," his father had said.

Phillip had stood at Ross Holland's side, the positioning apropos. The two men always seemed to be in synch, while Zack felt out of step.

"Why are you constantly trying to push Holland Farms in directions that distract from our product?" Phillip had asked.

Zack didn't see the addition of an inn as a distraction. He saw it as a complement, and a necessary one as competition grew fiercer for space on store shelves and in restaurant wine cellars.

One way or another, Medallion would have an inn, but he didn't want to cut into the vineyard's prime acreage to build one. He wouldn't have to if he could convince Jaye to sell. That realization had him frowning.

"Have you lost your appetite?" she asked.

Zack cleared his throat and reined in his thoughts. "Sorry. No. Just…thinking." He sent her the charming smile that had always distracted Mira. Jaye's eyes narrowed, so he changed the subject. "Which way to the kitchen?"

"Follow me."

As Jaye had said, the kitchen was generously proportioned and gorgeous, its decor leaning toward modern with granite surfaces and professional-grade, stainless steel appliances. It was big enough, functional enough to accommodate a chef's needs.

"Much better," he murmured.

"Not a fan of antiques?"

"They have their place, but not in a house like this. Anything Victorian clashes with its architectural style. But your stepmother acquired some pretty pricey pieces from what I could see. They should bring in a decent sum when you sell them."

She eyed him warily. "You know antiques?"

"What can I say?" Zack shrugged. "My mother is a fan of late-eighteenth-century French furnishings. I started going to auctions with her when I was in grade school."

Jaye grunted out an oath. "No wonder Margaret picked you to buy Medallion."

He cleared his throat then, wanting also to clear the

air. "About that, Jaye. She never told me that you wanted to buy the vineyard."

"You know now," she said quietly.

He nodded but remained silent. What could he say, after all, that would soothe her bruised feelings? Unless he was going to offer to sell Medallion back to her. He wasn't. As much as she loved it, he needed it.

After an awkward moment she said, "I'll get started on the pizza."

"Need a hand?"

"No, but if you want to be helpful you can open that bottle of wine."

"Sure. Happy to."

She told him where to find the corkscrew and glasses and set to work constructing their pizza, first rolling out the premade dough and then slathering it with store-bought sauce. As she chopped mushrooms, green pepper and pepperoni on the island, Zack settled onto a stool on the opposite side and sipped his wine.

"Very good." He held up his glass to inspect the ruby color.

"It's one of our best." She set aside the knife so she could reach for her glass. After taking a sip, she let the wine sit on her tongue for a moment before swallowing. "Mmm."

Zack watched her throat work. She had a slim neck, long. The word *graceful* came to mind again. Despite her rough edges and mannish attire something about her appealed to him. Attraction? No. Merely curiosity, he assured himself. He appreciated strong emotions, strong convictions. Jaye certainly had those in abundance. She was so outspoken and so passionate about the vineyard.

Just about the vineyard?

He realized he was staring. Jaye stared right back at him, eyebrows cocked in challenge.

"It finishes well," he said and took another sip.

"Yes. Unfortunately, not everything does." She set her glass aside and started chopping again.

"No."

When the toppings had been arranged on the pizza, she popped it into the preheated oven and arranged two place settings on the island.

"So, why Michigan?" she asked without preamble.

He blinked. "Sorry?"

"Why did you decide to move to Michigan? What made you decide to buy my vineyard?" She settled into her seat, picked up her glass and gave him her undivided attention.

The wine's aftertaste soured as he formulated his answer. "I liked what I saw here. The potential as well as the challenges."

He also liked the physical distance. The miles he'd put between himself and California had been part of the lure. Jaye rolled the stem of her glass between her fingers and studied the swirling wine.

"You mentioned celebrating freedom earlier. I wasn't going to ask, but…" She shrugged. "Even though it is none of my business, I am curious. Freedom from what?"

"The past," he supplied. "I guess you could say I needed a new start."

"You'll understand if I tell you that your new start is damned inconvenient for me."

It was more than inconvenient. She'd made that very plain. And so he said, "That wasn't my intention, Jaye, so I'm sorry for that."

She nodded, apparently accepting his apology. He thought the subject might be dropped. It wasn't. She tipped her head to one side, "Sorry enough to sell?"

"No."

"Well, I had to ask." Her green eyes grew bright until she blinked and then half of her mouth rose in a sardonic smile that did little to erase the heartache he'd seen. "I didn't think you were, but I figured I'd give it a shot. I think it's only fair to warn you that that won't be the last time I ask."

"I know. And I think it's only fair to warn you that my answer isn't likely to change."

She sipped her wine and regarded him over the rim of the glass. "I guess we'll see about that."

CHAPTER THREE

THE wine was nearly gone and only one slice of pizza remained. The clock on the stove read eleven-fifty. Zack set his napkin aside and stood.

"Well, I guess I should be on my way. It's almost midnight."

"Afraid I'll turn into a pumpkin?" Jaye rose to her feet, as well.

"Actually, I'm afraid I'll overstay my welcome."

The man was in no danger of doing that. Jaye had enjoyed his company, so much so that she was sorry to see the evening end. Even as she wanted to chalk her feelings up to loneliness, a small voice kept contradicting her. Zack was smart, funny, an interesting conversationalist and an attuned listener. He'd make a good friend. He'd make an even better…

"You'll be okay to drive?" she asked hastily.

"Fine." He cocked his head to one side. "You're not worried about me?"

"Well, you know how it is. Wouldn't want to get sued for providing you with the wine."

"Gee, that makes me feel special." But he laughed.

Jaye couldn't help it; she did, too.

Zack's expression sobered. "You know, that looks good on you."

"What looks good on me?"

He walked to where she stood, stopping just in front of her. "A smile. I don't know that I've seen you do that before."

"I haven't had much to smile about lately." She said it lightly, going for glib.

Zack nodded. He was oddly serious when he replied, "Perhaps I can remedy that."

He leaned forward slightly. Was he going to kiss her? His pose, the heat simmering in his gaze, both suggested as much. Jaye wanted him to, she realized, and so it came as a vast disappointment when his lips merely brushed her cheek.

"Thanks for dinner and the good company."

"You're welcome," she replied.

"I'll return the favor sometime."

"Oh, there's no need. Really. It was just pizza," she said, struggling to remain nonchalant.

"Another time," he persisted. "It would be my pleasure."

She shrugged and walked him to the door, feeling ridiculously out of sorts. It was just a kiss on the cheek. It barely rated as platonic. Hell, if he'd added one to the opposite cheek, it would have qualified as a polite gesture of welcome in many parts of the world. Why did her body seem intent on making more of it?

The night had grown colder, but she followed him outside and stood coatless on the porch in her stocking-feet.

"See you on Monday," she said.

"I'll probably be in over the weekend." The wind caught his hair, tugging it this way and that. His smile turned wry. "I'm not much for sitting in a hotel room playing solitaire."

As she watched Zack drive away, it hit Jaye that even though the man still had family, he was every bit as alone as she was.

Zack lay in the center of the king-size bed, hands stacked behind his head, and stared at the textured ceiling. It was past two in the morning, but he was wide-awake. He was still running on California time, he told himself, even though his insomnia had less to do with the clock than it did with Jaye Monroe. The woman intrigued him.

God help him, but there had been a moment that evening when she'd more than intrigued him. He'd come close to kissing her—and not just on the cheek.

"Not a good idea, Holland," he muttered, rolling to his side so he could flip off the lamp. "Not a good idea in the least."

Even having made that determination, however, when he finally slipped off to sleep, he dreamed of her, indulging in the kiss he'd denied himself earlier.

"So, what's he like?" Corey Worth sat across from Jaye in a Sutton's Bay coffee shop, her grin turning sly when she added, "Mom said she saw a Mercedes with California plates at the gas station the other day. According to her the driver was incredibly hot."

"Your mother needs to get out more."

"Oh, please," Corey scoffed. "The woman already goes on more dates in a month than I do."

Corey's father had died during their freshman year of high school. The girls had been acquaintances at the time, but because Jaye understood how it felt to lose a parent, even though her loss had not been the result of a death, they'd become fast friends. They'd remained close ever since, even sharing a dorm room during college.

"Then *you* need to get out more," Jaye said.

"Why don't I stop by the winery later today? You can introduce me to Mr. California and then maybe I will get out more."

Jaye's eyes narrowed. "You would date the man who is making my life miserable?"

"Depends on how well he fills out his clothes," she teased. Then Corey turned serious. "Is he really making your life miserable?"

Jaye wanted to say yes. But she blew out a breath and shook her head. "No. Not exactly. I'm not happy that he owns Medallion and I'm just an employee now."

"That goes without saying. But?" Corey prompted.

Jaye added a little more creamer to her coffee and stirred it. The man made her nervous in a way that had nothing to do with wine and everything to do with being a woman. She wasn't about to tell Corey that, though. So she said, "Well, he's not the jerk I assumed he would be. He hasn't spelled out the changes he plans to implement, but I'm no longer worried that he's going to drive the place into the ground or do anything stupid."

"High praise indeed coming from you," her friend said dryly. "So, let me ask you this—if you met him somewhere else, under other circumstances, would you be interested in him?"

"Maybe," she allowed. She thought back on the conversation they'd had over pizza in her kitchen. "He's got a dual degree in viticulture and viniculture from UCLA. He knows grapes. He knows wine. He understands and appreciates the complexities of the business end of things. We actually have a lot in common."

"Work." Corey's mouth puckered on the word.

"Sure. It makes conversation easy."

"There's more to life than work or wine, Jaye. Shall I give you a for-instance?"

"If I say no are you going to anyway?"

"Yes."

Jaye sighed and waved a hand in resignation before picking up her cup. "Then, please, by all means, Corey, enlighten me."

"What does his butt look like?" her friend asked just as Jaye took a sip of coffee.

She nearly choked on the steaming beverage, laughter sputtering out even as she grabbed for a napkin. "That's one heck of a for-instance," she finally managed.

"Well, are you going to answer the question?"

One word came to mind and slipped out from

between Jaye's curving lips before she could think better of it. "Prime."

Corey chuckled. "So you do notice more than grapes."

"I notice plenty of things, but Zack Holland is my boss—at least for the time being. We didn't meet under other circumstances, so my interest in him is and will remain limited to professional."

"Hmm. Too bad."

The waitress came by and refilled their cups. Jaye added creamer and stirred her coffee again. "Besides, I doubt I'd be his type."

"And what would that be?" Corey asked.

"Probably you."

"Really?" Her friend grinned. "Do tell."

"I figure he'd go for someone petite and pretty." Corey was blond, slender and all of five-three. She also loved clothes and wore them well, so Jaye added, "And someone who looks like she just stepped out of a fashion magazine."

Corey teasingly batted her long eyelashes. "Well, thanks. I try. But you're pretty, Jaye. You have great bone structure. You just need to play it up more."

Jaye held up a hand. "I don't have time for fussing."

"A little mascara, eyeliner and a sweep of blush hardly qualify as fussing. And your hair—"

"Is easy this way."

"It doesn't have to be one or the other, you know," Corey said in exasperation. "With a good cut it could be easy *and* more flattering. God, Jaye, you've already got a color that a lot of women would pay big bucks to achieve, and yet all you ever do is tug every last strand back in that tired-looking braid."

Because she was feeling tempted, Jaye crossed her arms over her chest. "No."

"My treat," Corey coaxed. "We'll go to that new day spa in Traverse this weekend, get a manicure while we're at it."

Jaye resisted the urge to look at her callused hands and close-cropped nails. Instead she grumbled, "Next you'll be adding that mascara, eyeliner and sweep of blush you mentioned."

Corey grinned. "I was thinking facials first. But, sure, makeup, too. Why not?"

I'll show you how to apply cosmetics when you turn thirteen. Jaye's mother had made that promise, but then Heather Monroe hadn't been around to keep it. Jaye pushed the memory away. She had makeup, an entire drawerful of products, most of which she'd bought at Corey's urging. She just preferred to go without.

"…and then I'll take you shopping at the mall. Your wardrobe could use an overhaul," Corey was saying, her gaze dipped meaningfully to Jaye's oversize shirt.

"This was my dad's."

"I know, honey."

Because she was uneasy with the sympathy she saw in her friend's eyes, she added, "I use his things for work clothes."

"Work clothes that you also wear out in public to meet your best friend for coffee," Corey said pointedly. "I don't want to seem critical, but you've really let yourself go since your dad died." She softened the words by reaching out to lay a hand over Jaye's. "You've lost weight, too. I'm worried about you, honey."

"I'm okay. Besides, you know me. I'll never be accused of being a fashion plate." Jaye shrugged. "I guess I'm still a tomboy at heart."

"I'm not expecting you to start wearing organdy skirts and high heels to work, but you used to take more care with your appearance. When was the last time you bought yourself a killer outfit and went out for a night on the town?"

Jaye scrunched up her face. "It's been awhile."

"We need to change that."

Her friend's idea continued to tantalize. It had been ages since Jaye had done anything remotely self-indulgent. From the moment she and her father had decided to start the vineyard, work had sucked up most of her time and energy. Since his death and since learning of the sale of Medallion, she'd barely taken time to look in the mirror.

Until Zack Holland had come along.

She shook her head, dismissing the man, dismissing her friend's idea. "I've got to get back."

"Of course you do." Corey's tone was resigned. "At least think about the weekend. It would be a lot of fun."

"I'll think about it."

But Saturday came and went. When Monday dawned, the harvest began in earnest at Medallion, and Jaye barely had time to take personal calls let alone the opportunity to head off to a spa for an afternoon of pampering. She did take some of Corey's advice, though, and started spending an extra few minutes in the morning applying a little mascara and liner to her eyes. But she donned the same loose-fitting clothes, since for the foreseeable future she would be up to her elbows in grapes—literally.

Medallion's operation was small, and they did things the old-fashioned way. They picked the grapes by hand, carefully snipping bunches of fruit from the vines and placing them in baskets to be taken to the crusher. It was a time-consuming process, and every available employee helped out. So even with the new title and duties of manager, Jaye found herself in the vineyard, traipsing the rows of grapes. She wouldn't have had it any other way, of course. But she was a little surprised to see Zack amid the workers the second morning.

It was the first time she'd seen him in blue jeans and she couldn't help but recall Corey's question about his backside. When he turned to talk to one of the other workers, her gaze dipped and her mouth gaped open for a moment before she thought to snap it shut. The man definitely did extraordinary things for a pair of faded Levi's.

A moment later he was walking in her direction. He actually looked excited, as if he felt the same sense of anticipation she always did this time of year.

"Good morning, Jaye," he called.

"Morning."

"Great day, huh?"

It was in fact overcast and threatening to rain. Still, Jaye found herself nodding in agreement.

"I told the workers that once things settle down and most of the grapes are in, we'll have a party to celebrate. We always did that at Holland."

At his words Jaye felt her stomach drop. "It's…it's been a tradition here, too."

"Oh, terrific." He offered an engaging grin, oblivious to her turmoil. "Then maybe you wouldn't mind adding the planning to your list of things to do?"

"Sure. I can handle the arrangements." Without warning, her eyes misted.

"Jaye?"

She glanced away, feeling foolish. "Sorry, it's just that my dad always took care of the party personally. With him gone, I…I just forgot about it."

"Understandable." Zack lowered his voice and reached out to lay a reassuring hand on her arm.

Jaye wanted to shake it off. But, God help her, she had an even greater urge to step closer and have him wrap his arms around her. She didn't just feel lonely. At times she felt unbearably alone.

"Zack…"

She didn't move, but he did. As if he'd heard her unspoken need he settled his around her shoulders. "I can see to the details if you'd like."

She blinked, seeking to banish the unshed tears along with her vulnerability. "No. Thanks for offering. I appreciate it. But I'll see to it."

"It hasn't been that long, Jaye. Cut yourself some slack."

His sympathetic tone had new tears threatening. "Dad loved the harvest." She glanced past Zack to the rows of vines that stretched across the horizon. "You know, I almost expect to see him out here."

"If you'd rather work at your desk—"

"I can pull my weight."

"I wasn't suggesting otherwise," Zack said. The arm around her shoulders tightened, pulling her closer against his chest. She swore she could feel the steady thump-thump of his heart. "I'm not questioning your professional ability, Jaye. But you're entitled to grieve."

She gave a jerky nod. "I know that."

"No one will think less of you. It's not a weakness."

"I know that, too." Her throat had gone tight, but she managed to say, "Thanks."

"No problem."

Then, to her mortification, a tear slipped down her cheek.

"Aw, Jaye," Zack brushed it away with his fingertips. "You're such a strong person. But you don't always need to be so tough."

But she did. She did. She was alone now. Who was she going to lean on? Zack? Because she actually was at the moment, she forced herself to step away.

"God, just what I need, to start blubbering while wearing mascara." She tried to laugh. It came out a hiccupping sob.

"I thought something seemed different. You have incredible eyes." After making that assessment, he appeared embarrassed. Reaching into his back pocket, he produced a clean handkerchief, which he handed to her. "Here."

"Thanks. I owe you."

"No. You owe me nothing." He saluted her with his clippers. "See you later?" It came out a question, sounded almost like an invitation.

"Sure. Later."

And she did. Once again that evening Zack and Jaye were the last two people to call it a day. They dined together again, too. This time the pizza was delivered and they ate it off paper plates while sitting in the small break room down the hall from their offices. They'd forgone wine, but the conversation flowed as easily as it had in her kitchen, and this time it veered into personal territory.

"Are you from this area originally?" Zack asked.

"No. I was born downstate in a suburb just northwest of Detroit. We lived there until I was in middle school."

"And your mom?"

As a general rule, Jaye never talked about her mother. Only Corey knew the details. But she heard herself say, "She left us a month before I turned thirteen. In her note she said she needed to find herself. As far as I know, she's still looking."

He made a sympathetic noise. "Sorry. That had to be tough."

"Nah. Dad did an incredible job as both mother and father, even if his face did bleach white the first time I asked him about sex." Jaye laughed, recalling Frank's stricken expression. Then she wanted to cry.

"Sex is a dicey subject," Zack said softly.

Jaye glanced over, distracted from her grief by the gleam in his eyes. "Isn't it, though? Some people have a tough time talking about it."

"But not you?"

"I'm pretty forthright."

"So I noticed." His lips twitched.

"Why beat around the bush?" She shrugged, but couldn't help wondering if that wasn't exactly what they were doing at the moment.

After a long pause, Zack changed the subject. "So, do you have other family?"

"No. Well, an aunt and uncle downstate, and some cousins scattered about the Midwest. I don't have any contact with my mother's side of the family, though. And I don't consider any of Margaret's relatives to be kin, a feeling that I can assure you is mutual."

"I didn't realize you were so alone."

"I've got the vineyard." She felt her face heat after saying that and she decided to redirect the conversation. "What about you? Brothers? Sisters?"

He dabbed his mouth with a paper napkin. "An only child, but I was raised with my cousin. My parents became his guardians after his folks died in a car wreck."

"How horrible for him. You must be close," Jaye said.

"You'd think, but no. Not especially." Zack's mouth

twisted. She thought he might expand on that intriguing response, but he changed the subject. "You know, I never would have taken you for a former city girl."

"Because I have more important things on my mind than the latest trends in fashion, hair and makeup?" Her tone turned chilly to compensate for her self-consciousness.

"No." He frowned. "You just seem so at home here. I can't picture you fighting traffic jams on the interstate during a morning commute."

"I can't picture me doing that, either." Then she admitted, "But I missed the city at first."

"Really?"

"We moved here in the dead of winter and lived in an old farmhouse just up from where we later built. The place was drafty and a little creepy." She shook her head. "I thought my dad was crazy."

"So what happened to change your mind?"

"Spring. And then summer hit." She glanced down at her work boots. Mud was caked on the soles. Seeing it there had Jaye remembering the early days when she and her dad had traipsed through the fields and begun making their plans. It had been just the two of them then and they both had felt bruised and a little disillusioned in the wake of her mother's bombshell. Little by little, though, they had patched up their hearts and moved on with their lives. "By the time fall came along I was good and hooked. I didn't even care that winter would be coming next."

"I know the feeling."

Because he sounded like he did, she asked, "What about California? Don't you miss it?"

"Sometimes," he averred. "My mother called the other day. Hearing a friendly voice made me a little homesick."

"And your vineyard? Don't you miss it?"

His tone was curiously flat when he said, "It was never *my* vineyard. My dad and Phillip—my cousin—we owned it together, but the changes I wanted to make, they weren't interested in."

"And so you bought Medallion and plan to make those changes here."

"Yes."

"And what are those changes? As manager of Medallion, I'd like to know."

"I have a proposal," he began, but then he stopped and shook his head. "I want to work out all of the details before I go over it with you. You're pretty key to the implementation of some of the changes."

"Really? Well, now you've got me good and curious. Can you at least offer me a time frame on when you'll get back to me?" she asked.

"End of the week."

She nodded. "I suppose I can wait that long since apparently I have no other choice."

"Eager?"

"Very. Maybe you can give me a hint."

"It sounds like the anticipation is killing you." His gaze dipped to her mouth when he said it.

She moistened her lips. "Chalk it up to fear of the unknown."

"Fear? No need for that," Zack assured her. "I think everything will meet with your approval."

"I don't know. I have high standards."

One eyebrow rose. "Are you hard to satisfy?" he asked.

"At times." Their double entendres had the room growing uncomfortably warm. Then to her mortification Jaye blurted out, "Are you involved with anyone?"

She watched his lips curve and his eyes seemed to darken. "No. Not any longer."

Something in his tone had her remarking, "It sounds like it was serious."

"It was for a while. We'd already booked the reception hall." He shrugged, and she figured the subject was closed, but then Zack added, "She's engaged to my cousin now. A spring wedding is planned."

"Ouch. That had to sting."

He nodded. "It did."

"But you're over it?"

"Over her." It seemed to be a clarification of sorts, as if something from his breakup had stayed with him. Before Jaye could ponder it, however, he'd turned the question around. "What about you? How close have you gotten to the altar?"

"How close?" She snorted. "Actually, I prefer to stay as far away from it as I can manage."

"Ah." He nodded. "Sounds like someone broke your heart, too."

She thought of her mother. Jaye wasn't willing to give the woman that much credit. "No. No broken heart. I just don't figure myself the sort cut out for matrimony."

Both of Zack's eyebrows shot up in surprise. "I can't say I've ever met a woman who shared your view. Most are eager to find Mr. Right. They make it their mission."

"What can I say?" She shrugged. "I'm one of a kind."

"Yes, Jaye," he said slowly, "I'm coming to realize that."

CHAPTER FOUR

WHEN Jaye arrived for work just before dawn the following morning, Zack's car was parked in its usual spot. The previous night, when she'd gone to close the blinds in her bedroom, she'd noticed that the light was still on in his office. The man certainly was putting in long days. Even as she was passing sleepless nights.

She was muttering to herself as she stomped up the stairs. What was he going for? Workaholic of the Year? She ignored the little voice whispering that she was the defending champion.

The employee break room was just down the hall from their offices. That's where she found Zack. He was standing at the coffeemaker, hands braced on either side of the countertop, and looking a little desperate as the carafe took its time filling with steaming brown liquid.

He flicked a bleary-eyed glance in her direction but said nothing. His face, however, spoke volumes. His jaw was shaded with stubble, and dark smudges bruised the skin below his eyes. It was just her luck he still managed to look gorgeous.

"What time did you finally leave here yesterday?" she asked.

He shrugged and scrubbed a hand over his prickly chin. It hit her then: the tousled hair, the rumpled clothes and bristly jaw. "My God, Holland. You slept here, didn't you?"

The coffeemaker gurgled, momentarily snagging his attention. Even though the pot was only a quarter of the way filled, he snatched it from the warmer. "Good enough," he muttered.

After he'd emptied what had already brewed into a large mug emblazoned with the words You Had Me at Merlot, he sighed and held it under his nose, as if testing its bouquet. It wasn't until he'd taken a sip that he finally answered Jaye's question.

"Yeah, I slept here." He pointed toward the lumpy brown sofa that was against the break room wall. "By the way, that couch has to go. It's hell on the back."

"Not if you use it for sitting," she replied.

One side of Zack's mouth cricked up in a smile that even a nun would describe as sexy. "What can I say? Sometime around three I felt an overwhelming urge to be horizontal."

At his words a picture of him in said position sprang to mind, accompanied by a completely inappropriate sizzle of awareness that zipped along Jaye's spine with all the subtlety of a lightning strike. Afterward, a tingling sensation lingered, as tantalizing as the man's smile. She swallowed and opted to ignore both.

"Maybe you should consider getting a room at a bed and breakfast in Sutton's Bay until you find a house. You'd be closer to the vineyard that way," she told him, pleased to find she sounded matter-of-fact.

"I've thought of that." He sipped his coffee. "But, actually, I've found a house I'm interested in buying. It's perfect for my needs."

Needs. Her own began to simmer. Jaye cleared her throat and inquired, "Is it nearby?"

"Very." He sipped his coffee again and seemed to study her. "But it's not on the market."

"Oh. Too bad." She tugged her braid around to the front and fiddled with the end of it, stroking it over the palm of one hand like a paintbrush. It was an old habit—a nervous one. Zack watched.

"Do you ever wear your hair loose?" he asked.

Jaye stopped fiddling. "Wh-why?"

He shrugged. "No reason. Just curious what it would look like."

"It would look long."

He didn't appear to be put off by her curt tone. "I'm sure," he murmured.

She felt the gooseflesh rise on her arms. "It's a pain in the butt to manage. Too thick. Too wavy. I'm thinking of having it cut."

"Don't."

The quickly issued command had her blinking. "Excuse me?"

"I mean, it would be a shame. It must have taken forever to grow it to that length."

"I've only had it trimmed twice in the past half decade."

"Hmm."

That damnable awareness was snapping again. Only, this time he appeared to be experiencing it, too. She tossed the braid back over her shoulder. "You know, it wouldn't hurt to make an offer."

"M-make an offer?" he sputtered.

"On the house," she clarified, trying to work up indignation over the way he was regarding her, when the only thing she was feeling at the moment was overheated.

The corners of Zack's mouth twitched. "Oh, right. The house."

"Why don't you contact the owners and tell them you're interested?"

"I'm thinking about it. So, you think that would work?"

She shrugged. "I don't know. But at this point what have you got to lose? A lot of people have a price at which they're willing to sell."

"That's exactly what I'm afraid of." Zack's rich laughter rumbled out.

"So, you think the asking price will be steep?"

"Think?" He shook his head. "I'm sure of it."

"It must be on the water." Even modest homes went for outrageous sums if they had frontage on the bay.

But he was shaking his head again. "No. It's got one hell of a view, though. One plenty of people would pay good money to enjoy."

She was truly curious now, her mind busily flipping through every nearby inland property she could think of. Nothing seemed worthy of such interest, though. "It must be some place."

Zack nodded. "As I said, it's perfect—"

"For your needs."

"Exactly."

"So, what are your needs, Zack?" Jaye wasn't sure what had possessed her to pose such a potentially provocative query, but she wished she could withdraw it when his eyebrows shot up.

"Now there's a question that could get a beautiful woman into a lot of trouble," he said quietly.

She gave her shoulders a negligent shrug even as her heart tapped out an extra beat. "Well then, it's a good thing I'm not beautiful."

"No. You're not."

Jaye's heart knocked unsteadily again, but for an entirely different reason. "Please, Zack," she said dryly. "Stop with the flattery. You'll give me a big head."

"You're not beautiful," he repeated. As if she needed to hear *that* a second time. But then he added, "You're striking, Jaye. You have a face that stays with a man."

He was studying her in a way that left her feeling self-conscious and exposed. The air in the room seemed to thin, making it hard for Jaye to breathe. She wanted to find an insult in his words, but, as compliments went, this was rated among the best she'd ever received. She couldn't stop herself from wondering: Had Zack found himself recalling her face?

"Striking, hmm?"

He nodded. "Striking."

As the silence stretched, she forced out a laugh. "Well, I guess that's better than being described as having a great personality."

"Jury's still out on that." But he winked and the mood thankfully lightened.

She decided to rephrase her original question. "Getting back to your house hunt, what exactly are you looking for?"

"Well, proximity to the vineyard is key of course," he began.

"I figured that much. And?"

"Well, it has to be large and well maintained. Architecturally, it has to have personality, inside and out. I want large rooms and plenty of sleeping quarters."

"Are you planning to have a lot of visitors, then?" She pictured a bunch of his equally stylish California friends coming by the tasting room and tromping about the vineyard. Maybe a gorgeous woman or two. He said he wasn't involved with anyone. That didn't mean the man lived like a monk. Because her upper lip wanted to curl, she nibbled on it.

"In a manner of speaking." The reply seemed oddly vague. But then he was saying, "This is a gorgeous area. I figure I'll get a lot of visitors."

Jaye snorted out a laugh. "Oh, that you will. Dad and I entertained our share of shirttail relatives and downstate friends over the years. Suddenly, people who couldn't make time for us when we lived a few miles away in West Bloomfield were eager to drive nearly four hours north to see us—usually at peak tourist times."

"Of course."

"I can't really blame them, though," she said. "The Traverse Bay area is a great place to get away. In the summer the main roads are crowded with tourists and seasonal residents. Pretty much every weekend in the fall is the same. The color brings them in."

"I can see why. The scenery is outstanding, especially this time of year," he agreed.

Jaye crossed to the window. The sun had just barely crested the horizon, but even shrouded in dawn's fickle light the landscape awed. "Fall's always been my favorite season," she confided. "Dad loved it, too."

Zack joined her at the sill. "It's a pity it doesn't last longer."

"Oh, I don't know about that. I think its limited run is what makes it so appealing. Kind of like Medallion's reserve wines." She smiled.

Zack's expression was a study in seriousness. "You've got a great smile, Jaye. A great…mouth."

He reached out and stroked the pad of his thumb over her lower lip. Unlike the kiss on the cheek he'd given her the other night, this gesture was intimate, loverlike. Apparently he realized that because his face flushed scarlet before he coughed and stepped back. "I'm sorry, Jaye. I shouldn't have touched you like that."

"No." *No?* She couldn't seem to make up her mind.

"I didn't mean to make you uncomfortable."

Try turned on, she thought, but waved a hand in dismissal. "Please. It would take a great deal more than *that* to make me uncomfortable."

"It would?" The simple question seemed to contain a subtle challenge.

Jaye decided to issue one of her own. "Oh, yeah. Much, much more."

"Such as?"

"I'll leave it to your imagination."

"You might regret that," he informed her. "I have a very vivid imagination."

"Then I'm sure I don't need to go into detail."

Jaye felt oddly empowered when his gaze turned smoky. This wasn't like her, engaging in verbal foreplay with a man she should consider off-limits. But, God, it felt good. It felt…liberating. It made her feel alive. Still, a smart woman knew when to leave, so she brushed past him with the hint of a smile tugging at her lips. Over her shoulder she said, "By the way, that's my coffee cup."

He lifted it, read the inscription and chuckled. "I didn't realize."

"I'm sure you just grabbed whatever was available in your sleep-deprived state."

He stopped her by saying, "No. I mean, I didn't realize you had a sense of humor. You keep it pretty well under wraps. Makes a man wonder what other things he might discover about you if you ever let your hair down." He grinned. "That's just a figure of speech, although in this case I wouldn't mind if you took it literally. Maybe I could watch."

Because the offer was tempting, she rolled her eyes. "Be sure to wash the cup."

"You can have it back right now if you'd like. Coffee's still hot."

"I'll get my own, thanks," she replied.

"Don't say I didn't make the offer."

Exactly what offer was that? Jaye wondered.

Zack watched her leave the room. He waited until he heard her heavy work boots on the stairs before he let out an oath. What had gotten into him? He had a feeling the question might be easier to answer if he asked himself *who?*

In the past few weeks at Medallion, he'd already become accustomed to butting heads with Jaye. She was stubborn, opinionated and used to doing things her own way. She also was dedicated, bright, a hard worker and a vital and valuable employee, even if she did sometimes still act as if she was running the show. But his interest in her seemed to keep straying well beyond business.

"Not a good idea," he told himself, and not for the first time.

Besides, she was far too single-minded. He'd been involved with a woman like that before. Neither his pride nor his heart had survived the encounter intact. He didn't plan to get serious with another woman for a very long time. When he did, it would be someone who could separate what he did for a living from who he was as a man.

The vineyard is my life. Jaye had told him that the

first day. At least she was up-front about it. Zack's ex-fiancée had left him to figure it out on his own.

And that brought him to another reason he needed to tread carefully. He owned the vineyard Jaye loved, and he planned to approach her about buying the home in which she currently lived. The home that had been willed to her by the father she still mourned. Those were excellent reasons to keep his relationship with her strictly professional. Involvement with Jaye on any other level surely would complicate matters. He couldn't afford complications.

Zack fully intended for Medallion to have the inn his father and Phillip felt Holland Farms could do without. Jaye's house was perfect for the venture. In addition to proximity and curb appeal, it was small enough to be exclusive and had rooms that were large enough to convey a sense of luxury.

Most people have a price at which they are willing to sell, she'd told him. For the first time Zack began to worry that Jaye's price might not be one he could afford to pay.

One hour and half a pot of coffee later, Zack was feeling more like his old self. The incident with Jaye in the break room basically came down to harmless flirting, he rationalized. He shouldn't have touched her in such a familiar manner and he sure as hell wouldn't allow himself to do it again, but it's not like they'd had sex or anything.

Oh, sure, he was attracted to the woman, but he could handle that. Besides, more than likely his interest in her would wane as time went by. Right now he found her captivating, enchanting, but that was only because she was a bit of an enigma. A woman who didn't want to marry? A woman who was sexy even when she wasn't trying to be? A woman who had him wondering what she would look like with all that glorious hair loose and her clothes tight? Of course he was drawn to her. What man wouldn't be?

He was standing shirtless in front of a small mirror he'd positioned on the windowsill as he shaved with an electric razor. He'd started keeping a change of clothes and other essentials in his office when his days had begun to stretch late. He'd figured at some point that torture rack called a couch would call his name, and it had last night.

He switched off the razor and passed a hand over his jaw, which was respectably smooth now. Just as he was reaching for his shirt a knock sounded briefly before Jaye opened the door. This wasn't the first time she had barged in without waiting for him to call, "Come in," but in the past he'd been sitting at his desk, fully clothed. He took his time tugging on the fresh shirt. It was small of him, but he enjoyed watching a flush creep up her cheeks.

"Hello, Jaye."

She didn't avert her eyes, even though she did mutter what sounded like, "Sorry."

"You know, I close my door for a reason," he told her.

"And I opened it for a reason." Jaye shrugged and then stuffed her hands into the back pockets of her ill-fitting jeans. The move pulled the baggy denim taut over a pair of slender but shapely hips and had him wondering about the contours of her thighs.

Zack dragged his gaze up to her face and forced his mind back to business as he buttoned his shirt. "So, what did you need to see me about?"

"I've got some bad news on the pinot noir grapes. We've got a mildew problem and it's not pretty."

He issued a mild oath. "How bad?"

"Bad enough. We're going to lose a significant percentage of the crop, I'm afraid. I've checked around at other local wineries. It appears to be a problem everywhere at county and peninsula vineyards this year."

It wasn't what he wanted to hear. A couple of recent vintages of Medallion's pinot noir had garnered promising reviews. There had been high hopes for this one. This time when he swore, his curse was not only more creative, but more explicit, and so he apologized. "Excuse the language, Jaye. My mother would be appalled if she heard me say that."

"I'm not your mother."

"Thank God." He hadn't meant to say that out loud, but it was the truth, given the thoughts he'd begun to entertain.

Jaye eyed him curiously for a moment before continuing. "Besides, that was my initial reaction, too."

"Any other varieties affected?" he asked.

"The cabernet franc and merlot look to be in good shape."

He nodded. "What about the pinot grigio and gamay noir?"

"They're fine." She came fully into the room, her gaze on the front of his shirt. "That's buttoned wrong, by the way."

Zack glanced down. Sure enough, he was one hole off starting from the third on down to the tail.

"So it is."

Jaye should have left then. She'd delivered the message she'd come to deliver. She had no reason to linger, but she remained rooted in place, fascinated as Zack began to unfasten the misbuttoned shirt, revealing a tantalizing bit more of that nicely muscled chest she'd seen a moment ago. He glanced up halfway through the job, and their gazes met, locked. His fingers stilled. Her pulse revved.

"Am I making you uncomfortable yet?" he asked, one eyebrow arching as he alluded to their earlier conversation in the break room.

"No." And because the one syllable came out sounding normal, Jaye added, "Are you trying?"

His jaw clenched for a moment and he shook his head. "I shouldn't be. Forget I said that."

"Sure. Consider it forgotten." Right. Like that was going to happen. Everything about the man seemed seared into her consciousness. Jaye was beginning to feel like a voyeur as she watched him continue with his task. But instead of excusing herself, she asked, "Need any help?"

His hands stilled at the offer, but he shook his head. "I think I can button a shirt on my own."

"I don't know. You didn't do so hot the first time," she noted.

He laughed tightly. "You have a point."

"Maybe I make *you* uncomfortable."

When he glanced up, his gaze was so potent it had Jaye's smugness vanishing.

"Maybe you do." He took a couple steps closer. "Are you sure this discomfort thing is one-sided?"

Jaye moistened her lips. "It would appear so."

He advanced again, close enough that she felt his breath warm her skin when he whispered, "What about now?"

"Nope. Still fine," she managed, even as his seductive taunt had fire shooting through her veins.

"And if I do this?" He lowered his head, stopping a mere inch from her lips. "Do I make you uncomfortable now?"

Something in his expression made her wonder if he was reconsidering, maybe even regretting his bold move. Or maybe he was giving her the opportunity to back away. Jaye knew she should. Like it or not, Zack was her boss now. In a very real sense, he controlled her future as surely as he controlled Medallion's. Even so she leaned forward, taking the initiative and sealing her fate.

Just before their mouths met she murmured, "Not even if you do this."

Nothing about the kiss could be called one-sided. Both parties were fully engaged. It quickly changed from a tentative exploration to an all-out sensual expedition.

Need flared and eclipsed reason. It made a mockery of Zack's previous belief that the more he got to know Jaye the less he would desire her. By the time the kiss ended a full five minutes later, his hands were tucked into the back pockets of her blue jeans, palms warming against a surprisingly curvaceous bottom; her fingers were tangled in the hair that brushed his collar; and he was sure of only one thing: he wanted more.

Green eyes regarded him with a mix of wariness and satisfaction. He couldn't decide which was the bigger turn-on.

"I've got to tell you, Holland, you do that pretty well," she said in a matter-of-fact tone as they extricated themselves.

It wasn't quite the response he'd expected, but then this was Jaye, so he said, "Thanks. And likewise."

"But it's not a good idea."

He knew exactly what she meant. Yet he heard himself ask for clarification. "What's not a good idea, Jaye?"

"Us…kissing or…anything."

Her hesitant response could hardly be considered a declaration. What's more, her use of the word *anything* posed tantalizing possibilities that his reckless libido was eager to explore. But he managed to grunt out an agreement as he began buttoning his shirt again. "No, probably not."

"Let's just call that a one-time thing." She blew out a breath and fidgeted with the end of her braid. He felt his shaky resolve start to falter.

"Want to make it a two-time thing?"

"No." But she moistened her lips and he could see the pulse beating at the base of her throat.

So he did what he swore he wouldn't. He reached for the braid and used it to pull her to him. "Liar."

This time when the kiss ended, his shirt was on the floor and he'd begun to work the bulky cable knit sweater she was wearing up over her head.

"I need a little help here, Jaye," he whispered.

He caught a glimpse of white satin and lace and some incredibly toned abs before she yanked the sweater back into place.

She pinched her eyes shut, looking pained. "Zack, we…we can't do this. Not here."

He backed up a step and tried to catch his breath. "Sorry. I wasn't thinking. I forgot this used to be your father's office."

"No. That's got nothing to do with it. We work together. Technically you're my boss."

There was no "technically" about it, but he didn't correct her. Ultimately she was right, even if he didn't want her to be.

"Let's just forget this ever happened," she suggested. "Not that anything really happened. I mean, we kissed."

He felt the need to point out, "Twice."

"Right, but no harm no foul. It was probably just a reaction to…to stress."

Zack wasn't sure what made him contradict her. After all, she was giving him a face-saving out. But he said, "And here I was thinking it might be attraction."

"A-a-attraction."

Her stuttering gave him courage. After retrieving his shirt from the floor he asked, "What? You don't agree?"

"It's not a good idea," she said again.

"Yeah, well, we've established that, Jaye. I believe we're debating the cause rather than the effect."

"What does it matter?"

A wise man would have dropped the subject right there. Zack was feeling strangely reckless. "Well, if you kissed me because you're interested in me that would make me feel better than if you kissed me as a way to, say, blow off steam."

"So, this is about male pride." She crossed her arms and angled one long leg out to the side.

"Call it what you want." He shrugged. "Well?"

"I'm not going to answer that question."

"Ah, pleading the Fifth?"

"This has nothing to do with self-incrimination." She huffed out a breath. "God! You make me regret acting on the impulse."

He grinned. "So, it wasn't just a reaction to stress."

"Yes, it was. It's the harvest. I've been working long days. I was releasing tension." She shook a finger just below his nose before he had a chance to speak. "And I'm not talking about *that* kind of tension, either."

"Okay, Jaye." She looked satisfied until he added, "If you say so."

Her lip curled. God, she could be a contrary woman. What did it say about him, Zack wondered, that it only made him want to kiss her again?

He loosened his belt and unfastened his pants far enough so he could tuck the tails of his shirt inside. When she swallowed and looked away, he decided he'd scored a victory of sorts.

"It won't happen again," she told him. "It never should have happened in the first place."

He nodded slowly, all of his smugness vanishing. "I know."

Long after Jaye had gone, Zack was left to wonder why it bothered him so much that she was right.

CHAPTER FIVE

JAYE bypassed her office and jogged downstairs. For the first time in her adult life she shifted work to the back burner and let her personal life take precedence.

"Corey?" She was placing the call from her cell phone even as she walked to her car back at the house. "Got time for lunch today? Yeah, everything's fine," she lied. "I just need a little advice."

Did she ever.

They met at a restaurant in Sutton's Bay half an hour later. Jaye planned to ease into the conversation, maybe pose a couple of hypotheticals to her friend first. Instead, a moment after their salads arrived she was blurting out, "He kissed me."

Corey blinked. "Zack?"

"Yes."

"He kissed you?"

Jaye scrubbed a hand over her eyes as the scene in his office replayed in her head. The mere memory of it had her pulse spiking. And so she said irritably, "Okay,

I suppose I kissed him. The first time. For heaven's sake, does it really matter who kissed whom?"

Corey's eyebrows rose. "There's no need to bite my head off."

Jaye fiddled with the cloth napkin that was spread over her lap. "Sorry. I'm just feeling a little…what's the word?" she murmured half to herself.

"Tense?" Corey supplied.

"Yes." Then Jaye's spine stiffened. "No! I am not *tense.* Definitely not tense."

"Oka-a-a-y," Corey said slowly. "Maybe I need to look that word up in my dictionary."

"Well, I am tense as in 'stressed out,' which is perfectly understandable given the time of year it is at work and everything else that has happened in my life during recent months." She leaned over the table and lowered her voice to add, "But I am not *tense,* if you know what I mean."

"Jaye, honey, I haven't got a clue. You're not making much sense."

"That's because *this* doesn't make any sense."

"This?" Corey's eyebrows beetled.

"Zack and me." Jaye exhaled sharply. "Haven't you heard anything I've been saying?"

"Yes, but apparently I missed something. Let me see if I've got this straight. Whatever is going on between you and Zack—and you do realize I'm going to require extensive details on that matter—doesn't make sense to you."

"That's the gist of it." Jaye glanced out the window. "Not that there is or could be a Zack and me."

"Why not?"

"Are you nuts, Corey? Isn't that obvious?"

"Apparently not. All I know is that my best friend, who hasn't been in a serious relationship since a three-month fling with Bobby Shumaker in the ninth grade, now has the hots for a gorgeous, successful man who shares her passion for winemaking. What's the problem?"

Jaye plucked at the end of her braid. Summarized like that it sounded so…possible. But she said, "I'm not his type. He's…he's not my type."

Corey rolled her eyes. "Oh, God. Not all of that type crap again."

"Well, you know me, Corey. I'm not a good bet for the long-term."

"Has he asked you to marry him?"

"Of course not," Jaye replied.

"Then what's the problem?"

"He's my boss, Corey. He owns Medallion and I work for him."

"That poses a bit of a problem," Corey allowed. "Why don't you give me those details now? Tell me exactly what happened, where, when, why and for how long." She bobbed her eyebrows on the last.

Jaye kept it short and to the point. "We kissed. In his office. Today. I'm not sure why and it lasted for, oh, about ten minutes."

Ten glorious minutes that still had Jaye's contact lenses wanting to fog.

"You call those details? God. I've heard you all but rhapsodize over chardonnay grapes. Give it up, girlfriend. What was the man wearing? What were you wearing?" Her smile turned devilish. "Where were his hands?"

Jaye couldn't help it. She sighed. Then she spilled everything. Afterward she touched her lips and admitted, "To tell you the truth, Core, I'm surprised that kiss wasn't detected on the Richter scale."

"That incredible, huh?"

"I'm still feeling aftershocks." Was she ever. "So, what should I do?"

"Well, you could keep your hands and lips to yourself, and pretend it never happened."

Jaye had already counseled herself on that approach. It was safe and it made the most sense. Still, she asked, "What would be option two?"

Corey's grin broadened. "What would it hurt to let nature take its course? You're both consenting adults. You're both unattached. He is unattached?"

"Yes."

"Well then, as long as all of the rules are spelled out clearly ahead of time, maybe the fact that you two work together won't be a problem. In the meantime, if you're not in any hurry to return to work, what do you say we run into Traverse for some shopping? Macy's is having a sale."

Jaye agreed, not so much because she was in the mood to try on clothes, but because she was in no rush to face Zack again.

Maybe the fact that you two work together won't be a problem.

She contemplated Corey's words as they traipsed from

one store to the next for the better part of the afternoon. Something told Jaye it wouldn't be as simple as that.

And it wasn't.

"You're not avoiding me, are you?" Zack stood in the doorway to Jaye's office, hands tucked into his pockets, a smile curving his lips.

It had been three days since their kiss, and she had indeed made every attempt to be in whatever location Zack was not. If he was out in the vineyard, she was at her desk. The moment she heard him coming up the stairs, she pulled on her jacket and headed out. She wasn't a coward, but Corey's plan to let nature take its course was too damned appealing, as unworkable as it ultimately would prove. Still, Jaye shook her head in response to his question.

"Avoiding you? What reason would I have to avoid you?"

He frowned. "None I hope. But I haven't seen much of you since…well, since the other day."

"It's harvest. You know how it is."

"Yeah. I know how it is." He stepped over the threshold. "I need to talk to you, Jaye. It's important."

"Oh, sure." But she stood and was already reaching for the coat that was on the back of her chair. "Can it wait, though? I have someplace I need to be in, oh, about fifteen minutes," she said, pretending to glance at her wristwatch.

He watched her intently for a moment. "It can wait for a bit. How about this afternoon? Got time then?"

"Sorry. We're short in the tasting room. One of the workers has a dental appointment. I agreed to cover for her."

"Fine," he replied. But her relief was short-lived. "I'll know where to find you."

What an awkward mess this was, Zack thought as he headed for the tasting room later that afternoon. What had he been thinking, kissing Jaye that way the other day? He wasn't one to act on impulse. Hell, he hadn't even made that kind of move on Mira until their second date. Yet he'd all but seduced Jaye in his office.

And she'd returned the favor.

Still it was unacceptable, he reminded himself. Unacceptable, inappropriate, untenable. He heaped on the adjectives in an attempt to convince his libido to cease and desist. It just kept pressing ahead.

Jaye was his employee and the one person who stood between him and his vision for Medallion. It was time to spell out his intentions—for the vineyard.

She was behind the large, circular bar when he entered the tasting room. He nearly tripped when he saw her. She looked…well, she looked different. Rather than her usual uniform of baggy jeans and a bulky unisex sweater, she wore a pair of fitted brown pants and a long-sleeved white blouse that tapered in at the waist.

Zack had suspected that Jaye had a nice figure. Hadn't his hands discovered some of those very curves? Still, he hadn't expected her to look quite so sexy. Of course, with most of the woman's height taken up in legs, how could she not?

Her hair was in its usual tidy braid, but even that had him wanting to groan. He'd entertained some incredibly erotic fantasies about unraveling it and running his fingers through all of that rich, cinnamon-colored hair. She'd applied more makeup, although nothing obvious, just a nice blush to soften the sharp angles of her cheeks and a neutral shade of eye shadow that emphasized her long lids.

He liked the subtle changes he saw. He liked them a lot, in fact.

As he watched, she poured a sample of Medallion's 2005 pinot gris into glasses for a couple of young women.

"This is a medium-bodied white. One of my personal favorites," she was saying. "You might detect melon and floral notes."

The young women sniffed, sipped and then nodded thoughtfully. He'd bet the vineyard they didn't have a clue what Jaye was talking about when she said the wine expressed the region's *terroir.* They looked like a couple of college coeds out for a weekend of fun rather than being true wine aficionados.

"Awesome," one said as her friend drew a smiley face on the paper menu they had been provided.

"What selection would you like to try next?" Jaye asked, recorking the pinot gris and putting the bottle back in the refrigerated case. Her movements were fluid and economical. They had him remembering the way she'd wound her arms around him that day in his office.

"Do you make any wine coolers?" the brunette asked.

A muscle twitched on Jaye's jaw. "Wine coolers?"

"I like strawberry or lemon-lime," the blonde added.

Zack stepped forward, deciding to head off an eruption. What the women were asking was sacrilege, but then neither of them was pretending to be a sommelier.

"No wine coolers, but we have an excellent barrel-aged chardonnay," he said. "It's one of my favorites."

All three women turned in his direction. Only two were smiling. Jaye's expression was guarded, her emotions impossible to read as she introduced him.

"This is Zack Holland. He owns Medallion Winery."

"I'm Mindy. We just love your wine," the blonde said.

"Yes. You do incredible things with grapes," her friend enthused. The brunette's smile turned flirtatious as she traced the lip of her glass with the tip of one finger and then proceeded to caress its stem. As signals went, it wasn't terribly subtle.

"Thank you," Zack replied.

She held out her hand. "I'm Stevie."

"Stevie. That's an unusual name."

"My dad wanted a boy, but I'm all girl."

He'd seen pinups with fewer curves. Behind the bar, Zack saw Jaye roll her eyes.

"Well, it's nice to meet you both. As for Medallion, it only recently changed ownership, so I can't take any of the credit for the finished product." His gaze veered to Jaye before adding, "Yet."

"We're in town for the weekend, staying just outside Traverse City. Maybe you could recommend a good place around here for dinner," Mindy said.

"And for dancing." Stevie smiled provocatively. "I'll need to work off all of these extra calories…somehow."

He'd have to be dead to misinterpret the invitation the attractive young woman was issuing. He was very much alive. In truth, Zack wouldn't mind sharing an evening with someone other than the news anchors on CNN, but Stevie was way too young for his taste—and far too obvious. He enjoyed subtlety. He enjoyed a challenge.

His gaze cut to Jaye.

"Well?" Stevie asked.

"Do you have any ideas for these ladies?" he asked Jaye. "I'm afraid I don't know the area well enough to make any recommendations at this point."

She rattled off the names and locations of several restaurants and night clubs in Traverse City. Something told him she had no firsthand knowledge of any of them. He stayed while the young women sampled the chardonnay. When they finished, the bolder of the pair handed Zack a paper napkin with her hotel name and room number scribbled on the back.

"I'll be up late if you're interested in coming by for a drink."

Stevie's smile told him that providing libations was the last thing on her mind. He coughed to cover his embarrassment, and tucked the napkin into his pocket. When he turned, Jaye was staring at him, her disdain obvious.

"Problem?"

"No." But then she said. "She's a little young, don't you think?"

"Old enough to drink, or are you going to tell me you didn't check her ID before serving her?"

"I checked," she assured him. "She was legal."

"Good."

"Barely."

"As a point of clarification, Stevie is not my type. I've made it a rule never to date a woman who was born while I was still in high school."

"But you took her number."

"I didn't feel the need to be rude."

"And they say chivalry's dead," she replied dryly.

"Don't tell me you've never been hit on."

"I discourage that kind of behavior when I'm working."

"Not always," he reminded her, and enjoyed the way she flushed.

"You said you needed to speak to me. Speak."

"I'm not a damned dog, Jaye."

"No. You're my boss."

Something about the way she said it turned his title into an accusation. He nodded slowly. "Yes, I am. As your boss, I'd like to speak to you. Now."

"Fine."

She stalked up the stairs, back ramrod straight, shoulders stiff. He followed at a more leisurely pace, hoping some of her irritation might dissipate. This wasn't the mood he'd hoped to find her in when he made his pitch.

She was leaning on the edge of his desk when he joined her in his office.

"Have a seat," he said, indicating one of the chairs.

"I prefer to stand."

He closed the door behind him and walked to the other side of his desk. The proposal he'd worked up was in a folder on the blotter. He picked it up.

"As I mentioned earlier, I have plans to expand Medallion's offerings."

"Do you mean wine?"

He thought he saw a spark of excitement light her eyes.

"Not exactly." And because he was in no rush to show his hand, he asked, "Do you have a suggestion in that regard?"

"Dad and I wanted to produce ice wine. There are only four locations in the world suitable for making it. We're on the forty-fifth parallel so this is one."

He rubbed his chin. "I hadn't thought about that."

"A couple of the other vineyards are doing it. One's had considerable success. In fact, one of its vintages was served at the White House a few years back. The label enjoyed a bit of buzz from that."

"I bet. But it would require some planning and the dedication of a portion of our vineyard. If all of the factors don't line up just right…"

"It could be a bust."

He studied Jaye for a moment. "On the other hand, I do like a challenge."

"I do, too."

"So, you don't believe in playing it safe?" he asked.

"Depends. I don't believe in taking unnecessary chances that aren't likely to pay off."

"That's probably smart," he agreed.

"So what do you propose?"

"I'm not sure," he said slowly.

"You're not sure? You're the one who called this meeting," she reminded him.

"Oh. That." Of course, *that,* he chided himself and then mentally regrouped. "Back in California I had a couple of ideas for Holland that my father and cousin unfortunately were not receptive to."

"Go on."

He decided to start with the less controversial of the two. "First, I'm going to add a creamery here. Medallion will offer its own wheels of European-style cheese for sale to the public. We can provide samples in the tasting room along with the wines and sell it at delis and to local restaurants for use in their menus."

Jaye nodded thoughtfully. "It certainly would be a complementary product and a good way to expand our brand." She pointed to the folder on his desk. "Do you have a detailed proposal worked up in there?"

"This is a proposal," he said slowly as he picked it up. "But it's for something else entirely. An inn."

"An inn?"

"Actually, more of a bed-and-breakfast, something small and exclusive and very luxurious. It would turn Medallion into a destination rather than a brief stop on an area vineyard tour."

"Where are you proposing we build this inn?" She

nibbled her lower lip. He found himself wanting to do that, as well. He forced himself to concentrate on what she was saying. "I'd hate to see acreage pulled from the vineyard to do it."

"As would I, which is why I propose to purchase a nearby site with a house already on it. The house could be converted with minimal fuss, I believe."

"Ah, this would be the house that is perfect for the needs you once spoke of," she supplied.

"Exactly."

She nibbled her lip again. "It must be close by or otherwise it would lose its appeal. Proximity is key, as I believe you said before."

"Yes, it is." He took a deep breath and decided to just say it. "Jaye, I want to buy your father's house."

Jaye couldn't make her mouth work. Words formed in her head, but they never made it past her lips to become audible. Zack's idea made sense. Perfect sense. It was something Jaye would have thought of eventually, she was sure. Still, selling the house would sever her last tangible tie to Medallion. She would have nothing left. Zack would own it all.

"This is the proposal I've worked up." He handed her the folder. "I haven't seen the house's bedrooms yet, but from what you've told me and from what I saw of the lower level, I'm sure they will be perfect after some changes."

Jaye opened the folder and skimmed through the proposal. The sum caught her eye. It was generous.

Make an offer, she'd told him. And he had.

Between it, the proceeds from the sale of her beachfront home and the money Margaret's antiques would raise at auction, Jaye would be set financially even were she not also earning a decent salary as the vineyard's manager.

"Well?" he prompted.

"I hadn't considered selling the house," she replied truthfully.

He apparently took her response to be a bargaining strategy. "The terms are negotiable. This is really more of a starting point than a final offer."

Jaye closed the folder and glanced up. "But you want my house. That's the bottom line. You want to buy it and turn it into a bed and breakfast."

"Yes."

And she wanted the vineyard. An idea began to form. An exciting idea that had her wanting to grin. She managed to bank her excitement and keep her expression bland. "And the terms are negotiable?"

"That's right," he said slowly.

"Good." She nodded. "I'll get back to you with my counterproposal."

He didn't look happy to hear that. "I see. Do you have a time frame?"

Jaye felt the balance of power shift and took a moment to savor it. For several months now she'd felt she had no say in her future, no control over her life. Finally she did.

Her lips curved with a smile. "Eager, are we?"

"Curious," he corrected. "Well?"

"I'll try not to keep you in suspense any longer than necessary."

"I appreciate that."

"Give me the weekend," she said.

In the end, of course, Jaye intended for the man to give her much more than that.

CHAPTER SIX

JAYE had asked for the weekend to consider his offer on her home, so Zack was surprised when she called him late Sunday afternoon and invited him for drinks in Traverse City to discuss her counterproposal.

"Sure," he agreed. "Have you eaten dinner yet?"

"I had a late lunch with a girlfriend. We've been in Traverse for most of the day, shopping."

It was such a typical female thing to do, yet he had a hard time picturing Jaye laughing with a girlfriend as they popped in and out of boutiques. He said as much.

"Generally speaking, I'm not one to waste time in a mall, but my friend's been after me to treat myself to some new things. I guess you could say I decided to indulge both of us today."

For some reason her reply made him nervous. Maybe it was her use of the word *indulge.* There were several things he wanted to indulge in when it came to Jaye, things that were strictly off-limits but still managed to slip into his dreams at night and toy with his sanity during the day.

"Well, I've seen what you eat for those late lunches of yours, so let's have dinner along with our drinks."

He almost expected her to argue, but she didn't. "Okay. Got a place in mind?"

"How does Minerva's sound?" The restaurant was adjacent to his hotel. He'd eaten there several times since his arrival in town.

"I'll meet you there at six," she said.

"Six it is."

Zack shaved for a second time that day and felt foolish when he couldn't decide what to wear. Should he keep it casual? Jeans and a sweater. Go for a slightly more sophisticated look by adding a sports coat? Or nix the jeans altogether and dress as he would for any other important business meeting? After all, that's what this was. He wound up going for option two. Showing up in a suit might put off Jaye, who clearly didn't buy in to the whole dress-for-success theory.

Having reached that conclusion, he still changed sweaters three times and dithered between a couple of sports coats until he finally grabbed one off the hanger and headed out the door before he could change his mind again. He blamed his indecision on excitement. He was eager to hear Jaye's response to his offer. He ignored the small voice that kept insisting he was also eager to see Jaye.

When he arrived at Minerva's she was already seated on a high stool at the bar, but it took him a moment to recognize the sexy siren sipping wine as the same blunt-spoken woman who held the key to his expansion plans for Medallion.

She'd said on the telephone that she'd been shopping with a friend. She hadn't mentioned that in addition to buying a new outfit or two she'd had a makeover of sorts. Her hair was different—shorter, although only by a few inches. But in place of the trademark braid, she'd left it loose. It fell in long layers around her face before cascading down her back in a tumble of cinnamon-colored curls that invited a man's hands to touch them.

Of course, her hair wasn't the only thing Zack wanted to touch. The cashmere sweater rated high on his list, too, especially given the way Jaye's slender curves filled it out.

She'd paired the sweater with jeans. Unlike the ones she wore to work, these fit. Even though she was sitting, he could tell they hugged her body in all the right places. Her long legs were crossed, one foot swaying lazily in time to the bluesy Norah Jones tune that was playing. He took a moment to admire the sleek boots below the hem. Their daggerlike heels would put Jaye at eye level with him when she stood. Of course, he'd already come to realize that, employee or not, the woman was his equal in every way that counted.

She glanced over, and their gazes locked. When she smiled his heart knocked out an extra beat. She'd never lacked for confidence. At the moment, though, she looked more than self-assured. She looked…satisfied. She lifted her hand to wave and he caught a flash of red. Her nails, he realized. God help him, she had them done. He'd always had a thing for blood-red fingernails. How was he supposed to concentrate on business now?

"Sorry I'm late. I hope you weren't waiting long," he managed in a normal voice when he reached her.

"You're not late. I arrived early and I've had a very respectable cabernet sauvignon to keep me company."

He took the glass from her hand and sipped from it, watching her over the rim as he did so. Something flickered in her eyes, as intoxicating as the wine he allowed to roll over his tongue before swallowing. "Medallion's 2003, I believe."

A smile curved her lips. She'd gotten far less stingy with those.

"You're very good at that. I'm impressed," she told him.

For some reason he found the need to say, "I'm very good at a lot of things, Jaye. And not all of them have to do with wine. I try to be well rounded."

"Do I detect a note of censure?"

He shrugged. "That wasn't my intent. Just stating fact. There's more to life than wine or work."

"Well, wine and work are one in the same for us, aren't they, Zack? And they are the reason you and I are here to have dinner."

She was right about that. "Well then, let's see about our table."

They were seated in the dining room and ordered an appetizer and drinks, but he found his mind on something other than business. "Your day of female bonding was quite a success. I almost didn't recognize you at first."

"Thank you. I think." She pursed her lips. "That was a compliment right, right?"

"Definitely." The word was spoken with a little more vehemence than he'd intended.

Jaye's eyes narrowed. "So, what you're saying is that how I look right now is a *vast* improvement compared to how I looked before."

Nearly too late he realized the boggy territory into which they were heading. "Do I have to answer that?" he asked.

"A smart man wouldn't."

"Well then, consider me a genius."

Even so, in the room's low light he studied her face—the high cheekbones, wide mouth and proud tilt to her chin. She still wore a minimum of makeup, but then she didn't need much to enhance what God had given her.

"You're staring," Jaye said.

"You're stunning." Zack hadn't meant to blurt it out like that, but then finesse, much like business, had gone the way of her braid. "Sorry."

She tilted her head to one side. "Does your apology mean you're taking back what you just said?"

He chuckled. "No. I said it and I meant it. I stand by my word."

Her smile was forthright rather than flirtatious. "And a good word it is. You know, I was flattered a while back when you said I was striking."

"I remember."

"Yes, but now stunning…" She made a little humming sound. "That's even better."

The waiter arrived with his wine, which Zack sipped gratefully. Business, he reminded himself once again. Business. But then he said, "I think it's the hair. I've never seen you wear it down. God, it's long."

"I'm beginning to wonder if you have some kind of fetish for long hair."

"Absolutely," he readily confessed. The obsession seemed odd, too, since Mira's blond curls didn't extend past her nape.

"Well, I did have mine cut today, but not by as much as the stylist would have liked. He wanted to bring it up even with my shoulders in some sort of layered bob." She indicated the length with her hands.

"The butcher. I'm glad you held firm." Zack saluted her with his wineglass.

She shrugged. "I've never been the type to let other people talk me into doing something I don't want to do."

"No, I didn't figure you were," he said.

He admired her for that, even as he found himself wondering if that particular personality trait was going to wind up dooming his plans. Anxious as he was to find out, however, they chatted about other things throughout dinner. Not surprisingly, when the meal ended it was Jaye who brought up the subject of business. The waiter had just cleared their plates when she reached for the portfolio that was balanced against the leg of her chair. She minced no words.

"I like the idea of an inn for Medallion. Love it, in fact. And I think my house will be perfect with some remodeling and, of course, new furniture."

"Of course."

"I've brought the building blueprint and some photographs of the bedrooms." She passed them to him across the table. "I've contacted an auction house in Traverse City. Once everything has been inventoried and appraised, they will send out a moving van."

"You've been busy."

"I've been motivated," she corrected with a smile that he didn't quite trust. "Until the antiques have been carted away, you'll have to use your imagination to picture what the rooms will look like with more suitable furnishings."

He grinned. "No problem there. I have a very good imagination."

"Yes, I believe you mentioned that before."

One side of her mouth lifted, but she appeared determined to stay focused on business. He should be, as well. So he said, "Of course, I'd like a tour of the place, too. It won't affect my offer, but I am curious."

"That can be arranged."

"When?" he asked.

"Whenever is convenient for you. I'm hoping to have the antiques out by the end of the week or the following week at the latest."

"They should bring you a good sum," he commented.

"Believe me, that's the only reason I haven't hauled them out into the front yard, doused them in gasoline and lit a match."

Zack chuckled. "They would make one hell of a bonfire."

"It would burn for days."

"You could probably see it from space," he said.

"Hmm, now I'm almost sorry I've made other plans." Both sides of her mouth curved this time. Then she cleared her throat. "Getting back to the house, every bedroom offers an incredible view. The master looks out over the vineyard and enjoys its own balcony."

"That's a nice touch. Romantic, too."

"I guess it could be." She nibbled her lower lip thoughtfully. It was a habit of hers that had a disturbing effect on his body. "You could advertise it as a honeymoon suite and throw in a complimentary bottle of our best sparkling wine," she added.

"What about bathrooms?" he managed. "Do all of the bedrooms have one of their own?"

"No. The two smallest bedrooms share one."

"Hmm. That poses a bit of a problem." He pushed the candle that was in the center of the table to one side so he could spread out the blueprint. "Paying guests of the caliber I'm hoping to attract aren't going to want to share facilities with strangers no matter how great the view from their window."

"Both rooms have large walk-in closets." She tapped a finger to the paper to indicate the area to which she was referring. "Perhaps adding a second bathroom would be feasible using the existing space and pipes."

"Perhaps. I'll see what a contractor has to say." He rolled up the plans and glanced up. "So, I take it this means you're willing to sell."

"Yes."

"Terrific." He smiled even though what he really wanted to do was pump his fists in the air. One major hurdle had been cleared. Of course, a second one loomed. "I assume since you mentioned a counterproposal that the terms I laid out don't meet your approval."

"Your offer is generous," she began.

"But you want more money."

"Not exactly." Her smile bloomed right along with his apprehension.

"Then what exactly do you want?" he asked.

She leaned forward over the table. The reflected glow from the candle flickered in her jade eyes. "Part ownership of Medallion."

"Wh-what?"

Zack's stunned and not particularly encouraging reaction was no less than Jaye had anticipated. She swallowed hard and forged ahead. "I will give you the deed to my house in return for a share of the vineyard."

Across from her, he straightened in his seat. "I'm not looking for a partner."

"Neither was I."

"Jaye, I know how much the vineyard means to you," he began.

She cut him off. "Then you know I'm dead serious when I say my house isn't for sale under any other terms. I'm not looking for a fifty-fifty split here, Zack. I know the value of the business and vineyard acreage versus the value of my house and its property. They are not equal. I'm not asking you to pretend they are.

You will remain the majority stakeholder in Medallion."

"Gee, that's considerate of you," he drawled.

She moistened her lips. "I can be a tremendous asset to the operation."

Her heart sang when he replied, "You already are."

"Thank you. That means a lot coming from you."

"Well, it's true." He looked slightly embarrassed. "If you were to leave, you would be very hard to replace."

"But you could. You would. I want to be irreplaceable," she said. The word seemed to mock her. She'd never felt that way in her personal life, she realized. Her mother had replaced her quite easily with a new, vagabond lifestyle.

"So, if you can't buy it outright, you'll be happy with just a piece of it?" he asked.

She nodded.

"Look, Jaye—"

For a second time she stopped him from speaking. "It's a good proposal. A very reasonable one, I think you'll agree, once you've had time to truly consider it. So, don't give me your answer right now. Look over my offer and study the photographs and the blueprints. Feel free to stop by for that tour. The pictures honestly don't do the bedrooms justice." With that she stood and gathered up her belongings. "I'll see you at work tomorrow."

Then she left.

Zack watched her go, his gaze lowering and lingering. He'd been right about the jeans. They fit her every subtle curve to perfection. He blew out a frustrated breath and slumped back in his chair. He certainly hadn't seen Jaye's partnership proposal coming, any more than he'd been expecting to see the woman who'd made the offer look like something straight out of one of his fantasies.

That ticked him off but good. In fact, the more he thought about it the more irritated he became. How convenient that her decision to get all dolled up and leave her hair loose had coincided with their meeting. He didn't appreciate subterfuge. Nor had he expected it from Jaye of all people.

"I'll take the check," he called out to the waiter as the man passed.

"No need, sir. The lady has already paid it."

That bit of news capped it for Zack. She was playing him. He didn't like it. He wouldn't allow it. He was on his feet in an instant and stalking toward the restaurant's exit.

By the time he'd retrieved his keys from his room and his car from the hotel parking garage, he figured Jaye had a good fifteen-minute head start on him. Still, he managed to pull into her driveway just as she was stepping out of her car. He rather liked the image of her caught in his car's headlights. She could be the one off balance this time.

"Zack. This is a surprise." She offered a wary smile.

"Don't talk to me about surprises," he snarled.

"Excuse me?"

"You've got a hell of a lot of nerve, Jaye." He

slammed his car door shut for emphasis and stalked toward her.

"I'm afraid I'm not following you."

"That's because you don't believe in following anyone. You blaze your own path and expect everyone else on the damned planet to just fall in line behind you."

She crossed her arms, angled up her chin. "I'm my own person. I don't pretend to be something I'm not."

"Yeah, that's what I thought, too. And I respected you for it, Jaye, even if I found it damned annoying at times. Then tonight…tonight you sashayed into the restaurant looking like—" His gaze skimmed down. He swallowed. "Like something edible, and you tried to seduce your way into a partnership."

Her arms fell to her sides. "Seduce my way into a partnership! I can't believe you just said that."

"Want me to repeat it?" he asked.

"Go to hell."

"Only if you'll join me."

Her top lip curled, which, perversely, Zack found sexy. "Have you even looked at my offer?" she demanded. Then she shook her head. "You couldn't have. There wasn't time. Besides, if you had, you'd know it's fair. It's more than fair."

"But you don't play fair."

"What are you talking about?"

"You…this," he said, pointing to her. "You decided to hedge your bets. You know that I'm attracted to you so you played up that angle, leaving your hair down, wearing clothes that actually fit and flatter your figure."

"You think I did this for you?"

"Was there someone else you called and asked to meet for drinks?"

"For your information, I did this for me!" she shouted, grabbing a fistful of her hair.

"Right. Excuse me for questioning the timing of your makeover."

"The timing may seem suspicious, but it's true." Her voice lowered, softened. "I've been dead inside for months, Zack. I finally feel alive again."

Funny, the same thing could be said for him.

Jaye continued, "I finally feel like the future holds promise rather than just more of the same…" She motioned with one hand as her voice trailed off. No words were necessary. He knew what she meant.

He believed her, but he hardly felt pacified, since she'd essentially told him it was the damned vineyard that was responsible for her rebirth. He cursed himself as a fool for thinking, maybe even hoping, for just a moment that it might have something to do with him. But that wasn't what he wanted. No, he assured himself, that wasn't what he wanted at all.

"So now your future looks bright," he said.

"I think so. I hope so. If you'll be reasonable and use your head instead of your…"

"My what?" he challenged.

"Your inflated ego," she replied pointedly.

"Believe me, sweetheart, *nothing* on me is inflated at the moment. You have a way of seeing to that."

She huffed out an outraged breath. "Are you saying I'm emasculating?"

"You're…something." And arguing with her was more of a turn-on than he wanted it to be. He shoved his fingers through his hair and then settled both hands on his hips. "I don't think a partnership between us is going to work, Jaye."

"Why not? Because I'm not interested in sleeping with you? Now, there's a good criterion for conducting business."

Her tone was steady, but she reached up to tug at the braid that was no longer there. Zack watched her loop one thick curl around her index finger before she let it go and crossed her arms. She was nervous.

He decided to call her bluff. "No. It's not a good idea, Jaye, because you *are* interested in sleeping with me."

Strong emotions coursed through Jaye. Anger was the only one she was willing to identify. The man accused her of having a lot of nerve. Well, he had no shortage of it himself.

"Tell me you're not interested." He lifted his chin. "Go ahead."

"I'm not."

His rumbling laughter mocked her. "You'd make a lousy poker player, sweetheart. Even in the moonlight your eyes give you away. You're as turned on as I am right now."

"This is ridiculous. I'm not having this conversation," she snapped, intending to leave.

“Coward.” The accusation was spoken so softly that it might have been mistaken for an endearment. It rooted her in place. “Come on, Jaye, admit it. You’re curious, too. That kiss in my office—”

“Was a bad idea and I believe I said so at the time,” she finished for him.

Zack wasn’t deterred. In fact, he looked downright smug. “Well then, this is probably an even worse one.”

Before she could fathom what he meant to do, he’d grabbed her by the shoulders and hauled her toward him. Her arms were still crossed and now they were effectively trapped between their bodies. She wanted them free so that she could shove him away, but a moment later they were and Jaye did no such thing. Quite the opposite, she wrapped them around Zack, reveling in his warmth and wanting so much more than could be had standing outside in her driveway.

When the kiss ended, Zack said the last thing she expected him to say. “I’ll take that tour of your house now.”

“Wh-what?”

“I need to know what I’m getting myself into.”

He wasn’t talking about the bed-and-breakfast. Jaye wasn’t either when she murmured half to herself, “Me, too.” Shoving the hair back from her face, she asked, “Does this mean you’re accepting my partnership proposal?”

“Yes.”

She should have been thrilled. This was what she was after. But something seemed off. “Why?”

"Does it matter? You're getting what you want, aren't you?" he asked.

She swallowed. "Yes. I'm getting what I want." And more than she bargained for. "What do you want?"

"Well, I want your house for starters. I don't want a damned business partner, but you've made it clear that's the only deal you're interested in making when it comes to this property. So, I've had to compromise." He shrugged negligently, but then his demeanor changed. "I also think we need to be clear on something else."

"And that is?"

"I want you, too."

She exhaled sharply. She wasn't as surprised by his words as the effect hearing them had on her body. Need rushed in even as her breath hissed out. "Jeez, Holland, and you call me blunt."

"It's a fact. One I don't seem to be able to change," he added, implying that he'd tried. "As your boss, of course, becoming intimate would be a bad idea."

"But as your partner?"

"Still not a good idea." He frowned. "But at least I will no longer be your superior."

"An objectionable word choice, but I get the point," she said.

"Good. Here's another point that needs to be made. I'm not any more interested in a long-term relationship at this time in my life than I am in a partnership."

She recalled the ex-fiancée he'd once mentioned. The ex-fiancée who was now engaged to his cousin. "She really hurt you," Jaye murmured.

Zack's expression hardened. "Mira wanted my birth-right more than she wanted me, so yeah, that hurt."

When he'd relinquished his claim to Holland Farms, his wife-to-be had relinquished his ring…and found a replacement.

"Now she's marrying your cousin."

He gave a jerky nod. "She's going to be a part of what was most important to her."

"That doesn't seem fair," Jaye said.

His rough laughter rumbled. "Life isn't fair, Jaye. Surely you of all people know that. If life were fair, you wouldn't be asking to become my partner." He swept his arms wide. "You'd own it all."

"I'd own it all with my dad," she corrected. "If life were fair, he would still be here with me."

"You're right." His expression turned contrite. "Sorry. I know how much you miss him."

"He was a good man. He taught me so much," she said softly.

"Mira taught me some valuable lessons, too. First and foremost she taught me to pay close attention to people's motives. I plan to be sure I know exactly what a woman is after when we get involved."

"And with me you know, is that it?" Jaye asked.

He didn't say anything.

"That makes me sound cold," she said after a moment.

"Not cold. I appreciate your honesty. You want this vineyard."

That was true enough, but for some reason hearing

Zack say it made her seem so single-minded, so obsessed. "I have a lot invested here."

"As do I."

"It's more than money with me." She needed him to understand that.

"For me, too, Jaye. I have more than money invested here, too. I need to succeed."

"So you can prove to your family that you were right all along," she added for him. Left unsaid was that in doing so he would prove to Mira that she'd chosen the wrong cousin.

He nodded.

"So we're partners."

"In business."

"And outside of work? What will we be after hours?" she asked.

"When we start sleeping together, you mean?"

She made a little humming noise in lieu of a reply.

"Exclusive," he said succinctly.

"That goes without saying," she huffed.

"Sorry. I didn't mean to offend you, but I don't share. I want to be clear on that."

"I don't share, either, and I appreciate clarity."

"As I recall, you once mentioned that you don't see yourself marrying."

"No." But her heart felt suspiciously heavy as she made the admission. "I'm not in the market for a husband. Is that a problem?"

"Not in the least. I'm not in the market for matrimony at the moment, either. So there won't be any hurt feelings."

"When it ends, you mean," Jaye said.

He nodded and she felt a traitorous twinge of disappointment, which she ignored, forcing out a laugh. "God, Holland, we're a cynical pair."

"Yes, but cynical looks good on you." His smile heated her blood.

"You know, here you are talking about how things between us will end when nothing has even begun."

"Nothing?" The word came out on a silky whisper.

"Well, not much." She took a deep breath and added, "Not nearly enough."

Zack's grin spread slowly. "Don't worry, Jaye. I plan to remedy that."

Her body caught fire, but her voice remained calm. "Now?" she inquired.

"Shortly." He chuckled. "I believe in taking my time. These things shouldn't be rushed."

"No." She moistened her lips, tasted him there.

"We're winemakers. We understand the value of patience."

"It can make all the difference," she agreed. "Ready for that tour?"

"More than. Let's start on the main floor and work our way upstairs."

"That's where the bedrooms are."

Zack held out his hand. "I know."

CHAPTER SEVEN

THE harvest ended and the winemaking began in earnest. The grapes already had been crushed, with most of the reds heading to the fermentor where the primary conversion of sugar into alcohol would occur. The whites were pressed and yeast added to start the fermentation process.

After this was complete most of the wines would be moved to large, stainless steel tanks or upright oak tanks. The red wines and some of the fuller-bodied white ultimately would be aged in barrels. Jaye always found it fascinating how different kinds of oak could influence the taste and texture of the finished product, and so she eagerly embraced Zack's suggestion to age some of Medallion's chardonnay in barrels made from American and Hungarian oak.

"It will produce a rich, buttery flavor," he promised. "Trust me."

She did. Even beyond winemaking. Jaye was learning that Zack had no shortage of integrity. The day they began the paperwork for their partnership, he called a staff meeting to announce Jaye's elevated status as Medallion's co-owner, leaving out the fact that he remained the majority stakeholder. He also was careful to keep their more-intimate relationship under wraps at the vineyard, even though now and again she would glance up to find him watching her, his assessing gaze hardly fitting for the workplace.

Jaye supposed some of the winery's employees, especially those whose jobs brought them into close contact with Jaye and Zack on a regular basis, were curious about what was going on between the pair of them behind the scenes. Thankfully, she heard not so much as a whisper, though.

At the house all of Margaret's antiques had been removed and an auction date slated for later in the month. The place felt bigger, huge in fact, and Jaye felt her excitement building as she and Zack began working on plans for its transformation from private dwelling to luxurious inn.

Jaye continued to live there. Renovations would not begin in earnest until after Thanksgiving and wouldn't be complete until late spring, so Zack said it didn't make any sense for her to find a new place until then. In the meantime, he'd purchased a sofa sleeper for the break room and he passed his nights there. Well, part of his nights. The actual sleeping part.

In the morning, after Jaye arrived at the office, he made his way back over to the house to shower and dress in fresh clothes, which were stowed with his other personal belongings in one of the guest bedrooms.

"You could just move in," she bolstered her nerve to suggest one evening as he pulled on his coat and prepared to head back to the winery to sleep. They'd had dinner together and a steamy interlude while feeding each other dessert. Jaye knew she'd never think of apple pie à la mode in quite the same bland way again. "You do own the house now and your clothes are here. You practically live here, anyway."

He studied her for a long moment in a way that had her knees going weak. "I know."

"Then why don't you move in?" She lifted her chin, raising the ante in what was becoming a high-stakes game.

"That's a serious step," he said.

"And we're not serious."

"You know what I mean. Living together would change everything between us. I'm not sure either one of us is ready for that."

"We agreed to no strings," she reminded him.

"That's right. No strings." He nodded. "That doesn't mean we should be careless with each other. I won't be careless with you, Jaye."

She liked his answer. It touched her deeply. And because it made her heart knock and her eyes sting, she smiled and forced her tone to be light. "Don't worry. I'll be sure to return the favor."

On the afternoon of Medallion's end-of-the-harvest party, the telephone rang just as Jaye stepped from the shower. After wrapping her hair turban-style in a towel and securing a second one around her torso, she dashed into her bedroom to answer it. Corey was on the other end of the line.

"So, are you going to wear the dress?" her friend asked in lieu of a greeting.

Jaye eyed the bold red dress that was hanging on the back of the bedroom door. Even on a hanger it managed to look sleek and sexy.

"No."

"Have you even tried it on?" Corey asked, sounding exasperated.

"I have."

"And?"

Jaye couldn't fault her friend's taste. The dress was highly flattering with its crossover neckline, three-quarter-length sleeves and a hem that fell to the knee. Still, she said, "It's too short."

"It's not too short," Corey contradicted. "It's the perfect length. It's the perfect dress. When I saw it in the window of that boutique in Sutton's Bay, I knew it would fit your body as if it had been made for it."

The dress did, too, which was oddly part of the problem. "I appreciate you buying it with me in mind. That was really thoughtful of you, Corey. But I'm just not comfortable wearing a dress. You know that. I've never been comfortable in one. I'm a tomboy."

"No. You *were* a tomboy, Jaye," her friend shot back. "And that was perfectly understandable when you were a gangly teenage girl without a mother around to show you how to be feminine or how to enjoy your femininity."

"My mother has nothing to do with my preference for pants," Jaye stated, but even she heard the defensiveness in her tone.

"Jaye, honey, I've seen pictures of Heather. Just because you look like your mother doesn't mean you are her or will become her."

Jaye studied her reflection in the mirror above her bureau. Her mother's face stared back. "I know that."

"Then start acting like you know that. Wear the damned dress tonight. You're an attractive woman with a successful career and a gorgeous man in your life." Corey, of course, was privy to the shift in Jaye and Zack's relationship. "It's time to move past your youthful inhibitions."

"Are you done, Dr. Phil?" she asked dryly, hoping to divert the conversation with humor.

Corey didn't follow her lead, though. For a third time she pleaded, "Wear the dress, Jaye. You have killer legs. Show them off. Zack will thank you for it."

"He does like my legs," Jaye murmured.

"He likes more than that, honey."

Jaye's heart fluttered at hearing the simple statement. The reaction made her nervous. In truth, a lot of things about her relationship with Zack made her nervous.

"So, are you going to wear it?" Corey asked, after a moment.

"I'll give it some more thought," she hedged.

Apparently mollified, Corey switched the subject. "What are you going to do with your hair?"

"I figured I'd braid it," Jaye replied dryly. Before her friend could sputter out a reply, she added, "Come early, okay, Core? I want to introduce you to Zack without a million people milling around."

Jaye decided against wearing the dress. Corey's irritation, though, was apparently forgotten when she saw what Jaye had selected instead.

"Nice. Very nice," her friend enthused when Jaye opened the door.

"You're not mad about the dress?" she asked, just to be sure.

"No."

"I left the tags on it. You can return it."

"Keep it. I'm sure you'll find another occasion to wear it for Zack in the future."

"Corey—"

"Keep it, Jaye. At some point, I promise you, you're going to feel comfortable in that dress. In the meantime, this outfit is stunning."

"Stunning," Jaye murmured, recalling that Zack had once used that same adjective to describe her. "Thanks."

Jaye felt stunning. The wide-legged black silk trousers had the same loose flow of a long skirt. She'd paired them with a jade-colored jacket of the same fabric. The cut was flattering, crossing over in much the same way the dress had and then nipping in at the waist before flaring out slightly at the hip.

She'd left her hair down, which she was doing more often lately, although she still pulled it back for work. She'd also applied a bit more eye makeup than usual.

"Is it too much?" she asked Corey when her friend continued to stare at her.

"No."

"Are you sure?"

"Jaye, you look incredible."

"But it's not…too much. I don't want anyone to think I spent the day primping."

"Would that be such a bad thing?" Then Corey shook her head. "Forget I asked that. To answer your question, it's not too much. Your look remains understated, but now it's also elegant and sophisticated."

Jaye's mood brightened. She liked those adjectives as much as she liked stunning. "Thanks."

"It's also perfectly fitting given your new status," Corey added.

"No one knows Zack and I are seeing each other," Jaye reminded her.

"Actually, I was referring to your status as Medallion's co-owner."

"Oh. That."

A grin bloomed on her friend's pretty face. Laughter followed.

"What's so funny?" Jaye demanded.

"I think that's the first time I can remember you letting something, or in this case some*one,* come before the vineyard in your mind. I can't wait to meet the man who managed that."

Jaye rolled her eyes. Inside, however, Corey's teasing comment further stoked her nerves.

Zack had been generous with the budget for the party, which in addition to celebrating the end of the harvest was intended to officially introduce him to the community, and Jaye had spent every dime he'd allocated. She had not only hired one of the area's top caterers to see to food and refreshments, she'd hired live entertainment.

Corey, who got out much more often than Jaye did, had recommended the band. Jaye took one look at the lead guitar player's tight jeans and ripped abs and figured she knew why. But actually the band was very good and played a range of music from classic rock and rhythm-and-blues to pop and even some jazz. Its members were warming up when Jaye and Corey stepped into the tasting room, which had been decorated with tea lights and hanging paper lanterns to create a more festive atmosphere. Zack was on the far side of the room talking with a couple of Medallion workers. He glanced up when Jaye and Corey entered.

"Oh, my God!" Corey grabbed Jaye's arm. "That's got to be him."

It was, but she still asked, "Why do you say that?"

"If it's not, the way he's looking at you could get him arrested." Corey fanned herself and muttered half under her breath, "I think I hate you," as Zack approached.

He was wearing a charcoal suit that accentuated his broad shoulders and lean hips. The white shirt and silk tie said businessman, but the hair curling up at his collar shouted something far less structured and stuffy. Sexy was the word that kept coming to Jaye's mind.

"Good evening, ladies," he said when he reached them. To Jaye, he added a simple, "Very nice."

"Thanks." God help her, she was pretty sure she blushed. "Zack, I want to introduce you to my friend, Corey Worth. Corey and I have known one another since high school."

"It's nice to meet you," he said, shaking Corey's hand.

"Likewise," Corey replied. "Jaye has told me a lot about you."

"Yes, well, don't believe half of it. You know how Jaye is prone to exaggeration," he teased.

"Not in this case." Corey grinned. "In fact, I'd say she played down some pretty key details."

His gaze flicked to Jaye, who felt her face heat a second time.

Mustering a thin smile, she asked, "Drink, anyone?"

Interesting, Zack thought, as they headed for the bar. Jaye appeared to be blushing. Again.

"Maybe we could have a toast," Corey suggested. "To friends, old and new."

Half a dozen black-vested bartenders were positioned behind the circular bar that normally only offered wine. Tonight, in addition to all of Medallion's vintages, the bar was fully stocked with every sort of beverage.

"What would you like?" Zack asked.

"I'll have a gin and tonic, please," Corey said. "Throw in an extra lime," she told the man.

"Just water for me," Jaye said.

"Make that two waters," Zack told the bartender.

"Wow. You two certainly know how to walk on the wild side," Corey teased.

"That will come later," he replied with a wink. His tone was light, but he didn't mean the words as a joke.

"Night's young," Jaye agreed.

She pushed a handful of hair back from her face so she could take a sip of water. The gesture was practical and ridiculously sexy. Zack had been looking forward to this night for weeks, happy to reward Medallion's staff for their hard work and eager to officially meet his neighbors and competitors in Leelanau's wine community. But at that moment all he wanted to do was cancel the party, send Corey on her way and retreat to the house so he could find out what Jaye had on underneath those flowing pants and that cinched blouse.

Truth be told, he'd expected her to wear a dress. The occasion called for it. The fact that she hadn't was somehow better. He liked that she remained a little defiant of convention. He liked that nothing about her was ever predictable. Even her moods couldn't be anticipated. Sometimes she was so vulnerable; other times nothing could shake her confidence.

"Why are you looking at me like that?" Jaye whispered.

Zack blinked. "How am I looking at you?"

"I don't know." Her laughter started bold before turning self-conscious. "Like you've never seen me before."

"I'm not always sure I know you," he whispered in

reply. The admission didn't trouble him as much as the fact that lately he'd found himself wanting to know Jaye's every last secret, dream and desire.

She gave him a funny look. "I'm not sure I know what you mean?"

Zack shook his head. "Nothing. Never mind." He smiled at Corey, who was pretending not to listen in on their baffling conversation. "So, you and Jaye have been friends since high school." His grin turned devilish. "Got any pictures from slumber parties?"

An hour later most of their guests had arrived and were milling about, enjoying drinks and helping themselves to the assortment of appetizers that had been set out on a long buffet table. For now the band had been asked to keep it mellow and the volume low enough to allow for conversation. Later in the evening they would kick it into high gear so couples could dance. During a lull between songs, Zack stepped to the stage area to officially welcome Medallion's guests.

"Good evening and thank you for coming tonight." He waited a moment until he was sure he had everyone's full attention. "As many of you know, I'm Zack Holland. I'm not new to winemaking. I grew up on a vineyard and worked my first harvest when I was still in grade school. But I am new to Michigan. I'm originally from California and I appreciate it that you've not held that against me." Muffled laughter greeted his quip.

"Tonight we're celebrating. We're celebrating a good

harvest thanks to the hard work of Medallion's crew. Frank Monroe knew what he was doing when he hired these people. They are smart, skilled and, above all else, dedicated. They've given me one hundred percent from the first day I came to Medallion. And so I want to thank them." He raised the glass of pinot noir he held and glanced around the room, taking care to make eye contact with as many of Medallion's people as possible.

He saved Jaye for last.

"We're also celebrating something else tonight. As all of you know, Medallion was a family-run business before, well, before Frank's untimely death. His daughter, Jaye, for reasons that don't really matter at this point, didn't inherit the vineyard at his passing. I don't think I'm talking out of turn to say that didn't sit well with a lot of folks around here, least of all Jaye. In fact, on my first day at Medallion she offered to buy me out.

"I told her no then and the other times she asked. I like what I see here. I like the Leelanau wine community and the friendly rivalry between vintners in the county and those on the Mission Peninsula. I have no plans to sell and go elsewhere. But Jaye, well, she can be pretty persistent."

As he'd anticipated, his understatement drew shouts of laughter. The woman under discussion, however, wasn't smiling, even when he winked at her.

Zack went on. "I came here with big plans for Medallion, things I've wanted to try in the past but was unable to implement. Jaye made me see the value of having a partner while attempting them. That's what she is now—co-owner of Medallion Winery."

Applause erupted along with chatter. Guests standing nearest to Jaye slapped her on the back or reached out to shake her hand and offer their congratulations. Zack waited until the room had quieted before continuing.

"So, in addition to raising your glasses to a good harvest, I ask you to raise them to Jaye. A man couldn't ask for a better partner. I count myself lucky to have her." The words were true…on more levels than he cared to consider at this point. He lifted his glass. "To Jaye."

While he'd made the announcement, her expression had changed from confusion to wariness and finally embarrassment. But she was touched, too, and rightly proud. He could see both in the way one corner of her mouth lifted and her chin angled up slightly. When he left the stage and joined her, stopping first to pick up a bouquet of red roses from behind the bar, her expression turned vulnerable.

The band had resumed playing and conversations returned to full swing when he reached her by the big window that offered a glimpse of Medallion's winemaking operation. Corey had seen him coming and discreetly excused herself.

"These are for you." He handed her the flowers.

"Roses." She buried her face in the blooms, her cheeks turning as richly hued as the petals. "I don't know that anyone has ever given me roses before. Thank you."

Because he wanted to lean over and kiss her, Zack cleared his throat. "You're welcome."

"Why did you do that?"

"Flowers seemed appropriate for the occasion," Zack said.

"No. I mean, why did you announce our partnership in such a public way."

"Does it bother you?"

She shook her head. "Hardly. But it wasn't necessary. Everyone at Medallion already knew."

"Yes, but the other Leelanau vintners didn't. I believe in playing fair," he added.

"Fair?" Jaye's brow puckered. "I'm afraid I don't understand what you mean."

"The competition has a right to know what they're up against." He grinned as he clinked the rim of his wineglass against hers.

"Thanks."

He sobered. "I meant what I said, Jaye. You make one hell of a partner."

"Same goes. I've never met anyone as passionate about the business as I am."

"I am passionate about wine," he agreed. "Among other things." His gaze dipped to her lips, lingering. "You know, it's getting warm in here."

"I noticed that."

"Yeah? Care to step outside for some fresh air?"

"Great minds," she murmured. "I was just about to ask you the same thing."

Jaye didn't bother with her coat even though the evening was chilly. Outside, a few guests milled about on the patio, indulging in a cigarette since smoking was prohibited indoors. When Jaye stopped at one of the tables, Zack took her hand.

"Come on."

"Where are we going?" she asked.

"Someplace a little more private," he whispered.

He tucked her hand into the crook of his arm. Moonlight lent a magical quality to the evening as he steered her down the brick walkway that led to the cellar where the wines were aged and stored.

"After you," he said, opening the door.

The cellar was built into the side of a hill. The building was utilitarian and not particularly pleasing to the eye, but it provided the privacy Zack wanted. No guest would see them here. Inside, the roof was made of variegated steel that curved in an arch and caused their voices to echo. Zack flipped on the lights and closed the door behind them, further ensuring that the wine-filled wooden barrels and moveable shelves of bottled vintages would be their only company.

Just to the left of the entrance, resting on the lid of a linen-covered barrel, stood an opened bottle of Medallion's semidry Riesling and two clean glasses.

Jaye's eyebrows cocked up when she spied the arrangement, and amusement shimmered in her green eyes when she turned to him. "A little presumptuous, aren't you, Holland?"

Zack shook his head. "If I were presumptuous I would have had the couch from the break room moved in here."

The suggestive comment earned her laughter.

He went on. "I prefer to think of myself as hopeful.

As in, I was hopeful that at some point this evening I would be able to steal you away for a few minutes."

"Ah. I see the difference."

"Do you mind?" he asked.

"Not in the least." She set the roses aside and picked up a glass and held it out for him to pour the wine.

He filled it and then his own. After taking a sip of the medium-bodied white he said, "You know, when we first met, I never would have guessed we would be so…compatible."

"I've changed a little." Her free hand slid over her hair in an absent gesture before tucking a hank of it behind her ear. "I think I've mellowed a bit."

"Mellowed?"

"A bit," she said again.

Zack couldn't help it. He laughed. "No you haven't, Jaye." Her eyes narrowed, so he pressed ahead. "Before you get your back up, that's a good thing. I don't want you mellow. Half of your appeal is your spunk."

"Spunk." Her lips twisted. "I think I liked it better when you referred to me as striking and stunning."

"See, there you go. You're opinionated and stubborn." When she frowned, he took her wine, set it aside with his and stepped forward. "Of course, your being so easy on the eye makes up for the fact that you're so damned hardheaded."

"Easy on the eye?" She was still frowning.

"Stunning," he corrected.

"Well, now, anyway. When we first met I was a bit rough around the edges."

Because she was being earnest he tucked away his grin. Vulnerable. That's what she was at the moment. "Then, now. You've always had my attention. Not that I don't especially like your appearance now. But something about you grabbed me from day one."

"I thought you were pretty hot, too." Her lips twitched.

"Yeah?"

"In a very California way," she amended.

"And what is that exactly, Ms. Midwest?"

"Oh, you know. Longer hair, relaxed style. And I thought you had a great butt." Her hands slid over the body part in question. "Still, I didn't expect us to end up involved, either in business or like this."

"Can't say I saw either coming myself," Zack agreed as he leaned in to kiss her. As their lips met, he added, "But I consider both to be a bonus."

By the time the kiss ended, Jaye swore she saw fireworks. The man certainly knew how to use his mouth.

"Do you think it would be bad form for the hosts not to return to the party?" she asked as the air sawed in and out of her lungs.

He rested his forehead against hers and struggled to catch his breath, as well. "Yes. Exceedingly."

"Damn. I thought so, too, but I figured I should get a second opinion. I guess this means we should return to the party." She stepped away, but he caught her hand and used it to tug her back into his embrace.

"We have obligations," he noted. His teeth nipped her jaw.

"Mmm." She sighed, because of those obligations and because of the effect his teeth were having on her heart rate. "People are probably already wondering where we are."

"I know." He stopped, but only so he could push her hair back for better access to her neck. His breath was hot on her skin. "What do you say we keep them in the dark for a few more minutes?"

"Only a few minutes?" she asked.

Zack chuckled and reached for the sash on her blouse. "Well, maybe a little longer."

It was a good hour before they returned to the party, slipping in from opposite doors.

CHAPTER EIGHT

As the weeks passed, their relationship changed, taking on greater depth and character, much like the wines that were aging in Medallion's cellar.

They had a lot in common—much more than Jaye could have imagined at the beginning. They liked the same film noir movies and were both fans of old *Seinfeld* reruns. When they had time they preferred reading medical thrillers to nonfiction, and when it came to dessert anything containing chocolate appealed to their palates.

Their views diverged on politics, but even in this they had something in common: they enjoyed debating the issues. The side bonus was that their passionate arguments often inspired heat of a more basic nature.

Jaye thought she finally understood why her father had opted to attempt matrimony again after her mother's heart-shattering abandonment. It was good not to be alone. It was good to have another adult to share meals with and evening conversation.

And then, of course, there was the sex…

Zack was a considerate and thorough lover, giving as much as he demanded in return, and Jaye matched his passion. Sometimes she took the lead, initiating their lovemaking. Other times she was content in the role of pupil, eager to discover what Zack would do next. The man was nothing if not inventive in bed, and it turned out she had quite a creative streak under the covers herself.

For the first time in her life, Jaye felt confident in her femininity. She enjoyed being a woman, so much so that she no longer thought of herself as a tomboy. She wasn't dressing the part, either, not even at work. Her father's oversize shirts had been relegated to a closet. She didn't need them to feel close to Frank. He was all around her—in the wines, the grapevines, the tasting room, the house.

Her dad would be pleased with the changes underway at Medallion, Jaye was sure. And he would be proud of the role she was playing in them. She knew he would like Zack, too, even if Frank wouldn't approve of the couple's intimate relationship, given the lack of a long-term commitment.

In truth, that was starting to bother Jaye, as well. Sometimes, in the wee hours of the morning, when Zack roused from slumber and slipped from her bed, she found herself wishing that he would stay. Indeed she found herself wishing for something far more permanent and enduring than their comfortable dinners and passionate evening encounters. She, the woman who had always assumed she wasn't cut out for marriage.

A couple of times during their lovemaking she'd nearly blurted out feelings that were much bigger and far scarier than anything she'd experienced before. On both occasions she'd managed to tamp down her wayward emotions before she embarrassed herself. She chalked up those weak moments to hormones and sex. After all, everyone knew that during the height of passion people often said or thought things they didn't really mean.

Thankfully, during the day, work kept her too busy to ponder her personal life. Word of their partnership was spreading. They had been besieged with media requests for interviews. Already a nice feature article had appeared in the Traverse City newspaper. The piece not only discussed Jaye's buy-in to the vineyard she'd helped begin, but Zack's decision to trade his stake in the venerable Holland Farms and gamble on a smaller and much newer Midwest operation.

The publicity was free and far-reaching. One such story ultimately was picked up by a wire service and made its way into wine columns and feature sections across the country. Zack's mother had even called to say she had read about their plans for Medallion in a publication there.

"We're creating buzz," he told Jaye.

Were they ever, and in local wine circles not all of it had to do with the vineyard. Despite their best efforts to be discreet, people were talking and speculating about the exact nature of the relationship between the two new partners. Corey was among them, even though she had a better understanding of what went on behind closed doors than most.

As she and Jaye chatted over coffee one Saturday afternoon in late November, apropos of nothing she mentioned, "I look good in most shades of blue."

Jaye stared at her blankly for a moment. "Sorry?"

"Blue. You know, for your bridesmaid dresses. No peach, please." Corey pulled a comical face. "It washes out my complexion."

"Ha, ha. Very funny." Jaye rolled her eyes and then sipped her coffee. The hand that held the cup wasn't quite steady, though.

"Actually, I'm serious, especially about my color preference."

"Corey, come on, you of all people know it's not like that between Zack and me."

But her friend was shaking her head even before Jaye finished speaking. "It's *exactly* like that. It's the Big *L*."

Love. The word hadn't even been said in its entirety and Jaye felt panicky. She choked down a mouthful of hot coffee. Outright denial seemed the best defense. "We're not falling for one another. We're just..." She shrugged.

"Just what? Having sex?"

"I was going to say having *incredible* sex, but yeah." Somehow Jaye managed to sound casual.

Corey wasn't put off. "So, you don't think you might be falling in love with him?"

"No. No!" she repeated a little more forcefully when her friend merely raised her eyebrows. "Zack and I like each other, sure, and we're compatible in many regards."

"Yes, I noticed that the other day when I walked into his office and he had his hands on your butt." Corey's tone was dry.

Jaye cleared her throat. "We try to keep it professional at work, but sometimes we become a little… affectionate."

"Honey, I'm a little affectionate with my cat. What you and Zack were getting ready to do in his office was—"

"What?" Jaye challenged.

"Well, let's just say after seeing the way the two of you look at each other I can understand why the polar ice cap is melting. It's the Big *L*," Corey announced for a second time.

Nerves tap-danced up Jaye's spine. "Oh, please. You're mistaking sexual chemistry for…for l-love." It was appalling, but she had a hard time getting out the word.

"I am not. I know all about sexual chemistry," Corey replied. "Even if it's been a while since I've actually experienced it firsthand with a man."

"Well then, you know it's a perfectly normal and healthy adult reaction that doesn't require a long-term commitment as a prerequisite. People have sex all the time without professing their undying devotion or making any plans to pick out china patterns."

"But I'm not talking about 'people,' Jaye. I'm talking about you and Zack. Your relationship goes well beyond sex."

"Of course it does." Jaye nodded matter-of-factly. "We own a business together."

"That's not what I'm talking about and you know it." Corey's tone softened. "It's okay to admit you're scared."

"Scared? I'm not scared."

Corey merely continued. "Sure you are."

"Okay, fine." She crossed her arms. "Of what?"

"You're scared of getting hurt. You're scared of being left or even that you might be the one to do the leaving, like your mother did to your dad." She ticked off the reasons with too much ease for Jaye's comfort.

"Corey, stop. I've heard enough."

But her friend wasn't through. "I think Zack is scared, too, given what you told me happened with his ex-fiancée."

"You're way off base," Jaye insisted.

"Well then, you're going to really take issue with what I say next. Medallion is your dream, and I know being in the vineyard makes you feel closer to your dad, but I think the place is also your security blanket. You love it the way you're afraid to love a man. You don't trust people."

"Oh, please," she muttered, not liking in the least the way Corey's summation nicked at old wounds.

"Zack's short on trust, too. You guys certainly don't trust each other."

"I trust him," Jaye argued.

"Not with your heart, you don't."

Because it was true, Jaye evaded with, "My heart is not an issue here."

"I don't buy that. Just like I don't buy your explanation that everything going on between the pair of you is merely hormone-based. Why can't you just admit that maybe Zack is the one?"

Vulnerability turned her tone crisp. "There is no *one* for me. As for what's going on between us, it's not the Big *L,* Core, unless the *L* you're referring to stands for lust. Neither of us is looking for more than that."

Corey appeared both exasperated and sad. "Is that enough for you, honey?"

Jaye thought of the feelings both foreign and exciting that had her rolling over to reach for Zack long after he'd left her bed. "Let's just drop it, okay?"

"Okay." Corey sighed. "You don't need to answer that question for me. But do yourself a favor. Answer it for yourself."

As November passed into December, Zack and Jaye's days fell into a pleasant pattern. From sunrise until just after sunset, they worked side by side at the winery. She liked the fact that he had no qualms about tapping her superior knowledge of the area's climate and other factors that would affect the *terroir* of the wines they produced. In turn, she had no qualms about tapping his innate sense of style when it came to outfitting the inn. Renovations of a couple of the bedrooms were under way, with work crews adding a new full bath for one. The addition of Zack's living quarters just off the main floor would take more time, but the footings for the foundation had been poured.

In the evenings Jaye and Zack holed up in the kitchen, going over material swatches and paint chips and thumbing through the furniture catalogues the interior designer they'd hired had provided. Where Jaye would have played it safe with neutral color choices for bed comforters and window treatments, Zack and the designer were opting for drama and a far more opulent color palette.

"We make wine," Zack said in explaining why the vivid color choices appealed to him. "Why shouldn't we bring the greens, burgundies and other hues found out in the vineyard indoors?"

So, this evening, as the construction crew that was installing the new upstairs bathroom banged away, Zack and Jaye sat at the island in the kitchen and made the final selections from the choices spread out in front of them.

"Which color do you propose for the walls in Suite One?" She held her breath half expecting him to pluck one of the deeper-hued paint chips from the pile.

But he reached for the bottle of wine they'd had with dinner and levered out the cork. "How about this?"

"That's a cork, not a color."

"But the people at the paint store can match anything these days thanks to computers. It's a nice neutral shade that will complement the darker-hued accessories we've selected."

Jaye tried to picture it but couldn't. She shrugged, "You're the expert."

"No, Diane's the expert," he said, referring to the decorator. "We'll run it by her to see if she agrees."

"The pair of you have been in sync on everything so far. I think she might have a crush on you."

He grinned. “Jealous?”

“Not as long as she keeps her hands to herself.” Jaye’s tone was teasing, but she wasn’t sure she was. She opted to get back to business. “So, what about the floors? What should we do with them?”

“Diane and I think rich, dark wood with plush area rugs the color of champagne.”

“Mmm. Sounds decadent.”

“Very.” He leaned over to trace the line of her jaw with his fingertips, and she swore her blood began to bubble and fizz like sparkling wine. “They’ll be so soft our guests won’t want to sleep on the beds.”

“Who says they’ll be sleeping at all? This place will be far too romantic to waste time slumbering.”

“Romantic?”

“Very.” Jaye made a little humming noise. “You know, that’s how we should market it.”

“As a couple’s getaway?” he asked. “A place where a man and a woman can retreat from reality and concentrate on their most basic needs?”

The passion simmering in his eyes made it impossible to speak, so Jaye nodded.

“What do you find romantic?” He stroked her face again, his caress featherlight and full of promise. “What makes you go all soft inside?”

Before she could think better of it, Jaye whispered, “You.”

Zack was the one struck mute this time. Her reply touched him on a level he hadn’t expected—an emotional level that was much trickier to navigate than a purely physical one. He reached for her hand and brought it to his mouth for a kiss. Then he used it to tug Jaye out of her chair.

"Come here." He pulled her toward him until she stood between the vee of his thighs. His kiss was hot, urgent and it made his desire plain.

"I see I have the opposite effect on you," she murmured with a throaty laugh when he stood and pulled her flush against him. Indeed, there was nothing soft about his body at the moment.

"This seems to happen whenever we're together."

"So I've noticed."

"I take it you don't mind," he said on a grin.

"Not in the least."

Jaye gathered her hair to one side, allowing him greater access to her neck, which he nuzzled on his way down to her collarbone. When he ran into the fabric of her blouse he unfastened the first button.

She glanced toward the door. Anyone could just walk right in. "M-maybe we should take this someplace a little more private.

In answer Zack lifted her up until her hips were perched on the island's granite surface. The move brought her breasts nearly level with his mouth. She forgot all about modesty when he went back to what he'd been doing.

Jaye shivered visibly as the second, third and fourth buttons of her blouse gave way. Zack parted the fabric to reveal the perfection beneath it, and with reverent hands stroked the pale exposed skin. When his fingers found the front clasp to her bra he heard her breath hitch. When he nudged the lace aside, she shuddered. When he lowered her head to savor her sweetness, she moaned low and long.

"Zack, I love..." For one mind-blowing moment he thought she was going to say she loved him, but she finished with "...the way you make me feel."

"Like this you mean?" he asked. He lowered his head again and her control snapped completely, as evidenced by the way she wrapped her long legs around his waist and arched her back. Her fingers were fisted in his hair, holding on, holding him close.

"Yes," she murmured. "Please."

What blood remained in his head took a quick detour south. The hard surface of the island beckoned. In his desperation it looked as soft and inviting as a down-filled mattress. Even the floor's cool travertine tiles held potential as Zack levered away from Jaye's straining body and struggled with the snap of her jeans.

Over the roaring in his ears and their combined labored breathing, the sound of work boots thudding down the stairs somehow managed to register. Jaye stopped, stiffened, as she apparently heard them, too. As the sound's meaning dawned, she quickly extricated her legs from around Zack's waist and hopped down. She managed to get her bra refastened as well as a couple of her blouse's buttons done before the door swung open and the work crew supervisor entered the kitchen.

The man glanced between the pair of them. Jaye's

face was flushed, her neck mottled from its encounter with Zack's late-day stubble. As for Zack, he was grateful for the high counter that hid the more incriminating evidence of his arousal, although nothing could camouflage the fact that he was breathing as if he'd just run a marathon.

"I…I…probably should have knocked," the man said.

"Nah. No need. Jaye and I were just…we were just picking out paint colors for the bedrooms," Zack said. Too late he realized that the samples were scattered all over the floor like confetti.

The work supervisor eyed them for a moment before clearing his throat. "Well, I wanted to let you know we're done for the day."

Zack bobbed his head. "Fine."

"The plumber got the piping installed on the new upstairs bath, and the wiring is finished, too. Once everything passes inspection the drywall will go up. I'm shooting for end of next week on that, although it may get done sooner."

"Terrific," Jaye managed.

"Yeah, thanks for the update," Zack said.

"No problem." The supervisor's lips twitched when he added, "You two have a good night."

When he was gone, Jaye and Zack eyed one another from opposite sides of the island.

"That guy has lousy timing," Zack muttered.

"The worst," she agreed. She motioned to the flat surface in front of her. "Another minute and…"

Zack snorted. "Exactly."

They heard the clatter of more work boots and then the front door closed. They were alone in the house now. There would be no further interruptions. Zack didn't move, though. The urgent heat of a moment ago had cooled. Now something more consuming than sex weighed on his mind.

I love...

In the brief moment before Jaye had finished that sentence, he'd experienced myriad emotions, some more troubling than others. Afterward, he'd been confused, because he'd felt oddly disappointed with her words. He needed to think.

"I should be going, too," he said slowly.

A couple weeks earlier he'd moved his belongings out of one of the spare rooms, taking up lodgings at a bed-and-breakfast in Sutton's Bay instead. Even the new couch in the break room had become too damned uncomfortable. Jaye had offered to be the one to relocate. As she'd pointed out, the house was more his than hers but Zack had been living out of suitcases for a few months now. He hadn't grown used to it exactly, but he had enough chivalry not to displace her until the addition of his quarters to the main level of the house was complete. In the meantime, she'd hooked up with a real estate agent and was looking for a new place.

Of course, one of the reasons he'd relocated was to keep the construction crew, which consisted of local craftsmen, from talking. It was a good bet they would be now.

A less comfortable truth was that while he wanted to move into the house, he didn't want Jaye to move out.

He liked, a little too much, the idea of both of them under one roof throughout the long, winter nights.

His evolving feelings for Jaye worried him. In the beginning those feelings had been based almost exclusively on sexual attraction. He'd wanted her and she'd desired him right back. Thus the no-strings arrangement they'd agreed upon at the outset had been simple and safe. Then, a few minutes earlier, when he thought Jaye might be getting ready to say she loved him, he'd been forced to confront his concerns head-on: What if their relationship went beyond sex? What if it was the beginning of something bigger?

Then, when she hadn't said the words, a different set of concerns had arisen: What if he discovered he wanted far more from Jaye than she'd already made clear she was capable of giving or interested in having? Worse, what if when it was all said and done Zack once again discovered that his main attraction for a woman was the land he owned?

He didn't like the answers he came up with to any of those hypothetical questions, so when Jaye said, "It's snowing outside. The roads might be slippery. You… you could stay the night," he shook his head.

"I think it's best I go."

Tugging at the ends of her hair, she asked, "Why?"

"It's hard to explain." He scrubbed a hand over his face. "I…I just don't think it's a good idea for me to stay here."

"Tonight? Or any night?"

"I don't know. Sorry. I'm not making much sense."

Jaye nibbled her lower lip. “Scared?”

It was an odd question and Zack wasn’t completely sure what she meant by it. Even so, he didn’t ask for clarification. “Half to death.”

As he grabbed his coat and headed for the door, he thought he heard her reply, “I am, too.”

CHAPTER NINE

JAYE lay awake long into the night feeling lonely, feeling confused. God help her, she'd almost done it. She'd almost blurted out, "I love you" while she and Zack had been tearing at each other's clothing in the kitchen. She wanted to blame the near declaration on sex, as she had in the past, but she'd be lying. Laying a shaky hand over her thumping heart, she admitted the truth to herself at last.

She loved Zack.

Earlier, in the kitchen, she thought she'd covered her tracks well enough, but his hasty retreat after the construction supervisor's unfortunate interruption had her rethinking that assessment.

And that was why she couldn't sleep.

Zack hadn't looked too pleased about the possibility that her emotions might be more binding than the no-strings sort she'd professed entering into their relationship.

In truth, Jaye wasn't particularly pleased, either.

Scared?

She blamed Corey for planting the question in her

subconscious. The fact that it had slipped out wasn't nearly as disconcerting as Zack's response: *Half to death.*

Was that a good thing or a bad thing? In the end Jaye decided she wasn't ready to find out. Before drifting off to sleep at last, she convinced herself she was perfectly content with the status quo.

As Christmas approached, however, the status quo took another hit. Their quasi-couplehood proved awkward with the holiday season looming. They'd made it through Thanksgiving without too much fuss. Zack had stayed in Sutton's Bay. But then, flying to California for what amounted to a long weekend probably hadn't been all that appealing. They'd spent the day together, shared a not-so-traditional meal of lasagna, since the housekeeper had the day off, and other than pizza Jaye couldn't cook much else.

But Christmas was different. Jaye had no immediate family to spend the day with. Zack did. Strained though his relationship with his family might be, this was the time of year to put grievances aside and gather with loved ones.

By the second week of December, though, he still had not mentioned anything about going to California. Nor had he said anything about staying in Michigan. Jaye was dying to know his plans, but she didn't ask. As with so much else in their relationship, she opted to wait, wonder…and pretend the outcome was really of no consequence to her.

Finally the suspense ended.

"My mother called this afternoon," Zack mentioned as they ate dinner in the kitchen a week before Christmas.

The housekeeper had prepared the meal and then left the salad chilling in the fridge and the main course warming in the oven before going home for the day. All Jaye had done was set the table. Zack had poured the wine.

"Oh? Everything okay?" She had to raise her voice to be heard over the hammering coming from the back of the house. The construction crew was working late to frame the addition, since this would be the last week they worked until after the holidays.

"Everything's fine." He cleared his throat then. "She asked me to come home for Christmas."

The dried cherries in the salad turned sour in Jaye's mouth. Still, she worked up a smile. "That's nice. I can drive you to the airport if you'd like, save you the hassle of long-term parking. When will you be leaving?"

He studied her a moment. Then he said, "Actually, I haven't decided if I'm going."

Her spirits rose ridiculously. "Oh?"

"I probably should."

"Yes." She tried to sound sincere. "It is Christmas."

He pushed chunks of romaine lettuce around on his plate with the tines of his fork. "I know, and I wasn't there last year, a fact that my mother reminded me of today."

"Where did you go last year?" Jaye was too curious to wonder if it was any of her business.

One side of his mouth lifted as he glanced up. "Well, when I wasn't looking at vineyards to buy I was wallowing in self-pity on the ski slopes in Aspen. I spent the bulk of December at a friend's chalet waiting for my father to call, tell me I was right about the direction I wanted for Holland Farms and beg me to return. Obviously, that didn't happen."

"Holland's loss is Medallion's gain."

His laughter rumbled. "Bet you didn't think you'd be saying that when I first got here."

"Not then. No," she agreed. "But I mean it. Medallion already produced a quality product before you bought it, but now..." She shook her head in wonder and smiled fully. "This vineyard is on track to become everything my father and I always hoped it would be. I couldn't have done any of it alone."

Her heartfelt comments didn't seem to please him. In fact, he frowned. "Good to know I could be of use to you."

"Zack?"

He waved a hand. "Forget it. I'm not in the best mood. And the phone call from my mom didn't help." He shook his head. "She sent me on quite the guilt trip."

"I'm sure that's only because she misses you."

Jaye thought of her own mother. It would be nice to be missed. She hadn't heard from Heather in years, unless one counted the sympathy card she'd sent Jaye after Frank's death. Her mother had signed it with her first name only. Beneath the typed sentiment, she hadn't included a more personal note. Jaye's insurance agent had at least penned the standard, "thinking of you."

"I know she misses me, which is why I feel so lousy." He set his fork down, pushed his plate to one side.

Because he looked so miserable, she found it easy to say, "Go home for Christmas."

"Is that what you want?" he asked softly.

"Of course." She kept her tone upbeat and her smile bright. "What else would I want? Besides, the longer you put off going back for a visit the more awkward it's going to be to see everyone when you finally do."

"I'm not worried about it being awkward. Sure, I'm still ticked off about my father always taking Phillip's side in everything, and I'm not exactly thrilled my cousin hooked up with my ex, but I'm over all that. I'm long over Mira."

"I didn't mean to suggest otherwise," she replied.

Still, his words had Jaye's heart lifting. Sometimes she'd wondered…okay, maybe even worried. She'd come across a picture of the other woman in a growers trade publication that had done a feature story on Holland Farms. Mira was gorgeous, petite and ultra-feminine. In other words, she was everything that Jaye was not. Jaye hadn't cared at all for the stab of envy she'd felt any more than she'd appreciated the self-doubts that had ensued.

He didn't appear mollified. "I wouldn't be with one woman and pine for another, Jaye. That's not my style."

"Good to know. Just for the record, though, I didn't say that you were." She plucked up her napkin and fussed with it for a moment before repositioning it on her lap. "Still, you can be over someone and not be over what they did to you."

"Well, you'd know."

"What do you mean by that?"

He waved one hand, picked up his fork. "Forget it."

"No. What do you think I'm not over?" she asked.

He set the fork aside again. "Your mother's desertion."

His reply was so unexpected that Jaye's head snapped back as if she'd taken an unexpected jab to the chin. "Wh-what?"

"You heard me. She left when you were what…? Twelve?"

"Almost thirteen."

"A kid, but as far as I can tell, you've used the fact that she walked out on you and your father as the reason not to trust long-term relationships."

"That's not true." But it was. Hadn't Corey said the very same thing? And Corey had known Jaye for ages. After a matter of months Zack had pegged her exactly. Jaye didn't like how easily he'd accomplished that, so she shifted gears. "Besides, we're not talking about me."

"No, we're not, and isn't that handy? You've got some issues to deal with yourself."

"I don't have *issues*. And my mother has nothing to do with my relationships with men," she snapped. But she couldn't maintain eye contact.

"Liar. You all but said so yourself."

"When?" Her gaze collided with his again. Surely she'd never confided such a thing.

"Before we became involved. I recall very clearly you telling me that you weren't interested in marrying anyone."

She hadn't been…then. But now? Because she was feeling vulnerable, she tipped up her chin. "Yeah. So?"

"I've never met a woman yet who didn't want to hear the wedding march."

"Well, now you have," she bluffed.

"Why? Got *issues,* Jaye?" he asked softly.

Eager to steer the conversation in a different direction, she turned the question back around. "Why aren't *you* interested in a serious relationship?"

"Who says I'm not?"

"You are?" She blinked. Her heart rose again, lurching into her throat.

"Eventually, sure." He shrugged. "Unlike you, I haven't ruled one out completely." He seemed angry suddenly. "Unlike you, this damned vineyard isn't the be-all, end-all for me. Ultimately I want more from life than to have Medallion toasted in wine circles. When both the timing and the woman are right, I have no doubt I'll want to settle down and start a family."

Forget feeling sucker punched. Jaye felt as if she'd been KO-ed. Through a haze of emotions she could almost picture a referee standing over her counting.

"Well, glad I can help you kill time until then." Somehow she managed to sound wry rather than wrecked.

Zack grimaced, apparently realizing how utterly insulting his words had sounded. "God, Jaye, I'm sorry. That came out all wrong."

"No, no." She waved a hand. "You have no reason to apologize. We're both well aware of—" she swallowed before continuing "—the limitations of our relationship."

"Yeah. Right. The limitations. I guess I thought…" His words trailed off.

"What did you think?"

But he shook his head. "Forget it. It doesn't matter." He snatched the napkin off his lap and tossed it aside. As he rose to his feet, he said, "There's some paperwork back at the office I need to go over."

"But you haven't finished dinner."

"I'm not really hungry right now. I'll see you in the morning."

After he'd gone, Jaye had no appetite either. She threw the baked chicken breasts and herbed rice into the garbage and then set the dirty dishes in the sink.

As the first tear leaked down her cheek, she murmured, "What a waste." But she knew it wasn't the ruined meal that was making her cry.

Zack hadn't slept well. Hell, he hadn't slept at all. Ever since his dinner with Jaye, emotions had been bubbling, as uncontrollable and potentially dangerous as a volcano's eruption.

Something, he knew, was going to give.

When he arrived at Medallion's offices just after dawn the next morning, Jaye was already at her desk. She glanced up when he stopped at her door. Her eyes looked shadowed and her demeanor was reserved. She was winding one long cinnamon curl around her index finger. She always fussed with her hair when she was nervous or distressed. It was a small comfort to know she'd passed as miserable a night as he had.

"Good morning," he said.

"Morning."

He pointed to the cup on her blotter. "Need a refill when I go for coffee?"

"No, I'm good. Thanks."

Zack shifted his stance so he could tuck his hands into the front pockets of his pants. "Look, Jaye, I feel horrible about last night."

"There's no reason to. What you said was only the truth." She coiled the hair so tightly that the tip of her finger turned purple.

"It wasn't remotely close to the truth." That was what had kept him awake half the night. So, once again he opted to come clean. "You're much more important to me than I made it sound with my thoughtless remark. I'm not just killing time, as you put it. It goes deeper—much deeper—than that."

She uncoiled the curl. Her voice was a hoarse whisper. "For me, too."

He sighed and leaned against the doorjamb. "So, what are we going to do about those limitations, Jaye?"

She wound another curl around her finger. "I don't know. I want…I want…" Her lips compressed and shook her head.

It shouldn't be that hard to say, but then he'd hardly put his own thoughts into words. "It looks like we both have some thinking to do." He cleared his throat. "I've decided to fly home for Christmas."

Her eyes widened. For a moment he thought he glimpsed disappointment. But then she smiled. "Good.

I mean, you should spend the day with loved ones. Have you called your mother yet to tell her?"

"Last night. From the way she carried on I think she's planning to slay a fatted calf or something." He laughed.

"Nah." Jaye shook her head. "They only do that for prodigal sons. You weren't acting reckless by leaving. You had a very good reason. Just as now you have a good reason to go home."

She'd helped him see that, he realized. "So what are your plans for Christmas?"

"I don't really have any." She shrugged. "I'll probably have dinner at Corey's. I've got an open invitation there."

The answer wasn't what he'd hoped to hear. "What about…family? You have relatives downstate."

"My aunt asked me if I'd like to come for a few days, but I declined. It's not like we're super close or anything." She glanced toward the window. "Besides, there's plenty to keep me occupied with the house renovations and decorating."

"Jaye—"

But she cut him off. "If we plan to open the inn by the end of May to take advantage of the Memorial Day weekend crowds, we've got to get going on publicity. Mindy has been working on a press release and media kit," she said, referring to their marketing director. "She said she'd have the materials to me by the twenty-second of the month, the twenty-third at the latest. I'll go over everything, make any necessary changes, so that we can have them mailed out before the first of the year."

"You don't need to work through the holidays."

"I know I don't *need* to. I want to. Really." Then she admitted, "It will keep my mind off my dad."

It was her first Christmas without him. For a moment Zack contemplated asking her to come to California with him. They could stretch out their visit through the first of the year, tour Napa Valley and sample the competition's offerings. He could introduce her to his parents. The idea smacked squarely into those "limitations" they were supposed to be weighing.

"Well, I'll only be gone a few days," he told her.

Zack booked his flight, made his plans, all with a heavy heart. He needed to go home. His mother was expecting him and it was time to face his father, his cousin and Mira. But he didn't want to leave Jaye. So much between them was…unresolved. Of course, neither one of them was willing to make the first move. Maybe they'd never be ready.

Jaye drove him to the airport on Christmas Eve morning, keeping the conversation light on the way into Traverse City. He was due to return four days later. That seemed a lifetime away. When she parked the car, Zack stopped her before she open her door.

"I have something for you. I was going to leave it under your tree."

"I didn't put up a tree," she said.

"I know. That's why I brought it with me and decided to give it to you now."

"Do I have to wait till morning to open it?" He liked

the eagerness he heard in her tone and the excitement that brimmed in her eyes. Both had been lacking in recent days. Her father's loss weighed heavily on her, he knew. It was small of him, but Zack also hoped she was going to miss him, too.

"Nah. You can open it now." He pulled the small gift-wrapped box from his pocket and handed it to her. "You're a hard woman to buy for, by the way."

"You didn't have to get me anything." But she was gleefully shredding the paper as she said it. Then she lifted the lid on the box and gasped. "Oh, my God."

Her stunned reaction had Zack smiling, but just to be sure, he asked, "So, do you like it?"

"I love it." She lifted the silver necklace from the box and inspected the pendant. It was a small cluster of grape-shaped amethyst stones—an exact replica of the fruit that adorned Medallion's label.

"I know you don't wear much jewelry, but I thought you might make an exception for this. I had it custom-made by an artisan my mother recommended. I know how much you love Medallion. This way it will always be close to your heart."

"It's gorgeous. Perfect." Her eyes grew bright.

"Jaye?"

"Sorry." She blinked away the unshed tears. "It's a very thoughtful gift, Zack. I can't remember the last time someone gave me something so beautiful."

"Let me put it on you," he suggested.

She lifted her hair so he could reach behind her

neck and fasten the clasp. The pendant rested just above her breasts.

"It looks good enough to eat," he said, bobbing his eyebrows in an effort to lighten the moment.

Jaye leaned over to kiss him. Afterward, she said, "Medallion's not the only thing dear to my heart, Zack."

"Oh?" His pulse beat unsteadily. He thought he knew what she was saying, but he needed to know for sure. "And?"

"I'm not good with words," she murmured, lowering her head and sighing. "I'm not good at a lot of things when it comes to expressing my feelings."

"You're doing fine."

But she shook her head. "I put something in your luggage."

"A Christmas present?"

"In a way. And an explanation of sorts."

"I'm not sure I understand."

"You will. And if it's…it's not to your liking, well, you can return it and…" She motioned with her hand. "I'll be okay with that. I'll understand."

She wasn't making any sense. "Jaye—"

But she'd opened her door and was getting out of the car. "Come on. We'd better hurry or you'll miss your flight."

CHAPTER TEN

THE first thing Zack noticed when he arrived at his family's vineyard was how much warmer the weather was. In Michigan the temperature had been hovering in the teens for weeks. Here, it was a balmy fifty-eight. He took a moment to savor that and the familiar scents and sounds after he parked his rental car and walked to the house.

His mother was out the door before he reached the front steps. Judith Holland's eyes crinkled with delight as she bounded down the stairs and called his name. Zack dropped his bag and scooped her into his arms for a hug, resting his chin on the crown of her head as they swayed back and forth in the drive. God, he'd missed her.

"Hi, Mom," he said when the embrace ended.

She sniffed and knuckled away a tear. "You're a sight for sore eyes."

"Same here."

Zack grabbed his bag and looped his free arm around her shoulders. When they started for the house, he realized his father was standing on the porch. Ross

Holland's emotions were far less obvious and more difficult to read than Judith's had been. But he shook Zack's hand, held open the door and inquired politely, "How was your flight, son?"

The question seemed to be an olive branch of sorts. Zack decided to accept it.

"The airports were a zoo, but my flight was fine. It's good to see you, Dad."

"Why don't we go inside?" Zack's mother suggested. Her smile bright, her gaze full of hope. "We can catch up over coffee."

"Or a glass of wine." His father rested a hand on Zack's shoulder. "I bet Zack wouldn't mind tasting last year's barrel-aged chardonnay."

"Did it turn out well, then?"

"Better than well. You were right about the Hungarian oak." Another olive branch.

"Thank you."

Ross nodded. "I think it will be hard to beat in tasting competitions this year."

"Don't go counting your gold medals just yet," Zack replied with a grin. "Medallion has something pretty special for the judges to try, too."

Later that evening as they sat in the den, sampling a nice Sangiovese, talking shop and watching the flames in the fireplace flicker and dance, his father surprised him by saying, "I want you to come back."

Zack straightened in his chair, not sure he'd heard correctly. "Back to California?"

His father nodded. "Back to Holland Farms. This is

where you belong." Hearing those words meant the world to Zack, until his dad added, "Phillip and I have been giving your inn proposal some more thought."

"So this is Phillip's idea, asking me to return." Even though his cousin wasn't in the room, Zack felt his presence and resented it. Nothing had changed. Zack was still the odd man out. For some reason that no longer bothered him quite as much as it once had.

"It's not Phillip's idea," his father insisted. "It's mine." Zack's surprise must have been obvious, because his father shook his head in dismay. "I can see that you don't quite believe me."

"It's not a question of believing you. Let's just say prior experience has given me reason to doubt that what I have to contribute will be taken seriously around here."

"I know that's been the case in the past." Ross studied his wine. "I'm sorry about that. I'm not very good at accepting change. You always seemed to want to shake things up."

"But for good reason," Zack protested. "There's nothing wrong with keeping certain things the same. In fact, I'd be the first one to decry change for the sake of change. But you and Phillip vetoed every idea I offered to improve the Holland brand's name recognition with consumers."

"I know it seemed that way."

"It *was* that way, Dad."

He expected Ross to argue, but the older man didn't. Instead, his father seemed to change the subject. "Your mother really misses you."

Zack sighed. "I know. I'll…I'll try to get back more often once things settle down at Medallion." He'd already told his father about the luxury bed-and-breakfast they would be opening in the spring, and so he added, "You and Mom are always welcome to come out and see me. The inn will be ready for guests by the end of May." He winked. "I'll set you up in the honeymoon suite."

Ross chuckled. "Your mother would love that."

"The package includes complimentary sparkling wine and gourmet breakfast that can be served in the room."

"Sounds like you've thought of everything."

"I had a little help," Zack replied, thinking of Jaye. Missing her.

"So, you won't consider returning? Holland needs you. I need you."

He'd waited a lifetime to hear his father say that. Since selling his stake in Holland, he'd fantasized about just this scenario. But Zack shook his head. Someone needed him at Medallion, too. And he needed that someone right back. He loved Jaye. It was time he admitted that, not only to himself but to the woman in question.

Jaye was on his mind when he went up to his old room an hour later. He considered calling her, but the time difference had him hanging up before dialing. In the morning he'd phone. He wanted to hear her voice. He hadn't unpacked yet, so he hefted his suitcase onto the bed and unzipped it. That's when he spied Jaye's gift.

He ripped away the festive wrapping paper and frowned at the Greek fisherman's cap. The crown was faded, its felt lining worn. Why on earth would she give him this? Then he read the note and his heart lifted. The last of his doubts about her feelings and their future fell away.

Don't worry, I don't expect you to wear this. It was my dad's. He wore it each spring when he went to inspect the vineyard after the last frost of the season. He called it his good-luck charm, and I figure there must be something to it since Medallion's vines always seemed to make it through the harsh winters intact.

Anyway, I wanted you to have it. In a lot of ways, you're just like my dad: solid, dependable. Someone I can trust.

Solid. Dependable. Trustworthy. Some men might prefer the woman they were dating to use more exciting adjectives to describe them. To Zack, though, these were perfect and significant. Her relationships with men had been stunted by her mother's desertion. She was letting Zack know she trusted him as much as she'd trusted her father. She was letting Zack know she now trusted herself.

She finished the note with this telling play on words: "There's no *limit* to my feelings for you. See you soon. Love, Jaye."

Long before the sun came up the next morning, Zack was dressed and in the kitchen. His mother smiled when she came through the door wearing her robe.

"You always were the first out of bed on Christmas," she teased, walking over to give him a kiss on the cheek.

"The only difference now is that instead of sniffing around under the tree, shaking my gifts and trying to guess their contents, I brewed a pot of coffee."

"So I see." She poured her cup. After she'd sipped it, she said, "I'm grateful for the coffee, but I miss that eager little boy. It's not fair that children grow up so quickly and leave home."

Zack cleared his throat. "Speaking of leaving, I…I changed my flight plans. I need to get back, Mom. Today."

Her face fell and she protested, "Oh, no. Not today, Zack. It's Christmas. What's so important in Michigan that you need to fly out today?"

"It's not what. Actually, it's who."

"Oh?" Her brows rose.

"There's this woman, Mom," he began.

She was grinning long before Zack finished.

Jaye dined with Corey and her family, but begged off early even though her friend had asked her to stay. By eight she was wearing a pair of silk pajamas and curled up beneath the comforter on her bed watching television and trying to pretend she wasn't waiting for the phone to ring.

She hadn't heard from Zack since he'd left. It had only been one day, she reminded herself. Still, she felt as if he'd been gone a lifetime. She glanced at the clock. It was five in the afternoon California time. Zack was probably eating dinner with his family. Jaye's lips puckered. And Mira. She ran her fingers over the pendant on the necklace he'd given her and wondered what he thought of the gift she'd given him. Maybe he hadn't understood its meaning. Maybe he had and didn't know how to react to her bald admission that her feelings had no limit when it came to him. Maybe his luggage had been lost.

"Maybe I'm being an idiot," she muttered aloud.

Only a couple more days and he would be back. Then she wouldn't have to speculate. She'd know.

When the doorbell peeled a moment later, she was tempted to ignore it. She wasn't dressed for company, nor was she in the mood to entertain. Most likely, though, it was Corey, who would no doubt try to talk Jaye into coming back over. If she didn't answer the door, her friend would stand out there all night, ringing the bell and worrying. She pulled on a robe and headed downstairs.

"I'm not in the mood for more visiting," she announced as she opened the door. Then her mouth dropped open. Zack stood on the porch. He was wearing her father's battered cap. Its black brim pulled low over his forehead. His longish hair flowed out from underneath it at the back. He looked ridiculous. He looked utterly perfect.

"What are you in the mood for?" he asked with a grin.

"I…I…"

"I love it when you're tongue-tied." He winked. "For some reason I find it incredibly sexy."

"Wh-what are you doing here?" she finally managed.

"I thought that would be obvious." His jaunty demeanor ebbed. Zack took off the cap and held it in his hands in front of him. "I don't know that I've ever received a gift quite like this one."

"A lot of thought went into it. It didn't cost as much as the necklace you gave me, but—"

Zack stopped her. "It's far more valuable than that necklace, Jaye."

"I can't believe you're here."

"I had to see you."

"Yeah?"

"When a woman tells you there's no limit to her feelings, well, a smart man catches the first flight out."

Her smile bloomed, trembled. "Is that what you did?"

"I'm here, aren't I?"

He stepped over the threshold and kicked the door closed behind him as he reached for her. Jaye's emotions reeled and her pulse sped up, making her hands shake when she laid them on his chest. Beneath her fingers she could feel his heart beating as furiously as her own.

Joy bubbled through her with the effervescence of champagne. "But you're supposed to be in California spending today with loved ones."

His kiss was tender. His words melted his heart. "That's what I'm doing, Jaye. I love you."

EPILOGUE

SPRING was always a magical time at Medallion. This year it was especially so. Not only was another growing season at hand, another season of Jaye's life had started. She felt reborn right along with the vines that had begun to sprout leaves now that the weather was turning warmer and the days were stretching longer.

Since Christmas, when Zack had arrived on her doorstep professing his love and wearing the cap she'd given him as a symbol of her trust, Jaye had discovered that in sharing herself completely with this man, she felt whole for the first time in years.

They hadn't talked about marriage, but it was the next logical step, one she was no longer skeptical about taking. She didn't just trust Zack. She trusted herself. She wasn't like her mother. She wouldn't wake up one morning and decide she'd had enough of playing house or raising a child. Zack was the person she saw herself waking up next to for the rest of her life. Like her dad had been, Jaye was the sort who took her commitments seriously.

In the meantime they had a wedding to attend. Phillip and Mira's. Jaye decided to wear the sexy red dress Corey had given her before the harvest party. She had the confidence to wear it now. She didn't mind attracting attention, as long as the attention she attracted was Zack's.

She and Zack arrived in California the day before the nuptials were to take place. Jaye had known that Holland Farms was a much larger operation, but it wasn't until she saw it firsthand that she understood the vast scope of Zack's family's vineyard. It was massive in comparison to Medallion, with five times the acreage, three times the staff, and of course it enjoyed a much longer and richer history.

He could be part of it again. All he had to do was say the word and his stake in Holland would be restored. He'd told her that himself after Christmas. Just as he'd told her how much it meant to hear his father say, "I need you."

"I can't recall him ever using those words," he'd said, sounding a bit awed.

Twice since then his father had made the pitch for him to return, sweetening the deal a little more each time. Zack steadfastly refused, but now that she was at Holland, Jaye felt the first twinges of regret. Maybe this was where he belonged, especially now that he could have a real say in the operation.

They were just leaving for the church, driving past the seemingly endless rows of vines, when Jaye reached her decision.

"Stop. Stop the car," she told him.

Zack pulled the rented sports coupe to the side of the road. Its tires spat gravel in his haste.

"What's wrong? Are you okay?"

"I'm fine. I just needed to tell you something."

He glanced at his watch. "Right now, Jaye? The wedding starts in less than half an hour."

"I know it does. I'm sorry. But, yes, I need to say this right now." Her tone was urgent, matching her feelings.

"Okay," he said slowly.

Jaye unbuckled her seat belt and got out of the car.

"Hey, where are you going?" he called, switching off the ignition and doing the same.

She didn't reply. Instead, she motioned with one arm for him to follow her and crossed into the vineyard, unmindful of the way her heels sank into the soil. Once there, she stood between two rows of trellised vines, put her arms out and turned in a semicircle.

When she was facing him again, she smiled. "This place is incredible, Zack."

He put his hands on his hips and eyed her as if she'd gone mad. "That's what you wanted to tell me?"

"Yes. I mean, no." She shook her head, trying to think of the best way to put her thoughts into words.

He tapped the face of his watch. "Jaye, we're going to be late."

"I know. Bear with me, please." Then she plowed ahead. "When we first met you told me that vineyards are just soil and vines. Pieces of real estate that represent more of an investment than anything else."

He frowned. "Yeah, I said that."

"And you believed it?"

"At the time," he admitted.

"Do you still believe it?" she demanded.

"No." Zack wasn't sure where she was going with this conversation, but Jaye had changed his mind about that. She'd changed his mind about a lot of things.

"I didn't think so." She appeared both relieved and sad.

"Jaye?"

But she shook her head. "I know I'm not making much sense, but humor me a minute longer, okay?"

"Sure."

"If my mom came back next week. If she just showed up on my doorstep, what do you think I should do?"

"Has she contacted you?"

"No. I'm just asking your opinion."

He rubbed the back of his neck. "I'd guess I'd encourage you to listen to what she had to say."

"If she wanted me to be part of her life again, and if she wanted to be part of mine, would you encourage that?"

"Sure, Jaye."

"Because family is important."

"Exactly."

She nodded. "And because you love me."

"I think you're acting a little nutty right now, but yes, I love you."

"And because you love me, you'd do what you could to make me happy. You'd make sacrifices for me."

He stepped closer, reached for her arms. "I'd move heaven and earth for you," he said simply.

Her eyes filled with tears even as she smiled. "I think you should sell Medallion."

Zack took a step back, sure he'd misheard her. But she was saying, "A buyer would be easy to find."

His blood ran cold at the statement. Old doubts bubbled to the surface. "You?" he asked quietly.

"No." She shook her head sending cinnamon-colored curls dancing. "I don't want to buy you out. I'm going to sell my share, too."

He blinked. "Jaye, honey, you've lost me. Why would you sell? Medallion means everything to you."

"No. I thought it did, but I was wrong. *You* mean everything to me, Zack. I can be happy living anywhere. Well, as long as it's at a vineyard and as long as I'm with you."

"What exactly are you saying?"

"Your father wants you to return to Holland Farms. Your mother misses you terribly. This place, it's been in your family for generations. You belong here."

He nodded, even though he didn't agree. "So, you'd sell Medallion, you'd trade in your dream, so that I could come back here, reclaim my birthright, so to speak."

She swallowed, but that was the only sign she gave of regret. "Yes."

If Zack hadn't loved her insanely already, he would have then. "But you once told me that Medallion was your life?"

She stepped closer and framed his face with her hands. "Turns out I was wrong, Zackary Holland. You're my life."

There was only one way to respond to a declaration like that. And so when he finished kissing her, he got down on one knee.

"You're my life, too, Jaye. You know I love you. I love Medallion, too. It's not just soil or real estate. But it is an investment and a dream. One I want to share with you."

"But Holland—"

"Is my past," he finished. "I'm more interested in looking ahead. Will you marry me?"

She was laughing and crying at the same time. When he reached out to wipe away her tear, she said, "Most definitely."

They didn't make it to his cousin's wedding. They did manage to put in an appearance at the reception hall, arriving just in time for the best man's toast to the bride and groom.

A smiling Zack and Jaye raised their glasses with the rest of the guests, but the future they drank to was their own.

* * * * *